Arthur, the Bear of Britain

More Titles from Green Knight

Pendragon™ Fiction

The Arthurian Companion
Percival and the Presence of God
To the Chapel Perilous (forthcoming)

Pendragon™ Fiction

Arthur,
The Bear of Britain

Epic Battles and Legendary Romance

by

EDWARD FRANKLAND

INTRODUCTION BY RAYMOND H. THOMPSON,
SERIES EDITOR

A Green Knight Publication 1998

Editorial by Raymond H. Thompson. Cover layout by Charlie Krank. Interior layout by Shannon Appel. Map locations by Roderick Robertson; map layout by Eric Vogt and Charlie Krank. Project, additional editorial / layout Lynn Willis.

Please address questions and comments concerning this book, as well as requests for notices of new publications by mail to Green Knight, c/o Chaosium Inc., 950-A 56th Street, Oakland CA 94608.

Visit our web pages at: http://www.greenknight.com, and at http://www.chaosium.com.

Green Knight publications exclusively distributed world-wide by Chaosium Inc.

FIRST PAPERBACK EDITION

10 9 8 7 6 5 4 3 2 1

Green Knight publication GK6202. Published in 1998.

ISBN 1-56882-102-6

Printed in Canada.

Table of Contents

FOREWORD

Edward Frankland was born in 1884 into a family of distinguished scientists, which offers no clue as to why his intense interest in King Arthur developed. It did so at an early age, however, for my father used to tell me that on their walks his parents would allow him to talk about King Arthur only until they reached a certain cottage. His interest in the legend survived into later life, and eventually led him to write *The Bear of Britain.*

In later years, I asked him what he would most like to do, and he said, "Excavate Pendragon Castle." This Norman keep, built about 1160 in the Westmorland Dales near where he lived, stands on the site of the legendary home of King Arthur's father, Uther Pendragon, and it must have helped to foster his interest in the legend. Sadly, he was unable to buy it from the descendants of the builder, the Norman knight Hugh de Morville. When it finally came on the market in 1963 as a lot in a very large estate, it was described only as "three small pasture fields near Kirkby Stephen" with no mention of the castle. It was knocked down to me for 525 pounds, a sum that was below the then agricultural value. Now it is conserved and partially excavated, and it draws many visitors from all over the world.

My father had another wish, that *The Bear of Britain* would be published in the United States, and it is a great joy to me that this too has at last come about.

Raven Frankland
Ravenstonedale, Cumbria
7 June 1997

INTRODUCTION

Dazzled as we so often are by the splendid deeds of King Arthur and his Knights of the Round Table, deeds celebrated so gloriously in the romances of Chrétien de Troyes, Sir Thomas Malory, and others, it is easy to forget that the legend first emerged in the much darker world of post-Roman Britain. This is a world less brightly illuminated than the High Middle Ages that produced the romances, but its outlines may be guessed at from the fragments of those few early writings that have survived the toll taken over the centuries: heroic tales, obscure poems, improbable saints' legends, historical chronicles of doubtful authenticity, and, most especially, that darkest of Dark Age documents *De Excidio Britanniae* (*The Ruin of Britain*), in which the monk Gildas castigates the vices of the rulers of sixth-century Britain. This is the material from which the authors of historical fiction have reconstructed a picture of a British war leader rallying his followers with resounding, albeit tragically short-lived, success against the invaders: Irish from the west, Picts from the north, Angles, Saxons, and Jutes from the east. Its influence upon Edward Frankland's *Arthur, the Bear of Britain* is acknowledged not only in his Afterword, but also in the headnotes with which he starts each chapter.

That Arthur's army fights on foot in this account rather than on horseback may come as a surprise to those who attribute his victories to the use of cavalry. Evidence for the continued use of cavalry after the withdrawal of Roman garrisons is inconclusive, however, and until the 1960's most historical novelists who trace Arthur's career in the Dark Ages choose, like Frankland, to attribute his victories to the superior discipline of infantry trained on the Roman model. Only since the publication of Rosemary Sutcliff's *Sword at Sunset* (1963) has it become customary for Arthur and his companions to operate as a fast-moving cavalry unit.

This Dark Age world is strikingly different in other ways also from that portrayed in the romances. Here are no chivalrous knights offering mercy to a defeated opponent with grave courtesy, but rather savage warriors driven to rapine and slaughter by blood lust and the casual cruelty that comes from supping too deeply upon the horrors of war. They encounter, not saintly hermits offering healing both physical and spiritual, but fanatical churchmen raging against sins of which they themselves are too often guilty. They pass through a landscape, not of quiet forests and solitary castles in which dwell lovely, if perilous, chatelaines, but of once-fertile farmland reverting back to wilderness, of pillaged villas and crumbling cities in which sullen refugees lurk amidst ruined splendour. The bonds of loyalty and brotherhood that unite the Round Table until its final dissolution are replaced by the treachery and ambition of arrogant princes, readier to attack one another than to combine against the invaders who threaten to overwhelm them all.

This is the world that Frankland creates for us in *Arthur, the Bear of Britain*, the second novel in the Pendragon Fiction series, and a dark world it is. First published in England in 1944, it reflects, perhaps, the savagery of a new dark age in which total war threatened the wanton destruction of all that was held dear. The nobility and heroic self-sacrifice of Arthur yr Amherawdyr, Arthur the Emperor, also known as Artos the Bear, stand out in this world in a contrast made all the more striking by the enveloping darkness. When his nephew Medraut advises him to seize absolute power after his great victory at Badon, Arthur, who had earlier vowed to fight against the invaders instead of other Britons, insists upon adhering to his principles: "A man may take it upon him to do as you counsel me to do and good may come of it; but for good or ill I am not that man," he responds. He pays the price for his decision on the battlefield of Camlann where, as she washes the blood from the face of his corpse, Garwen laments, "Of all the heroes that come up out of the race of Britons, this man sought least for himself and was most basely betrayed."

Despite Arthur's nobility, the dominant mood of the novel is sombre, recalling the world of Old Norse saga that influences Frankland's other historical novels. The very principles that rally followers to his cause prevent him from taking the ruthless actions that might have saved Britain from the invaders, and he is left to watch in frustration—"the saint, perhaps, most certainly the fool," in Medraut's cynical judgement—while the fruits of his twelve hard-won victories are squandered by men moved only by self-interest. This political failure is reflected by the internal struggle within Arthur's own family. Almost the first words that Arthur utters in the novel proclaim the importance of "kinship in blood": "Even as you and I stand side by side with Uther," he tells Medraut, "so the whole British race is bound together by blood and must stand or fall as one man in battle." Despite these sentiments, he is fated to kill by his own hand many of his kindred, as Bedwyr sorrowfully recognises at the end of the novel. This outcome is anticipated from the outset as Arthur and Medraut look upon each other with "tenderness and reassurance dimmed gradually by a tragic presentiment."

This tragic presentiment—found in both the disturbing visions of Medraut and the ironic comments of many characters, particularly Arthur himself—casts a dark shadow throughout the entire novel, preparing us for the eventual downfall of all that Arthur has struggled so valiantly to achieve. What dooms his efforts is not, however, the working of some inscrutable fate, but rather the failure of those in power to live up to their responsibilities in a time of crisis. Time after time, the British leaders choose to act out of jealousy, self-gratification, and ambition, plotting treachery with a callous disregard of its long-term consequences. Even those who should be staunchest in their support of Arthur conspire against him: His half-brother Modron connives in the murder of their father Uther and serves as a guide to the Saxon raiders; his wife Gwenhyvar resentfully yearns for a life of sensual indulgence and eventually runs off with Medraut; his nephew Medraut, torn between loyalty to his uncle and envy and ambition, lays the schemes that lead to Arthur's downfall. Since events are frequently viewed through the eyes of these and other foes and traitors, even Arthur's successes are undercut.

Despite the atmosphere of doom that pervades *Arthur, the Bear of Britain,* the awareness of opportunities irretrievably lost through short-sighted greed and ambition, Frankland nevertheless refuses to dismiss Arthur's achievements as merely futile. Though he is not prepared to allow us to forget the heavy price we all pay for our selfishness, he does remind us that there are alternative courses of action: the heroism of the Cymry and their champions, marching into battle against heavy odds with a song on their lips, "Cymry in victory, Cymry in woe!"; the heart-warming devotion of Olwen to Gwalchmei, of Garwen to Arthur; the visionary and artistic side of Medraut, raising the spirits of the army with his music. Even the corrupt British rulers are presented with choices, and though they almost invariably choose amiss, the battle of Badon Hill demonstrates what might have been achieved had they laid aside their differences.

There is too the note of heroic defiance, reverberating most powerfully in the words and deeds of Arthur himself. When his nephew recites the *Song of the Graves,* he responds, "If you believe that I am a doomed man, setting my hand to a hopeless task, I shall only push on the faster and strike the more fiercely." He is honest enough to recognise his own failure, that he "had not been great enough to bind the kings together or to break them, not great enough to renounce the stupid lusts of the men he strove to lead, not great enough to win the love of the most beautiful woman in Britain." When Garwen earlier tries to comfort him by arguing that he is more sinned against than sinning, he points out, "That they are base does not make us better." Yet though battered, his spirit remains unbowed when put to the final test. Thus at the last, fatal battle of Camlann he exhorts his sorely outnumbered followers, "A man's death should be worthy of his life; so shall his story become deathless among his countrymen and his fame leap up like a bright beacon when darkness lies over the land."

Arthur's heroic self-sacrifice does indeed leap up like a bright beacon amidst the darkness that lies heavy in *Arthur, the Bear of Britain,* filled with regret over what might have been. That this beacon has continued to shine so brightly down through the ages and across many lands, inspiring new generations with its story, is a tribute to the tales of those many writers who have kept the flame alive. It is well to remember, however, that the darkness out of which it shines still threatens to engulf us all if we fail to learn the lessons of Frankland's book.

Raymond H. Thompson
June, 1997

FOREWORD TO THE ORIGINAL EDITION

In the annals of history and legend there is no figure more haloed by romance than that of King Arthur, the last monarch of the British peoples in the culminating stages of their struggle with the Saxon invaders. Yet there is none of whom our picture is more hazy, or, in its conventional features, more untrue.

What manner of man was he, this legendary hero of the Cymry and early champion of Christendom? In the writings of Geoffrey of Monmouth he is already becoming unrecognisable. Geoffrey's account, though loosely based, no doubt, upon a substratum of old folk-lore, is obviously romantic fable, and the Arthur who appears in it is a character of fiction, tricked and embroidered to fit the fashion of a later age. When we come to the pages of Malory, the real Arthur, the tough Celtic warrior, has disappeared entirely, and we find a completely imaginary figure of mediaeval chivalry. In Tennyson's verses he has suffered yet another metamorphosis, and become an embodiment of the genteel notions of mid-Victorian Society.

Dr. Frankland has made in this historical romance a daring, diligent, and brilliant effort to re-create for us the real Arthur standing forth ruggedly against the actual background of his times. Historical research has given us considerable data from which to recover some notion of the state of Britain in the sixth century A.D. The author has used this with skill and effect to reproduce the savage confusion of the Dark Ages when the last vestiges of the Roman culture, once stamped upon Celtic Britain, were disappearing as the people slid back into barbarism, no longer one realm, but a chaos of rival local kingdoms, too prone to mutual treachery to combine in resisting the Saxon invaders. The tone of doom is well sustained in this picture of a twilight age, swiftly heading for the blackness of a long night.

For the actual details of Arthur's life and character Dr. Frankland has far scantier resources, for no contemporary historical record preserves them, and he has had to make such use as he could of subsequent accounts, of local place-names, and of lingering traditions. None the less, he has succeeded on the basis of such slender data in giving us a portrait which, if not historically authentic, yet bears the stamp of truth. Such was the sort of life which in that age a military leader like Arthur would live and such the kind of character probable in a man who could win mighty battles, and survive in legend and folklore for after-ages, yet could not hold Britain in unity against the invading Saxons.

Although King Arthur has become the supreme figure of romance, and the heritage of all races, he is essentially a Celtic hero, and Welshmen must feel a special gratitude to Dr. Frankland for clearing away the lumber of incredible mediaeval fantasies under which the personality of their mighty chieftain has been buried for centuries, and substituting a character historically intelligible. To that he adds the final merit of giving us a stirring and gripping narrative, which in atmosphere and incident is worthy of its magnificent theme.

D. Lloyd George

Glossary of Place Names

ABERGLEINWY: confluence of the Glen river with the Till, Northumberland.

AFON COCH: River Rawthey, Westmorland and Yorkshire border.

ALCLUYD: Dumbarton.

ALETH: St. Servan, Brittany.

ANDERIDA: Pevensey Castle, Sussex.

AQUAE SULIS: Bath, Somerset.

ARDERYDD: Arthuret, Cumberland.

ARFON: Caernarvonshire.

ARMORICA: Brittany.

BADON: the Downs from Liddington to Uffington, Wilts and Berks.

BANGOR YS COIT: Bangor ys Coed, Flintshire.

BERNEICH: Northumberland and Durham.

BREGION: "Beregonium" on Loch Etive, Argyll.

CAER CARADOC: hill fort in Shropshire.

CAER CERI: Cirencester.

CAER DAUN: Doncaster.

CAER EBRAUC: York.

CAER GLOUI: Gloucester.

CAER GWENT: Caerwent, Monmouthshire.

CAER ISC: Exeter.

CAERLEON: Caerleon-on-Usk, Monmouthshire.

CAERLUEL: Carlisle.

CAERMYRTHIN: Caermarthen.

CALLEVA: Silchester, Hants.

CAMALODUNUM: Colchester.

CAMELOT: Cadbury Castle, Somerset.

CAMLANN: near Queen Camel, Somerset.

CANDIDA CASA: Whithorn, Galloway.

CANTUCH: Quantock Hills, Somerset.

CARRUN: Carhampton, Somerset.

CASTEL YS COIT[1]: between Beaminster and Bridport, Dorset.

CERDICSFORD: Chardford, Hants.

CLANOVENTA: Ravenglass, Cumberland.

CLAUSENTUM: Southampton.

COIT ANDRED: the Weald, Sussex and Kent.

COIT CELIDON: occurs twice on the map: a wood in southern Scotland; also the Chilterns.

COIT GWENT: Wentwood, Monmouthshire.

COIT MAWR: Old Forest on borders of Wilts, Dorset, and Somerset.

CONWY: Conway.

CRAIG ARAN[1]: Cautley Crag, Yorkshire.

CUNETIO: Mildenhall, Wilts.

CYMENSORA: Kynor, Sussex.

DEGANWY: near Conway.

DEIVR, DEIR: Yorkshire.

DINDRAITHOV: Dunster, Somerset.

DINGUARDI: Bamborough.

DIN LIGWY: Din Lligwy, Anglesey.

DINMELIOC: Damelioc, Cornwall.

DIN UTHER[1]: Pendragon Castle, Westmorland.

DUGLAS: river in southern Scotland.

DURNGUEIR: Dorset.

DURNOVARIA: Dorchester.

DYFET: Pembroke and Caermarthen.

DYVNAINT: Devon and adjacent parts ("The Dark Valleys").

EIRÉ: Ireland.

ELMET: part of West Riding, Yorkshire.

ERCING: Archenfield in south Herefordshire.

GLEVUM: Gloucester.

GUINION: above Wedale, southern Scotland.

GWENT: Monmouth and adjacent parts.

GWYNETH: North Wales.

ISCA: Exeter.

ISCHALIS: Ilchester, Somerset.

KERNOU: Cornwall.

LINDUM: Lincoln.

LIS PENGWERN: Shrewsbury.

LONGBORTH: Langport, Somerset.

MOEL: Mull.

MOEL FRE: Wildboar Fell and Mallerstang Edge, Westmorland.

MON: Anglesey.

MORGANUC: Glamorgan.

PEN ARD: Pennard, Somerset.

PENWITH: country near Land's End.

PORTUS MAGNUS: Portchester, Hants.

POWYS: central Wales, Shropshire, and adjacent parts.

REGED: Cumberland and Westmorland.

REGNUM: Chichester.

SARUM: Old Sarum, Wilts.

STRATHCLYDE: S.W. Scotland.

TRAETH TREUROIT: the Fords of Frew, near Stirling.

VENTA BELGARUM: Winchester.

VENTA ICENORUM: Caister, near Norwich.

VERULAM: near St. Albans.

VRICON: The Wrekin, Shropshire.

VRICONIUM: Wroxeter, Shropshire.

VALENTIA: a Roman province in S. Scotland and Northumberland.

YNYS GWEITH: Isle of Wight.

YNYS GUTRIN: Glastonbury.

YSTREVELIN: Stirling.

The reader is reminded of changes in the county names of England since this book was written.

---

¹Name devised for this story.

Britain

OF ARTHUR YR AMHERAWDYR

NORTH SEA

EIRÉ

Moel •

• Bregion

Traeth
Tresroit
Ystrevelin •
Alclyd/Dunbarton •
Clydesdale •
STRATH-CLYDE

Duglas •

Carlida Cassi •

COIT CELIDON

Amandale •

Blatobulgium •

Aberglenwy •
Dinguardi •

VALENTIA

BERNEICH

Arderydd •
Caerleiol (Carlisle) •
REGED
Penrith •

Afon Coch •

Llanoventia •

DEVIR

Caer Ebrauc
(York) •

Caer Daun •

Din Uther •
Moel Fre •

• Crag Aran

ELMET

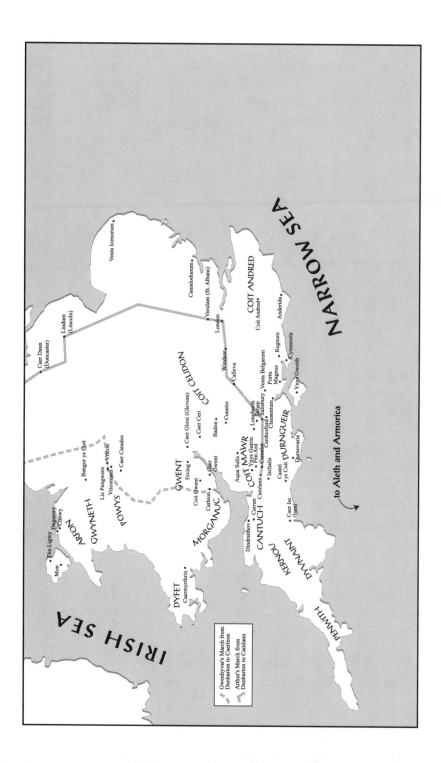

IRISH SEA

NARROW SEA

to Aleth and Armorica

Gwenhyvar's March from
Dunbarton to Caerleon

Arthur's March from
Dunbarton to Camlann

GWYNETH

ARFON

Din Ligyw
Degannwy
Conwy
Mon

DYFET

Caermyrthin

POWYS

Bangor ys Coit

Lis Pengwern

Vriconium

Caer Caradoc

GWENT

Ercing

Coit Gwent

Caer Gwent

Caerleon

MORGANWG

CANTUCH

Dindraithov

Currun

Camlann

KERNOW

DYFNAINT

Caer Isc (Isca)

PENWITH

Caer Daun
(Doncaster)

Lindum
(Lincoln)

COIT CELIDON

Caer Gloui (Glevum)

Caer Ceri

Badon

Cunetio

Aqua Sulis

COIT MAWR

Ynys Gutrin
Pen Ard

Camelot

Ischalis

Castel
ys Coit

Durnovaria

DURNGUEIR

Camalodunum

Verulam (St. Albans)

London

Windsor

Calleva

COIT ANDRED

Coit Andred

Anderida

Regnum

Cymenesoria

Ynys Gweith

Venta Belgarum

Portu
Magnus

Longbeath
Sarum
Salisbury

Cerdicsfort
Clausentum

Venta Icenorum

THE ADULTEROUS FINGER OF A TIME
THAT HOVERED BETWEEN WAR AND WANTONNESS.
        —Tennyson.

A GRAVE THERE IS FOR MARCH,
A GRAVE FOR GWYTHYR,
A GRAVE FOR GWGAWN OF THE RUDDY SWORD:
UNWISE THE THOUGHT—A GRAVE FOR ARTHUR.
        —*Song of the Graves.*

Arthur,
The Bear of Britain

Chapter I

The Roman Road

BRITAIN IS A LAND FERTILE IN TYRANTS. — Procopius.

The Roman road lay like a brown thread drawn taut across the green wilderness sunk deep among the mountains of Reged. A pair of ravens, soaring lazily from their nest on the blue-shadowed ledges of Craig Aran, croaked hoarsely as their gaze swept along that brown line and rested on a dark stain slowly filling the narrow cleft in the carpet of oakwoods. A creeping mass that glittered faintly in the August sunshine, it seemed from that outlook in the upper air like the blind unreasoning advance of a swarm of insects, ants following a trod in meadow grass on a nuptial flight, or a living chain of bees mounting to a hive. The birds knew well enough what to expect of these dark columns that moved from time to time on the old road, wearing down the droughted grass and breaking the fronds of encroaching bracken; men shouldering spears and axes, coming with a muffled tramp through the gloom of the great forest, men urging forward weary droves of sheep and cattle, women with burdens on their backs and dragging children by the hand, hordes of living creatures that shredded out as they went through this deep trough under the bleak indifferent gaze of the bald-headed mountains of Reged, leaving behind them fallen bodies stirring feebly at the roadside, a spent beast, a man with a mortal wound, a woman overtaken by the pangs of childbirth. Occasionally two columns would meet, and then amid the low murmur of rustling foliage and trickling water there would be a sudden uproar, the clanging of weapons, screams, and groans, and then in a little while the living would have passed on and the ravens would come circling down upon stripped corpses and pools of blood. There had been ravens on Craig Aran when Agricola's men hewed the track through the forest and set it with broken stone. Then, for three hundred years the ravens had fared meagrely on the creatures of the wilderness, but for the last hundred years mankind had come squandering itself, greatly to the ravens' profit, among the dark woodland lairs of wolf and wild boar.

The column of marching men drew nearer, topping a long ascent. The croaking of the ravens died away as they rose higher and higher, becoming black specks against the blue vault of the sky. A herd of deer emerging on to the road threw up their heads and dashed across into the tunnel-like gloom of the forest. Five hundred men, perhaps, in helmets of the old Roman pattern and hooped corslets of rusty iron, with plated shields on their backs, swords at their belts and spears at the slant, lean, wolfish-looking men with dark drooping moustaches. In the foremost rank was a gigantic figure with matted fair hair hanging over his shoulders; he held aloft a pole from which swayed a tassel of feathers below the carving of a red dragon. A little way behind the warriors rode a thick-set, grey-bearded man in a scarlet cloak, an evil-looking man with tight-pressed lips, bushy brows and eyes that gleamed angrily as they followed the languid sweep of the ravens far overhead: Uther Pendragon, the Guletic of Britain, now that Ambrosius Aurelianus had fallen in battle against the Saxons on the south coast, where the road went inland from Portus Magnus towards the chalk downs. . . . Ambrosius had been a link with the old days of the Empire; behind him was the prestige of a long line of Roman officials, men of wealth and culture; he himself had been able to speak Latin and he had made some attempt at training an army on the Roman model. They were men of Ambrosius that marched now with Uther, as shabby a band of legionaries as ever tramped a Roman road. Beyond their equipment there was little kinship with the men who had won an empire for Rome and guarded it for centuries against barbarian onslaught. They were British-speaking Celts, with scarcely a word of Latin, with no consciousness of the Roman world save for misty folk tales of the tyrant Constantine, and "Maxen Guletic," that Maximus who had led the British Army to disaster overseas. There was no cohesion, no ingrained discipline among them, except for the tribal loyalty of the Celt to his chieftain. Ambrosius ("Emrys," they called him) had led them against the hordes of Saxons swarming about the ruined walls of Clausentum, Regnum, and Portus Magnus, and against the stubborn Jutes who sat fast in Kent; on his death they followed Uther, the man of Reged, the hardy old fighter who had shed more Celtic blood than Saxon in his climb to power, who had lately forced his title of Pendragon upon the British princes with spear and torch.

If there was some small semblance of Rome about Uther in his scarlet cloak and the armoured men that marched before him, there was none about the motley host that came behind, leather-coated peasants in loose breaches, barefoot, shock-headed, armed with knives and axes, scarcely changed from the tribesmen who had yielded the country to Agricola. The legionaries marched in grim silence, but from the peasant ranks came a babble of high-pitched voices that rose and fell like the surge of the sea; sometimes there was a snarling as of wild beasts, a moaning that spoke of hunger or weariness, or a hush of foreboding at the sight of these forested hills mounting endlessly one beyond another in the narrow vista, some vivid in sunshine with a mocking beauty of foliage patterns, some wrapped in the tacit menace of cloud shadows. Last of all in the long column rode two young men, so nearly of an age, and so unlike in looks, that none would have taken them for uncle and nephew. Medraut, the younger by a year, had a delicate girlish beauty: small regular features, dreamy brown eyes, a paleness of complexion that was startling in its setting of lanky coal-black hair escaping under his green cap. He was clean-shaven save for a moustache which fell like a dark shadow at the corners of his mouth; his clothes were splendid and little stained with travel, green cloth embroidered skilfully with gold thread, a black riding cloak fell away from his shoulders, pinned with a brooch in the form of a cock, a bronze-hilted sword in a scarlet leather sheath hung from his belt, in his right hand he held a harp; he sat his white stallion with a careless grace and he hummed an air, slow and fatal-sounding, while his eyes wandered with an indolent pleasure from the sun-splashed stems by the roadside to the pillared blackness of untrodden woods. Arthur, the elder, was, next to Kai, the standard bearer, the mightiest man in the host, tall and broad, rugged-featured and grimly handsome, with long bushy hair and a beard that was a mass of auburn curls. His arms and knees were bare and sunburnt, covered with golden down, scarred with old wounds. Unlike Medraut, he wore armour such as the legionaries had, his clothes were sad-coloured, and he sat listlessly on his black stallion, his gaze on the ground before him.

The road dipped down; for a moment the woods fell away into undergrowth, wave-like crests purple with ling, monstrous brakes of gorse and juniper, winding glades of bracken. Far below, on the left hand, the forest thickened into a narrow lake of tree-tops and ran like green foam up the heights opposite. For the first time the host saw the dark beetling wall of Craig Aran, ringed about with the bald, rounded crests of grey-green mountains, some like the upturned breasts of a woman, some sprawling like monstrous hips and upthrust knees, and one peering over these anthropomorphic curves with a face of purple scree, a corpse-like face with tilted eyebrows that leered across the valley, impassive under the play of sunlight and shadow.

"The mountains frown," said Medraut laughingly, "the ravens croak, and Arthur's eyes are downcast while Uther Pendragon rides into Reged. Have you the second sight, uncle, and know that we ride to our doom in these endless leagues of oakwood?"

Arthur looked from the elfish profile of Medraut to the face across the valley; slowly he answered:

"I have no vision of what comes to meet us; yet a feeling I have that we are in a hostile land."

"The land is well enough in my eyes," said Medraut. "What pleasure it were to gallop on these hills with hounds and hunting horn chasing the deer, or ride down a boar at bay on some dusky forest path! What pleasure, uncle, to throw oneself from the saddle by some brown pool, to lie in the hazel shade and strike the harp to the tune that murmurs in rushing water, and perchance at nightfall to ride into some dewy glade where smoke streams from the huts and girls watch shyly from dark doorways. Horns of new milk they would give us, uncle, and kisses, and love-play while darkness falls on the mountains of Reged."

"So might it be, some day, when these wars are ended," said Arthur absently.

"When will wars end in Britain?" Will Uther end them any more than Emrys did?"

"Luck goes with Uther, so they say. Was he not the only Briton that came alive out of Anderida when the Saxons took it? Single-handed he brought my mother, Igerne, out of Gorlois' hall in Kernou, three ambushes Conan set for him in Coit Mawr and he rode scatheless through them all."

"Your mind is deeper than your speech, Arthur. The whole host knows that Uther is fey since he set out on this ride to Reged, and who should know it better than you, his son?"

"I know what the monks say, at Bangor and Ynys Gutrin, that for his sins God will punish him in the end, but I know that there would be few monks left alive if men such as Uther had not led our armies against the Saxon."

"And I know the monks too well to care what they mumble against us, the princes of Britain. Five years I spent in Bangor ys Coit for the sin my parents did in giving me birth, and there I heard the monks sing praises to Christ, but I found that even the highest of them were but men such as we are, full of pride and hatred, with lying tongues, and lusting after women. Life has been good for me since I broke my vows and went with a harp in my hand and a sword at my belt, to guest with Maelgun, the Dragon of Gwyneth."

"Sin . . ." said Arthur, frowning, as he thrust out his lower lip and stared at the ugly visage on the mountain side: "It may be that the monks are right. For the sins of our people God has let the Pict and Saxon waste our land of Britain. But I know something that may defy sin, and that is kinship in blood. Even as you and I stand side by side with Uther, so the whole British race is bound together by blood and must stand or fall as one man in battle with the savages from the North and the heathen from beyond the sea."

"Your mind is set on the old Britain that lived in peace and plenty under the Roman rule," said Medraut mockingly. "You have a Roman name, Artorius; your mother came of an old stock that was great in the land, men who were masters of fleets and armies when Uther's stock herded cattle under Moel Fre, but what are you today but Arthur the Bear, a Briton like all the rest of us, bred up in our beehive huts and drawing life from the shaggy halls of the West?"

"The Roman cities are wrecked, their halls are roofless, their columns thrown down; we see briars and nettles where once folk sat at ease anointed with oil and drinking the red Gallic wine, men who reckoned their wealth on parchments and read books in the Latin tongue brought from Rome itself, yet the land is ours and we shall keep it if we quit ourselves like men."

"What land shall we keep, Arthur? Do you mean this Reged, my father Modron's land, that we come to rid of the Saxons?"

"Not Reged only, but all Britain, from sea to sea."

Medraut laughed. He dropped the reins on his horse's neck and ran his fingers over the harp, striking a few full chords and then the little eerie-sounding melody that had been on his lips as they rode up under the boughs of the oakwood.

"I know Gwyneth," he said, "where Maelgun sits at Deganwy, and Dyfet, the land of Vortipore, the Protector, and Powys, the heritage of Cuneglas who dwells in the loop of Severn at Lis Pengwern: I know the land of Conan—the woods of Gwent—the thistly fields and the green downs beyond Caer Ceri, and I know Dyvnaint, the red sea cliffs and the land of purple ling and thorny forest, where rules Gereint among your mother's kinsfolk; I have heard that there is a

British kingdom among the deep woods of Elmet, and that there are men of our race still sheltering within the walls of London, but beyond this, uncle, there is nothing of ours any longer. Our folk are wasted away by the Saxon spears, and Britain is gone."

"We shall win it back," said Arthur obstinately.

"Not while Maelgun fights against Cuneglas and Conan against Gereint. Is Uther the man to wield the kings like a mighty axe to lop the Saxon tree rooted in the East? Why are our men so glum of face, lagging like jaded beasts on this march to Reged? Do they not know in their hearts that Uther's plough draws to its last furrow, that like a sick wolf he makes back to die in the place where he was born?"

"I shall wield the kings of Britain, and you shall help me, Medraut, for though I have the strength of my right arm, you have the strength of speech and music. You can lay a spell on our people so that they forget their fear of the Saxon and their hatred of each other; with you beside me I can deliver Britain, black as she is with sin and misery."

Medraut laughed and his eyes glistened. "See, uncle! We are at the march: before us lies the ford of Afon Coch. Yonder flat mountain touching the clouds is Moel Fre. In the plain behind the pass are camped the Saxons, lulled by peace-words from my father Modron. Let us set our hands to the axe to strike a blow for Britain! Let us be the first men into Reged!"

The two riders gathered up their reins and let their horses feel the spurs. One on each side of the long straggling column they thundered ahead at full gallop, past Uther, past the legionaries and the Red Dragon Standard, on and on, down the water-worn track between glittering hollies and grey-green plumes of juniper. More and more steeply the road went down till it ran out on an open space by the river bank where stood a circle of grey stones. Hard by the stones was a knot of men in grey cloaks, some fifty

strong. They sat or sprawled idly on the turf while billowy blue smoke rose from a cooking fire in their
midst. The riders held on at the gallop till the nearest
men scrambled to their feet to face them, men with
fair hair and sleepy blue eyes, men who stared open-
mouthed in dull wonder, slowly picking up spears
and axes that lay scattered beside them. The riders
came near enough for them to see the glint of bronze-
hilted swords in scarlet scabbards, of gilded spurs
and enamelled stirrups, then in a moment they
wheeled about and went back side by side the way
they had come, up the hill and out of sight, leaving
behind them churned-up turf and the sweaty reek of
horse-flesh.

Chapter II

The Saxons

THE FIRE . . . FED BY THE HANDS OF OUR FOES IN THE EAST, DID NOT CEASE, UNTIL, DESTROYING THE NEIGHBOURING TOWNS AND LANDS, IT REACHED THE OTHER SIDE OF THE ISLAND, AND DIPPED ITS RED AND SAVAGE TONGUE IN THE WESTERN OCEAN.

—Gildas, *De Excidio Britanniae.*

Eadwald, the leader of the Saxons, sat among his warriors by the ford of Afon Coch. He was a man in the late twenties, fair-haired and fair-skinned, with watery-blue eyes, a big moustache and a receding bristly chin. His expression was dull and inert, like that of some formidable wild beast entirely assured of its own strength and security. He had laid aside his coat of mail, stripped off his shirt and hung it inside out over one of the upright stones so that the lice might drop off in the hot sunshine. Naked to the waist he sat with his grimy hands clasped round his knees, the great muscles of his back and biceps had a pale oily sheen, and there was a dark sweaty ring on his neck like the tide-mark on a beach. Close beside him the carcasses of two deer were being skinned and disembowelled, a fire roared upwards through a heap of dry brushwood, but Eadwald's gaze shifted continually to the motionless woods and stark barriers of mountain amid which the clearing with the grey stones and the pillar of smoke might have been the arena of a vast amphitheatre. He stared at those mountains with a sullen distaste, holding at bay a faint sense of awe. The mountains of Reged were the first that he had seen in his life; they were alien, inimical to these folk that came from the flat heaths and sandy shores of Saxony. Evil spirits housed in them, no doubt, but what harm could they do to stout-hearted men who put their trust in Woden and Thor? As for the men of Britain, the dark strangers, the Welshmen, he had no fear of those folk. Once they had been a mighty race, so legend said among his countrymen, but now that their cities were ruined, their forts broken, their signal towers thrown down, there was no fight left in them. Three months ago he had landed with his war band at the mouth of the Tees; he had gone far and wide over Deivr and Berneich, seeing only starving wretches who turned their backs at the first sound of a Saxon war-cry, crowding in panic along these straight smooth roads that led to the mountains in the West. At last he had gone boldly on in the track of the fugitives and found himself in a new land that was as yet unharried, the land of Reged. Already his men were spreading out, firing the villages and rounding up cattle, when a host came to meet them, a poorly armed, shifty-looking multitude headed by a handsome chieftain. The Welshman rode forward lance in hand and spur at heel: he greeted the Saxons with friendly signs as they stood arrayed for battle under the ruined walls of an empty fortress, but even as he spoke and a fellow interpreted for him in a few words of Saxon, he had the air of a man ready to wheel his horse and fly from the line of brawny, beef-fed warriors who shook their spears and raised a jeering shout. He gave his

name as Modron, Prince of Reged, and in the end
Eadwald clasped him by the hand and took his offer
of all that country that lay about them, meadows and
woods and tilled fields from the mountain sides to the
river they called the Eden, and a thousand head of
cattle for their maintenance. It seemed to Eadwald a
good offer, for though he showed a bold face to this
chieftain Modron, he had only the half of his men
with him (the rest were not yet returned from a foray),
and the Welshmen were a great multitude. Even as
they spoke together, more and more showed on the
skirts of the forest, some to north and some to south.
The price of the land was but to chase away a host of
Picts that had begun to harry in Reged. Eadwald
gathered his men together and with an equal number
of Welsh they set out northwards. There was a fight
and the Picts fled. They followed them across the hills
till they came to a great wall of stone set with turrets,
but the Picts they never saw again, for they went so
swiftly afoot that not even a man on a good horse
could keep up with them in that wild country. So
Eadwald and his Saxons came back and camped
beside the Eden, waiting for Modron to deliver the full
number of cattle and to fix boundaries to the land
they were to have, and as a pledge of friendship Eadwald gave his sister Eadgyth to Modron in honourable marriage. . . .

As he sat on the turf by Afon Coch Eadwald's
mind wavered uncertainly from mood to mood, react-
ing sluggishly to imprints made on him by what he
had seen and done in Britain. A suspicion grew in
him that he had been a fool to make this pact with
Modron and seal it with the gift of Eadgyth, the girl
who had been his playmate as a child and who had
refused to be separated from him as they grew up,
riding side by side with him to hunting and even to
war, and now she alone, of all the women by the
Weser shore, had crossed the sea with him to Britain.

. . . Modron: he had sworn an oath to give the Saxons the land, but what was an oath? A breathing space, maybe, for the Welshmen. Why not for the Saxons also? With more warriors they could take more than a strip of land by the Eden: they might take all Reged. And so Eadwald had already sent men on swift horses to Berneich where other bands were on the move, Saxons and Frisians. Let them join him across the mountains. . . . Meanwhile, there might be something worth having here along this road. Even if peace-word had gone between him and Modron, that was no hindrance to his raiding outside Modron's land. It was more in accordance with his nature to go on from place to place living on plunder, battling with new men, raping new women, spreading the terror of the Saxon farther and farther into Britain; but that was not the desire of his comrades. Many of them lusted for the land itself; all they asked was to be left in peace to plough and sow, build themselves houses, turn the Welshmen into slaves, and breed up sons and daughters for whom this land would be a pleasanter home than the barren heaths of Saxony. . . .

The men lay thick on the ground about him, waiting for the meat to cook. Eadwald heard their talk while he himself sat silent, aware of a slowly mounting tension, not of fear but of foreboding that some difficult task lay ahead of him. To start off along this road to the south-west with fifty men had been the sudden impulse that came to him when he heard a growling among the warriors that Modron kept them short of food and drink. As yet he had followed all his impulses blindly, as though obeying some preordained destiny, ever since he came ashore from his galley on the Tees, and all had been well, so far. Now the sight of these mountains rearing their ugly heads about him on every side oppressed his spirit. A premonition stirred in him that good luck, or the favour of the gods, did not last for ever. A man had to be ready with a plan, even if he went along an empty road with no care but to bring down a few deer with his arrows and pluck himself a few herbs and handfuls of blaeberries, but what plan?

"Profitless it is, to my mind, to follow this road deeper and deeper into the woods. We can shoot deer and drink river water where we lie camped by the Eden."

"A road would not be made if it did not lead to some haunt of men."

"It is women we are short of."

"I have had my fill of women since we came ashore; my desire is to try this good axe on the skulls of the Welshmen."

"I would have cracked Modron's skull before I sent Eadgyth to his bed."

"There will be axe play if we follow this road far enough. Know you where it leads to, Eadwald?"

"It is said it leads to the sea," answered Eadwald, rubbing his chin.

"Since we left the ships we have come farther and farther towards the sunset and we march the same way today. How can this road lead us back to the sea?"

"There is another sea, beyond these mountains, and it is said there is another land beyond that sea, a rich green land full of cattle, a better land than this," said Eadwald.

"We shall build new ships and take it. I have no mind to stay here among these Welshmen."

"Reged is a good land," said the man who had spoken first. "The soil is deep and strong by Eden water, not loose sand as it is with us. No man need go hungry in that land."

"It is trees we need to fell. Let us make the Welshmen work for us and we shall sow the land thick with halls and byres and haystacks."

"Women we must have to bear us children."

"The Welsh women are good breeders. Their homesteads are full of children, and girls go with child younger than they do with us."

"They live like beasts in their little round styes; a filthy race I call them, beastly as swine and treacherous as serpents. I would burn them out and have in shiploads of women from oversea, our own folk that do as we do."

"Oswulf has left a sweetheart in the burg at Stade," laughed one.

"I heard such talk as this when I was in South Britain," said an older man with a great scar right across his face. "Our folk were spread out over the land, each in his own hall, tilling the good earth, hunting in the woods, and brewing ale and mead for the winter drinking bouts. And then a Welsh host came down on them, men in plated armour, riding hard on mettlesome stallions. Some of our people were roasted in their new halls and some gathered together and fought, but they had the worst of it. Not a few ships I saw put out to sea laden with men that were scarred as I am by the Welshmen's steel. Some made back for the Saxon coasts and some came north to try their luck afresh in Deivr and Berneich."

"Luck is with us who go with Eadwald!" said Oswulf jeeringly. "Never have we fled before Welshmen, but we have worked our will on the land, on its men and women, on its homesteads and on its beasts. I took a good horse when we first went ashore and rode him till he fell dead under me, and now it will not be long till I find another."

"As for horses, here come two with men on their backs," said a warrior raising himself leisurely on one arm.

"Bold riders are these! Chieftains by the look of them."

"Welshmen for sure."

"Let us kill them!"

Everyone was getting to his feet, reaching for weapons. A wolfish howl came from the mass of Saxons as the riders swung round and rode away as they had come with a flapping of cloaks and a thudding of hoofs.

Eadwald watched them in silence; a flush came to his cheeks, his teeth clenched, the great muscles of his arms swelled up as he gripped his axe. Fury swept over his dull brain like a blinding smoke shot with tongues of red fire. Those two riders were men of another world, a world that had to be trampled to death that he and his people might take what they desired, take and squander and build afresh. So near they had come and yet his hands had not been quick enough to tear them down.

"They came and went like two dragonflies," muttered a man.

"That black stallion!" burst out Oswulf.

"Slow you were to lay your hand on him!" said the old man with a hollow laugh.

"If my bow had been strung, I would have tumbled the big man from the saddle, the other, too, perhaps—he who had a face like a girl and a harp in his hand."

"Shall we follow them, Eadwald? What is your plan?"

"I have no plan," said Eadwald gruffly. "The meat is cooked. Let us eat it."

The Saxons sat in a ring sharing out the meat that was half blackened and half raw. They tore it from the bones with their teeth and the hot, blood-stained juice streamed into their beards and dripped on their leather coats and shirts of mail. They ate hurriedly, without speaking, with frequent glances over their shoulders at the watching forest and the bald-headed mountains. A croaking of ravens sounded high above them.

"Woden's birds seek their food from us," said a man.

No one answered. A gloom had fallen on that band of carefree savages since they set eyes on the sinister figures of Arthur and Medraut. It was as if, through the cloud of their simple preoccupations with hunger and lust, a vision had penetrated to them of gods riding to battle.

The sunlight faded, a moist chilly air eddied through the valleys and on the bare crests above appeared marching streamers of mist. Eadwald stopped eating. The thought grew in his mind slowly like a paralysing disease: those men in strange armour and splendid clothing, they rode like any good riders, gripping tight with the knees and ruling their horses with rein and spur, yet there was a light on their faces, a glint of something gay and terrible that Eadwald had never before seen on the face of Welshman or Saxon. Were they mortal men, galloping out of the wilderness and vanishing again like magic? Were they not avenging spirits that had sallied forth from the blackness of the forest, from echoing gills where water lapped stealthily against moss-grown cliffs, from dusky trails of scree that slid like purple torrents from the mountain crags? A faint whizz and a dull thud: an arrow stood fast in the turf beside Eadwald. It had just grazed his right arm, the merest scratch, but the blood welled out and ran down to his fingers. He stared for a moment, then sprang to his feet.

"Take your weapons!" he shouted.

The Saxons rose in a ring. At once another shaft came and struck the old warrior, he who had faced Emrys, full in the mouth, passing downwards into the throat. He fell with a crash and was dead directly. A chill went over Eadwald; the man had fallen whom he could least spare, a man who might have given good counsel when danger threatened. . . .

"There they are!" shouted a dozen men about him. They pointed to heads rising above the gorse brakes high up on the hill, where the road went on into the unknown. Now they could see more and more men, crouching like wild beasts as they came through the thickets, a long line descending in an arc from the heights to the river above and below the clearing with the grey stones. Arrows began to come in a steady shower. Many pierced the raised shields of the Saxons, with a sound like hammer-blows on a board, but some sank into flesh with a soft crunch, like a stone striking a mud bank.

"Shoot back!" growled Eadwald.

A dozen men drew their bows, but their arrows, discharged uphill, failed to reach the Welshmen. The advancing line halted. A converging flight of arrows continued to rain on the Saxons, of whom a few were killed and many wounded. With each man that dropped there was a triumphant yell from the enemy, though as yet he ventured no nearer.

"They draw stouter bows than we do," muttered Oswulf. He threw down his bow and pulled out a sword. "What is your plan, Eadwald? Shall we close with them hand to hand?" But Eadwald was silent, stroking his chin. Behind the archers he now saw a horseman on the hill, a big man in a scarlet cloak, and around him stood motionless a solid mass of warriors whose spears bristled against the sky thick-set as the teeth of a comb. Slowly the Saxon groped in his mind for a decision. They must go back across the river, out of reach of these bowmen, back along the road into the shelter of the forest. Then they would have the advantage of the ground and a few men could hold off an army in the narrow cleft between thorny brakes. He would send a runner to warn the host camped by the Eden—they might last out till help came. He turned to look back and saw the road behind filled with armed men. For a moment he thought his comrades had come unbidden, then he saw that these were men such as he had never seen before, men all dressed alike with helmets on their heads, square shields, and hooped corslets—a host sent by Modron to destroy him? No, these were no men of Modron's, for thrusting their way through the ranks came a rider on a white stallion and a rider on a black. He was trapped; the host in front had slipped round him under cover of the woods, they were between him and the Saxons, his comrades, who doubtless sat feasting on oxen by Eden banks, gulping down ale and throwing the gnawed bones in each other's faces. Still there was no fear in his heart, only a suffocating rage. He picked up Oswulf's bow, laid an arrow on the string and shot as the mass of armoured men splashed into the ford. Hah! that fellow's breastplate had not saved him. He shot at the rider on the white stallion and hit the beast, making it rear for a moment. A horn blew; there was a roar of voices behind him. The bowmen were coming down the hill like flying foam, a disorderly line brandishing knives and axes, and behind them, like an advancing wave, came the bristling mass of spearmen with the rider in the scarlet cloak. Shout and counter-shout; the scraping clang of steel on steel, the smash and crunch of steel on head and limbs. Eadwald saw weapons rising and falling in desperate haste all about him and blood flying in the air like rain. He gripped his short-shafted axe in both hands and swung it up as the white stallion came at him with bared teeth and ears laid back. The girlish-looking youth leaned forward in the saddle poising a javelin, the axe came down and clove the horse fairly between the eyes. Blood and brains poured over Eadwald's naked chest, he stumbled sideways and got his axe free. There was the rider, struggling up on one arm, trying to drag a leg from under the fallen beast; his eyes glared at the Saxon in helpless fury as Eadwald

trod him down with one foot and swung up the dripping axe. . . . Here came the big man on the black
stallion like a dark ship cleaving the tumbled waves
of war; a sword whirled in the air and Eadwald
turned his axe stroke at the grim bearded face
impending over his. He gave a great bellow of defiance; he would prove whether this was a mortal man
or not . . . he staggered as the fallen rider heaved
frantically to rise under him, the big man went by
with a backhanded sweep of the sword that fell on
Eadwald's bare neck. The roaring voice ceased suddenly as darkness comes when a light is blown out;
the head with its flaxen tangle of hair dropped upon
Medraut with a dull thud and the mighty trunk slid
down after it, spouting a dark torrent.

Already the din of battle was lessening; there was
nothing now but a one-sided hewing and thrusting
as the waves of Britons closed over the sinking bodies of their foemen. Uther himself pushed forward on
foot to stare at the grisly sight; behind him Arthur
and Medraut, bloodied and breathing hard, gave
each other a long searching look, a look of tenderness and reassurance dimmed gradually by a tragic
presentiment.

Chapter III

Evening at Din Uther

LET UTHER PENDRAGON DO WHAT HE CAN;
EDEN WILL RUN WHERE EDEN RAN.
              —*Westmorland folk saying.*
MODRON, UTHER PENDRAGON'S MAN.
              —*Black Book of Caermarthen.*

Uther Pendragon rode slowly through the pine forest that climbed the northern face of Moel Fre. High above him the snout of the mountain rose into the air, a black knob of rock like a skerry in a cloud sea, overwhelmed again and again by heaving billows of mist. How often in his wild life had his mind's eye beheld that crag, a landmark for all Reged, the dark beacon-stead above the place where he had been born! It had stood to him as an emblem of his own rugged strength, the harshness and arrogance that he had shown to man and woman, friend and foe, to the vacant, ferocious faces of Saxon warriors and the crafty, smiling looks of Celtic princes. All day the peak had stood out clear and sharp as a hammer-head against the blue sky, but now, in the evening, when the day's work was done, it was drowning in the rising tide of vapour that rolled over the mountains, as though God were no longer willing to behold this bloodstained and sin-smirched land of Reged. A chill crept into his heart, a superstitious dread, as his mind turned from the deeds of that day to what was to come on the morrow. He had achieved the task which he had set himself when his son Modron's messenger reached him feasting with Gereint in the shelter of the great stockaded ramparts of Sarum.

Reged had been delivered from the Saxons. Eadwald's head hung by the hair from Uther's saddlebow, all his chosen band had been destroyed at Afon Coch; the remainder of his host had been encircled in the night. In the grey of morning the attack had begun on the unsuspecting mass of warriors still plunged in drunken sleep. Dazed and unresisting, most of them had been hewn down or burnt alive in their wooden huts by the Eden, a mere handful had got clear. With the fury of despair they had hurled themselves on Modron's folk that barred their way to the east, and Modron, like the coward he was, had given way. Thirty men, perhaps, had burst through like wild cattle scattering the rotten stakes of a fence. It was a small matter that a few Saxons had escaped to join their kinsfolk across the Pennines, but it was one more proof of the worthlessness of Modron, Uther's eldest son, the man he had set to rule Reged, though his mother had been no more than a girl herding goats out westward where the limestone scars broke like foam on the verge of the Great Heath. Falser than most men in a land where all were false, Modron had held his own by cunning. He had never stirred to help his father in all these years of dubious war, against Saxons in the east and against Britons in the west; against the fierce sons of Hengist, against brutal Cuneglas and the malignant Vortipore. He had sailed in a ship to Deganwy to be the guest of the arch-plotter, Maelgun, the dragon of Gwyneth, and then when he had let the Saxons into Reged he sent a whining prayer to his father for help.

Modron—the old man glanced at his son riding beside him, a fine figure of a man with lank black hair and downcast eyes under a broad-brimmed hat, a chain about his neck strung with gold coins of Roman emperors, the man who had held Reged, by guile, maybe, but in peace, for thirty years, ever since Uther had gone south to master Britain. A man whose strength was eaten out by sin, like this land of Reged tunnelled by underground waters and sinking down in ghastly chasms—the monks were never silent with that dark story that as a boy of fourteen he had lain with his own sister . . . and Medraut was the fruit of their unnatural lust, a lovely poisonous fruit that delighted the eyes of all the princes of Britain, the boy who did good and evil with the same careless grace, who could charm any woman with his ready tongue, who drew tears from the eyes of warriors by his skill on the harp. . . . As though aware of his father's sullen gaze, Modron looked up. A smile flickered over his sombre face and he said gently: "It shall be a joyful homecoming for you to-night, Father! You shall feast well under Moel Fre. The best mead and the fattest cattle in all Reged are hidden here out of sight of the Saxons; wheaten bread we have, and salmon from the Eden, and flesh of deer from the forest. To-night you shall not lie in camp on the hard ground, but in a soft bed in the firelight under a roof of heather thatch, and I shall send a woman to you, a woman whose hair shall be as silk in your hands, a woman with soft breasts and shapely hips, a wild young thing, to be used roughly, as a stallion subdues a wayward filly, the sister of the man whose head hangs from your saddle."

"The woman you have taken to wife?"

"Even so, but now my treaty with the Saxons is ended."

Uther laughed unwillingly. "A smooth-spoken, treacherous son I have in you, Modron. Is any man or woman safe in your keeping?"

"Surely you shall be safe in Din Uther under Moel Fre, the place where you were born?" Modron laughed in return. "Am I not in your debt, now that you have made an end of the Saxons?"

"The Saxons will come again and you are not the man to keep them out of Reged."

"Who then?" Modron glanced furtively at the stalwart figure in the scarlet cloak. But Uther was silent. He thought to himself: 'I shall sit in Reged to the end of my days and then Arthur shall have it. His fame will overtop mine and he is worthy to be Pendragon of Britain, but the kings will choose Modron because they have no fear of him. And if I leave Modron in Reged he will betray me as he betrayed the Saxons, and if I send him forth he will go to Maelgun and Cuneglas and tell them that the old boar lies asleep in Din Uther. The night will come when I shall see him in the circle of those that hate me, ringing me in with spear and torch. Better it were for me and better for Britain if I have him put to death, this very night, while I lie with his wife, the Saxon woman. . . . My men are with Arthur, camping by the Eden, but Kai I have with me; he would kill Modron to-night if I gave him the word.' Uther stared thoughtfully at the huge figure of the standard-bearer who strode ahead on the forest path, carrying the Red Dragon, and then he said to himself: 'These black thoughts spring up in my mind, taking shape like the monstrous stems of these pine trees sprouting upwards in the forest gloom, twining together like dragons over a floor of dead needles, brooding on death and decay. All my life I have seen men trodden down in death, death by hunger, and death by steel, and death by fire, and death by drowning, and death by poison. Can I hope to escape all these deaths and yield only to old age, as these trees do, withering slowly year by year and falling rotten at last on the top of rottenness? And what follows on death? What do these monks know when they tell us of a purging of sins, of eternal torment for those whose sins cannot be washed away by the mediation of God's Son? Do they know more than the heathen who believe in eternal feasting and battle for the brave man, no matter what his sins have been? No man is ashamed in times like these to bring down an enemy by strength or guile; but what if that enemy be his own son? Shall I break the bond of blood and go scatheless into the next world?'

And Modron thought: 'My father's strength is nearly gone, broken with thirty years of war, his looks are bent to the earth like those of a man carrying a heavy burden; the witches and druids of the western mountains foretell his death within the year, reading fate in the stars, in water under the moonlight, in the entrails of beasts. And when he is dead I shall be the Guletic, the Pendragon of Britain, for so Maelgun promised me if I bring the men of Reged to battle against Cuneglas and Conan. But Uther has as little love for me as I for him. What if he gives Reged to Arthur while he has this army at his beck and call? His end is near, but maybe not near enough. Were it better for me to strike first, while he is in my power? The Church turns its face from the man who is father of his sister's child; will the people follow the man who strikes down his own father?'

Side by side, Uther and Modron rode in the footsteps of Kai bearing the Red Dragon, out of the deathly stillness of the pine wood into the light of sunset by the Eden river. The shoes of the horses clattered suddenly on shingle and boulders; dogs barked and a shout went up from Din Uther, the ring of moss-grown walls on the knoll across the water, topped by beehive roofs and streamers of blue smoke.

* * *

Eadgyth stood in the doorway of the largest hut, watching the rush of women and children towards the gate, vaguely troubled by that cruel exulting shout coming at the end of a long day of disquiet. The men had all gone the evening before, and ever since morning there had been an excited muttering among the women and jeering cries from the children who pointed their fingers at her, grimaced, and ran away when she turned on them angrily, sometimes chasing them over the courtyard, stick in hand. How she hated these Welsh, whose tongue she could not understand, whose slovenly and filthy habits disgusted her, bred up in the Saxon timbered halls, for the true savages were then seemlier in their mode of life than the civilised that had relapsed into savagery. Modron was different. For a time he had enchanted her by his suave, courteous manner, his fine clothes, his gold and jewelled ornaments, his skill in the arts of love, yet lately she had glimpsed something sinister in his brooding looks; there was something incomprehensible to her in his sudden chuckling laugh when he spoke with his men, in his obvious pleasure in the vicious usage of servants or beasts, matters to which she, in the rawness of her experience, was callous and indifferent. And now something was afoot, something menacing to her and her kinsfolk; her slow wits could divine that well enough. What was the meaning of those clouds of smoke that went up over the tree-tops to northward in the early morning? The sight of it had sent all the women climbing on the rampart, pointing, gabbling, and gesticulating.

Slowly, with a sense of fatality, she went out at the gate, between the tall stoups of limestone and over the fosse by a path among heaps of evil-smelling refuse, that fosse which, long years before, Uther had vainly bidden his men deepen until it was flooded by the Eden water. The women and children had made a lane through which a big fair-haired man came with

a swinging stride holding aloft a standard pole.
Behind him came two horsemen, Modron and an old
man in a scarlet cloak, like some malignant troll from
the forest that rose in black pinnacles against a crimson sunset and monstrous shapes of purple-bellied
cloud. A snarling laugh came from the old man as
Modron bent over and muttered a few words to him.
Now she was between the two horses that brought a
chilly reek with them from the passage of the river;
the riders drew in their reins and looked down on her,
dark against the sky, their teeth gleamed in the dusk
as they laughed again, a hollow mocking laugh, while
Eadgyth stared at them under knitted brows. The
jabber of the women, the shrill voices of children
ceased suddenly, the standard-bearer leaned on his
pole, the two riders sat silent; Eadgyth found herself
in the centre of a ring of peering faces; sagging
mouths and eyes gleaming wolfishly.

Her gaze dropped to something that hung from
the saddle of the old man, a severed head hanging by
long flaxen hair. A cramping pain shot from her heart
to her throat. She put out a hand and lifted the head
so that the sunset light fell on the hollow cheeks, the
lips dabbled with blood, the wide-open eyes . . . Eadwald's head, the trophy of this man in the scarlet
cloak, some great king, perhaps, among the Welshmen to whom Modron had betrayed her brother.

The colour flooded back into Eadgyth's face. With
steady fingers she unloosed the knot of hair and took
the head under her arm. No one hindered her: still
silent, they opened out and let her lead the way into
Din Uther, the tall, stately-looking woman holding the
head which bore a ghastly likeness to her own. By the
door of the great hut she paused and turned to face
the throng following her, she opened her lips to
speak, but what was there to say, and would any
there understand her? The men who spoke her

tongue were doubtless dead with Eadwald; she might
be the only Saxon left alive in Reged.

With a sudden thrust of the spurs Modron came
to her side.

"Fetch us mead, woman!" he said in a loud jeering voice. "It is thirsty we are, after the slaughter of
the Saxons. Fetch our strongest mead for Uther Pendragon, the Guletic of Britain, who sleeps to-night in
Din Uther."

Eadgyth stood motionless; then a light seemed to
come into her face, a gleam from the crimson glow in
the western sky. Without a word she walked across
the courtyard to a hut that had barrels of mead
ranged in a circle within. A table stood there covered
with drinking horns; she pushed them aside and set
down the head, passing her hand over the features
while she stood in the half darkness. No one had followed her; a crowd swarmed about the great hut,
before which Kai planted the pole with the Red Dragon.
Her pulses began to hammer; a mist floated before
her eyes. Suddenly she ran out and went to the rampart where brushwood was stacked up and spear
shafts stood against the wall to season. In a corner
among sodden chips and fallen stones was a tuft of
foxgloves. She wrenched up the plants, crushed
them together and hid them in her cloak. Then she
went back to the hut, took a stone quern and put in
it the mass of dark leaves and purple flowers. She
poured in a little mead and began to pound with a
pestle. . . .

Modron stood in the courtyard, his hands thrust
in his belt, his face upturned to the dew that was
falling under the green vault of the sky. Like two
monstrous waves on a stormy sea, the mountains
rose on either side of Din Uther, their tops lost in a
foam of cloud. The air was stagnant and heavy with
the smell of wood smoke, a heavy suspense hung in
the deepening dusk, in the silence broken by the

clatter of a solitary horseman crossing the ford, by the faint thudding sound from one of the farther huts. Modron set his teeth in a mood of devilry; he drew a long breath as though to fortify himself with all the powers of darkness that hovered over Din Uther. Slowly he drew near the hut where the mead was stored, he looked in at the doorway, letting his eyes grow accustomed to the gloom. Now he could see Eadgyth leaning over something on the table, the paleness of her face and of the two plaits of fair hair that fell forward from her shoulders. A little trickling noise, as though something were being poured into a horn, the splash of a beaker in one of the mead barrels, the gurgling sound of a horn being filled to the brim.

"Eadgyth!" he said in a low voice, little more than a whisper.

She came to meet him in the doorway, a long, curved drinking horn in her hand.

"A horn for Uther," he said, backing slowly away from her and staring at her hands to see whether they held a weapon.

"A horn for Uther," she said tonelessly, repeating his words, and moving forward. He let her pass and stood for an instant irresolute.

"Not for nothing do men call me Modron the Quickwitted," he muttered to himself. He stepped inside the hut, felt for a horn and thrust it quickly into the nearest cask, spilled a little back and came out, following Eadgyth. In the glow of light from the door of the big hut he saw a man dismounting from a shaggy pony, a man with a harp in his hand; his son Medraut.

Meanwhile Uther sat with Kai, on couches spread with deerskin, the cheerful glow of the fire between them and the steady pillar of smoke going up to the hole in the high peaked roof. The old man twisted the strands of his beard in his horny fingers.

"The drink is long in coming!" he said, staring questioningly at Kai.

The standard-bearer reached for his unbuckled sword and laid it across his knees.

"It is a small following that Uther Pendragon brings to the House of Modron," he said.

"I have heard it said that Kai has the wits of five men and the strength of ten; am I not safe with him?"

Kai shrugged his shoulders and was silent.

The fire fell together, the flames died down: darkness seemed to drop like a veil between them from the blackened rafters.

"What shall I do, Kai?" said Uther, after a long pause.

"Beware of the Saxon woman."

"I have handled many women in my time," said Uther scornfully.

"Beware, then, of the man who thrusts her into your bed."

"A weariness grows in me as the years pass, Kai. It is a joyless task to rule Britain, yet the blood leaps still to the taste of mead and the kisses of women, and there is Medraut's harp. Life is sweet, Kai."

"Yet to my mind it hands by a thread in Din Uther."

"Give me good counsel, Kai."

"You shall do one of two things. Either mount your horse and ride back to Arthur, where he sits in his tent among the slaughtered Saxons, or send me to kill Modron."

"It sits ill upon the Pendragon of Britain to do either of these things." Kai was silent.

"There is enough British blood on my hands, Kai. You shall get my horse . . . but stay, who comes?"

Medraut stooped under the doorway and came in. He kicked the fire so that flames sprang up again.

"I see small cheer in my father's house," he said laughingly. "Only two grim faces where I had hoped for a sight of the girls of Reged, for meat and drink, and voices raised in song."

"Is Arthur with you?" said Uther, leaning forward.

"The Bear stays with the army: he goes among the men sorting out weapons and binding up wounds." Uther sank back on the couch. He raised his hand as though to signal to Kai, but let it fall again as Medraut took his harp and began to caress the strings. "A song came to me as I rode through the forest," he said, puckering his brows and staring at the fire. Throbbing chords filled the hut and began to drug the senses with an elfish air of gaiety, an ironic accompaniment to the words that followed:

> "Cold the feast by Eden ford,
> Mead nor maid for man providing—
> Uther sits at Modron's board—
> 'Neath the stars the Bear is biding!
> Uther sits at Modron's board.
>
> Swathes there lie on moor and mire
> Where the sword has done the reaping—
> Uther sits by Modron's fire—
> On the dead the wolves are leaping!
> Uther sits by Modron's fire.
>
> Shines the moon on faces cold.
> Dew has silver'd o'er the slaughter—
> Uther sits in Modron's hold—
> Dark as blood is Eden's water!
> Uther sits in Modron's hold."

"A grim song to a gay tune!" said Modron, stepping through the doorway and holding aloft a horn of mead. Behind him came Eadgyth, pale now, with parted lips and glassy eyes. "The feast is cooked, but first shall you taste our brew of mead, Uther! A strong mead spiced with strange herbs that grow in the shadow of Moel Fre—herbs that kindle man's lust like a spark in dry bracken. Bear the horn to Uther, Eadgyth."

The old man leaned forward, his eyes glittered like black beads. With a sudden movement he caught Eadgyth's left hand and spread out the fingers.

"A dangerous playmate you give me, Modron!" he said snarlingly. "No weapon in her hands, but let us see what she has hidden in her dress!" He drew Eadgyth down beside him on the couch, plucked out a dagger and slit her tunic so that her breasts came out into the firelight. His hand groped under her skirt, searching her body—a malignant grin spread over his face, while Eadgyth sat impassive and unresisting, holding the horn with care so that not a drop was spilled.

"A meek heifer she seems, to be sister to that bull Eadwald," he muttered suspiciously.

"Buxom she is in all ways that a woman should be," said Modron, smiling.

"A lovely woman in the fair, barbarous manner of the sea folk," said Medraut, gazing at Eadgyth, while his fingers strayed over the harp, twanging out a new melody.

"Will you ride now to Arthur?" said Kai gruffly.

"Not yet . . ." answered Uther. His hand passed slowly along Eadgyth's arm until it closed over the horn.

"Taste the mead, Modron!" Kai's voice came sharply from the other side of the hut.

"Ay, for sure . . ." Modron grasped the horn in a steady hand, raised it to his lips and took a sip. At once he raised his own horn in turn and brought it likewise to his lips. . . . "Let us drink," he cried, "to the glory of Uther Pendragon, Guletic of Britain. Long life and glory to the conqueror of the Saxons!" He handed back the horn to Uther, who took it and rose to his feet, looking Modron straight in the eyes.

"And I drink," he said in a loud voice, "to my son Arthur. Bravely has he gone before me in every battle! Not more than a ninth part can I claim of the valour of Arthur. I call on you, Modron, and you, Medraut, and you, Kai, to witness that I name Arthur to take my power when my day is done. He, it is, who shall be Guletic of Britain when I am laid in the grave."

None of the men spoke or moved while Uther drained the horn, but Eadgyth slipped quietly to the door of the hut, watching with set teeth and gleaming eyes.

"A bitter brew you have here in Din Uther." The old man threw the horn on the floor. His head sank forward; slowly his body crumpled like an emptying sack and he fell sideways on the couch. Kai rushed to him and raised him up; he thrust a hand into the bosom under the scarlet cloak, he laid his fingers on a skinny wrist.

"The mead has been too strong for him," muttered Modron, gazing, as though fascinated, into the eyes that were still fixed in a scowl of hatred.

"To my mind he is dead, and dead by poison!" said Kai, staring hard at Modron.

"Poison! I tasted for him . . . if there was anything amiss it was the woman's work!" stammered Modron, as Kai laid a heavy hand on his shoulder. The undrunk horn of mead fell to the floor, and the liquor ran hissing among the embers of the fire.

"Ah!" said Medraut, and then: "I ride back to fetch Arthur."

A group of women pushed in carrying steaming joints of meat and loaves of bread. They set up a wailing cry as they saw Uther lying on the couch, his mouth open, one hand trailing on the floor.

"Where is Eadgyth?" shouted Modron. "We must get the truth from her! She drew the mead. Fire or steel will make her speak. Quick! fetch torches!" He ran out into the night. Kai stayed behind with the dead man. Medraut went to the main gate where the horses were eating hay, tethered to crooks in the rampart. He leaned on the back of Uther's stallion and watched. Torches flashed here and there among the huts, lighting up narrow passageways and running figures. Suddenly a man came past holding something in his hands. He ran through the gate and down to the river. In a moment he was back again, breathing hard. "A quickwitted man is my father," said Medraut to himself. A sinister smile crept into his face as Modron came presently with a torch, held it aloft over the uneasy horses and stared at his son.

"I thought you had gone to Arthur," he said menacingly.

"There is time yet. Have you caught the woman?"

"I have searched everywhere—I ran down to the river to see if she was at the ford."

"You have searched the brewhouse, like enough? If it was poison, something might be found."

"I have been there, but let us go again."

Together they crossed the courtyard, they stooped under a doorway and Modron held up the torch. Casks round the walls, a table on which stood a human head, dark shadowed in the flickering glare, and a stone quern. Medraut put his hand inside. It was moist, but empty.

"Those herbs that grow under Moel Fre," he said indifferently.

"We waste time here!" said Modron. "The woman may be hiding among the brushwood; she may have climbed the rampart and taken to the forest. If we could lay hands on her we could get the truth. . . ."

"And tell it to the army."

As Modron led the way out of the hut, Medraut stooped quickly and picked up a tiny object on the floor. His hand closed over it and did not open again until he stood in the light of the full moon. He gazed hard and again his face lit up with a subtle smile. In his palm lay a foxglove bell.

Meanwhile Eadgyth toiled slowly up the mountain face behind Din Uther. She steadied herself against sapling oaks and tore her dress free from sloes and brambles, mounting step by step in the moonlight on a chaos of boulders, wreckage from the crags above. Now she looked back at the lights that flickered to and fro in the lake of darkness beneath her. A keening of women, a faint tang of cooking and wood smoke reached her on the gentle breeze.

"Eadwald is avenged!" she burst out exultantly, yet her savage spirit longed for a more ample vengeance. If only she had the strength of a giant and could tear down these crags and overwhelm that nest of cruel, treacherous people as children stone a viper! As it was, in some instinct of passionate defiance, she lifted her clothes and eased her body in their direction. Then she climbed on, into the mist and over the topmost ledge of the mountain, setting her face towards the sea in the east.

Chapter IV

On Moel Fre

YR AMHERAWDYR[1] ARTHUR. — *Dream of Rhonabwy.*

It was a morning of dazzling sunshine and black clouds racing before the east wind. On the table-like summit of Moel Fre was a great multitude of men, some sitting on small ponies, some standing on foot, leaning on their long spears; there were Uther's legionaries in a solid mass like a big rock set among loose stones and shingle, there were sullen-faced peasants from the little clearings that broke the green mat of forest far below with patches of grass and corn, there were sharp-eyed women and hordes of children squatting in clusters, weary with the long climb on woodland pathways. The crowd formed an arc around the snout of the mountain, an out-thrust headland dropping away sharply in bare screes and precipices. There, on the last few yards of level ground, a hole was dug through the fleece of purple ling and beside it stood Uther's stallion with the dead

---

[1] The Welsh equivalent of the old Roman title "imperator" or general.

body of his master roped to his back, a bulky bundle lapped in a scarlet cloak. Between the crowd and the grave was the Red Dragon standard, planted in the heath, and about it, watching Kai unloose the rope that bound the corpse, stood Modron, Medraut, and Arthur, their heads bare, their cloaks flapping in the wind. A murmur spread from the sea of faces, a murmur that had in it something of grief but more of a blind, emotional response to the cataclysms of nature, like the moaning of a forest in a gust of wind. Kai lifted the body in his great sunburnt arms and laid it in the shallow grave. The crowd surged forward, but the legionaries thrust it back with rough words and levelled spears while a hundred of them gathered stone from the loose edge of the mountain and passed it from hand to hand, setting it up edgewise over the corpse. For a while the scarlet cloak showed among the gritty slabs of rock, then it vanished under the rising dome, and at last, when earth and sods were thrown on top, there was a landmark to the folk of Reged for many centuries to come.

"Some priest of God should be here to put his blessing on the dead man; so is the custom in the south," said Arthur to Modron.

"There are no priests left in Reged," said Modron indifferently. "A few there may be still at what they called Candida Casa, across the sea in Pictland, but there have been none here since the days of Cunedda."

The legionaries moved back, Kai stood with his hand on the standard pole. There was a clear space round Uther's barrow. An old bent man pushed his way forward and struck the mound with a crooked staff, a hollow-eyed man with white locks falling in ringlets over a dirty white robe. He turned and waved a bony arm towards the sun.

"Woe to the House of Uther!" he shouted in a feeble croaking voice. "Woe to the proud princes of Britain! You bloody-minded men steeped in guile and evil lust, doomed to work each other's doom, stinking carrion you are in the sight of gods and men, for you have set the faith of Whitechrist above the faith of your fathers and flouted both! Man's likeness sits upon you, but what are you three princes but evil beasts preying upon each other and upon our whole nation! The Bear, the Fox, and the Serpent! A fire is kindled in this land from one end to the other, and fire shall drive out fire and be quenched in blood, and blood shall be washed out with more blood, and when the land greens again it shall not be for our people! Their bones shall be dust under the feet of those that hate them—our poor hungry folk shall perish for the sins of their princes."

"A druid from the western mountains," said Modron, with a disdainful scowl, but his hand shook as he twisted the ends of his moustache.

"There is some truth in what he says," muttered Arthur, with a grim smile.

"Too much truth!" said Medraut, laughing. "It shall be my task to answer him."

"The best answer were to throw him down the crag," Kai interrupted angrily.

"The words are spoken; we must abide them," said Arthur.

"The people are not moved," said Modron. "They murmur uneasily, but his thin old voice has not reached them. Let the man be—it is a dangerous thing to lay hands on a druid before the eyes of half Reged, but afterwards we will do away with him, out of sight in the forest."

The murmuring from the crowd increased to a menacing roar of voices. Even the legionaries set up a clamour; their ranks wavered to and fro, they seemed to be swallowed up in the masses of angry bewildered people pressing in amongst them.

"It is a leaderless host that stands on Moel Fre," said Kai.

"Speak to them, Medraut," said Modron calmly. "Tell them that Modron, Uther's eldest son, is Guletic of Britain, that he shall make all the tyrants bow their heads before the Red Dragon of Reged, even as his father did before him."

"The Fox shall never be the master of Britain!" said Kai fiercely.

"Evil brings forth more evil!" mumbled the druid. "The House of Uther shall be washed away by its own blood! The strength of the mountains, the darkness of the forest, the fury of the sea shall not avail to shelter our race from the doom that is spoken over it."

"Stand high on the mound, Arthur and Modron; I shall speak to the people!" Medraut leaned against the Red Dragon standard, his harp propped against his waist. He raised his hand and there was a hush. Kai drew his sword and stood beside him. The druid sank down on the heather and covered his head with his robe. "Hear me, you mailed men who have marched with Emrys and with Uther!" shouted Medraut. "Hear me, you folk of Reged, men of the heath and forest who reckon their wealth in cattle and sheep. Uther is dead, and here on his grave mound stand two of his sons. One you know well; he is Modron, my father. His kin are of this land and for thirty years he has ruled Reged in peace, hidden from the flaming torch of war behind these rough mountains. The other is Arthur, whom you know not so well. His kin are in far Dyvnaint, of a noble house that has done mighty deeds against the spoilers of Britain. A man of war is Arthur; he it is who has gone before Uther in battle under this Red Dragon standard; it was his right arm that saved my life at Afon Coch and struck dead the Saxon chieftain—the man who would have made a smoking wilderness of Reged even as his folk have done already in Berneich and Deivr.

"It is Arthur whom Uther has chosen to stand in his place as ruler of Reged and Guletic of Britain, for so he said to me and to Kai and Modron but a moment before he fell dead with the drinking horn in his hand, drinking mead in Din Uther where he was born . . ." Medraut paused for a moment, then went on, stilling a gathering hum with a gesture of his hand: "Do you ask why Arthur shall take his brother's place? I shall tell you, you who know him not. To-day the sun shines on this land of Reged, but black clouds are in the eastern sky. The storm comes driving across Britain; already it has leaped these mountains, touching your huts with flame, ravishing your women, hewing down your flocks and herds. Then came Uther in his scarlet cloak and Arthur on his black stallion, and you mailed men, well practised in war. The storm passed; but it gathers afresh, it will come again with fury tenfold, eating the life out of our land till the Briton is gone from the face of it, trampled to death under the feet of Picts from the northern mountains and Saxons from across the sea. Who shall save you from this storm of steel, this whirlwind of fire? Is it Modron, my father; is it Maelgun, sheltering behind Penmaenmawr, or Cuneglas, ringed about by the dark waters of Severn? I tell you there is but one man in Britain who has the might of arm and strength of spirit to beat back this ruin that swallows our people, and that is Arthur."

He stopped and waved a hand towards the figure of Arthur, massive and motionless, with folded arms, like some rough-hewn wooden image on top of the mound. There was a brandishing of weapons and knotted fists, a doubtful and discordant roar of voices out of which sprang a mighty shout from the legionaries: "Hail! Arthur Guletic."

Arthur did not move, but Modron sprang down from the cairn and rushed to the standard. He clasped the pole in both hands and began to shout:

"They are lies that Medraut is telling you, men of Reged! Mine is the power after Uther! I am his eldest son. Hear me, you howling wolves! I have the might of Maelgun behind me, the Dragon of Gwyneth. He shall smoke you out of your cots and clearings as men smoke out a skep of bees. I doom to death you who will set up Arthur in my place—this Bear from Dyvnaint—no true-born son of Uther, but a fatherless boy reared in the cliff castles of Kernou. . . ."

Foaming with rage, Modron strove to make himself heard, but his voice was drowned by louder and louder shouts:

"Arthur! Let us hear Arthur!"

Medraut laid a hand on his father's shoulder.

"The tide runs against you to-day," he said, with a cold gleam of malice in his eyes. "It would run faster yet were I to show them this—what I found on the floor of the brewhouse in Din Uther." He pointed a finger in his father's face, a finger capped by a foxglove bell. Modron backed away, clutching a dagger; he stepped back farther and farther till he was swallowed up in the crowd. In a while his blue and gold cloak disappeared and few recognised the Prince of Reged in a dirty leather jerkin and a moth-eaten squirrel-skin cap.

Meanwhile Arthur, alone on the grave mound, sought slowly for words. He turned his eyes from the roaring crowd to the vast landscape out of which Moel Fre rose like the paired, empty seats of giants, facing one another across the dark forest floor more than a thousand feet below. His gaze swept the purple wilderness to northward, the Great Heath, blacked by yet greater forests, behind which were the dim hills of Pictland; it swept the long curving face of the Pennines, foaming with limestone scars like a blue wave arrested in its crash downwards upon the Vale of Eden. To westward he saw the rounded heights about Craig Aran, like the brown backs of monsters stooping to drink in glens untrodden by man; far beyond he saw the crests of yet mightier mountains tossing among clouds and grey curtains of rain, and to the south-west he saw the sun gleaming on salt marsh and wet sands and a winding arm of the sea—the path to Gwyneth and Eiré. This land, he thought, lovely in sun and shadow like the face of a woman laughing through her tears, this land of purple heather and green forests and blue hills, bearing in its lap the homesteads of our people clustered together in their little fields and folds like limpets on rocks in the sea, is it in my power to stay the destruction that rushes upon it? Even if I beat back these Saxons, can the people save themselves? Can they ever be otherwise than fierce as fire, weak as water, and wayward as the wind? Can any man deliver them from these princes of Britain that tread them to dust and from the folly and wickedness that devour a people whose spirit is broken by misery?

Suddenly he drew his long heavy sword and held it high in the air, pointing upwards from the cairn of Uther Pendragon.

"Legionaries!" he shouted. "Men of Reged! I claim to be no Guletic of Britain. I am a simple soldier, skilled only in the art of war, but I will be your leader. I shall not lead you to battle to cast down Maelgun or Cuneglas that I may be foremost among the Britons as Uther, my father, was, for a few short years. I shall lead you to war against the enemies of our race, the men who seek to root us out and take our land into their own possession. I give you war that I may give you peace and a breathing space to build a new Britain on the ruins of the old. But the war will be long and desperate, for we have to do with men who are hard as the mountain crags, and men who are fierce and treacherous as the sea from which they come. We shall triumph only if we stand together as comrades from end to end of Britain, comrades knit by the tie of blood, of speech, and of faith in Christ. A sinful man am I, yet I call on God in good hope that He may forgive us our sins and grant us victory, that we may tread down both our evil-minded enemies and the evil that is in our own hearts." For a moment he held aloft the crossed hilt of his sword, then put it back in the scabbard.

Again the confused uproar of the multitude was dominated by a great shout from the legionaries.

"Hail! Arthur yr Amherawdyr!"

The sound rolled away on the wind—making a faint stir among the atmospheric patterns that streamed out over the forest tops and played upon the lifeless crags and screes—a sound quickly lost to human ken yet reverberating afresh century after century in the consciousness of the British race and of many other races as yet remote in space and time.

Arthur raised his hand and in the hush that followed he said: "Medraut shall sing a song to the army, a song that they shall carry on their lips in the war to come."

Medraut climbed up on the mound beside Arthur. He took his harp and struck out the air that he had played day after day on the march towards Reged. His voice rose, sombre and terrible, in tones of passionate defiance:

"Cymry[1] in victory, Cymry in woe!
See those clouds that *darken the sky;*
Pow'rs of evil *riding on high!*
Fiercer yet the storm shall blow;
Cymry of Arthur, face your foe!"

"Blood on the bracken, see, blood on ling;
Roars now storm of *steel upon steel!*
Blow on blow for Britain we deal!
Daring doom, our swords we swing:
Arthur our leader, Christ our King!"

---

[1] Welsh for comrades; pronounced Cumry. Hence Cumberland.

Chapter V

The Slaughter in Berneich

THE FIRST BATTLE WAS AT THE MOUTH OF THE RIVER GLEIN.
—Nennius, *Historia Britonum.*

Arthur and Medraut rode at the head of the army in drenching rain down the forest banks towards the white rumbling torrent of the Tees. They had hoped to encounter and destroy a powerful band of Saxons known to be marching on Reged, doubtless to join Eadwald, but there had not been a Saxon to be seen on all that weary road over the wilderness, past old Roman fortresses half buried in briars and saplings. They had met not a man, woman, or child till they came to the river gorge and saw a few refugees huddled by cooking fires under the beetling cliffs and dripping roofs of foliage. A shrunken, stooping figure came to meet them now, a man covered with a few sodden rags, hollow-cheeked and bright-eyed with fever. Behind him crouched a woman half hidden in volumes of smoke from a fire of wet sticks; she stirred something in a pot, mechanically, with a dull rhythmic violence that seemed inspired only by desperation. On the slimy stones beside her sat two children, naked save for swathings of birch bark, spindle-legged children with protruding bellies and chattering jaws, who stared silently at the oncoming army—the helmeted heads and bare brawny arms, the Dragon Standard, the swaying spears, the tired horses.

"The Saxons have come and gone," said the man in answer to Arthur's curt questioning. "They killed a few folk farther up the river and went forward swift-footed on the road to Reged, but next day they were back again and turned northward into the forest. There was a man on a horse guiding them—a man of our race maybe. Not a few of our people have joined the Saxon bands rather than starve, but the Saxons themselves have little enough. There is scarcely a cow left in all Berneich, south of the Wall, so they say, unless cattle be hidden far up in the valleys where no folk have dwelt before."

"Where shall we find the main strength of the Saxons?"

"A few days ago some men came here too spent with hunger to go farther. They said the Saxon ships are in the bay by Dinguardi, beyond the Wall's end, and that a host is camped inland at Abergleinwy, seizing beasts and harvesting corn as though they meant to winter there. Farther north a great host of Frisians is on the move, but whether they be with the Saxons or against them none know. It is said they have a treaty with the King of the Picts and go to take up land in his country."

Arthur looked significantly at Medraut.

"The Saxons have a warning from Reged," he said, "but we shall bring them to battle at Abergleinwy.

You," he turned to the man, "you have been someone of mark in this land in years gone by?"

"My father was the chieftain over many villages near the sea, where the old signal towers stood. We could get some sort of living there till five summers ago when the Saxons began to come again. Since then we have wandered far over Deivr and Berneich searching for food."

"Will you help us to win back the land for the Britons? We go hungry, yet not so hungry as you do, for we have a hundred cattle on the hoof with us. A man such as you can guide us to Abergleinwy."

"Gladly would I go with you!" The man straightened himself a little. "I know the way, and someone will doubtless lend me a spear, yet I have a woman who has been with me for many years—ailing, she is, now, and weak with hunger."

"It is women we lack in this host," said Medraut with a laugh.

"Forward!" shouted Arthur impatiently. "We must cross the river and follow the trail of the Saxons! It is time our weapons were wet with something else than rain."

Kai went ahead with the standard; waist deep he struggled through the foaming river, the few mounted men pressed their beasts after him, the legionaries followed in a dense column, linking arms and steadying themselves with their spears against the current. With one accord they took up the chant: "Cymry in victory, Cymry in woe!"

"I come!" shouted the fugitive in a hoarse voice, and splashed in beside the armoured men. The woman set up a scream: she ran to the bank shouting prayers and curses.

"What is left for us?" she cried. "You leave us to starve! All these years, and now . . ."

A legionary threw her a bit of oatcake.

"Follow the army!" he said roughly. "The only hope is to follow Arthur!"

"How can I follow with these children?" she cried, frantically stuffing a bit of the oatcake into her mouth.

"Leave the children," said another man. "There is no chance of life for them."

The woman stared at the swaying stream of men pouring down to the ford, churning up the mud, brushing aside the interwoven branches of alder and hazel, men limping and in rags, but each carrying a weapon, and each with a light on his face upturned to the rain in a kind of ecstasy. The song swelled to a loud triumphant roar. She turned back, clutched the children to her and burst into sobs. But late that night, when the army was camped among burnt-out stockades above the Wear, a solitary woman came staggering into the firelight, empty-handed, apathetic as a dumb beast broken down with want and hard usage.

On the next day they reached the Wall. A fortress with blackened, crumbling walls rising out of scrub and lush grass and purple spike of fireweed, and then the Wall itself, a monstrous barrier of masonry, splitting here and there under the pressure of tree roots, tufted for miles with green turf and wind-blown bushes. A tunnel-like archway which had been built up and roughly broken open again. The army climbed over heaps of wreckage that no one had troubled to clear away: they left the Wall behind them and marched due northwards on a straight road. It plunged down into forest and climbed out over heathery wastes, on which were forts, hut foundations, little fields and burial cairns. All was desolate—there was no sign of living man until a day later a tumbled group of high hills rose up on the left and out of their deep recesses sprang a dozen trails of smoke—not the thin blue streamers from cooking fires but dense dun-coloured plumes with here and there a momentary gout of red flame. Even as they watched, some of these plumes died away, disintegrating into a grey veil, while others spurted up miles off to the west and north.

"War work!" said Medraut gaily.

They turned away from the Roman road and struck into tangled tracks along the valley of the Till. Another river wound out of the moorland heights and where the waters met was a green plain dotted everywhere with grazing cattle. Now they could see clusters of huts roofed with turf and half-withered branches, groups of men thickening into dense crowds; they could hear a squealing and bellowing of beasts, a barking of dogs and suddenly the warning note of a horn that echoed from the dreary hills.

"This is Abergleinwy!" said the man who had struggled along with the army ever since they left the Tees.

The Britons answered the horn with a blast of trumpets. Arthur galloped hither and thither on his black stallion. In a few moments he had halted the legionaries on a hillock, screened by thickets of broom. More slowly he got the light-armed men gathered in a long line on the level ground. They moved forward, urging each other on with screaming cries, while the Saxons closed up in a dingy mass, silent save for a low, scornful muttering. Now the bows began to twang with a dull, continuous hum and arrows flew high, descending in a spattering shower on the Saxon ranks. The muttering changed to angry shouts. A chieftain sprang forward waving a sword, the sun broke through the clouds and flashed on the big metal bosses of the Saxon shield wall, on helmets here and there, on a thousand uplifted weapons. The mass of warriors stirred, swept forward with a deep-chested yell. The arrows still whizzed, but the British line began to waver and buckle inwards, it stiffened again and the Saxons crashed into it. For a few minutes the venomous rage of the Celt made head against the blind fury of the Teuton, then the tide of battle rolled on, into the Glein river and across it, spreading out fanwise towards the dark rampart of hills. The trumpets blew again and the legionaries burst through the broom, following Kai with the Red Dragon and Arthur on the rearing black horse. Down they came on the right flank of the rushing crowds of Saxons, stabbing and lunging with short sword and spear, warding off slashing blows with the shield, cutting through the unprotected Saxon ranks like mowers in corn. They came on the inner side of the high bossed shields, plying their weapons on men in linen clothes and leather jerkins, men reeling under the sudden shock, jammed together in masses, hardly able to use their long spears and swords. The Saxon host split up into knots of stubborn but bewildered fighters; the legionaries wheeled this way and that in a solid mass, shield to shield, destroying first one group then another. Meanwhile Medraut was across the river rallying the Britons who had broken in the first charge. With redoubled fury they rushed in upon their disordered assailants, like a pack of hounds closing with a wounded boar, snapping, snarling and worrying. Here and there a few Saxons sought to sell their lives dearly, standing at bay, back to back, among hard-driven arrows, till the legionaries closed in and trampled them underfoot. Others streamed out of the fight and gathered, bleeding and breathless, in front of the camp; they stared sullenly at the level plain strewn with heaped-up corpses and wounded crawling away on hands and knees; inert they watched the Britons advancing. Groans and screams and shouts of rage rose here and there and ceased abruptly as the dark mass flowed on in the wake of a man on a black horse, a broad-shouldered, bushy-bearded man splashed with blood from head

to foot. The trumpets blew again. Already the bowmen were spreading out and letting fly their trial
arrows; the helmeted men were coming on shield to
shield like a living wall. With one accord the remnant
of the Saxons turned and ran. They plunged into the
Till, scrambled out and made for the lower heights to
eastward, behind which lay the sea.

The black ships were hauled up on the beach
between Lindisfarne and Dinguardi. The fugitives
clustered about them, striving to thrust them out on
rollers across the sloppy shining sands, like a horde
of ants struggling with twigs or pine needles. But the
tide was out, and strong men's strength ebbed away
through unbandaged wounds. Not a ship was afloat
when the Britons came swarming out on to the beach
in hot pursuit. The gulls circled over the dusky sands
with their pitiless cries, while once more men faced
each other in rage and despair, their nostrils full of
the tang of the sea and the tarred ships, their feet
caressed by the incoming wavelets that scoured away
the blood-stains and smoothed out the trampled
sand with nature's kindly indifference to human
violence and passion.

The last knot of Saxons fought desperately by the
stern of the ship that was farthest out. A few more
minutes and they would have got her afloat. Wounded though they were, they might have climbed in and
rowed away, perhaps to prolong their lives for a while
on these coasts of Britain, but they were all doomed
to die here, taking their last look at the sun as it
sank, a crimson disc in the haze, flashing redly on
uplifted swords and battered helmets.

Arthur was in the forefront of the final rush. Knee-
deep in the water he hewed down the last Saxon with
his own hands. A wave surged past him and lifted the
ship, and at that moment a man who had hidden
himself on board leaned out with an oar and thrust
off. The ship swung away, but Arthur heaved himself

up over the low gunnel. The man crouched and sprang in with a knife. They wrestled together over the rowing benches. Bleeding from a stab in the cheek, Arthur dropped his sword and fixed his teeth in his enemy's throat; the sinewy figure relaxed its grip and Arthur stepped clear. With a shout of triumph he picked up the sword and slashed the head off the body writhing face downwards in the water that chuckled to and fro in the bottom of the boat. Standing in the bow, he held up the head to the mass of warriors that crowded into the sea, blood-drunken, howling like wolves.

"So perish the enemies of Britain!" shouted Arthur.

"So be it," answered Medraut. He stood right below the prow, leaning on his spear and gazing upwards at the severed head. "Look on that face, Arthur."

Arthur twisted round the head that he held by a handful of long black hair. In the heat of the struggle he had felt something phantasmal hovering on the verge of consciousness, something of vast and ominous import submerged for the moment by the fight for dear life. The face, distorted with terror and hatred, was the face of Modron, his half brother. Below him were the staring eyes of Modron's son, lit with the dawn of a ghastly prevision.

Chapter VI

The Fort of the Legion

GWENHYVAR[1], DAUGHTER OF GWYTHYR.
—*Red Book of Hergest.*

It was on a morning early in summer that Arthur climbed the mountain that bears his name to-day[2]—the double-headed monster, southernmost of all the wild mountains of Pictland, that looks down on the entrance to the Clyde. Without a backward glance he pressed on through the bronze-leafed oak scrub, up among the stunted pines and the tufts of ling that quivered in the wind like brown flame licking the grey boulders, higher and higher on the narrowing crest where old snowdrifts lay ebbing away in dark stains among the crags, till he stood on the topmost peak. Beside him climbed a single companion, Gwythyr ap Greidiawl, the Guletic of Strathclyde, a man double Arthur's age, red-haired, with the build of a giant, but slovenly dressed and kindly, almost simple in his looks. "It is a measure of our

---

[1] The spelling of this name has been slightly simplified.
[2] Ben Arthur.

work, Arthur," he said, with a humorous twitch of his
bushy brows, "that we two can come thus far unat-
tended, when a year ago it was a foolhardy man who
went a dozen yards from his fellows for nature's necessity, camped by the Pictish march."

"To my mind our work will not be done till we have
dealt with the Pict as we have dealt with the Frisian
and the Saxon." Arthur stared broodingly at the grim
array of mountains to northward, peak beyond peak
and crag beyond crag till they faded in the summery
haze, leaving their snowdrifts like streaks of foam in
a uniform sea of grey.

"It is a bloody-minded man that you are!" said
Gwythyr with a sigh. "Can we put a whole nation to
the sword in a land such as that?"

"These are the men that have wrought the ruin of
Britain, these vermin lurking in their wilderness like
rats in a stone heap. These, and the Scots from
across the sea, have made the path that the Saxons
tread to-day."

"There is room for them and room for us; turn and
look upon the land we have won, Arthur." He pointed
southward to the silvery wedge of the Clyde, narrowing at the foot of a double-peaked rock, a tiny replica
of the mountain on which they stood, to the flat,
forested plains of the Forth, and the far-flung line of
rounded hills behind which lay Reged and Berneich.

"We have ploughed but one field of the many that
are overgrown with weeds," said Arthur gloomily.
"What is this but Valentia of the Roman time, the
least regarded province of Britain?"

"A fair land I call it, well stocked with sheep and
cattle and hardy men. A powerful prince was my
grandfather, Ceretic, ruling from sea to sea in his hall
by the Fort of the Legion, under the rock of Alcluyd."

"I shall build a new fort on that rock," said Arthur
suddenly. "Arthur's Castle it shall be called, and I

shall set you in it, Gwythyr, to be a fierce watchdog at the gate of Britain."

"I should be better pleased if you sat in it, Arthur. Then the terror of your name will give peace to this land. We shall lie at ease like men in the pleasant shade of a tree when labour is over in hayfield and harvest. I have no son, but I have a daughter, Gwenhyvar. Take her, Arthur, and breed up a line of kings to enjoy what we have won with the sword."

A slow smile spread over Arthur's harsh face; he sat down on a rock and said:

"Perhaps I shall rest awhile."

His eyes wandered over the vast landscape—the hills, plains, forests, and deep shadowy valleys won back for the British race in three years of war. 'I have done much,' he thought, 'more than Uther, more perhaps than Emrys. Many a man would be content.' He thought of the hard-won victory at Abergleinwy, of the destruction of the Frisian host by the banks of Nith, the long struggle with hordes of Pictish raiders, light-footed elusive bands, savage as wolves and cunning as foxes. Gwythyr and his people had been chased into hiding by the headwaters of the Clyde, behind the Fire Hill, that far-away blue breast with a nipple on the top, but Gwythyr and Arthur together had turned the tide in four fierce fights by the Duglas water, and they had driven the Picts behind their mountain barrier after the tremendous slaughter of Cat Coit Celidon[1]—that desperate encounter when the Pictish king put forth all his strength in the dark glades of the forest and corpses lay in great drifts about the scaly trunks of primeval pine trees. Perhaps there had been slaughter enough, perhaps the land was safe now for the people who had grown out of it century after century as trees, flowers and grass grew out of the earth. 'Once we have taught these

---

[1] Literally "The Battle in the Forest of the Woody Hills."

enemies of ours,' he thought, 'that there is no profit
to them in coming to take our land from us, to rape
our women and spoil our goods, then we shall be at
peace. But will Briton dwell in peace with Briton? If I
give the land peace will the princes cherish it? I can
make peace in Strathclyde and Reged; but can I make
it in Gwyneth and Dyvnaint?'

And then he thought: 'This man Gwythyr, with his
smooth tongue and his smiling eyes, he deceives me,
talking of peace and rest and the pleasures of love.
Have I forgotten that only yesterday a message came
from the east saying that Saxon ships had been seen
battling with a storm off the shore of Berneich? Did I
climb this mountain to-day to look back on what I
have done in the past three years and dream of peace
for Britain? Was it not rather to watch for the signal
of war smoking from some height on the rim of
Strathclyde? Gwythyr and I, we are two men who sit
at ease at the drinking board planning how we shall
bestow our goods on those that come after us, while
the enemy draws near with a ring of steel and fire to
burn us in our beds.'

That night there was a feast in the Fort of the
Legion, for Gwythyr had just finished raising a hall in
the ruins of the Roman barrack buildings and covering it with a roof of reed thatch. It was a council and
dining hall, but it had no resemblance to the elegant
triclinium of a Roman governor, being a mere barn
with benches and tables and a fire on the floor, after
the fashion of the Saxon halls that were springing up
at the river mouths of Eastern Britain. Still, there
was shelter from wind and rain, there was roasted
meat and rye bread and oatcake and ale. At the high
table sat Arthur with the most notable champions of
his host. Kai was there, and Bedwyr, a kinsman of
Arthur from Dyvnaint, and Medraut, silent, with his
eyes on Gwenhyvar who sat beside Gwythyr, and
Mabon, a younger son of Modron, who had come

north with a fresh army from Caer Luel, and many more were there; chieftains from the glens of Strathclyde and legionaries who had won fame by daring deeds at Abergleinwy or in the Wood of Celidon. And when the feast was over there was laughter and boasting and part-singing of songs, as was the custom of the Britons, and save for the ready wit and a certain pride of bearing that was a shadowy legacy of forgotten culture, there was not much but this singing to mark their difference from some band of Saxons at a drinking bout, for the Saxons shouted their rough alliterative lines in unison. Then Gwythyr called on Medraut to play on his harp, but Medraut refused, saying that his mind was only tuned to gloomy melodies that night, and even when Gwenhyvar called to him to sing them the Song of Cat Coit Celidon, the air that had put life into the weary host on dusky forest pathways through the Pictish marsh, he shook his head, pushed aside his drinking horn and went out into the night.

Now he stood in the warm darkness by a gateway of the fortress, watching the flickering radiance of camp-fires rising against a looming black mass that clove the starry sky, the great rock of Alcluyd.

This is Arthur's work, he thought, Northern Britain won back in seven great battles, peace for the peasant to plough and sow, peace for the chieftain to ride through the Straths with hound on leash and hawk on wrist, to drink and sing at the ale board and give away girls in marriage. . . . This Gwenhyvar, golden-headed, with eyes like the blue of the distant mountains, whose face was changeable as the sea, sullen or gay as the talk eddied about her like smoke from the fire, as her thoughts sped this way and that and her blood leaped, stung by the heady mead, kindled by the hot breath of wantonness that swept over men and women alike now that hunger was appeased and death held his hand. Gwenhyvar who was to be the bride of Arthur. . . . But what thought would Arthur the warrior give to this lovely playmate, this sweetly tuned instrument on whom a man such as he, Medraut, might play a thousand delicate airs, laying up glamour for a lifetime? She would signify nothing to Arthur but a momentary wakening to lust amid the labours he had set himself, a hope now and then that heirs might follow him to hold fast this land of Britain that he meant to wrench from the hands of Pict and Saxon. It was Arthur that men saw as the saviour of Britain, not his kinsmen: Uther who had humbled the pride of the princes, Modron whose head had fallen in the slaughter after Abergleinwy, Medraut who smote hard in battle but was tainted in blood. He was brushed aside—men called on him for a song, but they did not offer him the leadership of armies, and a girl of the house of Ceretic in marriage. . . . "It is my work," he muttered to himself. "Arthur wields the sword, but it is I who have tempered it and laid it in his hand. I sang to the people on Moel Fre and their hearts will stir to that music so long as the British race endures, I foiled my father when he would have taken the power from Arthur, my harp fired the host when it was faint with fear and weariness. Am I to have nothing and Arthur all?"

A woman came across the open spaces of the camp, moving slowly past the groups of men that sat by the fires shouting over their ale, gnawing at bones, or crushing girls in their arms. With her face turned to the stars she climbed the broken stairway beside the fortress gate. Medraut followed her. They stood side by side on the turf of the ramparts, looking out over ruined parapets to the silvery sweep of the Clyde rippling silently in the moonlight.

"What is it you seek, Gwenhyvar?" he said gently. "Do you leave Gwythyr's hall to feel the dew on your face and breathe the air that comes from the moun-

tains, or do you too seek love, like all these women
that have flocked to the army?"

"I think my wits are clouded with the heat and the
strong mead," she answered, pushing the hair back
from her forehead. "My father has promised me to
Arthur—and I found nothing to say."

"And does your heart not burn for the champion
of our people, Arthur yr Amherawdyr?"

"There is no man like him," she said simply, "yet I
am afraid."

"There is no woman like you in the land between
Forth and Tees, nor in Maelgun's hall at Deganwy,
nor among those that lie in the arms of Cuneglas at
Lis Pengwern."

"Maybe; a mighty man would be my choice, a warrior feared by his foemen and just and generous to
his friends, but not one who is more than man."

"Is Arthur more than man?" said Medraut, and
his voice had a mocking tone. "Is he stronger than
Kai, has he won greater victories than Emrys? Is
his race more glorious and honourable than that
of Ceretic?"

"Tell me, Medraut." She laid a hand on his
arm. "Were not the old rulers of Rome called
Amherawdyr?"

"It is our word for Imperator, so the monks say."

"And these men were gods, worshipped in temples, before the Christian faith grew to power?"

"Yes; it was wise to hail them as gods."

"To my mind there is something god-like in Arthur.
He seems to stand above the passions and the weakness of ordinary men as a dark rock stands in the sea;
the strength of the hills is in his heart, and his eyes
mirror death, not gladness and love-play."

"Your mind is simple, Gwenhyvar, untrained in
the subtleties of life; your eyes see shapes but not
their structure, as when you look toward the Rock of
Alcluyd by night and see only a black wall which

might defy all but the birds of the air. But when day pierces the darkness you may see many a green ledge and trodden path on which a man may climb to the top. So, too, with rocks standing out in the waves, you have seen Ailsa, but I have seen other rocks of unlike quality, tall pinnacles, red and white, like proud statues along the shores of Dyvnaint, and the breakers fret them away so that there are fewer now than there were in man's memory. So it is with the heroes of Britain; their strength passes and in time they will be gone. You must be the mother of fresh heroes, Gwenhyvar, men whose eyes shall mirror death to Britain's enemies when Arthur is fallen."

"Are not our wars ended?" she asked wearily.

"Only for those who hide their heads in the deepest glens of Gwyneth, or for those that cross the sea to the oakwoods of Armorica. Britain is like a honeypot set between three nests of wasps—the Picts, the Saxons, and the men of Eiré."

"And must I stay here and bear children that will never see days of peace, only blood and fire and the flashing of weapons?"

"It is only Arthur that can give the land peace; and he, perhaps, only in his lifetime."

"The land!" she echoed. "Why should we die for this land when we can live elsewhere?"

Medraut was silent. 'I go blindly on,' he thought, 'helping Arthur to power, risking my life again and again, and to what end? I owe a debt to my kinsman, but I have repaid it many times. I love this land, and music leaps up in my mind when I think of the wind roaring in the forest tops and breakers flinging spray upon the cliff walls of Britain, yet it is true there are other lands where a man need not live sword in hand, and where Gwenhyvar could have all that she desires, mated to a man such as I am, and not to a demigod, such as Arthur . . . .'

"Give me counsel, Medraut!" she said pleadingly. "Surely your heart is not hard towards women—you are not as all these men who have lived in war and snatch pleasure with greedy arms as a dog snatches a bone, you who stand long watching sunset colours behind blue hills and whose harp brings forth music magical as the song of the birds in spring."

And Medraut thought, 'Pleasure is a small thing when we glut ourselves with it at the first wanton stirring of the flesh. Happiest is he who has the power to drain the untasted horn, to pick the unpicked fruit and who holds his hand, sporting with his desire as a cat may play with a mouse.' And then he thought: 'The time will come when I shall take a price for my father's head. Blood calls for blood and dishonour is quenched in dishonour, even as the druid foretold on Moel Fre. The only thing worth having is power—power to work good and power to work evil, to do and undo, to make and mar. The common man loves the sun and fears the darkness, but my delight is in both.' He drew a deep breath and answered in a gently mocking tone:

"Is it so hard to be the wife of a hero?"

"It is hard to sit on some windy hilltop within guarded ramparts, or in some deep forest dale among women and old men, waiting for news of the battle."

"Then you should go with your man to war, as the Saxon women do, riding a good horse, a spear in your hand and your breasts shielded with mail. Far from Strathclyde you will go, safe yet unsafe in a host of men who have their faces set towards new lands and doubtful issues. And life will beat more fiercely in you, Gwenhyvar, when death may lurk behind the next hill. The tramp of marching men will be music in your ears, no mead will taste like the spring water in some forest glade, no bed will seem so soft as the heather where we fling ourselves down to rest, no dawn will seem more lovely than the one when the host wakes to the trumpet blast and the low sunshine glitters on the round shields of the Saxons. And after the battle what pleasure will be greater than to do what woman can for her lord who comes wild-eyed from the slaughter, reeking with sweat and blood, joyful in having dealt another famous blow for Britain?"

"It is easy for you, Medraut," she said, and her hand reached towards him as though to draw some reassurance from his dark figure leaning with folded arms against the fragrant moss and fern of the parapet. "What are danger, wounds, and death to you? What are the swaying fortunes of our people but a theme for glamorous words, a stormy tale to be told on the strings of your harp?"

"Listen, Gwenhyvar!" he answered fiercely. "We live in the most fateful hour of our people's history, when all hangs by a thread whether we beat out the storm that has drowned the Roman world, or whether we plunge downwards, a rotten ship swept by the waves of the Saxon sea. And if our race lives on in the ages to come it will tell of three figures that stand out in the twilight—the dusk before night or before the dawn—three figures like stark mountains overtopping a tangled forest, caught in the glow of a waxing or a waning light; Arthur, Medraut, and Gwenhyvar."

There was a long silence. Then a murmur of voices rose from the hall, dark shapes stirred about the camp-fires, flame and smoke leaped out in a moaning gust of wind.

"The folk are uneasy," said Medraut. "It is time for Gwenhyvar to pledge herself to Arthur the Warrior."

"I shall play my part," she said in a toneless voice.

Like a dark shadow she glided noiselessly away from him, down the steps and across the trodden wreckage of the fortress towards Gwythyr's hall. Medraut leaned against the parapet, his eyes fixed on the blackness of the rock of Alcluyd.

"Arthur!" he said under his breath. "Have you the same forward vision that I have? Do you see as I saw at Afon Coch and on the beach after Abergleinwy?" He set his teeth and with a vicious impulse conjured up the phantom that he could summon at will, as from some rent in a veil—the veil that hid the years to come, impenetrable to some men, but tenuous to others. . . . Slowly the darkness became transfused by the shape of a man looming above him, a monstrous figure, pale, bloody, corpse-like, yet whirling a sword.

"Where shall it be?" whispered Medraut, striving to avert his gaze from that hollow-eyed spectre, death-dealing in the moment of its own dissolution.

Now there was a glimmering of water, a low hillside on which stood out a few wind-blown trees against a crimson sky with mounting wisps of flame-coloured cloud.

"Where?"

The word crossed his lips, but his mind flashed suddenly to overwhelming dread, to horror and self-disgust. The vision faded.

Chapter VII

Cerdic at the Broch of Guinion

THE EIGHTH BATTLE WAS NEAR THE CASTLE OF GUINION, WHERE ARTHUR BORE THE IMAGE OF THE HOLY VIRGIN, MOTHER OF GOD, UPON HIS SHOULDERS, AND THROUGH THE POWER OF OUR LORD JESUS CHRIST AND THE HOLY MARY, PUT THE SAXONS TO FLIGHT.

—Nennius, *Historia Britonum.*

It was the morning after the wedding night of Arthur and Gwenhyvar, a morning of thick mist followed by rain. The mountains were lost in a lowering drift of dun-coloured cloud; only the great rock of Alcluyd rose like a knotted fist out of the waste of sodden tree-tops and slimy sands, its precipices burnished with grey gleams from a wan radiance in the east. The smoke hung low in Gwythyr's hall and rain dripped through the roof into sooty puddles on the uneven floor. Mud, filth, broken bones, the reek of spilled ale and unwashed clothing—the seemliness of life had gone into eclipse behind the darkening fortunes of the British race, yet the flame of life itself still glowed fiercely amid gloom and squalor.

The champions of Britain emptied their horns of drink, their eyes shone, their hands gesticulated eagerly, their voices rose, loud and passionate, in genial fellowship, and in the high seat sat Arthur and Gwenhyvar, their golden heads close together, talking low, their faces calm with a dreamy content.

"What is to be my morning gift, Arthur," she said playfully, "now that I am the foremost woman of Britain?"

"All that you desire, that shall I give you, if it be in my power," he answered, smiling and slipping an arm round her waist.

"And who has such power as you have?"

"My power rests on my sword and on the swords of those that follow me; maybe on the prayers of the Christians, but more, maybe, on the magic of the spoken word and the harp music of Medraut."

"Is song mightier than the sword, Arthur?"

"It is the passion of our people. Even a weakling has the courage of ten champions when music beats in his blood, for this music comes like the scent of flowers and the murmur of water, out of the very heart of our land, and when we hear it the land seems to us a jewel to be guarded more jealously than gold or goods."

"Blue hills and hazel brakes and golden gorse, are they dearer to you, Arthur, than the love of woman?"

"It is magic that makes them seem so, and yet, what can man and woman be to each other unless they have the land for food and shelter?"

"The land drinks the life-blood of our people; their strength ebbs away when their veins are opened at Abergleinwy and Coit Celidon. There is another way of life—the way of the Saxons and the men of Eiré—to live on the sea in ships, and passing from land to land, to take what they need and what pleases them. Build me a ship, Arthur, let us sail together with a guard of champions, free as birds of the air that spread their wings, skimming from isle to isle in the western sea!"

"An unwise thought, Golden Head!" said Arthur indulgently. "The men that live by ships become no better than wild beasts, building nothing and spoiling all. Our strength has not ebbed so far that we need quit our heritage and seek fresh homes among the faint-hearted in Armorica. Our swords are sharp and our women go heavy with child—fresh champions shall follow in the footsteps of those that fight and fall. Will you bear me sons that shall be towers of strength for Britain, Gwenhyvar?" His hands gently lifted the breasts under her tunic.

"What needs be, I shall do," she said with a sigh.

"Do you give gladly to Arthur?"

His voice seemed to strike some chord in her heart—a deep, ominous note, and she answered quickly, bright-eyed, thrusting herself nearer to him.

"Gladly I give! Would any woman deny herself to the Bear of Britain?"

"And what shall I give you in morning gift, my Gwenhyvar? Shall I put a gold chain about your throat, shall I cover you with a silken mantle, or will you have hawks and hounds to sport with when I build you a house far from the Northern March, perhaps on the green plains of Usk or in some deep combe of shaggy Dyvnaint?"

"Build no house for me till your wars are over and you can dwell in it in peace! The gift I ask is a good horse, a saddle and a coat of mail. Let me ride with the army when you march to battle."

Arthur laughed and shook his head; he drew her fondly towards him, but she stiffened in his clasp and turned up her face to his, flushed and angry-eyed.

"Am I Arthur's mate or Arthur's plaything? Am I to share pleasure only, never danger and hardship? I, the daughter of Gwythyr ap Greidiawl! You say there is magic in Medraut, that his words put fire into our folk—is there no magic in this face of mine, Arthur, magic to stir men to desperate deeds? Or am I a girl such as other girls, bred up only to milk and make hay, to spin and weave, to lie in bed with men and suckle their children?"

Arthur's hand grew heavy on her shoulder; he pushed her back and stared at her with a grim smile.

"You are indeed the daughter of Gwythyr," he said shortly, "but your place is not in an army marching to war."

There was a sound of splashing and chattering outside the hall, a sudden hum of voices, a crowding of men towards the door. Arthur was on his feet in a moment, his hand dropped away from Gwenhyvar.

"Little luck shall I bring the man who leaves me penned up like a sow in a stall!" she threw at him, but he was gone, thrusting his way among the champions, clapping the hard-faced legionaries on the shoulder and shouting: "What news? Is it war?" Across the hall she saw Medraut sitting at a table where lay a horn and a harp, his chin resting on his hands. Alone he sat there, his eyes fixed on her in stealthy appraisal so that her heart began to beat heavily and her limbs shook as they had never done under the gaze of Arthur.

She turned away, clenching her fists, forcing herself to listen to the confusion of voices in the hall.

"News from the East!" "The Saxons—three hundred ships or more at the mouth of Tweed."

"The Saxons!" she thought, and suddenly the leaping flame of anger in her died down. The harsh, god-like figure of her husband shrank in her mind's eye, so that she could almost hear it. The simple soldier, the Amherawdyr, the Bear of Britain—did he think that his only enemies were the Saxons? Had he no eyes for Medraut sitting alone and weaving his spells, the man who waited and watched, with music in his voice and some dreadful purpose in his heart? "Strongest of all is the bond of blood," she had heard Arthur say, when he and Gwythyr were camped by the Duglas and a fair stranger had come into the army, a strong and steely man, Cerdic by name, with thin lips and the fierce gaze of a bird of prey, carrying a Saxon shield, but speaking the British tongue. A wise saying, she had thought then, glad that Arthur welcomed the splendid-looking warrior, though Gwythyr eyed him askance. But foolish, she thought now, when she could read the mind of the man who was nearest of all to Arthur in blood. . . .

Cerdic—they were speaking of him now. "Cerdic stands fast at the Broch of Guinion, but few folk gather to him."

Surely Arthur had been right to trust Cerdic even if he was wrong to trust Medraut. The man had fought like a lion on the Duglas and at Cat Coit Celidon—he had been among the bravest of the brave in the Pictish war and Arthur had made him guletic of the land between Tweed and Forth. And Cerdic had come to the Fort of the Legion and asked for the hand of Gwenhyvar. And she—yes, she would have gone with him to the Broch of Guinion, the old tower built by some Pictish prince high above Gala Water—she would have chosen Cerdic the eagle rather than Arthur the bear or Medraut the serpent, but Gwythyr had refused him very shortly, and Cerdic had gone back alone to the east.

"Blow the trumpets!" Arthur was shouting. "Gather our people together! Before midday we must be on the road to join Cerdic."

But Gwenhyvar heard nothing of this; at the first mention of Cerdic she had seen Medraut's face turn to her with a smile that seemed half pitying, half filled with a devilish malice.

* * *

Cerdic stood on the top of the Pictish tower, a tall, tapering cylinder of masonry that rose like a finger pointed to heaven on the rugged hills above Gala

Water. He stood motionless, with folded arms, his
cold blue eyes sweeping the landscape like those of a
bird hovering in mid-air. On all sides of the tower was
a wilderness mottled here and there with green
patches in which were huts and folds. To northward
there was not a sign of life, not a beast or man on the
clearings, not a wisp of smoke rising against the quivering birch woods and fading into the blue sky. To
southward, down the winding valley towards the
blunt cones of Eildon, there were abundant signs of
man's activities, but they were signs of death and
destruction. Trails of moving figures on the bare
moors, broad pillars of smoke swaying up from a
dozen villages, a dense mass of men jostling their way
up a narrow track between forest slopes and the valley bogs. The Saxons were coming. Here was half
their host feeling its way up Gala Water and Cerdic
knew that the other half was going up the Lauder, a
few miles to eastward across the rolling heights of
Guinion. They would unite in the low country by the
Forth and spread ruin from sea to sea; then perhaps
they would recoil towards their ships, mark out land-
takes, build themselves halls and houses with the
women and cattle they had swept together after a
summer's harrying. They would send back boasting
messages to their kinsfolk by the Elbe and Weser, and
next year there would be more of them, fresh harry-
ings, fresh groups of timber halls with brawling dull-
faced men sitting over their drink or sallying out, axe
on shoulder, to fell the forest and split the skulls of
any Britons they found in it. It was the beginning of
the end; the Saxons were coming and the Celts were
going back and back, their hearts eaten out with rage
and despair, towards the high mountains and the
western sea. A tide was rolling in from the east, lapping over the green fields and the ruined towns, and
there were no chieftains in Britain that could turn it,
not Conan and Gereint in the south, nor Arthur and

Gwythyr in the north. But Cerdic had no fear of what was before him. The men he had been set to rule over, they had scattered and sped away light-footed to the deepest glens of Ettrick and Yarrow and Teviot Head. He alone remained on the Broch of Guinion, watching coolly the tokens of approaching war. Why should he fear the Saxons when he had spent half his life among them, and what cause had he to love the Britons? His grandfather had been a landowner in the Thames Valley with a mansion in London, a man of wealth, speaking the Latin tongue, a descendent of Roman officials. He had been put to death and his property seized by Vortigern, the tyrant who had admitted the Jutes to Kent. In the wars that followed Cerdic had sought safety with the invaders, not with the defenders of Britain. Before he was twenty he had been the leader of a band of South Saxons raiding the big estates on the fringes of the Forest of Anderida, he had helped in the sack of Venta, he had been wounded in a fruitless assault on Sarum. Alone of his company he had escaped from the slaughter made by Emrys, and sailed away with beaten warriors to Germany, come back to the North when Berneich was raided, and found himself alone on the hills above Abergleinwy when the Saxons were rolled back to the sea. There was nothing for it but to bow the knee to Arthur or else perish in the wilderness. His fortunes rose again in the Pictish war, he won broad lands for himself, the title of guletic, but he did not win the hand of Gwenhyvar. Now a fresh wave of ruin was advancing on Britain and Cerdic was resolved that it should bear him on its crest to still greater power. A man such as he was born to rule—a Saxon soothsayer had foretold that he would found a line of kings— a druid foretold that his house would rule all Britain and many other lands besides. He was not going to perish in this dark rat-haunted tower, hoping against hope that he would see, before it was too late, Arthur on his black stallion and Kai with the Red Dragon coming over the hills from Strathclyde. Here were the first Saxon spears bristling on the brow of Guinion. . . .

Cerdic climbed down a narrow stairway in the thickness of the wall. He crawled on his hands and knees along galleries where a hound could scarcely have stood erect, through little sleeping rooms with loops to the roofless well of the tower, and finally he crept out of a hole on to a ladder and descended to the circular floor at the bottom of the shaft of masonry. On hands and knees again he made his way out by a tortuous passage to a courtyard littered with tumbled ruins and black with fires. A bunch of grimy, frowsy-headed ruffians was scrambling in over the outer wall. They came on with guttural shouts, waving their axes drunkenly, their greedy blue eyes fixed on the gold-hilted sword that hung at Cerdic's belt, on his silver buckles and polished steel helmet.

"Hah!" a bestial, bloodthirsty yell echoed from the blank face of the tower, but Cerdic only smiled, as though the sight of these savages awoke pleasant recollections in his mind.

"Hail, Saxons!" he shouted. "Welcome to the Broch of Guinion!"

"What is your name, you stranger, who speak our tongue?" answered a big man with a beard the colour of ripe corn. He strode heavily to within a spear's length, spat on his hands and took a firm grip of a short-shafted axe.

"Cerdic I am called."

"You are a Briton by the look of you." The axe rose in the air.

"Maybe, but I have fought side by side with you Saxons in many parts of Britain. I have made havoc in the south and havoc in the north."

"Cut him down!" growled the men crowding behind their leader.

"Fell him, Ceolred! We deal in blows, not in words."

"I am more use to you alive than dead. Do you know the Britons as I know them? Do you know where their strength is and where their weakness? Where they hide their women and their cattle, where you may lay your hand on horses, on coats of mail, on gold-hilted swords?"

"How shall we know whether your words be true?" The yellow-bearded man lowered his axe uncertainly.

"You can take my life when you find them false. It is power that I seek, power over this land of Britain, and I seek it with the help of you Saxons. Why else should I wait for you here when all others have fled? But now that we are face to face I doubt whether luck goes with you. Few you seem, and ill armed for such an enterprise as I have in mind. What chieftain rules over your host?"

"That man am I. Ceolred is my name. Ceolred, son of Ceolbert," said the big man gruffly.

"I have heard of you in the Burg at Stade—a land-waster, well spoken of," said Cerdic in a detached tone.

"This is the third time that my ships have brought me to Britain and it shall be the last time!" the Saxon began to shout. "I shall stay in this land and master it. I shall make myself a king!"

"I shall be a king before you are, friend Ceolred."

"How so? You stand here a single man with a single sword, though maybe a good one," Ceolred looked inquisitively at the gilded hilt and the scabbard bound with interlacing serpents in bronze. "I have a thousand warriors with me: they are a match for thrice that number of cowardly Welshmen."

"It is wit you lack, more than warriors," said Cerdic bluntly.

Ceolred gaped, he twisted his beard, but finding no answer to this, his eyes began to blaze with fury.

Cerdic thrust his hands in his belt, took a step nearer the Saxon and said significantly: "Where are your
men, friend? I have watched for awhile from the top
of the tower, but from what I have seen of them I
reckon them at far short of a thousand."

"Five hundred are on the march through the dale
to the east of us, following a trusty guide. Three hundred are here." He pointed to the ever-increasing
mass of men climbing into the courtyard and staring
at the tall windowless tower. The word "Treasure"
began to be muttered on every side.

"You are two hundred short," said Cerdic.

"A few are watching the ships; the rest have gone
farther up the main river, seeking cattle. They will follow us to-night, and to-morrow we shall stand a
thousand strong on the far side of these hills."

"If I know anything of the men you make war on,
I doubt whether you will reach the other side of the
hills with a thousand men. Two hundred of your men
are as good as lost already."

"Do you foretell ill luck for our men? Beware, or
my axe shall cut short the spoken words!"

Again Ceolred swung his weapon, but his rage
turned to bewilderment as Cerdic smiled in his face.

"I do but seek to save your men from their own
folly," he said calmly. "Have you heard of the champions of the Britons who sit feasting under the rock
of Alcluyd? Have you heard of Arthur?"

"I have never troubled to learn the names of Welsh
chieftains," said Ceolred scornfully.

"If I mistake not you will have learnt something
about Arthur before sunset to-morrow. He is warned;
he knows of your design, he has made plans even
while your ships were being buffeted back to the
mouth of Tweed."

"The sooner we fall on him the better: then the
land will be ours."

"It is he who will fall on you. I have certain knowledge that he will cross the hills from Strathclyde into the glens of Tweed. As for your men that have gone that way . . . " Cerdic shrugged his shoulders.

There was a pause. "What counsel do you give us?" said Ceolred sulkily. Cerdic's face lit up.

"Wisely you speak now, friend, and I shall give you good counsel. Call off these men that have burrowed into the tower seeking treasure. There is none there that I know of. Set them to piling stone on these outer walls! Let us have a strong burg that will daunt even the Red Dragon of Arthur; bring your booty within, fetch water from the spring on the hillside, and, before all, send swift messengers to summon your men here from east and west."

"We have no skill in laying stone on stone," grumbled the Saxon. "I am for a good fight on clear ground, not for hiding our heads behind old walls."

A murmur began among the men on the hillside below; it swelled to a roar of rage and defiance. A single warrior pushed his way into the courtyard, his face black with blood, a broken arrow sticking in one shoulder.

"News!" said Ceolred, his eyes beginning to glint like those of a dangerous wild beast.

"I can guess it," said Cerdic.

"We have fought, Ceolred," said the man in a dogged voice. "We had taken a flock of goats in a little dale north of the river when Welshmen came upon us, many a hundred of them, singing a song and following a big man on a black horse. They ringed us in and I was the only man that broke through. The rest are dead."

"My son Ceolric is dead, and Wulfstan and Eadwulf?" The big Saxon stood with his hands fallen.

"They all died facing their foemen."

"So be it." Ceolred clenched his fists: a row of broken teeth showed through his beard. "Hear me, men!"

He turned to the surging mass of figures on the hill-
top, helmeted heads, spears and axes rising darkly
against the clear greening sky. "Make good these
walls. Let them be our shield to blunt the weapons of
the Welshmen. We shall stand here and make a
slaughter of our foes as a boar at bay deals out death
to a pack of hounds."

* * *

Dusk had fallen when the British army, pressing on
from the slaughter in Caddon, entered the Torwood,
a hoary forest that hid the union of Tweed and Gala.
The long column of armed men came swaying forward, dim-eyed and drunk with weariness, like sleep
walkers following the Red Dragon and the sombre
shape of Arthur on the black stallion. Clink of
armour, the dull rumble of dragging footsteps on turf,
a steamy vapour rising in the tunnel-like passage
under monstrous boughs of oak; the breath of war
rolled on into the silence of primeval woods. Two figures stood in the bracken at the path side, a youth
and an old man, shrinking backwards into the gloom,
as Arthur pulled in and hailed them.

"Where lies the main body of the Saxons? Speak
up and fear not! We come to deliver the land, to strike
a blow that shall give it peace."

"The Saxons are gathered on the Broch of Guinion," answered the youth, a shepherd in a sheepskin
cloak, a crook in his hand, weaponless save for a
bronze knife.

"What news of Cerdic?"

"I know not whether he be alive or dead."

"You shall be our guide. Fast as we have come,
night overtakes us and we must camp at the Broch of
Torwood. To-morrow we shall bring the Saxons to
battle. You, old man, what have you to tell us?"

The bent, bearded figure came to Arthur's stirrup.

"A priest of God am I, Amherawdyr, living in a hut in this wilderness," he said in a high, quavering voice. "Once I served in the church over the tomb of the holy Saint Alban in Verulam; I am the last of a little band of brethren wasted away by the swords of the heathen— I have wandered far over field and forest, meeting only folly and wickedness, bloodshed and unbelief. The rocks and trees are kindlier companions than the sons of men in this dying realm of Britain."

"Britain shall not die while we are here to defend it," said Arthur sternly.

"You speak as a man of blood, glorying in the lusts of the flesh," said the priest, "yet it may be that you are the saviour sent to deliver the faithful, and to lead the people back to Christ. I will give you a precious relic that may bring you victory when you go against the heathen." He drew a roll of cloth from his tunic and held it up before the grim, mail-clad man on the wicked-eyed horse. The red glow of sunset streaming into the opening of the forest showed faintly the figure of a woman and child embroidered in coloured silks.

"This is a picture of the Holy Virgin and the Son of God that once hung behind the altar in the great church of Verulam," said the priest. "Wear it over your heart, Amherawdyr, and it shall guard you better than plates of iron and nail-studded shield."

"I would sooner trust in a quick wit and a keen blade than in the magic of priest or druid," said Arthur, smiling. "Nevertheless . . . ." He drew his sword, slit the fabric and put his head through the hole. Casually he tucked a tasselled fringe into his belt.

"Blood and yet more blood poured out on the green hills of Britain will not avail to save our nation," said the priest warningly. "There must be a change of heart, a kindling to the true faith, a shaming of the powers of darkness."

"Forward! Forward!" shouted Arthur fiercely. He gathered up his reins and pressed the stallion with the spurs. The long column of men leaning drowsily on their spears woke to movement again and lurched on into the blackness of the forest.

* * *

All morning the tide of battle swayed to and fro about the Broch of Guinion. In vain the Saxons strove to hold the twin summit of the bare hill where there were no ramparts; the legionaries fighting shield to shield thrust them off it and back over the tumbled wall of the fortress. Here, hour after hour, the invaders stood immovable, disdaining the whizzing volleys of arrows, holding off their assailants with a hedge of spears, with showers of stones and sweeping sword cuts. Often their heads turned to scan the long rolling heights behind the outthrust headland on which they stood—Guinion—the White Moor, and old pine forest swept by fire and now a wilderness of grey deer grass. But there was still no sign of their comrades coming to the rescue. Three hundred Saxons sheltered by the loose stone ramparts of the broch; but outside there might be a thousand Welshmen, half of them legionaries, hard men to talk to, with shields from knee to chin, stout helmets, and darting swords. The light-armed men came swarming up the wall like cats, spitting and snarling, maddened by the roar of their own voices, still hacking, stabbing and throttling in maniacal fury while life drained from them in frightful wounds. The Saxon line grew thinner. Sometimes it was thrust back against the tower itself, but here and there it held like steel and the breathless, sweat-drenched warriors broke into jeering shouts as the Britons recoiled down the slope, daunted by the ghastly heaps of maimed and mangled bodies, fallen men and fallen stone making a stairway from which blood and entrails oozed out over the bruised thyme and lichened crags. Cerdic leaned over the parapet, a dripping sword in his hand. He shouted in Welsh to the wavering ranks below:

"The Saxons are the better men, Cymry! Where is Arthur your leader and Christ your King?" Among all the scowling, infuriated faces his eyes lit on Medraut, pale and beautiful, his lips twisted in an icy smile.

"If you fight to have your way with Gwenhyvar your labour is in vain," he shouted back. "For all your cunning you are on the losing side, Cerdic!"

"To-day, perhaps, but not to-morrow!" Cerdic looked over his shoulder. The legionaries were in the courtyard now, bearing all before them. In their front rank, hewing with both hands as a man rains blows upon a forest tree, came the dark figure of Arthur like some implacable angel of doom. Round his neck hung the tatters of an embroidered cloth. Cerdic ran to the tower . . . He saw Ceolred leaning against the wall and clutching a gash in his throat. The blood spurted through his fingers and made a crimson arc in the air, spattering down on the body of a dead legionary . . . He dived in at the doorway, scrambled through the passage, climbed the ladder, and crawled up into the honeycombed cylinder of masonry. Up a stairway he saw a rectangle of blue sky blocked presently by the figure of a desperate Saxon lifting off loose stone and dropping it on the heads of the Welsh below. The fearful uproar outside the tower was dying down—the fight was nearly over, but now a confused shouting began far away on the moor. Cerdic climbed the stair and put his head out into the sunlight. Yes, there were the men from the eastern valley coming at last, a long string running, bunched into little groups of ten or a dozen here and there—to lighten themselves they had thrown away their shields and mail. And there were the legionaries moving out to meet them, a dark phalanx wiping away the trail of exhausted warriors as a cloth mops up a trickle of

spilled mead. Cerdic slid himself down into darkness
again. He felt his way to a passage blocked at the far
end by a flat slab of stone. He pushed it back, crawled
over it and set it up again, wedging it fast with loose
stone from within. He was in a sleeping room little
larger than his own body with a slit to the open air
not more than an inch wide between two vertical
blocks of stone. There he lay, contending with hunger
and thirst while he heard men rummaging in the
tower, the occasional crash of a stone thrown down,
and now and then a yell from some fugitive speared
in a dark passage. The tower grew silent; he heard
trumpets far away on the moor, shouting that became
fainter and fainter. The battle had rolled away to eastward—probably it was now nothing more than pursuit and massacre; another great victory, another
lightning counterstroke by the defenders of Britain.
Yet to Cerdic's mind as he lay cramped in his stone
cell, these mighty blows—Abergleinwy, Coit Celidon,
the Broch of Guinion—were but the last frantic struggles of a mortally wounded race.

'The Saxons are a broken weapon in my hand,' he
thought, 'but I shall forge them afresh. There is no
steel in Britain that can withstand them in the end. A
time will come for me, or if not for me, it will come for
my children!'

He shifted the stones that closed him in and listened. He heard only the feeble groans of the dying.
Swiftly he made his way out of the tower. With hardly a glance at the body of Ceolred, he ran faster and
faster, leaping over dead men and men that still
clasped their wounds, staring upwards at him with a
flicker of recognition. Over the rampart he went and
down headlong into the shelter of the friendly woods.
A flock of goats scattered before him in a brackeny
glade; he flung himself on the nearest animal,
dragged it down and set his lips to its teats. For a
while he lay there, sucking the sweet milk and think-

ing: 'I alone of all that host of stiff-necked Saxons have had the wit to save my life.' A wild exultation went to his head like strong mead. Never yet had he felt so confident in what the future had in store for him. 'Arthur was born to be the shield of Britain,' he said to himself, 'but I am born to be the axe that will split that shield. The champions of Cymry shall be tumbled from their seats and I shall mount above them, the first builder of a new Britain that shall care nothing for Christ or Rome, but shall be strong with the strength of a new people. Let Arthur's men pray to their crucified Christ and their wan-faced saints, we shall draw our power from devils, from the images of Thor and Woden black with caked blood.'

The satanic head of the goat lifted itself and stared at him with malicious yellow eyes; the creature yielded its milk freely now, sprawling beneath him, passive under a hand that tickled its skinny ribs.

After a while Cerdic got to his feet. The goat stood up too and continued to regard him with an enigmatic stare.

"You have saved the Bane of Britain!" he said to the animal.

And then a chill went over him as he stared back into those yellow eyes. The powers of evil were mighty indeed, but legend said that mortals often failed to profit by them. For that matter, the Christians prayed and were disappointed over and over again. Had he the wit to juggle with the forces that he invoked so recklessly, to use them as a man may use a torrent to turn his mill? He was suddenly aware that this little glade with the goat was seething with midges, that clegs had planted themselves on his bare arms and neck, that a cuckoo was perched above his head uttering its enchantment in the silence of the wood. Looking up through a rift in the motionless tufted plumes of pine branches he saw many black birds swooping high in air towards the Broch of Guinion.

"Power, Power!" their hoarse croaking seemed to say to him in tones of grisly mockery.

Cerdic set off at a slow run, sword in hand, in and out among the giant stems of the forest to eastward. On the evening of the next day he came down to Tweed Mouth and saw vast columns of smoke going up from the beached ships of the Saxons. A few half-manned vessels lay at anchor in the river, waiting in the hope of more survivors coming from the fight. Cerdic thrust himself off in a fisherman's currach; he rowed out to one of the black galleys and climbed on board.

"Who is your leader?" he said to the blond-haired men that stared at him dumbly as brute beasts.

"We have none," they answered. "None has come back alive."

"Then I will be your leader. Luck I have with me, even as Ceolred had ill-luck. Let us leave these banks of Tweed and try our fortune afresh on the Thames!"

Chapter VIII

The Storming of Bregion

THE ELEVENTH BATTLE WAS ON THE MOUNTAIN BREGION, WHICH WE CALL CAT BREGION.

—Nennius, *Historia Britonum.*

Arthur did not pursue the flying Saxons to the sea. The trumpets blew and slowly the British host streamed back to the Broch of Guinion. News had come in the very moment of victory that the Picts were in the field again. They were across the Forth, they had burnt Gwythyr's Hall, and the men that guarded the Fort of the Legion had fled with Gwenhyvar towards the wilderness of Clyde Head.

There, behind the screen of waving birchwoods, the fugitives stayed, watching the smoke that rose from beacons on the bald, round-headed hills, listening to rumours that came with herdsmen shifting their beasts to the high glens. Arthur was gathering fresh bands of fighting men under the rocky height that looked over the Forth—some day to be known as Arthur's Seat. Then, confused but unmistakable tidings of victory. Half the Pictish forces had been routed at Traeth Treuroit, not far from the Rock of Ystrevelin. Then, almost immediately, came the reverberations of another mighty blow. Arthur had given battle again—he had scattered the Picts in the shadow of the Rock of Alcluyd. The Fort of the Legion was once more in British hands. East and west there were no enemies left to fight; Gwenhyvar and her company rode out again into Strathclyde. The Fort of the Legion was still desolate when they came to it. The blackened timbers of Gwythyr's Hall stuck out gauntly from heaps of ash and carrion and patches of dried blood, but a felling was going on in the forest that swelled gently towards Loch Lomond foot, and there came a rattle of hammers and mallets from the Rock of Alcluyd. Rows of oak poles were planted in the green turf, a vast wall of ragged stone was rising across the pathway that climbed up between the twin peaks.

Gwenhyvar sat on her horse, riding slowly with loose rein over the saltings by the Clyde, her eyes fixed dreamily on hundreds of figures toiling like ants at the will of one man—the man on whose mind lay like a spell the past greatness of Britain. The ring of axes on wood, the crash of iron on stone, the chorus of voices raised in song as great trunks were hauled from the forest—something was being created here that would be a rallying point for the Cymry in long centuries of wavering fortune, a citadel flinging back the waves of war, Dunbrettan. . . .

All this Gwenhyvar felt as she rode slowly, unwillingly, towards the dark figure on the black horse round whom eddied crowds of upturned faces, faces alight with a vision, a faith in some power mightier than that wielded by Roman emperors with their paid armies of alien soldiers, the power of a man who was the champion of his people, knit to them by the bond of blood, the captain of a ship labouring in darkness against mountainous seas.

'What part have I in all this?' she said to herself. 'No one heeds me—not even Arthur. All these folk are bewitched; death has come so hear them that they have forgotten how to live—oxen dragging a plough at the will of the driver, so are the Cymry. Will the time never come when I, the wife of the greatest man in Britain, shall lie as women did in old days, on silken couches in painted rooms, with a fountain playing in the courtyard, eating wheaten bread and oysters from the southern seas, free to wear splendid clothes and jewels, and hearing no more than a rumour of war far off behind forests and mountains? It is a hard lot for us women of Britain to live filthily in little beehive huts and see even these poor homes go up in flames behind us as we toil through the heather carrying the children of men whose brows are ever dark with rage or terror, knowing that the children we bear must live ever more brutishly than their fathers. Or is the night passing and we are near the dawn? Was it against dawn or sunset that three great figures should stand out like mountain peaks above this clouded land, Arthur, Medraut, and Gwenhyvar? You have no eyes for me to-day, you hard-faced leaders in war and you Cymry toiling with wood and stone, but some day you will see what I am—not the woman to be clasped in lust for a night or two while armies rest from battle, nor the woman to bear children and turn a spinning wheel, blindly striving to make good what men have squandered, but the woman who turns the wheel of fate, raising up or casting down the whole of Britain.'

All that summer labours went on at the defences of Alcluyd and on the shore below rose gradually the framework of a dozen ships. They were not like the beaked galleys, patched-up survivors of a Roman fleet, with which Ceretic had raided Eiré within the memory of man; perforce Arthur had to take as models the long low Saxon ships seen on the east coast. What would do for the Saxons would do well enough for the Cymry in the enterprise he had in view. He meant to deal one more blow at the Picts that might bring the war to an end. He would strike at Bregion, the capital of the northern king, far away on a rock where Loch Etive widened to the sea, a rock crowned by the Fortress of the Sons of Usnoth. Not even the Roman armies had been able to win a passage through the secret passes to those green shores looking westwards to the mountains of Mull, but the sea offered an easier approach. The Gaels of Eiré knew it well enough by sight, the blunted pile of rock ringed with ramparts and spouting a hundred pillars of smoke from huts large and small. Boldly crossing the sea in their little currachs, they were already masters of the islands; their eyes were set greedily on the land across the water, green-nooked among bulging crags, dark with forest, purple with heath; knotted crests rising higher and higher until they sprang out against the sky like mighty paps, broken teeth, and battered helmets. It was with the men of Eiré that Arthur made a league for the conquest of Bregion.

When October came the ships were launched on the Clyde, packed with legionaries, rowed not by slaves as in Roman times, but by free tribesmen and fishermen from Kyle, Carrick, and the Solway shore. They were not bold seamen like the Saxons, but the voyage was through landlocked waters and the wind was light, scarcely filling the big square sails. At Tarbert they went ashore, felled pine trees in the forest and laid them as rollers on the narrow neck of land. One by one, the ships were hauled across and thrust out with their prows towards the Atlantic. Here the wind freshened and they sped before it, swaying and crunching among the green waves, while the spray came stinging across the low gunnels. Soon they were in a narrowing sound with slim evil-looking

peaks rising against the sunset sky. The sea grew
still again and suddenly from the shadow of the western shores emerged a great fleet of currachs with a
churning and creaking of oars and a high shrill
music of pipes. The leading currach came alongside
Prydwen, the big galley where Arthur stood beside the
steersman, and two chieftains climbed on board, Fergus MacErc and his brother Angus, broad-shouldered
men with bare legs and long sinewy arms, dark-eyed,
with dark lanky hair escaping under leathern helmets.
They wore no armour, but were wrapped in richly
coloured chequered cloaks; their brooches and buckles were of gold wrought in fantastic patterns of
writhing beasts, their voices were soft and lilting, their
bearing was courteous as they fronted the grim figure
of Arthur; it shone with dignity, and sparkled with a
reckless grace, that was alien to the smouldering fire of
the Cymry.

"Kingly are these men, beyond all the leaders of
Britain," said Medraut in a low voice to a warrior who
leaned over the gunnel beside him, high in the prow
of the next ship; a beardless youth with cropped gold-
en hair, a green cloak, shield on back, and a long-
skirted leathern coat. "Do they stir your fancy, Gwenhyvar?" he added with a subtle smile, and at his words
the disguised Gwenhyvar felt a qualm of strange and
horrid excitement. She turned away her face and
answered coldly: "They have the beauty of mountain
cats, but Arthur has the might of the bear."

"Does the bear's eye never rest on this slip of a
warrior adventuring among the picked men of the
Cymry?"

"His eyes are on the curves of Prydwen breasting
the waves, on the play of wind and current, on the
beacons that begin to smoke among the Pictish hills.
He has no thought of Gwenhyvar left behind on the
Rock of Alcluyd."

"It is a heavy burden for the man who takes on his back the fate of Britain."

"Do I not carry it too, and you, Medraut?"

"Our hearts lust for life, but Arthur's only for the destruction of his enemies. We have ears for that thin wild music of the pipes, but Arthur only for the blare of the Roman trumpets."

She looked at him swiftly. "Does that music please you?" she said.

"It is in my blood, maybe, for Modron's mother was of Eiré stock, so they say, a girl got by some Gaelic raider hewing his way over the walls of what was Clanoventa. It is a sad music that comes from the harp, the voice of a people whose day is done, but these pipes have the spirit of youth, the fire of a race that has never bowed its head to a foeman; it is wayward music, changeable as the surge of wind or sea, savage as the smell of misty moors, keen and pitiless as whirling steel."

"Splendid they are to the eye, these people," said Gwenhyvar, gazing at the chieftains on Prydwen and the warriors crowding alongside in the little currachs, "but I have heard it said that they are falser than the Britons and more ruthless than the Saxons."

"Christians they are, some of them, and companions of Arthur, even as I am," he said, smiling.

"Is it their race that will master Britain?"

"It is a race that will never be mastered except in death," he answered.

That night they cast anchor in a little bay among the islands and went on shore, and next morning the combined fleet of the island currachs and the galleys from Alcluyd ploughed its way northward through the glassy Sound of Kerrera. A dimness of light rain moved away on the wind and the sun came out, throwing long shadows from rock-crested hills, waking hot colours on rusty heath and faded bracken, lighting orange flames in rolling seas of birchwood. Of man there was hardly a trace on those desolate shores, unless it was the bottle-like tower of a broch in a patch of green, or a trail of blue smoke rising over walls that merged with living rock on some upthrust precipice. Desolation it was, but kindly and beautiful, dreamily at peace, not sinister, full of a devilish menace, as were the high mountains of Reged and Gwyneth. The water widened out, glittering in the low sunlight; the soft air was clamorous with gulls, tall peaks rose and chuckled musically along the curving sides of the ships, but a hush lay on the crowded masses of men staring over the gunnels. It was as though some melancholy enchantment spread over the army from these shores of unearthly beauty, shores on the edge of the known world, a land seemingly undefiled by human greed, fear and hatred.

They rounded a promontory, and there at the head of a bay lay Bregion, a dense cluster of thatched roofs on an isolated hump of rock that looked as though it had rolled from the mountain above and plunged down into the sweep of moss and forest beyond the pale strand drifted with dark lines of seawrack. Now they could see herds of cattle and goats stirring uneasily on tawny moors, they could see clusters of men mounting here and there on the knolls, and from the Fort of the Sons of Usnoth sounded the long echoing blast of a horn. To Gwenhyvar, in the prow of Medraut's ship, there came a sudden breathlessness; her heart seemed to leap into her throat, her eyes swam with tears, as she heard the answering blast of Arthur's trumpets and a screaming unearthly yell from the warriors of Eiré. Her senses reeled with the awakening surge of human passion, the mad lust for blood and destruction that swirled above sunlit water and silvery shore. Senseless, she thought in her heart, but her mind was intoxicated by its splendour. What followed seemed to pass in a series of flashes, glimpses of things familiar in word or deed, but never before realised with such painful intensity. It was as Medraut had foretold—in these moments of peril both beauty and horror beat upon her senses as though she stood unclothed amid driving snowflakes. A grating of keels on shingle, cold sea water gurgling about her knees, a stumbling run in a jostling crowd, a babel of shouts, the whizz of something past her face, a man crumpling up in front of her, heads ducking suddenly, the sharp rap and clang of missiles on shields and helmets, Arthur, ahead of everyone, clambering over a grey lichened crag, pushing on among little white-stemmed birches and dark thickets of broom. Green turf now, steep as a house roof, and great stones leaping down it, splintering as they came on ledges of rock. A ladder reared in the air before her, a hairy-legged man of Eiré scrambled up a wall hand over hand with a sword in his teeth and slid down again drenched in blood; wild laughter and screams of agony, weapons whirling against the blue sky, a sudden crush of sweaty bodies carried her forward, recoiled, and gained ground afresh with a snarling roar. A hand came up out of the press and dragged down her shield, then lost its grip as hot blood spurted suddenly into her face. The crush thickened, it seemed as though her lungs could no longer draw breath into her body; vaguely she saw a gatepost above her, men wrestling together on the broad top of a wall, a stone hurtling through the air— it was coming right at her, but she could not move to avoid it—and then the crowd flowed forward again and the stone came down with a crunch on someone behind. Through rising and falling weapons ahead she saw the peaked roofs of huts, and now she heard the savage yelling of women in front and a gathering uproar of voices on either side. A torrent of men was pouring in over the walls; close beside her she saw a line of legionaries, exultant faces staring over the rims of shields. Pipe music shrilled in the air above the growling and gasping shouts; braying, screaming notes of defiance that flew up like sparks from the keen edge of life laid on the grindstone of death. Gwenhyvar stumbled over something that squirmed violently; she plunged on hands and knees through a dark doorway. She saw a fire and a cooking pot; a beam of light fell through the smoke hole on deerskin rugs and a man lying motionless in a great pool of blood. Her body began to spew ungovernably, she crouched in a heap, violently sick, then screamed frantically as the doorway went dark and a hand caught her by the belt. Instinctively she covered herself with her shield and felt it driven hard against her. A knife blade pricked her in the breast, she fell backwards and felt herself gripped brutally between the thighs.

"Cymry!" she cried. "I am of the Cymry!"

The hand left her, the figure drew back with a reedy laugh.

"Gwenhyvar!" said the voice of Medraut. "Are you hurt?"

She flung her arms about his knees and burst into tears.

"I thought I was grappling with a wounded Pict. You parried my dagger well, Gwenhyvar! Forget you are a woman! You are safe now, but it is an ugly sight outside. . . . Arthur has won again, but it was a near thing that I did not slay his wife." He still chuckled softly, wrenching the dagger out of the round shield in which it stood fast.

"Come, was I too rough with you?" He bent down and kissed her on the lips.

"Oh!" she said. "I want to see no more of war!"

"Harden it out till you can bend your knee before Arthur. He will forgive you for coming in man's dress to see him victorious. Till then you are a warrior among warriors, honourably reddened with blood,

and only I know your secret. Come with me now and
see what work has been done here."

She shuddered a little, but followed him out of the
hut, shield on arm and grasping a light javelin.

"Is the fight over?" she asked between set teeth.

"The town is ours, but the Picts have fled out of
the landward gate towards the mountain." He
pointed to the beetling heights above, now bristling
with spears.

"Arthur means to strike them another blow.
Meanwhile here is the King's hut. Here is booty, by
the looks of these men coming out."

"Here is more than booty!" said Gwythyr, letting his
hand fall on Medraut's shoulder. "Here is the King of the
Picts taken unwounded! The man who made us bleed at
the Duglas, at Coit Celidon and Traeth Treuroit."

Gwenhyvar slipped away. Unnoticed she went in
and out among the huts till she came to the great
stone rampart, greened over the top, vitrified at its
base by hundreds of years of cooking fires. She
climbed up and lay on the turf among harebells and
sweet thyme, watching both Islemen and legionaries
mounting the hillsides in an irresistible wave, bearing
back the Picts in a fainter and fainter clamour of voices
and clash of arms till they vanished over the purple
shoulders of the Ben. She watched unseeingly as her
mind ran back over her dreadful experiences during
the assault, the crescendo of horror that had been
ended by Medraut's kiss. And suddenly at the
thought of his lips on hers after the savagery of his
hands upon her a flush came to her cheeks and her
body quivered in a hot stealthy ecstasy such as no
sight or expectation had yet unlocked within her. His
words—they had been rough and indifferent like
blows to awake her mettle, to force her to play out the
part she had so rashly chosen for herself—but his
laugh, low and vicious-sounding, called to something
other than pride, and her senses had leaped to it as

they had never leaped to the voice of Arthur. She felt an amazed delight in her body that it could respond so violently to lust in a moment after being at grips with death. 'What a fire in me this man can kindle even when I am chilled by the sights of war,' she thought. 'All this would have been hidden from me if I had stayed behind on the dreary top of Alcluyd, waiting for Arthur. . . . I should have gone on my way through life, unmastered as a horse that has not been taught with blows and harsh usage, but now I know who it is that can hold me with reins or drive me with sharp spurs.' She stretched herself on the soft turf, sunk in dreamy visions, caressed by the gentle breeze from the sea, unconscious of the dead men that sprawled not far away with clenched hands and staring eyes. Gradually she became aware of three great mountains towering up to the west, with mist hanging motionless like locks of white wool in their furrowed flanks. "Arthur, Medraut, and Gwenhyvar," she murmured to herself, and then abruptly she raised herself on one arm. For the first time a picture flashed before her eyes—a vision that had hovered about her ever since she had spoken with Medraut on the ramparts above the Clyde. Subconsciously she had held it at bay, but now she could do so no longer. She saw in what guise those three figures would become famous to the generations that followed them.

A footstep sounded softly beside her, she turned her head and saw Medraut regarding her; his mouth was set, his eyes smouldered gloomily. At once she realised that he knew what she knew, that they had both taken a step on a path that was soft to tread but darkly shadowed with guilt. Swiftly she spoke, snatching at thought that came to her out of those vague sunlit spaces of sea flowing about the mountains:

"Tell me, Medraut, what lies yonder out West?"

"Moel it is called," he said indifferently, as though he, too, saw what her mind envisaged, but knew that she was on a hopeless quest.

"What people dwell there?"

"These Gael, the allies of Arthur."

"They are far-away mountains, dim and peaceful like the depths of mighty woods."

"But an hour's sail would bring Prydwen to those shores."

She sighed and said: "What lies beyond?"

"The sea," he said.

"Are there no lands in that sea beyond the ken of dwellers in Britain?"

"Legend says so, but I know not whether it says truly."

"You have a ship, a company of armed men, a sail and oars. Will you adventure on that sea with me, Medraut?"

He stared at her fixedly, shrugged his shoulders, and turned away.

"It is another path that we must tread," he said at last.

"Can you see the end of that path, Medraut?"

"I see what has to be done here and now, and that is to lead you to Arthur. The battle is over; now is the time to count our gains and losses."

"What is it that you brood upon, the desire that eats out your heart? Is it for me, or for power in Britain such as Arthur has?"

"There are three foundations for happiness; a suffering with contentment, a hope that it will come, a belief that it will be," he said, evading her question. For the moment he did not know the answer.

Arthur came down from the mountain in company with his champions, Kai, Bedwyr, Gwgawn and many another wearer of the golden torque, and with them came the Islemen, Fergus and Angus, making light of wounds, and boasting of much splitting of heads and shearing of limbs.

They swung in at the landgate of Bregion, a little battered body of men, bloody and spent, thinking much of what mead or milk might be found in the Pictish huts, and little of the fact that in an hour or two of confused fighting they had changed the history of northern Britain.

At the cross roads in the middle of the town three figures awaited them, standing before a crowd of men who were heaping up plunder—Medraut and Gwythyr, and Gwenhyvar between them, still holding her spear and buckler. It was Gwythyr that spoke first:

"We have taken the King of the Picts; the war is over."

"And we have laid our hands on his eldest son," said Arthur. "He is wounded, but he will live. He shall go with us as a hostage and we shall make a good peace with the Picts. How say you, Fergus?"

"The reddening of swords is like the reddening of the sky to our warriors. A dark summer it will seem to them if the sun shine but for a single day," answered the Gaelic chieftain.

"Our work here is finished. The business of the Cymry lies in the south. We must fight the Saxons without having to look back over our shoulders at these Picts. We leave you Bregion, Fergus, the key to the land, and half the plunder taken in it." Arthur leaned on his long sword and looked reassuringly at the man with the soft, musical voice and the dark, bloodshot eyes that still seemed to reflect a murderous lust for killing.

"We have set our teeth in Alban to-day," said his brother, Angus. "We shall eat up the land and all that is in it from the sea to the highest mountains."

"Erre Gaedhil[1] it shall be called and I shall be its king, I, Fergus MacErc, of the House of Hy Nial!" Fergus's voice rose to a sudden wild shouting; it echoed from the blank face of the cliffs; his sword flashed out menacingly towards the heaved-up carpets of golden forest and far-away crests, copper-coloured in the glow of sunset.

"He should bow the knee before the Amherawdyr; this Wolf of the Isles should wear a collar and chain," muttered Gwythyr.

"We should be fools to trust in an unwilling word from men such as these," said Arthur. "Their blood is not our blood—we are but as wolves and eagles striking down the same prey . . ." His words were drowned by the skirling of the pipes, by ferocious yells from the Gaelic warriors crowding round Fergus and Angus.

"You have planted a seed in Alban that will grow to a mighty tree," said Medraut, with a crooked smile.

"We shall divide the booty and then get back to our ships; but first I will see the King of the Picts and bind him with an oath and the sight of his son ringed about by the Cymry." Arthur turned away and Kai strode with him, carrying the Dragon standard, and then at last Gwenhyvar stood in his path and went on her knees. His eyes brooded on her, he laid a hand on her head, but was slow to speak.

"I had to come," she said desperately, and then she thought: 'Why did I come? Was it because I could not be parted from the man I love; the dog following his master? And who is my master—the man to whom I have pledged my body or the man who can command that body if he will? The man who has honour and power and such fame that in time to come all will know that his sword was Caledvulch and his ship Prydwen and his wife Gwenhyvar—or the man that may go unhonoured to his grave, famous only in that he loved Gwenhyvar and she him?'

---

[1] Argyll—the Land of the Gael.

"It was a wanton deed of Gwenhyvar to set her life in such peril." Arthur spoke slowly, his eyes on the sun sinking behind the great mountains in the west. "Did you do it in love of Arthur, child, or was some strong spell laid on you that you could not rest secure within Alcluyd's walls, shielding your honour and Arthur's unborn child?"

Tears rushed from her eyes and dripped about his feet; she could not answer him.

Arthur stood motionless in a silent glooming circle of faces, the well-tried champions of the Cymry, weary but watchful, seeking a sign from the man who had given them victory in eleven great battles with the spoilers of Britain.

"My deeds bring forth mighty fruit," he said with a sigh, "yet the full fruit will not be gathered in my lifetime. When this sword drops from my hands there must be fresh hands to wield it, to finish what I have begun, or else my labour is in vain. A man must come forth who stands not for Reged or Gwyneth or Dyvnaint, but for the whole race of the Britons. Where shall I find such a man unless he be my own son, walking the same road that I tread to-day? I hope little from men like this Fergus MacErc or Maelgun at Deganwy or Cuneglas at Lis Pengwern, but I hope much from Gwenhyvar, the daughter of Gwythyr. It is through her that my work shall go forward, or it may be through her that it will become a thing of naught, a tale lingering on men's lips when our enemies' feet stride over the graves of the Cymry."

Gwenhyvar looked up. Her eyes rested on the haggard face of Arthur and suddenly her heart went cold, for she saw that he too had glimpsed some vision, gazing towards those mountains in the west, such as she had seen with a dreadful clearness as she lay day-dreaming on the walls of Bregion; the same vision, perhaps, that Medraut had called up out of the blackness of night under the Rock of Alcluyd.

Medraut heard it, and she heard it, but Arthur still
strove to be deaf to that distant thunder that muttered on the wind. . . . And then she thought, with a
dull, despairing anger, 'I have given myself to a
doomed man, thinking that he was more than mortal,
but now I know that his race will perish through me,
whereas other men that I might have chosen will triumph, their seed will be mighty in Britain, but not
through me. A word here, a look there, I might have
guessed that Medraut knew with whom I should lie if
I would give what I shall never give to Arthur—heirs
that will beget a line of kings, men of the sunrise, not
of the sunset. . . .'

Many times afterwards did Gwenhyvar think of
Medraut's mocking words when she first set eyes on
Fergus MacErc, and his cruel burning gaze when
men spoke of Cerdic at the Broch of Guinion.

Chapter IX

The Vision

NEVER WAS SLAUGHTER MORE
IN THIS ISLAND
AFORE YET
OF FOLK OVERTHROWN
BEFORE THIS
WITH THE SWORD'S EDGE.

—*Song of Brunanburh*
(E. A. Freeman's translation)

The woods still bore their covering of bronze and gold when Arthur's army moved out of Strathclyde and through the Strath of Annan, heading southward again for the land of Reged. Gwythyr was left to hold the Rock of Alcluyd, the tribesmen had gone back to their villages in the hills, to count depleted flocks and herds and to see what harvest had been garnered by women and old men, but the legionaries still marched with Arthur. Their harness was even more battered, patched and rusty than it had been when they came north with Uther Pendragon, but there were more men, not fewer, for the gaps in the ranks had been filled and many a bold fellow, whose home had been burnt, whose kinsfolk had perished in

the sweep of armies backwards and forwards from
sea to sea, chose now to follow the Red Dragon standard no matter where it led. The great champions
were still with the army, Kai and Bedwyr, and Mabon,
son of Modron, and March who was first through the
gate into Bregion, and Gwgawn who carried a shield
split by a Saxon axe in Strath Gala. Medraut was
there, picking out airs on his harp, and Gwenhyvar
rode with a little company of women, moving by easy
stages on the road to Caerleon-on-Usk. There, far in
the west, where no Saxon had yet set foot, she would
await the coming of her first child, but Arthur and the
army were bound for Caer Ebrauc and London.

The host halted at the old Roman fort of Blatobulgium, with their backs to a bleak hill, deep in
brown heather with three humps against the sky,
dyked and pared to serve as a fortress long before the
Roman day. In front of them, over the forests, was a
glitter of water, the Solway, and beyond, smoking
with cloud like some vast beacon, rose the blue
mountain mass of Reged.

A little vaulted building remained intact amid the
ruins of the fort and in it lay Gwenhyvar on a couch
of dead bracken, listening to Medraut playing a new
air on his harp, an air to which he had as yet put no
words. The sun was going down behind low hills,
glimmering between the mighty stems of oak and
pine; the men had eaten and drunk, they rolled themselves in green cloaks and lay everywhere among the
tumbled heaps of ruddy stone, their senses drowned
in weariness; only the standard stood upright, planted over the southern gate, and Arthur leaned his
elbows on the back of the black horse, his eyes on
that far cluster of mountains, the homeland of the
race of Uther. A band of yellow sky lay remote and
tranquil on the low south-western horizon—a curtain
against which cloud wreaths loomed up in slow procession, monstrous spectres suffused with dove grey

and amethyst, footed in crimson and gold. Swiftly they turned ashen and formless, the yellow curtain became a silver streak on the threshold of night. The harp playing had stopped; Medraut and Arthur lay wrapped in their cloaks at the round arched entrance to the vault in which slept Gwenhyvar.

In the grey of morning she awoke, chilled by a sharp breeze that blew from the sea, flapping the standard over the gate, making the sleeping warriors huddle closer to earth, thrusting their hands between their thighs for warmth. The girls lying in the bracken beside her moaned and muttered uneasily, one of them lifting her arms as though to clasp the lover she had left behind in Strathclyde. Arthur already sat up, his chin resting on his hands, watching a flush of pink on the cloudlets drifting to eastward. Slowly Medraut raised himself, yawning and rubbing his eyes. Suddenly he stood up and gazed across the ruins to the triply humped hill. Tonelessly his voice sounded in the silence:

> "Bet y March, bet y Gwythyr,
> Bet y Gwgawn cletyfrut;
> Anoeth bid, bet y Arthur."[1]

"What words are these?" said Arthur sharply, and Gwenhyvar crept near to the arch to listen, reluctant and shivering, while her heart cried out: 'What have I to do with these men whose minds hover about each other like two eagles in mid-air, watchful and grim, I whose task it is to bear a child?'

"They are the words of my dream," answered Medraut, "words that fit to the air that I have played ever since we turned our faces southwards from

---

1 "A grave there is for March, a grave for Gwythyr
  A grave for Gwgawn of the ruddy sword;
  Unwise the thought—a grave for Arthur."
  —*Song of the Graves.*

Alcluyd, words that will be on men's lips many a hundred years hence."

"Can you read the future in dreams, Medraut?"

"When a storm blows do we not all taste salt on our lips before we come to the sea?"

"We may have warnings of what to avoid."

Medraut shook his head. "What I see must come, strive as you will, Arthur."

"Then it is you that will it to come, you that shall bring it to pass."

"Not so: I set my will against it." He stared gloomily at the face of Gwenhyvar set in golden locks against the blackness of the vault, a lovely face, but sullen now, withdrawn into itself, not eager and imploring as he had seen it on the sunlit rampart of Bregion.

"If you believe that I am a doomed man, setting my hand to a hopeless task, I shall only push on the faster and strike the more fiercely," said Arthur, rising to his feet.

"This dream tells me nothing of you except that you shall sleep only, when your champions lie dead in their graves—sleep, maybe, as the bear does through a long winter and arise again in the spring." Medraut smiled subtly. "Listen, I shall tell you what I saw. I seemed to pass in mighty strides out of this host of sleeping men; and yet they were not these men that slept, but men that lay dead by the side of a little brook with a gleam of sunset above blackthorn trees—a place in some far distant part of Britain. Four strides I took, and each stride was the passing of a hundred years, and then I stood on that hill crest that reddens now in the light of dawn, among a host of sleeping men far greater than the one that lies about us here. They lay on the western peak of the hill, many a thousand warriors; there was a Red Dragon standard and about it lay men of our race, men of Reged and men of Strathclyde; there were men from Gwyneth too, and some from Dyvnaint. I saw next to them a host of Picts and Gael under an Eagle standard, and farthest forward a Raven standard with a host of fair-haired men the like of whom I had never seen before. And then across the heath on the eastern peak lay a great host under a standard that bore a Dragon and a Fighting Man, and they were Saxons. And while I watched, the armies rose up and in a while they gathered in line of battle and came out of the old ramparts on to the heath and there they fought a long autumn day. There was a mighty man under the Red Dragon, black-bearded and strong as a bull, with a crafty smile on his face, and as he stepped before his men he sang in a clear voice the Song of the Graves, to the very tune that I played last night on the harp. Under the Eagle was a grey-haired chieftain, his brow seamed with scars and wrinkles, and in the front line of the men with the Ravens were chieftains with staring blue eyes and long thick hair pale as flax. Fierce as birds of prey they looked, in their mail shirts, whirling their axes, tossing swords in the air and catching them by the hilt. With the Saxons came two men, brothers, in purple cloaks, noble-looking men, calm and smiling as though they went among friends to a wedding feast, haughty men and fearless, seemingly well used to victory. All day they fought on the heath, those two great hosts, and the fallen lay thick as leaves on a wintry forest floor. And towards evening the fight rolled towards the west and first the old hoary-headed chieftain turned his back and his men streamed away over the heath like sheep that fly before a pack of wolves. Then our people were broken; the Red Dragon showed no more above the whistling arrows and the whirling steel, and a great shout went up: 'Slain is Owen the Tall! Dead is the King of the Cymry!' And at last back went the Fair Strangers, with their Raven, like a rock rolling down a mountain

side, splitting and shattering as it goes, and a long
trail of them fell dead or dying on the plains of Vina
and all the way through the woods to the sea,
where dragon-headed ships thrust out with handfuls of hacked and bleeding warriors raising the
sails or drooping over the oars as they set their
course for Eiré."[1]

"In vain I shall bear children to Arthur," said Gwenhyvar in a loud voice. "In vain, if the Cymry go down in
ruin and the Saxons triumph in the end."

"A curse it is for a man to have the second sight,"
muttered Arthur, clenching his fists. "Cursed are you,
nephew, in your birth—your powers come of evil,
working wantonly on the fortunes of our people, bidding them hope or despair as the spirit moves you.
Yet even if you speak truth and what must be must,
your words do not daunt me. What is the loss of one
battle, the fall of one king? Our race shall not perish;
the fire that glows in us shall not be trodden out.
Even as your music goes forward into the darkness of
ages to come, a token of our strength, and our weakness, so our spirit shall prevail, flaming more fiercely
as the wind blows upon it, so long as there are
dwellers in Britain, so long as there are folk overseas
that strive to bring us down."[2]

"Unwise the thought—a grave for Arthur," said
Medraut with a slow smile, yet his eyes kindled a little.

---

[1] At this place in the year 937, four hundred years after
the Battle of Camlann, the English King Athelstan and
his brother Edmund defeated with enormous slaughter
an army of Welshmen, Scots, and Vikings from the
western seas, as is told in the contemporary poem of
the Fight of Brunanburh and in the Saga of Egil Skallagrims-
son.

[2] Few can doubt that a Welshman averted the defeat of
Britain in the war of 1914-18.

Chapter X

The Round Table

FIST ARTUS LA ROONDE TABLE
DONT BRETON DIENT MAINTE FABLE.
—Wace, *Geste des Bretons.*

The army passed on over the mosses at the head of Solway, it saw the Wall before it, a long red line, turret beyond turret feathered with fern and brambles, it filed through an archway and mounted a sudden slope dotted with tree stumps, grazed green by shaggy herds of cattle. With a blast of trumpets it poured into the city of Caerluel, along streets where fountains still played and porticos rose among heaps of wreckage and overthrown statues from the days of imperial Rome. Folk swarmed about the columns of armoured men with shouts of welcome, women came from their doorways staring with eager eyes, bare-legged children rushed ahead of them brandishing sticks and bits of broken board after the fashion of spears and bucklers. Here was no

shambling uncertain host of tribesmen pressing to
war from forest cots and mountain folds, but a hard-
faced mass of warriors marching in step with the
confidence of victors and singing a song that echoed
defiantly among bulging walls and roofless colonnades. "Arthur our leader: Christ our King!"

For a few days the champions of the Cymry
housed within the smoke-blackened walls of the great
basilica, they went to the baths and splashed and
scrubbed each other amid shouts of laughter in the
weed-grown tanks, while the people of Caerluel
looked on admiringly at their scarred brown bodies,
learning the names of the heroes who had given a
new lease of life to Britain. "That great fair man is Kai
who carries the Red Dragon—Bedwyr they call him,
that black hairy man with charms in his ears; some
kinsman of Arthur is he, from far Dyvnaint—there
stands Gwgawn who fought single-handed against
ten Saxons in Strath Gala. That broad-shouldered
youth sitting alone, with a bloody binding round his
neck, he is Brude, the son of the King of the Picts,
taken by Arthur on the Mountain of Bregion. That
frowsy-headed man rubbing tar on his skin is Coll, a
famous warrior given to Arthur by the King of the
Islemen. See there that man with hooked nose and
greying hair—that is March, whom the Christians call
Marcus Cunomorus—a mighty guletic in Kernou.
They say he married a young wife and then killed his
son Drystan out of jealousy. . . ."

Bathed and fed and swollen in numbers, the army
pushed on to southward through a great forest of
oaks. They left the straight cut of the Roman road
marked by its mossy milestones and lines of kerb
sinking into slime and rush beds, they thrust their
way in little parties through man-high bracken, hunting deer and wild boar in and out among the vast
trunks of the trees, shooting arrows after the hares
that leaped up in heathery glades. And Arthur, riding

ahead on his black stallion, came upon a little reedy
lake ringed round on every side by the bronze or rus-
set bastions of the oaks. There was a hut by the
water's edge with goats grazing round it and a wisp
of pale smoke going up into the languid air. At the
door of the hut a young man looked up from skin-
ning a boar, a merry-faced young man with black
curly hair. He looked quickly at the rider, away again
at woods and water, then coolly went on with his
task. A woman came out and stood beside him, a
strangely beautiful woman for such a wild setting.
Her clothes were coarse and stained, but there was a
gold bracelet about her arm, her cheeks had a delicate bloom, her eyes had the dreamy softness of a
young hind.

"Do you know me, young man?" said Arthur, looking down on him from horseback.

"I can guess well enough," answered the youth.
"The race of Uther is good to tell."

"Are you of that race?" said Arthur, looking at
him keenly.

"I am Gwalchmei, your cousin, Arthur."

"It is not good enough for you to be a huntsman in
the forests of Reged when Arthur, Mabon and Medraut
lead an army against the foes of Britain."

"Little cause have I to fear the foes of Britain, but
much have I to fear from her rulers. I have stolen a
precious jewel from one of them, even from the
mightiest, the Dragon of Gwyneth. I hide among
Reged's oaks because I have taken Olwen, Maelgun's
daughter, out of the Castle of Deganwy, and his
vengeance is more deadly to me than the swords of
Picts or Saxons. A long arm has Maelgun and he has
grasped after me from the banks of Dee to the streets
of Caerluel."

Arthur gazed sombrely from the man to the girl.
Lovely these two were to look upon—what they had
done was utterly right in their own eyes, and yet it

was a pitfall in his path when he turned for help to the princes of Britain. He wheeled his horse without a word, and then the woman spoke:

"Safe we should be where Arthur rides with Gwenhyvar."

Arthur pressed the horse to a gallop through the dark tunnels of the forest. Angrily he told himself that the friendship of Maelgun Gwyneth was more precious to him than the youthful might of a kinsman such as Gwalchmei. It was madness to drive the wedge of family feuds into the timber of the British oak, and yet he was turning his face from a champion—a youth who would hearten the Cymry with his laughing eyes, who had the spirit to dare and dare again where others hung back. . . .

The army feasted in the overgrown ruins of Voreda; on the next day it crossed the Eamont under the grim walls of Brovacum and moved to meet men that Mabon had summoned from the Lakeland glens and the heaths that stretched to the Lune. These were enchanted glades that lay in the heart of Reged between Lowther and Eamont, still green and summery with flowers on the threshold of winter, and the great trees spread their branches with a faintly ominous grace and significance. Man had set his hands on this land in the past; Roman engineers had cut ways through the woods and laid out one of the great square forts that were a commonplace in Northern Britain, and in dimmer ages folk had come in from the West and made a temple of tree trunks on a round platform of earth—a place of worship and sacrifice. The patterns of nature wove themselves gently about these works of man and the wilderness bore a faint, glamorous imprint of human passion and endeavour, as when the sea breaks in a white surf over a sunken wreck.

A monolith lay in the yellowed bracken on the temple site, and, waiting for Mabon's folk who could be seen on the hills to southward, Arthur took his seat on the fallen pillar.

"Let us rest with our women," he said, beckoning to Gwenhyvar and the girls with her who were sliding stiffly from their horses. "We have come to the parting of the ways, for we men march on a great enterprise across yonder blue hills"—he pointed to the dark wave-like wall of the Pennines—"and the women shall go well guarded on the road that leads on the mountain crest above the lakes of Reged and down to the western sea. Southwards they shall go and guest with Cuneglas at Lis Pengwern, and farther yet to Conan at Caerleon-on-Usk. No safer places do I know in Britain to-day. To Caerleon shall we go, champions, when our work is done, those of us that are yet alive. Our meeting by Usk shall be merrier than our parting here by Eamont!"

Then Gwenhyvar came and sat by Arthur, and the champions crowded close beside them, some with the girls of their choice who would be suckling children, perhaps, before the warriors returned to the west. But at once voices were raised in anger, for the champions could not agree who should sit nearest on the stone to Arthur and Gwenhyvar.

"I have carried the standard in every battle beside Arthur and Uther his father," said Kai. "Mine is the seat of honour."

"A kinsman am I of Arthur; this land of Reged is mine; trees, grass and hills and winding waters. Here in Eamont Woods I should be next the Amherawdyr," said Mabon, pushing through the cluster of scowling champions.

"Who is braver than March, he who broke the gate of Bregion?" said a voice.

"Bregion was child's play to what we did in Coit Celidon. There it was Bedwyr who hewed down the standard of the King of the Picts."

"It was I, Gwgawn, who went forward side by side with Arthur at the Broch of Guinion. Biting weapons there were behind Cerdic's shield wall and there were many of you butchers of the Picts that liked not the taste of Saxon steel."

"If Gwythyr were here none would deny him a seat next to Arthur."

"It was I who spoke to the people on Moel Fre; my words have made us Cymry; side by side with Arthur have I been in battle and council ever since we spilled the first blood at Afon Coch." Medraut stared defiantly at the sullen faces around him and all at once he was aware of a silence, a silence of ill-will and fear. But the silence was broken by the voice of Arthur, cheery and confident as men heard him when greatest danger threatened.

"There shall be none first and none last among us," he said, and rose from the fallen stone. "Let us sit in a circle on the heath, here in this round space that likens a table. Here is a table with no head and no foot, and all that sit about it have places equal in honour." Leading Gwenhyvar by the hand he sat down on the old temple platform covered with dry, faded ling. There were smiles now and the champions sat down without more ado, and as they did so the thud of horses' hoofs sounded on the turf under low sweeping branches of oak and two riders galloped up to the ring, a man and a girl. Flushed, gay and breathing hard, they sprang down. The man laid an arm about the girl's waist; they thrust into the ring and sat themselves next to Arthur and Gwenhyvar.

A murmur rose afresh from the grim-faced warriors, but the youth shouted challengingly: "Untried I may be in war, but my name is known from Solway sands to the mountains of Gwyneth; when shields clash and steel flashes against steel you will find me among the foremost. I have luck with me, Cymry!" His eyes shone with merriment as he clasped the girl closer and looked boldly round the ring.

"You shall go with us and prove your words, Gwalchmei." Arthur laid his hand on the young man's shoulder; he thought to himself, 'This cousin of mine has all that I lack, the headstrong passion of youth, the joy in living life to the full, the recklessness that will venture all for a whim, the power to kindle women so that his clasps and kisses are dearer to them than life or honour. It may be that he brings us luck,' and then, unwillingly, his eyes wandered to Maelgun's daughter and to Gwenhyvar, and he thought, 'These are surely the loveliest women in our land, the sight of them heartens us to great undertakings, and yet their beauty has a fatal ring, like Medraut's music on the harp, and I doubt they will be the doom of Britain.' But now Mabon's servants brought meat and ale from his fortress on the hill where Eamont issued from the lake, and all round the ring of champions there was laughter and song and good fellowship again, and in a little while a band of trusty men set off with the women, riding up the track that climbed the mountains, and the army swung away eastwards into the Vale of Eden, bound for Caer Ebrauc.

Chapter XI

The March
on London

THE MORE THE SAXONS WERE VANQUISHED, THE MORE THEY
SOUGHT FOR NEW SUPPLIES OF SAXONS FROM GERMANY; SO
THAT KINGS, COMMANDERS, AND MILITARY BANDS WERE INVIT-
ED OVER FROM ALMOST EVERY PROVINCE. AND THIS PRACTICE
THEY CONTINUED TILL THE REIGN OF IDA, WHO WAS SON OF
EOPPA; HE OF THE SAXON RACE WAS THE FIRST KING IN BER-
NICIA AND IN CAER EBRAUC.
                              —Nennius, *Historia Britonum.*

The weather changed as they turned their backs
on Reged and crossed the great moor into the
valley of the Tees. Snow came drifting in their
faces, muffling the wilderness in a pall. The ling
became a grey dusky sea stretching endlessly into a
grey void, juniper bushes bowed over the track
imprisoned in fantastic plumes, drifts piled up man-
high within the ramparts of the ruined forts. The
mood of the men hardened as they tramped forward
in a long ghostly column, heads bent to the blast,
whitened spear shafts slanting from their shoulders
like quills on a porcupine. They muttered how they

would warm themselves at burning huts and halls when they came down into Deivr; but no enemy contested their passage as they plunged on into forested plains. A few huts they found here and there, but they were clearly huts of Britons. The folk had fled at the coming of the army from the North. The snow turned to rain and they broke out into open country, sodden and desolate under leaden skies. The squat towers of Caer Ebrauc rose like dark symbols of power in an empty world, the hard shell of a city that had died and rotted away. There were no gates in the round archways and tall trees stood up above the roofless buildings within instead of trails of smoke. Yet the place was not as deserted as it looked; from the thorny scrub that covered old graveyards outside the walls emerged a silent mass of men. They formed up across the road, barring the way to the Cymry, and out from their ranks rode a chieftain on a white horse. The westering sun broke through the clouds, throwing a sheaf of wavering rays upon the plain; it lit up a glint of weapons here and there in the throng gathered before the walls of ancient Eboracum.

"An army," said Mabon, "but it has little stomach for battle, by the look of it."

"We taste now the fruit of what we did at Abergleinwy and Guinion," said Kai, raising the Red Dragon aloft. Arthur had the trumpets blown; the Cymry halted and spread out, fronting the men of Deivr. Archers bent their bows, swords rose in the air, a snarling roar came from the legionaries who had fought the bitter wind and the snow on the Pennines. Then the man on the white horse rode forward, holding up an empty hand; an unarmed man walked beside him. They came right up to Arthur where he sat on the dark stallion backed by the champions of Britain. The rider looked Arthur in the eyes, then slowly he dismounted, a big fair-bearded man in a leather coat and cross-gartered hose.

"Eoppa am I, lord of this land of Dere," he said in the Saxon tongue, and the man beside him translated his words into the British language. "Do I speak to Arthur, the ruler of the Britons?"

"You speak to Arthur, but we in this host are not accustomed to answer men of your race with words."

The Saxon looked again at the big man in the crested helmet, at the long line of grim faces to right and left. He said: "We come not to hinder your march, but to make peace. Willing am I and all my men to take you as overlord of Dere. But if you will not give us peace, then we shall do what men can to guard their homes, their wives and children from the stranger."

Arthur rode nearer to the host that followed Eoppa, and Medraut went with him. "There are as many of them as there are of us, but we shall shatter them at the first blow," said Arthur moodily. "These men are not the same breed as they that met us at the Broch of Guinion."

"True Saxons they are not," said Medraut, "by their looks I can tell that they are Engel; I do not doubt that you can break them, Arthur, yet you will not easily drive them overseas. These men have let their ships rot, they have built themselves halls of British timber, they have ploughed British earth, they have bred from British women. The British folk of Deivr are so mixed in them that we shall be hewing our own flesh and blood; ever since we came down from the hills the people have fled before us and joined themselves to this Eoppa. If we fight now we may stay for years in Deivr harrying here and harrying there, up one valley and down another. We can empty the land, as men deal with wolves, yet it will fill again with our enemies, for they are many across the sea, and we are few."

"Full of folk are the vales of the West. What might we not do if we had the strength of Maelgun and Cuneglas?"

Medraut should his head. "Too few," he repeated. "The best of the Britons are bled away in the wars or gone in the ships that sail to Armorica."

"It irks me to leave these people masters of Deivr," said Arthur. His cheeks flushed and his eyes glittered as he looked at the sullen-faced mass of men before him, the half of them British born, but no friends to the Cymry, with no consciousness of the bond of blood.

"The storm blows up in the South, Arthur. There is Cerdic, our greatest enemy; there is the main danger to Britain. Have you not summoned the Kings of the West to meet you before Christmas in Verulam? Will you let our army waste away in the wilderness of Deivr?"

"Your mind is subtle, nephew, but your heart is cold, your words carry a chill of doom as we stand here in the setting sun, doubting our strength for the task before us."

Medraut shrugged his shoulders. "Let us take hostages and pass on," he said briefly. They turned back and spoke again with Eoppa.

Then, between both the armies, the big fair-haired man went on his knees and kissed the foot of Arthur as it rested in the stirrup. He bade the champions of the Cymry to meat and drink in his hall by the river bank on the far side of Caer Ebrauc. It was dark when they came from the ruined city to fenced fields and long low buildings of timber and thatch. Firelight glowed in the doorways, there was a smell of roasting and baking, but Arthur rode on. "I shall not house under a heathen roof," he said, "nor shall I eat the bread of men that bow to us with hate in their hearts." His men followed him without a word, only Medraut wheeled his horse and rode into the firelight.

He stooped his head and rode in at the hall door, looking about him as though in a dream. Eoppa pointed to an empty seat before the fire, but Medraut sat still in the saddle, dark thoughts drifting through his mind as smoke drifted to and fro in the hall.

"These are the men that will master Britain in the end," he said to himself. "The men that will undo Arthur's work and bring down the pride of the Princes. It is through them that the path leads to power, the path Cerdic has chosen. What if it should be my path also? My first step was when I spoke with Gwenhyvar on the walls of Bregion; my second now when I saved Eoppa and his folk from the swords of the Cymry, but there are many steps to tread yet before I can glut my desire and Britain knows me for what I am."

A woman brought him a horn of mead. He took it from her, looked long in her face, then passed it back untasted. The woman was Eadgyth, the sister of Eadwald, with whom his father Modron had lain in Din Uther. It was as though a hand beckoned suddenly to him out of the gloom, luring him towards something which he longed yet dreaded to see. He felt the fierce heat of the fire upon his face as his horse snorted and edged away from the leaping flames. 'The blast of hell,' he thought, 'but the path to power.' He saw the dull faces of the Engel staring at him from the long benches, and before them all, two children on the rush-strewn floor, two boys, the elder dark and shifty-eyed, the younger fair and smiling. They came nearer on all fours like young puppies, they dived under the horse's belly and sported round him, plucking at the reins and fingering stirrups and spurs.

"Are they your children?" he asked Eadgyth. She nodded.

"Bold men will they be when they grow to manhood. What are their names?" His meaning was clear to her though she understood few of his words. She pointed to the younger child and said "Ida."

"And who is he?" Medraut pointed to the dark boy.

She did not answer, but her eyes gleamed at him with a frosty sparkle.

"I shall give him a name," said Medraut. "Brawd-bach[1] he shall be called, and I shall take him with me among the Cymry where he belongs. You will hear of us again, Eadgyth! Modron is dead, but his sons may live to throw mighty shadows from the fire that burns up Britain."

The woman laid a hand on the shoulder of Eoppa, who stood with arms folded on his broad chest like a pillar in the midst of the long low hall. Neither moved as Medraut took up the boy in his arms, set him astride the saddle-bow and wrapped his cloak about him. The horse leaped suddenly at the touch of armed heels, it churned the rushes under its feet and went at a bound through the doorway into the winter's night.

* * *

Southward went the Cymry through the ruins of Caer Daun in its marshy moors and Lindum set high on a wave of gorse-covered hills; they skirted the fenland, full of broken people of the British race who won a living as fowlers and fishermen, and crossed a heathery wilderness to a rising country of deep earth dotted everywhere with burnt-out farms. The orderly prosperity of Roman times was gone, but there were folk here who ploughed and sowed, who shunned the old haunted ruins and live clustered together within oaken palisades, both Briton and Engel. A new community was spreading out over the good land, a heathen people, rough in their ways, but only asking to be left in peace by the wolfish-looking warriors

---

[1] Little Brother.

that came from the North. Now forests closed in
again, mounting the low ridges of chalk, and the
army swung to the right until it reached the road
that led to Verulam. The banks and ditches of the
greatest highway in Britain were lost in scrub, the
broad cambered surface had vanished under turf
and heather, marked here and there by the fires of
wandering folk coming from the high black wall of
forest Londonwards or from the dim blue horizons to
west and north.

It was growing dusk and frost was in the air. Horses
and cattle pulled greedily at the rimy turf; from the
brown-leaved thickets came the sound of axe strokes
and a snapping of branches as the Cymry collected
firing for another night under the stars. The champions stood in a group talking eagerly in low tones,
Arthur and Medraut sat side by side on a sack of
meal lifted from one of the pack animals, above them,
perched on a fragment of flinty wall coursed with red
tile, was the little impish figure of Brawdbach.

"The men are cheerless; tired they are and hungry, and there has been no fight to hearten them,"
said Medraut. "Friendless we seem under these wide
steely skies, welcome we are neither to man nor
woman."

"Then let your harp speak to the army. With our
people nothing has such power to lighten the heart
as music."

Medraut ran his fingers over the strings; he tuned
the harp and played, and as he did so the fume of
dark designs and evil passions ebbed from his mind.
He looked at Arthur, sitting beside him with bowed
head and hands hanging loosely between his knees,
and he thought with a sigh of relief, as though the
sun had broken in on a night of dreadful dreams,
'Why should it be my destiny to cast this man down,
to snatch at power which even he cannot bear on his
broad shoulders? Weak and mortal he is, like all the

rest of us, mighty only in his spirit which drives him
from one peril to another, seeking only to save what
is already lost—this land of Britain for the British
race. And we who go with him, we fight because we
are loyal to Arthur and the Red Dragon, or because
we find no pleasure except in killing and taking what
we can from our enemies, or because we hope to
grasp power in our own hands such as he holds to-
day. We are lesser men than he is; and if he be
doomed to fail shall any one of us fare better? But
must he fail in the end if we all stand by him, if the
Princes are ruled by the bond of blood and not by
envy and hatred? What if I cast away this lust to take
Gwenhyvar, to avenge my father whom Arthur slew in
the Saxon ship, to raise up my own tainted blood in
the face of all these champions who listen to my
words and music and yet hold themselves aloof,
shunning the powers of evil? These visions of things
to come, the beckonings by which I steer my course,
these may be pictures bred of my own desires, the
cunning devices of devils that try to entrap me. Need
I finish what I have begun, even though I listened to
Gwenhyvar at Bregion and took Brawdbach out of
Eoppa's hall to forge a weapon for a dark deed in days
to come?'

"You make us comforting music to-night,
nephew." Arthur raised his head as Medraut ceased
to pluck at the strings. "Music that heartens us for
our enterprise to-morrow across yonder hills. Coit
Celidon they call the wood that lies in our path, and
it is a lucky name for us." He pointed to the band of
deeper darkness to the south-east, in which showed
the red eyes of camp-fires answering to those of the
Cymry. "I doubt it is but a false comfort," said
Medraut. Suddenly he put his hand on Arthur's arm.
"There is a bond between us, Arthur—we are of the
same blood though sundered by fate and sin. I helped
you on Moel Fre, I put a weapon in your hand which

you have wielded well. Now I would help you again. Preserve your life and power; hold your hand till you find yourself backed, not by a dozen champions and a few hundred brave men in armour, but by the whole might of the West. What are we doing here, a little ship sailing farther and farther among unknown rocks in a rising gale? This is the very heart of the old Roman Britain, but what do we see about us? A few ruins, gorse and blackthorn, an untrodden road, and the fires of our enemies upon the hills. If we win through to Verulam shall we find Maelgun there, or Conan, or Cuneglas? There are no footprints of their armies on this road that leads from the Strath of Severn and the mountains of Gwyneth; they come not at your call. Will you go forward alone, perish, and leave Britain without a leader?"

"Even if they come not, I must do what I can," said Arthur gloomily. "The prize is London, the crown of Britain. The Saxons cluster about it now like a swarm of bees, but if we can deliver London it may be that we shall one day win back everything from Clyde to Kent."

"To my mind we come fifty years too late. Where Vortigern and Emrys failed shall we succeed with hundreds where they had thousands?"

"I trust more in the spirit of my men than in their numbers. Our foes are divided, jealous of each other, greedy for gold, for land, for women, but we Cymry are all of one heart and mind."

"United we stand, yet doubt presses us hard."

"It is your music, Medraut, that is our armour against false heart and doubting mind." Arthur rose to his feet and walked among the fires where the warriors lay warming themselves and eating their meagre rations. Medraut sat still, his fingers moving soundlessly over the harp, and Brawdbach came down from the ruin and crept in under his brother's cloak.

Next morning the men moved up the road into the hills, their feet scuffling through copper-coloured drifts of leaves, their eyes fixed on something dark in the narrow vista miles ahead. The forest thinned and suddenly they saw a great dyke and ditch curving away on to the heights to right and left and in the gap where the road went through was a crowd of armed men. They were Saxons for the most part, a brutal-looking band, staring vacantly like a herd of oxen, big brawny men bloated with good living, but before them stood a warrior in Roman armour who hailed the Cymry in their own tongue.

"Here begins the land of London!" he shouted warningly. "There is no passage for any folk that come armed, whether Briton or Engel."

It was Medraut that answered him. "A passage you must give, friend, to Arthur the Amherawdyr, guletic of Britain after his father Uther. He comes with a host of war-hardened men to bring help to London."

"We have plenty of stout men to guard London; we want no help from you barbarians of the Pictish march."

"Do you guard London with men such as these?" interrupted Arthur, scornfully, pointing to the Saxons. Something in his gesture seemed to infuriate the big brutish warriors. With one accord they gave a shout of defiance and a cloud of misty breath rose from them in the keen still air. The legionaries levelled their spears, they maintained a contemptuous silence, but the London leader did not care for their looks. He liked it still less when he saw a solid mass of men swing out to right and left, taking the unguarded dyke at a run. All around him now were men laying arrows on their bowstrings, ready to shoot into the slowly heaving mass of bewildered Saxons. Tauntingly Medraut called to him: "You will have a busy day, friend, for when you have slain all of us you will find Cuneglas and the men of Powys following in our footsteps, and behind him Conan from Caer Ceri, and somewhere farther back on the road will be the men of Dyvnaint and those of Gwyneth and Dyfet. What can you do against all the Princes of Britain when they seek a passage through Coit Celidon?"

The man made no answer to Medraut, but he began to speak hotly and blusteringly to a big Saxon who stood out before his comrades, leaning on a battle-axe. After a while the Saxon stirred and shouted, he began to push the warriors back, he even felled an obstinate fellow with a blow of his fist. Growling and grunting like a drove of wild beasts, the Saxons shifted off the road and flowed away between the monstrous clustered shafts of beech trees towards their camp on a height above. The Cymry watched them for a while, then moved forward along the road. Their voices echoed triumphantly in the dim forest glades:

"Cymry in victory, Cymry in woe!"

"It is not worth while making a song about this Coit Celidon," said Medraut, smiling as he rode between Arthur and Kai with the Red Dragon. That evening, Christmas eve, they reached Verulam and marched unopposed into the city between a pair of huge round towers, on one of which still stood the rotting timbers of a ballista.

It was Caerluel over again on a vaster scale. Some quarters of the town were gone altogether, a chaos of wreckage half buried in a withered brush of nettles and docks, but mighty buildings still rose up around the forum; baths, basilicas, richly carved porticos of great mansions, colonnades that still contained shops. Here and there were marks of fire and plaster peeling from brickwork, pigs rooted in the courtyards, cattle wandered along the grass-grown streets, churning up mud and filth, clattering among heaps of fallen tile and broken crockery; nevertheless it was still a city, squalid indeed, but crowded with people.

Most were of the British race, chattering insolent folk who still wore costumes that savoured of Roman days, albeit patched and dirty; there were tonsured priests at the door of the Christian church, a bell rang for mass, but amid the swarms of slovenly men and pinched, febrile-looking women there staggered groups of yellow-headed Saxons, roaring drunk, elbowing their way carelessly among these British citizens that represented the ultimate degradation of Imperial Rome. The legionaries halted in the forum, they stared about them in surprise at the magnificence of the buildings, at the food and goods men offered them in exchange for money. Some of them remembered this way of life in Caer Isc or Caer Ceri, but now they had no coins to pay with, they had no possessions but foul clothes on their backs, rusty armour and sharp-edged weapons. These dwellers in Verulam were grasping and suspicious, there was none of the friendly hospitality here that had greeted the army in Caerluel. From the steps of the great basilica Arthur spoke sternly to the crowd of scowling townsmen.

"Men of Verulam!" he shouted, "we Cymry are no band of robbers and broken men roving abroad from the forests of the North. We are an army that has battered and beaten down the foes of Britain. Eleven times has our Dragon standard seen victory over Pict and Saxon, and given peace to men of our race that cling to the land—the land that was ours in the days of Rome and in long ages before the Roman came. We are here to do in the South what we have done in the North, to guard the Briton against his savage enemies from overseas, to give security to the peasants in the fields and the dwellers in the old cities of Britain. No violence shall be done to you by us Cymry—Christians we are, friends to priest and friends to trader— but meat and ale you shall give us, men of Verulam, as long as we house within your walls, and in return we shall give weapons to any of you that are men enough to join with us and help us in our task. If we fail, this city will soon be in a heap of rubble and ash, like Lindum, like Eboracum, and many another splendid jewel of the Roman world; if we succeed, it will rise afresh, wealthy and beautiful as it was before Pict and Saxon set their teeth in Britain."

A great answering shout went up from the legionaries and their weapons rose menacingly in the dusk under the columned piazzas of Verulam. "Hail, Arthur yr Amherawdyr! Hail, Arthur, giver of victory!" But the citizens answered only with a discontented muttering. Here and there a voice was raised:

"Safer we are with Saxons to guard us than with these mountain wolves."

"Armies came from the South to deliver us in the old days, but never from the North."

"We have walls and paid mercenaries; our rulers are the Council in London; we want no tyrants with their hungry armies eating us out of house and home."

Nevertheless the army got what it wanted from Verulam without blow or bloodshed, all the time that it rested in the great buildings around the forum, and that was for three weeks. All that time Arthur waited for news of the Kings. A rumour came that Gereint was mustering men at Sarum, but otherwise there was silence. Powys, Gwent, Gwyneth and Dyfed made no move behind the broad barriers of forest and wasted land. No enemy threatened their frontiers—what should they care whether a few more cities were sacked in eastern Britain? On the other hand there was news that great masses of Saxons were encamped on the Thames shores below London, and that day by day the east wind brought fresh ships up the river, ships packed with warriors, and, even more significantly, with women and children. A nation was pouring into Britain, not a medley of raiding bands bent on plunder. There was news, too, of a stir among the Saxon communities that for a hundred years had lived peacefully on the upper Thames, where the river wound lazily among rushy moors and level pastures before it entered the defiles under Celidon. These men, it was said, had come in on the rivers of the great fenland, pushing far upcountry in their flat-bottomed boats; they had settled down in desolate places during the vast upheaval in Britain due to the invasion of Nial of the Nine Hostages from Eiré. Now there was a leader among them, a man called Cerdic, and they were making ready for war. There came an evening, raw with mist that clung in the ghostly streets of Verulam, throwing a halo round every glow of light in window or doorway. Life beat with a more violent rhythm in the old city since the coming of the army; there were harsher tones in the hum of voices, louder laughter where drink was served, a hectic excitement in the eyes of the women. Wrapped in his cloak, Arthur walked through the narrow byways behind the great basilica where most of his men had housed themselves. In the wavering radiance of a lantern he saw a legionary with a ham under his arm, a fat priest slipping into a doorway with a girl who looked at Arthur over her shoulder as though more interested in the man of war than the man of God. From a dimly lit courtyard came a smash of crockery and hoarse chorus: "Arthur our leader; Christ our King!" Furious, brutish voices in the dialect of Strathclyde sounded from an upper window mixed with the whimpering of an ill-used woman—in a dark corner someone was violently sick—he heard the bellowing shout of an infuriated Saxon—girls' laughter and the maudlin tones of a priest: "*Domine, Domine, juva servos tuos.*" From a ragged opening in a wall came a rustle of hay and the strong stench of cattle; an overburdened mule staggered along the street driven by incessant jabs with a goad; a bell tolled mournfully, the chanting of a congregation could be heard like a whisper behind a cliff-like face of brickwork. A row of fluted columns went up into blackness. Arthur stepped between them and in at a door. He felt his way across a courtyard, where a dog barked savagely on a chain, and opened another door into a flickering radiance of firelight. He stood in a room with a superb mosaic floor, sunken in places and littered with bones and broken pottery. In the centre was a great blaze of beech logs set about with lumps of raw clay and close to the fire was a tub of steaming water in which a naked girl stood washing herself. She smiled unconcernedly, passing a strigil over her glistening white skin; her black hair was neatly coiled on her head, her firm young breasts stood out in sharp silhouette against the yellow glare of the flames. Smoke and steam hung heavily under the high ceiling and drifted out through a great rent in the plaster. Sprawling on the floor was a boy, toasting his feet at the fire and staring up at the girl with the dawning of a vicious curiosity; in the background was a row of pillars, once elaborately painted but now scored over with obscene charcoal drawings, and behind the pillars a couch on which lay Medraut, half stripped, a sword across his knees and one hand resting on a harp. His dark eyes left the girl and brooded on the tall figure standing in the room with arms folded under a black cloak. The look of sleepy, sullen contentment on his beautiful face changed slowly to something sombre and inscrutable. The steely bearing he had shown since he sat with Arthur under Celidon had relaxed during the weeks of ease and pleasure in Verulam; he was once more the vision-haunted man of the past, leaving his mind open indifferently to the promptings of good and evil as a roofless house admits both sunshine and storm.

"I shall march to-morrow," said Arthur. He looked about him, breathing deeply, as though struggling in

this room of ancient splendour against mighty elemental forces that mocked him with wanton smiles
and enigmatic silence. Here, he knew, was the corruption that ate out the manhood of the rulers of
Britain, this dalliance with lust, this inclination to
perverse pursuits that had lingered on from the days
of Rome, and from which the Saxons were immune.
The bestial habits they indulged in did not abate one
whit their natural fierceness and hardihood—creatures of instinct, they could not comprehend the
pleasures born of cynical sophistication . . . . Women
such as this dainty fragile creature who regarded
him, smiling and unashamed in her nakedness,
would they bring forth children who could save
Britain from the Saxons? This life that clung about
Verulam was surely doomed; it had outlived its time,
it would fall inevitably as the autumn-tinted leaves
dropped from the thickets in winter frost. London,
too; there were more folk there, mightier walls, still
nobler buildings, greater wealth and ease—possibly it
was not as far gone in rottenness—and yet, could he
save it with a few hundred Cymry? Medraut's words
came back to him, words spoken as they rode
towards Afon Coch: "Britain is gone." Medraut had no
belief in victory, and now he had no word to say, after
eleven great battles when they lay a day's march from
their goal, London.

* * *

The army was camped on a heath scattered with
huge oaks, the last wave of the forest before it died
away in green fields and ploughed earth before the
walls of London. From the brow of the hill Arthur on
his black horse looked down on the city ringed with
walls and towers, on a grey mass of hovels and vast
rectangular blocks of brickwork and masonry that
rose cliff-like out of a sea of thatch and smoke. Gilded crucifixes and bronze statues stood up in the

misty sunlight, there was a gleam on reaches of the
Thames winding through swamp and scrub, a faint
bristling of masts where Saxon fleets lay inshore
below the eastern end of the city.

About Arthur, washed and combed, in brightly
coloured cloaks, were a dozen champions. They got
on horseback and circled round him, laughing and
racing each other from tree to tree, hair flying in the
wind, their eyes alight with joyous adventure. Arthur
smiled to see their high spirits when the fate of every
man there hung by a thread. That morning a bedrag-
gled weaponless man had limped into the camp with
news from Gereint. The host that had marched from
Sarum was shattered to fragments like an earthen
pot under a hammer stroke. Cerdic and his Saxons
had lain in ambush for it on the scrubby heath outside Calleva. Of a thousand warriors from Dyvnaint
he was the only one who had got through to eastwards, swum the Thames, and reached Arthur.

"What is your plan, cousin?" said Gwalchmei, as
he rode beside Arthur down the hill towards London.

"If the men of the city join us we may rout the Saxons in the east, then turn back and try our steel
against Cerdic," said Arthur grimly. "If not . . . ." His
eyes swept meditatively over the low featureless landscape, drab-coloured now under lowering skies, fusing into fog breath that flooded up from the river.

"A hard task it will be, to teach the Cymry to run
from their foes," laughed Gwalchmei.

"This morning at least let us ride like conquerors,"
said Arthur. He stared challengingly at Medraut, who
came on with slack rein and downcast head, hum-
ming a little monotonous tune.

They all broke into a fast trot and Medraut raised
his voice; he sang in time to the hoofbeats on sodden
turf, a song of the Cymry before London:

> "Clouds come down in dark'ning pall,
> Dim and grey is London wall;

> Cymry, ride at Arthur's call,
> Though we all
> Fall!
>
> Death shall ne'er the brave deny
> Life in song till seas go dry,
> Life in fame till falls the sky;
> They who fly
> Die."

There was a shout of approval, but Medraut's face remained gay and indifferent. They sped on over weedy ploughland, past haystacks and sheepfolds. Where a broad road went straight towards the river they swung to the left among clusters of cabins plastered against the walls of long-ruined villas. They rode on through deepening mud and thickening mist, past tombs, heaps of refuse, and rooting pigs, into a hollow with grey tidal sludge and reedy pools overhung by pollard willows. On the top of the steep bank opposite rose two towers, sharp-edged as the day on which they were built, and between them twin archways under rows of window openings, a pediment with statues and a mighty inscription. They were at the Praetorian Gate in the north-west angle of London Wall.

CHAPTER XII

Constans, Dubricius, and Sigbert

So that all the columns were levelled with the ground by the frequent strokes of the battering-ram, all the husbandmen routed, together with their bishops, priests and people, whilst the sword gleamed and the flames crackled around them on every side.
—Gildas, *De Excidio Britanniae.*

Kai blew a trumpet and crowds of spectators on the walls stirred, pointed, and broke into an excited murmur. A gate opened and a little group of men came out backed by a show of soldiery. The Council of London looked warily at the champions from the North, the men whose deeds had resounded through the length and breadth of Britain.

"We need not have come," said Medraut mockingly, as Arthur dismounted and went forward on foot up the slough of mud to the gateway. Three men stood out to meet him. Foremost was Constans, handsome and grey-haired, with a deeply furrowed brow and a portly figure draped in the old-fashioned Roman toga. He came of a wealthy family of merchants who, with the ruin of Britain's trade, had maintained a shadow of their old prosperity by ownership of estates near London. The land had been plundered often enough by Saxon marauders, but Constans had generally been able to get most of its produce into safety. He had bought up the groves, orchards and waste land which lay inside the western gates, no small proportion of the whole area within walls, and there were his granaries, brew houses, stores of smoked fish and salted meat, his bales of wool, his trussed hay and straw, his herds of cattle and swine that went out to summer pasture on the skirts of the forest. The western part of the city was indeed nothing more than an intensive farm and storehouse, and from its surplus the city lived in time of need, repaying the family of Constans in goods and services. Next to the city magnate stood Dubricius, the Bishop of London, a hatched-faced, fanatical-looking priest, tonsured on the forepart of his head after the fashion of the British clergy. He had a nose like a pickaxe, a small tight-set mouth; his eyes, horribly inflamed by disease, seemed to blaze out a reflection of hell fire. His figure was bent and meagre as though eaten up by the passion which consumed his mind, a fury with his British flock for their miserable addiction to deadly sins, and a black hatred for the pagans both within and without the city walls. Their presence in London was, indeed, mainly the work of Constans, who hired a small army of mercenaries recruited cautiously from the thriving Jutish villages in Kent and from the newer and weaker Saxon settlements north of the lower Thames. The astute merchant hoped to keep this tough material in pliable condition partly by training a more numerous guard of British-born youth, and partly he relied upon the feud between Jute and Saxon to prevent any concerted action of the barbarians against their employer. Unfortunately the British troops had degenerated

into a thieving mutinous rabble. It was hopeless to pit
them against the raiders who were swarming into the
land of London from the east; the bolder spirits had
deserted and formed themselves into robber bands,
the more timorous could not be induced to show
themselves outside the city wall. Yet for the moment
the life of the city went on much as usual; there was
food and comfort, luxury even, for the streets of London had not as yet been trodden by the feet of
destroying hosts. For a hundred years there had been
recurring alarms; flocks of refugees pouring in from
the countryside, sometimes the sight of scowling or
jeering plunderers, flaxen-haired men with big round
shields, who came to the foot of the walls, made
insulting gestures and then drew off again, their
departure sometimes expedited by arrows and sling-
stones or a few shots from a ballista. Now there were
men of this breed in the service of the city. They
lodged in the old legionary barracks, dangerous men
when excited by drink, but generally docile enough,
contemptuously tolerant of the ill will which Dubricius raised against them among the Christians. They
had their own commander, the Saxon Sigbert, who
lived in rude magnificence in the gatehouse at the
head of London Bridge. He it was who stood beside
Constans and Dubricius, a short, bandy-legged man
in a white linen tunic and cross-gartered hose; red-
cheeked, with a long tawny beard and expressionless
blue eyes. He looked with critical interest at the
mighty figure of Arthur, a man from another world
where folk were inured to hard living and hard fighting, not like these Britons of London, cringing and
treacherous, with no thought but how to save their
skins—a dealer in magic, maybe, but not in the magic
of Dubricius, the sound and fury of words that blew
about the ears of the crowd like autumn leaves show-
ering down in a winter's gale. Here was a warrior who
might stir men's blood and nerve them to desperate

decision; he might even now turn the tide that was flowing from the East, the tide which Sigbert had resolved to let in through the gates of London, hoping for power in Britain such as he could never win as the servant of Constans.

It was Constans who spoke first.

"Are you this man Arthur who has come unbidden into the land of London with a war band from the North?" he said haughtily in the slurred Latin of the Celtic townsmen.

"I am Arthur yr Amherawdyr," came the reply, cold and significant.

"Are you a man of Christ?" asked Dubricius sharply.

"I am, father; and so are my warriors, men of Christ and smiters of the heathen."

"Then I give you my blessing, on behalf of the Church in Britain, in the name of the Father, the Son, and the Holy Ghost," said the Bishop unwillingly, and he raised three fingers in the air in a gesture that seemed more a menace than a benediction. Arthur went down on one knee for a moment.

"*Gratzagum.*"[1] His tone was short and disdainful.

The Bishop stared at him with increasing disfavour.

"What is your purpose in passing our boundaries with this host of men?" asked Constans.

"I come to give you help against the Saxons who gather for the destruction of your city."

"Our walls are strong, our moats are deep; London stands secure against any plunderers from the sea."

"I would make her more secure. By the looks of those men behind you the enemy is already within your gates. Britons are we, bred in the deep valleys of the West and on the Northern moors; our task is to

---

[1] A corruption of *gratias agamus*, 'we return thanks.'

win back Britain for the men of our race and our faith. A multitude of men you have in London; we shall be their spear, and by the might of us all united we shall drive the Saxons back into the sea from which they come."

Constans combed his beard with nervous fingers. He looked waveringly at Arthur and at the fierce faces of the champions behind him, hard weather-beaten men with the glint of battle in their eyes. 'This man would make himself tyrant of London,' he thought. 'I would be safer with Sigbert and his warriors—if I could be sure that they are true to me . . .'

"Ill reports come to us of how your men have housed in Verulam," he said tentatively.

"I fear that you folk from outer Britain are deeply infected with the vile Pelagian heresy," broke out Dubricius. "The true church can have no communion with such men."

"Yet you have communion with that man," said Arthur, pointing swiftly at Sigbert. "What is he but a whelp from the kennel of heathendom?"

"He is a baptised Christian," said the Bishop, in an angry voice that betrayed an inward struggle.

"He is a faithful servant of the city," said Constans, striving hard to appear calm and judicial. "Shall I bid him go forth and you come in? We have hundreds of law-abiding citizens here who have Saxon blood and glad they are to live in the shelter of London's walls and serve the state in field and forest and in bearing arms for her when needful. What are your men but wolves bred up to rapine in the wild hills? What bond can there be between them and the peaceful folk of London?"

"My men are the Cymry, and between all Britons there is the bond of blood," said Arthur proudly. The champions behind him stirred in their saddles, there was a clink of bridles and stirrups as the horses flung up their heads and pulled their feet from the sucking mud. The Bishop raised a hand warningly, his eyes seemed to shoot red fire, Constans went back a step, glancing over his shoulder; only Sigbert stood unmoved, his brown hairy arms folded on his chest. He cleared his throat and spat. In a low, gruff voice he muttered to Constans:

"A dozen men cannot take a city. Even if their whole force stood before the gate, seven hundred perhaps, they could not harm us."

Constans did not answer. His thoughts wandered distractedly to and fro like branches swaying in a mighty wind. He stood there in the darkening fog; conscious alternately of the huge outthrust towers to right and left and of the dim void beyond the little group of Cymry, a void that seemed to hide the face of Britain and all the forces lurking in it, active for good or evil, and all that fate had in store for this land of black woods and sodden plains, the leagues of spray-drenched shingle in the east and the high cloud-ridden hills of the west. And as he stood shifting from foot to foot, under the walls of London where everything was familiar and yet all of a sudden charged with some cataclysmic significance, he realised that for a brief moment fate held her hand and waited with an ironic smile for him to say his part like some actor pushed unexpectedly upon the stage before a nation in suspense. 'A dozen men,' he thought, 'but what men! Could they not kindle a fire among our people that would burn out these Saxons that come trampling in from the sea? Our people are weaponed only with the hate that Dubricius pours into their hearts, but Arthur could make them an army reckless of their lives for some mighty purpose. By a desperate stroke we can free ourselves or perish in the attempt. Or we can close our gates and put our trust in Sigbert. Perhaps, for my day at least, we can preserve London in peace, all will be as it was; the Saxons will flow past us as they have done before, but within these walls we shall be safe with our women and children, our slaves, our good houses, our Roman way of life, and our Christian faith. And when the confusion passes and a new Britain arises on the ruins of the old, we shall be a bright light shining in a dim world, a storehouse from which the waste places shall be replenished. I can say which it is to be, but not now—I must consult with Dubricius, I must get a fresh hold on Sigbert—a bargain . . . perhaps my daughter Helena . . . and if I can see a flaw in the man, if I get a sign that he thinks of betraying us to this hungry sea of savages lapping up to the eastern wall, then we must put ourselves in the hands of these Cymry. . . .'

Through the mist appeared the foremost ranks of Arthur's host descending to the marsh. A faint rattle of arms, the muffled tramp of hundreds of footsteps in the sticky clay, a pale gleam on helmets and armour under the dripping trees, a loud anxious murmur from the watchers on towers and wall. Arthur turned from the three men who stared in each other's faces with swift flashes of doubt, suspicion, and hardening resolve, he vaulted on to the black horse and made it plunge wildly along the ramp to right and left, churning up the foul refuse of the city, clattering among heaps of broken pottery. He threw up his right hand towards the lines of faces that leaned out between the battlements or were packed under the timber pent-houses, gesticulating Celts and surly Saxons.

"Men of London!" he shouted. "We come to do you no harm! We come to save you from fire and sword, from rape and pillage at the hands of the spoilers of Britain. We are a Christian host; we have triumphed in every battle, driving the Pict to his mountains and the Saxon to the sea. I call on you to open your gates to Arthur yr Amherawdyr!"

A confused uproar came from the walls, shrill cries of welcome, growling curses, and from the Cymry thronging up the slope from the bridge came a loud exultant yell. Spears, swords and axes swung up in the eddying mist. Sigbert stepped back and gave a swift order to a warrior standing behind him. The man turned and shouldered his way through the crowd of soldiery at the gate.

"Shall we let them come?" said Constans to Dubricius. He bit his lips, he was deadly pale and his knees shook behind the folds of his toga.

"These wolves! These heretics! Are they to be masters of London?" said the Bishop between clenched teeth.

"We shall close the gates!" said Sigbert violently. "What terms can we make with them once they are inside?" He caught Constans by the shoulder in a hard grip and drew him backwards, muttering in his ear. The Bishop raised his hand authoritatively. "We shall give you an answer in an hour's time," he said in a calm voice to Arthur and the champions on horseback who closed about him shortening their reins and leaning forward in their saddles as though to sweep on at the gallop.

"Forward now and put your fortune to the touch!" said Medraut with a short laugh. A legionary came to Arthur's side. "A great band of Saxons has come between us and our camp on the hill!" he said breathlessly.

"Men from the city?" Arthur looked over his left shoulder at the white billows of fog. A smell of burning drifted in the chilly air.

"Men from the ships. They are firing and killing as they come."

"If we had Maelgun here and Cuneglas . . ." said Arthur, irresolute for the first time since the passage of Afon Coch.

The Bishop had gone slowly back under the arch. The great oaken doors were beginning to move.

"There is still time!" shouted Gwalchmei. His horse reared up at a sudden thrust of spurs and bounded towards the gate. At that moment a big stone came down from an opening above, there was a crunch, horse and rider rolled over in a heap. In a moment Gwalchmei was up, seemingly unharmed, he rushed forward on foot and flung his spear at a group of grim-faced Saxons who crowded in the narrowing opening. The doors came together with a hollow boom and the spear stood quivering in the grey timber. Gwalchmei sprang back pursued by more stones and an arrow or two. He came up to Arthur, rueful at the loss of his horse, which lay between the gateway towers with a smashed skull.

"The first war-work since we left Reged, cousin, and I have won little honour," he said.

"Even as you were too late, so we are all too late. Let us get back across the bridge and stand ready for the Saxons should they aim at giving us battle." Arthur rode slowly through the ranks of the legionaries and led the way to groves of chestnut and sycamore trees on the opposite slope. Across the open country he could see here and there a redness of fire in the mist. There was an occasional cry or a chorus of guttural voices, but the city had grown strangely silent. The dusk of a winter's afternoon was closing in, the fog grew thicker, the tall columned façades of baths and temples had faded away; there was nothing to be seen but the mighty walls enclosing a formless gloom. An hour passed and the sounds of pillage grew fainter and fainter to northward, the city made no sign. Medraut rode once more to the gateway, then back at a gallop.

"There are few men on the walls now," he reported. "They pay us no heed; their heads are turned the other way. Something is happening in the city. Listen!"

A low murmur seemed to come out of the gathering darkness to eastward, a noise like that of surf breaking on some distant beach. It grew louder, spreading out, rising and falling, disintegrating into a jumble of separate sounds, a scream leaped out sharply and then suddenly a bell began to boom in quick strokes.

* * *

Meanwhile Constans, Dubricius, and Sigbert had gone to consult within the temple of Venus, not far from the Praetorian Gate. It had stood formerly in a little grove of sycamores, but these had all been felled for firewood and replaced by fruit trees now that the family of Constans had bought the site. The pillared portico had been partly walled up and turned into fowl houses, the temple itself was a barn for hay and straw. The windows high in the walls lit up mountainous heaps of fodder coated with dust and mould. At the far end, buried to the knees in hay, and with a scythe hooked casually over one shoulder, was a statue of the goddess, brutally and obscenely disfigured by Christian hands.

For half an hour the three men sought to read each other's minds, seated in a dim light on bales of straw, while over their heads the goddess, blandly unconscious of her degradation, extended a handless arm. Dubricius was for allowing the Cymry to march through and fall immediately upon the Saxons camped by their ships below the city. Sigbert shrugged his shoulders. The Saxons would be four to one, he said.

"Your men must fight too; we must enrol every citizen capable of bearing arms," said Constans energetically.

"I cannot answer for my men if they have to fight side by side with Arthur's," said Sigbert.

"Then will you lead your men across the bridge and drive back the Kentish host while Arthur goes out by the Eastern Gate?"

"Your plan is to make Arthur lord of London and bar us Saxons out of the city. Has not that man sworn to drive every man of our race from Britain?" Sigbert grew indignant—he got up as if he would leave the temple. Constans spoke soothingly, praising the trustiness of the Saxon guard while he threw a meaning look at Dubricius. The Bishop, however, sat with bowed head, his lips moving silently.

"There is nothing that I should like better than to keep the gates closed to Arthur if you have the strength to keep us safe from this host in the east," said Constans.

"I can make a treaty with these people," said Sigbert slowly. "What if I give them leave to march past us and join their forces with those of Cerdic?"

"Then Arthur will be a nut between the hammer and the anvil?" suggested Constans.

"It is London that will be the nut, crushed and eaten by the heathen!" said Dubricius, suddenly raising his head. "That is your plan, Sigbert."

"For five years I have served London faithfully," muttered the Saxon, his eyes wandering to the temple door.

"I have a mind to reward this faithfulness . . ." threw out Constans. At that moment a man rushed in, a stout man with terror-stricken eyes, his gown trailing behind him.

"The Saxons!" he shouted. "Save us, holy Bishop! Save us, Constans! The seamen are pouring in at the East Gate—the guards are gone—our people are being slaughtered like sheep!"

"Treachery!" muttered Constans. He sprang back as he saw Sigbert draw his sword.

"I go to have the gates opened to Arthur!" shouted the Bishop. Gathering up his black robe under one arm he rushed out of the building followed by the panting citizen. Sigbert stood with his sword in his hand watching them go. Then he turned with a grin towards Constans. "For five years I have kept you master of London," he said. "Now it is my turn."

The Briton stared for a moment at the broad, bandy-legged figure closing upon him as a spider might approach a fly caught in its web. He leaped into the hay and dodged behind the goddess. "Christ have mercy upon me! Christ spare my life!" he babbled. Visions crowded into his distracted mind of servants forking hay into this tall dim building on summer evenings, of his lying with a girl here at the foot of the statue only yesterday afternoon—soft flesh and a laughing mouth—but he was not going to clasp any more girls; he was going to be killed . . . Despairingly he snatched at the scythe and made a stroke at the Saxon round the smooth thighs of the statue, but the sword flashed out and cut the blade from the worm-eaten shaft. He gathered up an armful of hay and flung it in his enemy's face, but a sharp point sped through the fragrant mass and caught him under the chin. Constans went backwards, kicking and heaving, while blood spurted about him like a fountain. After a few more stabs Sigbert coolly shore away the golden belt buckle, he undid the toga brooch, harsh to the touch with cut gems, he wrenched at a golden seal ring inlaid with lapis lazuli, but the dying man's hands were swollen with gout, so without more ado he sliced off the finger with his sword. Methodically he stuffed the spoils into a leather wallet, then with a wolfish gleam in his eyes he caught the body round the waist, heaved it up and flung it over the goddess' outstretched arm. It hung there quivering in spasms, a dark stream spattering down over the voluptuous curves of the statue that stood impassive, its upturned face moulded in a faint smile of infinite understanding.

* * *

The uproar from the doomed city grew louder and
louder as Arthur and his men watched from across
the creek. It flamed up first in one quarter, then in
another, a prolonged wail of terrified voices, stabbed
by thin screams and despairing yells, urged forward
by gasping, growling shouts in Saxon: "Kill! Kill! Hew
the Welshmen!"

"Shall we burst in the gate?" said Gwalchmei, in a
frenzied voice. His handsome face was all distorted,
he trembled all over like a hound held on leash.

"It is useless now," said Arthur. His eyes wandered to Medraut sitting motionless on horseback,
pale-cheeked, with a bitter smile about his lips. Like
a dull echo in his mind he seemed to hear the words:
'All that we do is useless.'

Saxons were crowding back on to the parapets;
taunting words came through the mist. From a window over the Praetorian Gate a slack, lifeless figure in
a black toga was lowered on a rope. A struggle was
going on behind the great oaken doors, but they
remained closed. Farther away, however, a tumul-
tuous roar spread out into the open country; some
gate had been forced open, a mass of people were
fleeing into the sheltering fog, into the dark woods,
making blindly towards Verulam, towards any cover
they could find from the pursuing horde of blond devils insatiable in their lust for blood. The legionaries
broke from their ranks; they crowded round Arthur
and the Red Dragon hanging limply from its pole.
"Vengeance!" they shouted in harsh inhuman voices.
"Lead us forward! Let us die fighting!"

"We can do nothing for London," said Arthur stub-
bornly. "You shall have your fill of fighting, but not
here and now. We are the sword of Britain, not to be
cast away lightly."

"What is your plan, Arthur?" came Medraut's
voice from the group of champions.

"We march by the western road to join Gereint at Sarum."

"I shall take a last look at London!" said Medraut recklessly.

"I, too," said Gwgawn, waving a naked sword in the air. Side by side they cantered down to the creek, across the bridge and up to the gateway towers. They ducked their heads as some missiles flew, glanced at the corpse of Dubricius twirling on its rope, and held on towards the West Gate. Parapets and pent-houses were deserted here, but farther on there was a glare of fire and they could hear the miserable clamour of fugitives. Now they could see a sheet of flame leaping up behind the wall and black against it a little cluster of folk huddling between the battlements. They stared down helplessly at a tuft of willow trees that grew in the choked outlet of a culvert. The slender topmost branches were close under the parapet. Medraut heard a shrill gabble of women's voices.

"Jump down and save yourselves!" he shouted.

Just then there came a rush of heavy footsteps along the crest of the wall and immediately a chorus of dreadful screams. The cluster of figures vanished, all but one that shot over the edge and fell with a crash into the trees. Lower and lower it came, tumbling this way and that among bending and snapping branches. Medraut drove his horse forward and caught the writhing thing in his arms, he planted it across his saddlebow and found it was a girl. She lay still in his grasp, breathing in loud sobs, but not uttering a word. The two men rode on in the shadow of the wall. Great towers rose before them ashen grey in the radiance of the flames, veiled sometimes in billowy clouds of smoke. They had come to the West Gate. Suddenly they rode into a band of Saxons lurching out vaguely from the archways, evil ungainly figures, dazed with wine, but still shouting hoarsely "Kill! kill!" Gwgawn's sword whistled about their heads, warm blood splashed in all directions, heavy bodies fell grunting in the mud. In a moment the riders were through, letting their maddened beasts race on a paved road that swung to the right, down into chilly depths. They thundered over a bridge and laboured desperately up the opposite slope. London was behind them and their faces towards the west. Medraut called to Gwgawn and drew rein. He sat on his panting horse, passing a hand over the girl's face, her breasts, her thighs.

"Are you hurt?" he said.

"I am not," she answered in the soft British tongue.

"What are you called?"

"Garwen."

"How old are you?"

"Seventeen years old I am said to be."

"Easily you breathe now, Garwen, and your eyes are dry, yet there have been few things in Britain more terrible than what you have seen to-day."

"I have seen much in my short life."

"Are your father and mother living?"

"My mother died in the fall of some city east of London: my memory begins from that time. My father was killed fighting the men of Kent on London Bridge. I was in the household of the holy Bishop Dubricius."

"Have you known a man, Garwen?"

"A Saxon tried to take me a little while ago, but suddenly he gave a shout and lay still. I pushed him off me and saw he had a knife in his back."

"One Saxon the less; but there are not knives in Britain to make an end of them all. Are you glad that I take you among the Cymry, Garwen?"

"I must needs be glad," she answered.

"Torches!" said Gwgawn, pointing with his sword at flares of light in the gloom.

"It is Arthur seeking the western road," said Medraut. They galloped on and came alongside a column of marching men. A chant rose from them. "Cymry in victory; Cymry in woe." A man on a horse turned to look back at the flickering glow over London. Gwgawn came up with him, waving a sword streaked with blood to the hilt.

"Some at least of them are dead!" he shouted.

"Gwgawn of the ruddy sword!" said Arthur with the ghost of a smile, and wondered where he had heard the words before.

"Spoil I bring you from London, uncle," said Medraut gaily. "Here is at least one girl who has not yielded her body to the Saxons."

There was a grim chuckle from the men marching in a dense mass beside the riders. A torch was thrust forward and many faces turned to look at the girl with a torn dress all smirched with blood—a slim young thing with breasts laid bare, with black curls about her shoulders, with a profile of unearthly beauty set out in black shadows.

"Take her, uncle," said Medraut. "Garwen is her name; your horse can bear a double weight better than mine."

Arthur made no answer, but he let Medraut set the girl up behind him and he drew her hands round his waist and her knees close behind his own. A heavy load of anxiety, of disappointment and foreboding he carried with him as the army pushed on hour after hour into the forests west of London, and yet the gentle pressure of this girl against him, this warm living creature saved from the wreck of a city, was like a draught of water to a thirsty man.

At last they came out from under interwoven branches into open ground. The fog had lifted; the moon shone on fenced fields and newly turned earth. There was a great space made by man in the far greater spaces of untamed forest, and in the midst of it lay some mounds of darkness, a splendid country house from the old days of Rome. It had been burnt more than once, perhaps; part of it was a broken shell buried in ivy, but part had been roughly patched up and made weather-proof. There were pigs, sheep and cattle here, grain stores, thatched shelters where poultry sat thickly on the carts and wagons, a smell of wood smoke in the air, and voices of men and women newly wakened from sleep. They were servants of Constans in London.

That night there was a vast upheaval in this peaceful place, but in time it sank to rest again. It was not till towards morning that Arthur went, half dazed with weariness, into a long low room where the champions lay stretched out on straw and their horses stood tethered to the walls, munching hay and snuffling the floor for the oats spilled out before them. A lamp burned in a niche of the wall, and by its feeble light he saw a curtain at the end of the room. Mechanically he walked towards it and all at once a girl rose from a dark corner and drew it back for him. She brought the light and stood motionless in a little room where there was a couch with carved feet that still showed scraps of inlaid silver. Through a scattering of chaff on the floor could be seen a mosaic in black and red stone of Hercules fighting the Hydra. Arthur's eyes fell on it; he smiled sadly and pointed. "There am I, Garwen, in battle with the foes of Britain."

"It is a hero's task," she said simply.

Together they scraped away some of the litter with their feet to reveal the pattern; they stared at the floor that had seen the smooth luxurious life of three centuries earlier, then their eyes met in a long quiet gaze.

"We live in a dark age, where every light grows dimmer, and no dawn shows in the east," said Arthur. Instinctively, he laid his hand upon her in a light caress.

"Yet we must live," she whispered, and set to work to unbuckle his steel corslet and to unlace his shoes.

Chapter XIII

The Passage of Thames

"THE POOR REMNANTS OF OUR NATION, TO WHOM FLOCKED FROM DIVERS PLACES AROUND ABOUT OUR MISERABLE COUNTRYMEN AS FAST AS BEES TO THEIR HIVES FOR FEAR OF AN ENSUING STORM.

—Gildas, *De Excidio Britanniae.*

Next morning the army moved on in a freezing fog towards the crossing of the Thames, but as it marched it found itself in the heart of an ever thickening crowd of fugitives from city and countryside—men, women, children, with hollow cheeks and dragging feet, struggling blindly westwards. Terror was in their eyes, their hands grasped feverishly at some relic of household goods—here a silver cup, here a cooking pot, a broken loaf of bread, a sack of meal, a carved image of the Virgin. Out of the depths of the fog came a rising and falling murmur, doleful or petulant, the dying voice of a culture thrust out into a bleak wintry world lit up with red flames and the flash of steel.

Now the mist was blended with volumes of smoke. The tide of doomed humanity flowed on into the smouldering ruins of a little town. The murmur of voices swelled into a loud despairing uproar, for here was the river, barring the way to the West, and one span of the bridge was broken down. A lane opened in the recoiling eddying masses of weaponless folk and Arthur rode his black horse down to the bridge. He looked across the gap and saw a band of bearded men leaning on their axes, silent, impassive as a group of wooden idols. A tall figure strode out from among them and stood with folded arms on the bridge-head, a man in chain mail with black hair falling over his shoulders—Cerdic, whom he had last seen ringed about by desperate-faced Saxon warriors on the ramparts of Guinion. Now he stood, cool and confident, at the head of an army, heavy with food and drink, arrogant with victory; his hawk-like features relaxed in a sneering smile, slowly he raised an arm in the Roman salute. Arthur stared at him for a moment, he threw a glance at the stealthily flowing Thames, blurred with breaths of white vapour, he wheeled his horse and rode back among the crowds of dark, anguished faces, men that jostled round him shouting about fords and ferries higher up the river, women that raised their babies in the air towards him, calling in piteous voices, "Save us! Save us!" With a set face he urged the snorting and quivering black horse through this wreckage of misery banked up like flotsam and jetsam before an angry sea, a welter of human beings in the grip of elemental forces, dragged down suddenly to the level of the brute creation, scuffling and snarling over scraps of food, dropping asleep where they stood, yielding to nature's requirements without thought of shame or modesty. Now he was among men who stood in a dense mass under a forest of spear shafts, the mailed ranks of the legionaries, yet even here he could sense a wavering breath of dismay and panic. The champions came about him on wild-eyed horses with tossing manes and switching tails. "What is your plan, Arthur?" he heard on every side. Only Brawdbach seemed to be inspired with an impish glee. He sat up behind Medraut, jabbing the horse with his heels, screaming with laughter, spitting in the faces of cowering women, slashing at little children with a whip. Medraut made no effort to restrain the boy; alone of all the Cymry his face wore an icy calm, as though the horror and confusion that enveloped the army were of no more moment than a shower of rain on the day's march.

The trumpets blew; in a few minutes the warriors had thrust their way out into the open fields again, taking a course parallel to the river. In frantic haste the fugitives streamed after them, dragging their feet through the sticky clay of ploughland, plunging on into the black echoing depths of a forest that loomed out of the grey void of mist.

But the hard floor of the forest dipped down into reedy brakes and stagnant water. Despairing cries broke out above the splashing and floundering of thousands of feet, cries from folk sunk to the waist, covered all over with green slime, reaching out hands for help, or struggling desperately to get a hold on yielding branches of willow. The army drew ahead by its strength, by its well tried sense of wild places; recoiling from the deep swamps it swung out into drier if thornier thickets, it splashed boldly through clear running water, swarming like a trail of ants over fallen trees and along dusky glades. Foremost of all went Arthur on foot, the bridle over his arm, stooping his head under the low branches, and close behind him was Garwen on a white pony, a ghostly figure following the golden-haired man like some emanation of the mist. To the champions and legionaries crashing through the brakes she seemed a guiding angel threading that treacherous forest, a girl with a gently innocent face lit by some inward fire, one steadfast face among many darkened by a growing dismay. For there were as yet no tracks that made towards the river with the promise of a crossing—in that direction were only deeper and deeper sloughs of mud and scrub thinning away into ever thickening screens of withered flags and dun-coloured reeds. Ahead was no outlet into safety and behind gathered a rumbling tide of destruction. Sigbert had hurried the Saxons on across London and urged them in pursuit of the horde of fugitives. Now they had caught up with them. Through the grey fog of vapour and the black fog of interwoven branches came louder and louder shouts, the same dreadful shouts that had rung through the streets of London: "Kill! Kill! Hew the Welshmen!"

It was Garwen who came first on a path, circling round a great patch of holly and bramble through which she could not drive her pony. It was only a faint trod, smothered in drifts of fallen leaves, but it led at once to drier ground, and there, between the vast trunks of oak, appeared the river with a chain across it . . . She beckoned and in a moment Arthur was beside her, vaulting into the saddle. A few bounds of the black horse brought him to the river bank; under the bushes he saw a raft stuck in the mud and planked over with green, half-rotted wood. Nothing stirred on the shore opposite and the land rose in a high wall of scrub out of which, caught by a gleam of sunshine through dissolving mist, rose the broken skeleton of a roof and a gable-end built of brick and timber.

Arthur blew a horn, the trumpets answered, and soon the glade was crowded with the Cymry. Brawdbach capered about on the raft while a score of men thrust it out into the green languid water. He and Medraut were the first to spring to land on the western shore. A knot of men followed them up a tunnel through the undergrowth. Now they were climbing on the ruin and waving—all was well. Again and again the raft went across with a fresh load of men. The horses swam, men plunged in after them, hanging on to their tails, others worked themselves across clinging to the chain. Now there were only stragglers coming to the water's edge, but they came panting, white-faced, bleeding from wounds, and close on their heels came a rushing horde of fugitives, shrieking, stumbling, falling. Arthur looked round. Some fifty legionaries stood in a group beside him, men picked to be a rearguard, and there was March tossing a naked sword in the air and catching it by the hilt. The raft was starting across again; the water lapped over it and those on board fought desperately to throw off those who pursued it through the shallows; the river was full of folk swimming, clutching, drowning. Across the water the Red Dragon rose limply above the ruined house and Garwen sat her pony by the shore watching, waiting to see what was to be the fate of Arthur.

"Let us drive off these howling Saxon wolves," said March suddenly. He looked at young girls coming by with the clothes ripped from their backs by the thorny brakes, at wounded men struggling down to the water's edge on hands and knees, at mothers searching frantically for their children. "If we hold them at bay for half an hour some hundreds of these folk may get safe across."

"There are Saxons before us as well as behind," said Arthur grimly. "We have not done with Cerdic yet. Nevertheless we will show them that there are still Britons who can give back blow for blow." He and March sprang on their horses; at the head of the little band of legionaries they thrust a way through the fugitives, back into the dark woods whence came the echoing sound of screams, of blows, and devilish laughter. Here was the tail end of the mob floundering in slime and rush beds and among the hindmost waded a few Saxons striking and thrusting at their leisure, glutted with slaughter, ripping and maiming rather than killing outright. Behind them, as far as the eye could reach, lay moaning and writhing objects, struggling feebly in the mud or caught fast in tangles of briar and thorn. A maniacal fury came over the Celtic warriors—in a dense mass they ploughed through the Saxons, spearing and stabbing, dealing blows that went home with the pent-up, venomous hatred of the tormented for the tormentor, the dark fire of a doomed race transmuted into blind savagery. Farther and farther they went through brake and bog, irresistible in this sudden release of passion, hardly aware that the ranks of their enemies were thickening and surging about them with a dull roar like breakers beating shoreward in the thrust of wind and tide. It was Arthur who saw that no more could be done by a handful of mortal men. He slid off the black horse that was sinking with two Saxon spears snapped off in its chest, he blew his horn and shouted:

"Back, Cymry! Back to the river, step by step!"

Closing up in an ever-lessening band the legionaries went back from thicket to thicket, from bog to bog, while the big blond men poured after them with a brutish clamour. March, still on horseback, stuck fast in a watery place. He turned in the saddle and whirled his sword, lopping off spear heads and uplifted hands, but a Saxon caught him round the waist and dragged him down. Together they rolled over and over in the black bubbling ooze till both vanished from sight. The horse still plunged frantically to save itself till a Saxon, treading his way over corpses, rained blows on the creature with an axe as though he had been hewing upon a tree trunk. Laughing and yelling in berserk frenzy the shipmen went lurching forward, caked from head to foot with British mud, making their weapons crash and ring under the canopy of these primeval British oaks, yellow lichened, sprouting with ferns and moss, the tough handiwork of Nature that stood aloof and insensitive amid this brief cataclysm of human violence . . . .

Meanwhile, battle had begun across the river. Medraut, with the vanguard of the Cymry, burst into Cerdic's men, feeling their way in scattered parties through the fog. Here and there it came to a hard fight hand to hand where the forest gave space enough, but soon the armies lost touch with each other. On the whole things went well with the Cymry; they pressed on over the hills with a sense of victory and with them went some part of the horde of shivering and limping fugitives who had crossed the river. The trumpets blew, but the Red Dragon hung back at the ruin above the ferry. Where was Arthur? It was Gwalchmei who came thundering down the tunnel path on a blown horse. There was no one at the river bank except Garwen. Across the water a knot of helpless people shrieked to him to bring back the ferry, but as he stared at them they dissolved away into the thickets. No one was left on the opposite shore, but farther back in the woods he could hear the clash of weapons, shout and counter-shout.

"Is Arthur there?" he said to Garwen.

She nodded and stepped on board the ferry, beginning to work it along the chain. Gwalchmei followed and helped her. Before they were half-way across a little group of men appeared on the bank, crouching behind their shields, parrying, striking back, giving way step by step as a mass of yelling Saxons bore in on them, hewing as best they could under the low sweep of oak boughs. Gwalchmei sprang off the ferry, waded ashore, and flung himself into the fight; Garwen struggled painfully to get the clumsy raft nearer to land. Now it touched bottom

and she looked up. Five battered and bleeding men
flung themselves on board, then came Arthur, the
sixth, mud and blood from head to heel with just a
glint of the whites of his eyes and of white teeth
through his matted beard, and then Gwalchmei, the
seventh, still laying about him like a madman as the
Saxons came on like hounds baulked of their prey.

The men worked desperately at the chain, the
ferry drew away, and Arthur and Gwalchmei show-
ered sword strokes on those who clutched at the slip-
pery timbers or strove blindly to clamber on board. At
last they touched the western shore; they stumbled
up on land and Arthur sat down to rest on a bank
netted with tree roots.

"A grave there is for March, cousin," he said to
Gwalchmei, and some dim remembrance stirred in
his mind. "How goes the fight with Cerdic?"

"All is confusion; Medraut and half the army
have pushed on over the hill, the rest of us have
gone only a little way. It seems as though Cerdic has
struck at us and missed his blow in the fog and the
thick woods."

"Break down the chain and hew the ferry to
pieces," said Arthur. "Then we are not likely to have
yonder folk on our heels again." He pointed across
the smooth, dusky water to Saxons crowding thickly
on the opposite bank.

"I must bind up your wounds," said Garwen,
unbuckling the chin strap of the dinted helmet.

"I shall want a bathe before you can find the
wounds on me," said Arthur with a chuckle. "Never
was there a worse battleground for mud! No, Garwen,
I have a cut or two somewhere, but nothing that
bleeds enough to matter now. Give me a drink in this
helmet and drink yourself, for we must push on hard
and join Medraut. See, I am not so stiff yet!" He stood
up and whirled his arms. "You shall bathe and bind
me up to-night, Garwen, if all goes well. All must go

well." His face grew grave. "There is strength yet in the West if we can reach it. If the Princes of Britain will not come to me, I must go to them. . . ."

"This at least I shall bind." Garwen splashed water over an ugly gash above the knee, she dabbed it with her skirt, then tore off a piece and tightened a bandage with a bit of stick.

"The Saxon wolves worried the Bear hard to-day, but they have only given him a few rips of the skin," said Gwalchmei, smiling. Arthur rested a hand for a moment on Garwen's bowed head, then he clapped on his helmet and vaulted on to Gwalchmei's horse. The sun came through the mist in a coppery glow, a flight of duck went skimming up the river, plunging in with a swirl of foam. Arthur pointed to the dark tunnel in the wood. "Follow! Follow!" he shouted, urging the tired horse up the slough of mud. "Break through to the West!" Cerdic and his main force had blundered across the track of the Cymry and missed them. When Arthur went forward with Kai and Gwalchmei and a thick column of marching men, with Garwen on her white pony, and with a thinning trail of spent exiles from London, there were no foemen to bar their passage. By nightfall they were clear of the great woods that a later age knew as Windsor Forest, and they had caught up with Medraut on the wilderness knee-deep in fern and ling that lay about Calleva.

Chapter XIV

The Painted Room in Sarum

THE VESSEL PREPARED FOR THE SERVICE OF GOD IS NOW
TURNED TO A VESSEL OF DIRT.
—Gildas, *De Excidio Britanniae.*

For two days more they went at a steady pace
over the pale chalk downs where flocks of half-
wild sheep nibbled about the grave mounds and
mighty hill fortresses of forgotten tribes—an empty
country rolling uneasily under the dark winter skies,
dappled with gorse and thorn, sinking slowly into
columned woodland that broke here and there about
the crumbling ruins of towns and villas. A country
that had given life and strength to ancient peoples
and had lapsed into a battleground, an eerie no-
man's-land between Celt and Saxon, baring its white
scarred bosom to sun and rain like some corpse
seamed with old wounds.

They came down into the Avon valley before the
vast stockaded ramparts of Sarum and here at last
were Britons under arms, a dark-haired, shifty-look-

ing levy from Gereint's kingdom licking the wounds
they had got from Cerdic's Saxons. They stared suspiciously at the rough, haggard men who had gone
North with Uther, the savage faces from far Strathclyde, the woebegone stragglers from London, but
they raised a welcoming shout at the sight of Arthur
and Garwen riding beside him in the band of champions. In the thatched booths of Sarum a bard stood
up and sang to the harp an inconclusive poem full of
strange imagery, praising in stormy language the valour of Arthur, the glorious beauty of Gwenhyvar, the
flower-like loveliness of Garwen, interspersing his
lines with vague references to Abergleinwy, to Guinion, to Traeth Treuroit. The years of fighting on the
Pictish marsh had sent a confused reverberation into
the South and West—a legend was growing up that
here at last was a leader whose standard had never
seen defeat, a man who won the trust of warriors and
the favour of fair women, a man whose fame was
darkened by no black deeds of treachery to his own
kith and kin. And yet a gloom hung over Sarum, a
shadow of dark happenings that loomed up in the
east: the terrible slaughter of Gereint's men at Calleva, the fall of London, the gathering together of the
greatest host of Saxons that Britain had seen since
the first wild assault in the days of Vortigern. Any day
those bare horizons across the Avon might darken
with hordes of bloodthirsty folk raising their dreadful
chant of "Kill! Kill! Hew the Welshmen!" Arthur yr
Amherawdyr was a splendid figure of a man, a victor
in dim battles among the northern mountains, but he
brought with him less than a thousand warriors and
he had escaped disaster before London almost by a miracle. Was he a match for Cerdic, whom the West Saxons had made king after a resounding victory not fifty
miles from the ramparts of Sarum? After all, this Arthur
was mortal enough; he went gloomy-eyed to council
with his barbarous-looking champions, limping from

the stroke of some Saxon swordsman, and he lived, so the priests muttered, in sin with a harlot, though wedded to the daughter of a guletic in Strathclyde. The man was hardly more of a Christian than were the Saxons he fought against; he passed by holy shrines without so much as a glance, his fingers fumbled when he made the sign of the cross, he slept with his girl in the basilica that had been the chapel of a Bishop before the holy man and most of his deacons had gone westward with Gereint.

Early one morning Garwen sat on a couch beside Arthur, watching him stir in his sleep and reach out instinctively toward the place where she had been lying. It was chilly in the high stone building with its plastered walls covered with frescoes—a procession of robed and bearded men with haloes round their heads. In the light of the tiny oil lamp their eyes looked down on her big with menacing disapproval. Garwen shivered a little. She had a violent impulse to creep back into the embrace of those great sinewy arms furred with golden down—there lay the only joy, the only true significance that she had found in her short life. To give to a man who was kind to her, who was even gentle and grateful, who was yet the foremost man of her race in Britain. . . . She sighed, telling herself for the hundredth time that it was only for a few days that she would ride by his side in the keen breeze of the downs or in the dank silence of great woods, only for a few nights that she would sleep in his arms—his woman, unquestioned in her right by this host of rough men; men who glanced at her shyly, with superstitious reverence as the chosen of Arthur. For a few days more, and then Arthur would ride on with his champions to Caerleon, where Gwenhyvar waited for him, and she would be left behind in some safe place, far in the West, and then perhaps in time she would give birth to a child. . . . She clasped her firm young body suddenly and gripped the outstanding breasts—her heart seemed to leap up into her throat and blood rushed to her cheeks. Arthur's child—how many women in Britain would be lucky enough to bear a child to such a man?

The lamp flickered up and went out. She looked at the round arched window high in the wall and saw with a start that it was dawn. A curtain that hung in the opening fluttered inwards in a bitter wind blowing from the Plain and in the gap was a pink flush on racing clouds. She and Arthur had to rise early and ride—to-day the army was to leave Sarum, where there was scantiness of everything, even of water, and pass on to the green lowlands of Dyvnaint. There Gereint had gone to gather more men from every corner of his realm, from the heath country across the Stour, from the marshland about Ynys Gutrin, from the forest valleys of Exe and Teign, from the green hollows among the cliffs of Kernou. Quietly she went out and in a little while came back. She put out her hand to Arthur, smoothing away the curls from the broad forehead and suddenly he rose up on one arm and looked at her with a flash in his dark blue eyes.

"Is there news?" he said eagerly. "Is Cerdic on the road hither?"

"There is no news," she said softly. "The town is quiet, but the sun is up. I have been out and seen the horses fed, I have brought warm milk for you to drink and milk to bathe your body if you will; there is little water to be found within the ramparts when no rain comes, and it is far to the river where the beasts quench their thirst."

"Let us drink our fill, Garwen," he said with a laugh. "We have a long ride before we camp in Coit Mawr; but let us waste no milk on bathing—there will be water enough and to spare when we come down to the banks of Brue by Ynys Gutrin." In silence she combed his hair while he sat up, stretched himself, and suddenly laid his hand on her so that she smiled a little and blushed hotly.

"A kind companion you have been to me, Garwen," he said. "Your touch brings me gladness; perhaps the bard was right when he called you the fairest flower among the women of Britain. In some other time than this, child, we might have gone through our lives side by side, happy alike in sunshine or in storm, instead of snatching a few brief days at the head of an army under wintry skies, with death following in our footprints."

"These few days are worth a lifetime to me if I have had the love of Arthur." She passed a hand over his cheek. Suddenly he pressed her back and got to his feet.

"I have found you too late, Garwen. All that I do is too late—so Medraut says, and he can see further than most men. Power I have to do as I will, yet other powers are stronger than mine, driving me on the road that I must tread, perhaps to glory, perhaps to bitterness, to the spilling of many lives that shall avail nothing in the end. A warning came to me when I sat before the gates of London and our people would not suffer me to save them. It was not given to me, a sinful man, to deliver that glorious city, the pride of Britain. And so, in the dark mood that was on me, I added sin to sin and took you, Garwen."

"Sin?" she said, looking up at him with troubled eyes. "What evil have you done to me?"

"The priests call it sin. All the rulers of Britain are accursed, they say, because they yield to the urging of the flesh and not to the voice of God."

"Are the Saxons men of God?"

"They are but the weapons he chooses to punish us, to break our pride, to spoil everything that is our delight."

"The priests!" she said hotly. "I know what the priests are, even Dubricius, who was accounted the holiest man in London. Ah, the things that I have seen! Who are the priests to call this sin that we have done together?"

"That they are base does not make us better," said Arthur, smiling a little. "Who is perfect? An evil-minded man may win glory in fight and a bad priest may tell the people where lies salvation."

"Is it a time to talk of saving souls when the enemy is about us with fire and sword? These holy men!" She stared furiously at the sombre frescoes. "What do they know of the things that make life lovely and the heart sing, of the powers that are given us to strive for what is man's due, that light may break into darkness and go forward in ages to come?" She dashed her fist on the accusing faces so that the plaster cracked.

"It is passion's slave you are, Garwen. Like you, too, are all our people, though you burn with a clear white flame and they, most of them, with a red and smoky glow."

"Would you have me otherwise?" Her glance wavered, she sank down on the couch suddenly and hid her face.

"Not I. But there perhaps is the flaw in me so that I shall break in the task I set myself."

"I believe that if a man can save us, you are that man," she said, raising her head.

"Not all think as you do, Garwen. Do the Britons love me as you do, you who have given me your body? Not man enough am I, or the kings would have met me at Verulam and Constans would have trusted me in London."

"Can you be more than man? Can you blind your eyes to beauty, can you steel your heart against love, despise power, look on a woman without lusting?"

"There have been such men," he said moodily.

"Then there were no women found to love them!"

He laughed suddenly, took her in his arms for a moment, then began to throw on his clothes in haste. A clatter of horse hoofs sounded on the frozen ground outside, the clanging of a bell from some high gable, and then a rumble of voices coming up the street:

"Cymry in victory, Cymry in woe!"

Chapter XV

Through Coit Mawr

"THE WOOD WHICH IS CALLED SELWOOD, WHICH MEANS IN
LATIN SILVA MAGNA, THE GREAT WOOD, BUT IN BRITISH COIT
MAWR."

—Asser, *Life of Alfred.*

A s the army marched westward from Sarum in
a blaze of wintry sunshine the land blossomed
suddenly into life. The chalk downs were
patched with grey strips of ploughing, herdsmen
rounded up droves of cattle on valley pastures, stockaded dykes wound across the hills and beehive huts
clustered in hundreds on green shoulders above the
hanging woods. Here and there a blackened ruin told
of more luxurious living in Roman days, yet a Celtic
people still clung to the land, forgetful, seemingly, of
the desolation that lay to the east, and of that blast
of rapine that had swept Britain from the west in the
days of Nial of the Nine Hostages. A sense of security
hovered like the fickle cheeriness of sunlight on these
rounded hills swelling higher and higher against the
blue sky and then dipping suddenly into the vast
dusky carpet of Coit Mawr.

Now, however, came a breath from an older world in which man had no part. An air of menace and mystery hung over these forests, rolling on and on over yet higher hills; millions of tree-tops fading into a blue haze to north and south. Instinctively the army came to a halt and a murmur of surprise and awe broke from the refugees whose homes had been in the narrow echoing streets of London, as they stood on the flat brim of the last chalk down, scarred by the bleached ramparts of an abandoned fortress, and saw the trackway sweep down into a sea of wood so dense, tangled, and forlorn, that it seemed like some great cosmic barrier raised against the casual passage of mankind.

But Coit Mawr was not so impenetrable as it looked. The track, far older than any work of Roman hands, plunged into the dark labyrinth like a mine tunnel. With a snapping of twigs and a rustling of dead leaves the army forced its way on with a spasmodic rhythm and on the second evening after leaving Sarum it camped in a glade around a barrow of ancient days and saw the sun dipping towards a level plain out of which rose little heights in a feathery surf of fog. A gentle breeze full of the bitter-sweet tang of sedge and moss stole over the hills; the sharpness was gone out of the air, the harsh rancour of unending toil, strife and death were left behind on the downland horizons. Beyond Coit Mawr spread out a softer, wilder, friendlier land, shadowed by grey cloud masses drifting in from the western ocean.

For a few moments a sheen from the sunset colours seemed to fall upon the hundreds of weary faces gazing from the forest crest upon this dim country, alien yet welcoming, a lake of peace unruffled by the stormy winds of war.

Medraut climbed the barrow to where Arthur and Garwen stood beside the newly planted pole of the Red Dragon. He gazed at the rapt faces of the man and the girl, and some pang of envious rage made his heart glow like a fire in a sudden gust of air. These two were enchanted by a love that he would never feel for a woman, not even for Gwenhyvar if she bowed herself to his will as this girl did to Arthur's. Yet this glimpse of something lovely amid the terror and ruthlessness of a changing world was his doing. He had plucked that delicate creature from the wreck of London, he could have done what he would with her, and he had chosen to thrust her upon Arthur. Both good and ill will had blended in his deed, as in the subtle impulses of an artist—it was the right medicine for a man labouring under a fearful disappointment, to give him a plaything that in soothing his body might ease the ache of the spirit; it was a malicious thought to break the chaste austerity of the warrior at the moment when fortune went against him; it was a darker design to open a way to Gwenhyvar, with the ugly weapon of adultery.

It irked him, nevertheless, that what he had begun lightheartedly, sporting with cruelty rather than goodwill, should yield something so fair instead of something sullied and commonplace. At once he gave his mind to dark thoughts as a man contentedly yields his body to some pleasant vice. Generous he had felt when they camped below the wood of Celidon, when Arthur's star seemed likely to go into eclipse, but evil was in his heart now that they lay in peace and security awaiting the turn of fortune. He spoke in tones of faint mockery:

"There in that plain of Ynys Gutrin beats the quiet heart of the West, heavy and slow, drowned in idleness and easy living, soft with a hundred years of peace. Beacons blaze on the downs to eastward, but their flames are hidden by the tree-tops of Coit Mawr. Dyvnaint lies asleep, lulled by the bird songs of spring and the harmless music of the breakers fretting the coves of Kernou—she lies like some smooth-limbed maiden warm under downy coverlets, never dreaming that rough men are at her door ready to use her for their pleasure."

"Gereint rouses the land," said Arthur shortly. "To-morrow we shall look on his host. Not so sleepy will those warriors be that are gathered under his standard, from what I remember of my boyhood in Kernou, for the wildness of Eiré is in their veins as it is in yours, Medraut."

"But not in yours, Arthur. Far in the West your mother lived, but her stock came of the Artorian house—hard-headed men who did the Emperor's business in Britain and served him faithfully. From them you get this passion to serve the state and keep it as one bright jewel in the crown of the West when all others have been plucked out and squandered among these Franks and Goths and Vandals over-seas. And because you have old Uther's blood you are rough and stubborn as some mountain crag in Reged. So cold you are, Arthur, and strong of heart and mighty with weapons, that Gwythyr's daughter thought you more than man. She dreaded your embrace when she was pledged to you under the rock of Alcluyd, for in those days you did not stand alone with girls, loverlike, watching darkness come."

"Dangerous words you speak now, Medraut! Have you not seen that the bane of Britain lies in hatred and jealousy between kith and kin? A song you made for the Cymry, but you do not wear it in your heart, for your mind is always eager to mock our hopes and laugh at our sins."

"You and I, uncle, are stained as all the princes of Britain are stained. Why should we hold our heads so high above treachery and lust? For I turned the peo-ple against my father Modron and you struck off his head on the beach at Dinguardi, and both of us have slept with wantons."

"Is it a wanton that I am, I who love Arthur and have never known any other man?" said Garwen hotly.

"Do not answer him lest he spit forth more venom!"

Arthur turned and swiftly raised his clenched fist, but Medraut went back before him laughing, down the mound, and glided away like a black shadow among the cooking fires.

Next morning they came down from the heights to the southwest, following the old track from hill to hill, and down at last into a green nook below the forest walls, a valley full of booths and herds of cattle and companies of armed men. And there, smooth and bare, with a couple of clear streams springing from its steep flanks, was a hill carved out with ring on ring of mighty ramparts. Within these, like a citadel, was a platform of greenest turf and on it a rude palace of timber and thatch with a standard flapping in the wind.

Medraut rode ahead of the army. He gave a long look at the hill and went on past it, down the water-side until the plain narrowed below a little ridge where a few old thorn trees stood up against the sky. Here he drew rein and sat on his horse for a long time, indifferent to the shouting behind him, the welcoming shouts from the men of Dyvnaint as Arthur and the Cymry climbed the hill to Gereint's palace. A couple of shepherds came by leading a flock of sheep towards the camp ground.

"What place is this?" asked Medraut sharply, as though waking from a dream.

"This is Camlann," they answered in the thick slurring dialect of the West.

"A famous name it will be in years to come," said Medraut with a smile, but a shudder ran through him from head to foot.

CHAPTER XVI

Conan, Olwen, and Gwenhyvar

THOU LION'S WHELP, AURELIUS CONANUS, ART NOT THOU
SWALLOWED UP IN THE FILTHINESS OF HORRIBLE MURDERS,
FORNICATIONS, AND ADULTERIES, AS BY AN OVERWHELMING
FLOOD OF THE SEA?

—Gildas, *De Excidio Britanniae,*

Gwenhyvar lay stretched out on a couch, pale and listless, letting the late spring sunshine stream in upon her through an open doorway of an old house in Caerleon. Her body had lost something of its slim shapeliness, for her child would be born in the height of summer, but her face kept its arrogant beauty. Unseeingly her eyes looked outwards into a courtyard with the bases and stumps of many columns; it was littered with fallen stone, with broken pots and bones, and shaded by an enormous laurel tree, from which the lower branches had been hacked for firewood. Hens pecked about the middens, a cock crew, standing in a gaping hole which had once been a latticed window, a horse stamped somewhere in the darkness of the buildings, but

Gwenhyvar was not aware of these familiar sights and sounds. Her eyes were intent upon an inward vision, of a smoky hut with blood on the floor and a man thrusting her down with the savagery of a wild beast. She opened her dress and fingered a little mark on her bosom where Medraut's dagger had broken the skin, and again she felt the horror of what had happened to her; the desperate desire to cover her body against the hard driven steel, and then the wild impulse to yield herself utterly to the man who had stood over her in his bestial strength and beauty, laughing at the realisation that he had struck recklessly into a female body, that he had come within an ace of giving death to Gwenhyvar. . . .

Why had it not happened, what she wanted, what he wanted—there had been chance enough in Bregion during the sack of the town, while Arthur was slaughtering more and more Picts on the mountains? Then this child that oppressed her, that stirred her mind not to gentle thoughts but to sullenness and vicious imaginings, this child might have been Medraut's. But even though their bodies had seemed to be enchanted, wrought up for a fierce adventure of the senses, their minds were paralysed by a vision of the man they must betray, the bleak power and steadfastness that shadowed them as might some dark impending crag on the mountain side, a strength of spirit that could not be shaken by the gusty wind of passion. She was Arthur's woman, and it was only a mightier man than Arthur that could take her from him and keep her. Her heart had leaped up in a guilty sense of joy and dread when rumours came to Caerleon that Arthur had failed in the East. There were men here who had escaped from London through the forests of Middle Britain and they spread a story that Arthur and all his army had been overwhelmed between two hordes of Saxons when seeking for a passage of the Thames. Then came more fugi-

tives by the southerly route and they said that Arthur
had got through to Sarum; no one seemed much concerned in far away Caerleon. For twenty years there
had been fighting in the South and nothing much
had come of it. For a hundred years there had been
Saxons on the upper Thames, but it was only once
that they had showed themselves by the Severn, and
then Emrys had made short work of them. On the
other hand there was no little jubilation when news
came that Gereint, marching on London, had been
sent flying back into the West. Gereint was a most
objectionable neighbour, continually extending his
power over the downland villagers between Cunetio
and Caer Ceri; he had even expelled some Saxon settlers under Badon Hill, men who claimed Conan as
an overlord and protector. It was a good thing that he
had singed his wings, hovering further and further
afield, planning doubtless to make himself guletic of
Britain with the help of Arthur yr Amherawdyr. . . .
They spoke slightingly of Arthur here in Caerleon—a
man puffed up with pride over some victories among
the Pictish hills, who thought that the Kings of
Britain should squander their power waging unprof-
itable war in the East. There would always be Saxons
in the East; no one bothered about what had become
of places like Lindum and Venta Icenorum. Even London had only been a nest of greedy merchants. The
great landowners had mostly chosen to live within
easy reach of Aquae Sulis, and the wealthiest family
in those parts had been the ancestors of Conan—
Aurelius Conanus as he styled himself when confer-
ring with bishops and other learned men. A different
world was about her here from that which she had
known in Strathclyde, thought Gwenhyvar. Arthur
spoke of the might of ancient Rome; in a ruder guise
he seemed a reincarnation of fighting emperors, men
such as Severus and Theodosius, who had chased
barbarian hosts into the northern mountains; but

here was the nearest approach to the old orderly life of Roman Britain, cities where there was still a remnant of luxury and indolence, a fruitful countryside where men worked without scanning the hilltops for the smoke of beacon fires. Arthur and his champions had become dim, fantastic figures now that she lived in Conan's land, and yet she felt that this was but a lull in her life, a dreamy interlude leading inevitably to some great convulsion out of which would rise three tall figures, Arthur, Medraut, and Gwenhyvar, landmarks for time to come like the three carved columns of a ruined temple standing high over the huddled roofs of Caerleon.

The gate of the courtyard opened and Olwen came through, Gwalchmei's girl, treading daintily along the foul pathway in high riding boots, a red kerchief over her black locks, a green tasselled cloak pinned over one shoulder. In one hand she held a light spear, in the other a whip, and two deerhounds pranced beside her sending the hens fluttering wildly in all directions.

Gwenhyvar looked at the girl with a jealous glitter in her eyes. Olwen had lived with a man, but no care rested on her. She was not hampered by the coming of a child, she was going off on a good horse, sitting astride, and knee to knee with Conan and his wild companions—galloping through the budding woods of Gwent in chase of deer or boar. Gwalchmei was nothing to her now perhaps, for a mightier man than he courted her with gifts of horses and hounds, and lolled beside her on a couch draining cups of mead while fat-faced priests smirked together and harpers played the whimsical airs that had come into Britain with the men of Eiré. It was luck to be chosen out by a ruler such as Conan, gay, generous and pleasure loving where women were concerned, though subtle and malicious in his dealings with men. Yet it might be a dangerous game that Olwen played with him, accepting his favours, yet possibly baulking his desire. Gwenhyvar could see no change in Olwen all these months they had been together; the women about her surely knew everything there was to know, and yet it was hard to believe in honour or innocence in Caerleon . . . .

"News, Gwenhyvar!" said Olwen, gazing thoughtfully at the sullen beautiful woman who lay in the sun fingering a little red mark on one full breast. "News from the South!"

"Ah." Gwenhyvar sat up slowly. 'How like a boy she is but for those plaits of black hair!' she thought. 'How supple, slim, and full of life, small hipped and little breasted, even as I was when I sailed on Medraut's ship to Bregion.'

"A London priest has come by the ferry across Severn, aiming for some house of monks far west in Dyfet. Four days ago he sat with Arthur and Gereint in a hall under Coit Mawr."

"Is the war ended?" asked Gwenhyvar listlessly.

"Nothing is heard of Cerdic and his Saxons, but Gereint slowly draws in men to a great camp there at Camlann and meanwhile he and Arthur are as brothers, hunting day by day on the hills, feasting and drinking in the hall of Camelot."

"Are the champions there?"

"All save March, who fell near London. Medraut is there, but his tongue has turned bitter and his harp is silent. Wherever he goes there is a dark haired child with him, plucked from some Saxon hall by Caer Ebrauc, a proper limb of Satan, so the priest says."

"And Gwalchmei?" Gwenhyvar stared at the other woman and saw her chin go up and her lips tighten.

"He too is there. It is said he did some mighty deed by London." There was a short silence.

"Have they women with them, there in Camelot?" asked Gwenhyvar, striking hard at a hound that tried to lick her face.

"Not a few," said Olwen smiling. "Gay they are at Camelot as we are here in Caerleon. Even Arthur sleeps with a girl."

"What sort of girl may she be?" Gwenhyvar turned away her head, but Olwen could see her cheek flushing hotly.

"The priest said some harlot who had slipped out of London when the city fell."

"Young and lovely and unburdened with child-bearing, even as you are, Olwen?"

Olwen laughed and sat down on the couch beside Gwenhyvar.

"The priest is one of the holier sort—he spat when he mentioned her and looked angrily at me, even as you do."

"Would you be pleased to lie here like a great sow, waiting for your time to come? Is it magic or some brew of strange herbs you use, Olwen, or what art have you found to put aside the penalties of love?" Gwenhyvar's hands played sportively with Olwen's body, but her eyes were cruel. Olwen laughed on a deeper note.

"It may be that I am warier than most women in Caerleon," she said. "I have a man's clothing under my dress."

"What would that avail you when you are alone with Conan in those deep dark woods between Usk and Wye? There must be times when he can take you if he will, when none are near to see, or to help you if you be unwilling. Subtle you are, Olwen—how can you hold at bay the man who is foremost among the princes of Britain? Are not these hounds, these high boots, and the fiery horses that carry you like the wind from the gates of Caerleon, are they not all tokens of his pleasure in your body?"

"Armoured am I in another way," said Olwen calmly. She pulled down a gold bracelet from under her sleeve and held it in front of Gwenhyvar. There was an inscription, incised in Roman lettering: MAGLOCUNI DONUM.

"Gold," said Gwenhyvar appraisingly, "but what are the signs? We have no knowledge of letters in Strathclyde."

"The gift of Maelgun," said Olwen briefly.

"I heard that there have been men here sent by Maelgun. Will Conan let them take you back to Deganwy?"

"That he will not; and yet he fears my father's vengeance if he do me violence. Thus it is that I dare to sit here with you and let Conan wait for me."

"Then you are true to Gwalchmei?"

"As you are to Arthur. Glad he will be when he sees you far gone with child. Even now he and the Cymry may be on the march hither."

"This child will never be a joy to Arthur!" said Gwenhyvar impulsively. Olwen stared at her without speaking. She got up abruptly and gathered her cloak round her, calling to her dogs that were busy cracking and gulping down eggs in the hen nests.

"Why should we women be faithful to men that content themselves with harlots?" said Gwenhyvar in a furious voice. "What faithfulness is there left among the British people, either men or women? It is the same everywhere, in Caerleon, Caermyrthin and Camelot, in Deganwy and Lis Pengwern, every city is smeared with lust and stinks of treachery!"

A barrier seemed to have sprung up between the two women; the one nurturing her dark thoughts on the wickedness she saw around her, the other shaking it from her with smiling indifference because her spirit soared upwards in an ecstasy of love, like a lark against the blue sky.

* * *

Conan rode at a fast trot beside Olwen through a round tunnel-like archway in the walls of Caerleon, a king and a king's daughter in dyed cloaks, with stirrups sparkling in the sun and spirited horses moving in step. Behind them came haughty-looking young men, some few women, and huntsmen running on foot with hounds on leash. They swept along the verge of the city fosse, past the squat bulk of the amphitheatre which was now a milking pen for cattle; the hoofs thundered on a trestle bridge above the silvery mud banks of Usk—now they raced eagerly over the flat pastures to eastward till they came with panting horses flecked with foam to steeply rising woods. Horns blew and dogs bayed; beaters circled round the hills shouting at the sight of deer. On the open spaces about the Roman road there was a twanging of bowstrings, a charge of mounted men upon a wild boar. Conan and Olwen rode on through the heat of the day, down glades rustling with last year's bracken, among thickets twined with leafy strands of honeysuckle, in and out they went among vast stems of oak, treading down the bluebell buds into the black earth, while far away in the steamy gloom sounded the first shout of the cuckoo. They rode hard, seemingly impatient with the labouring horses, the thorny brakes, the echoing blasts of horns and huntsmen's voices far behind. It was as though a feverish desire possessed them to bring their conflict of wills to a crisis before they rode back from these virgin woods into the dingy streets of Caerleon.

Olwen's eyes were constantly on the man beside her, gauging the design hidden behind that handsome yet crafty face, the man who wore a golden torque on his head, who was clean shaven after the old Roman fashion, fastidious in his dress, perfect in his horsemanship, yet fused in spirit with these mighty woods that were his heritage, secret, savage, passionate with the reckless passion of Spring that quivered in bird song and hung enmeshed in the

green haze of unfolding leaves. But for Gwalchmei
she thought that she would have let herself drift with
these ardours that she felt about her; but for the
sight of Arthur marching steadfastly against the foes
of Britain she would have been in tune with this gallant figure of a man who idled away his days in the
West, taking his pleasure with women and with all
the good things of life, drink and music and witty talk
and swift horses, and the colours, sounds, and
scents of hills and forests in which the Celtic spirit
found comfort like a child in the arms of its mother.
How easy to let herself be caught up in this fierce
careless life and take what came to her—how easy to
let her tired limbs relax, to slide out of the hot saddle
and lay herself on these cushions of bronzed moss,
pressing her cheeks to the cool friendly earth; but
even as she watched and waited, spellbound by the
leafy caress of the brushwood and by the rhythmic
movement of the eager beast under her thighs, she
saw a vision of herself galloping joyously beside
Gwalchmei as they burst through the woods of Reged
to where Arthur and Gwenhyvar sat in the ring of
champions. . . .

And Conan rode with a smile on his face, but with
angry longing in his heart. This girl was a jewel
among all the bright-eyed women in Gwent, lovely in
body but wild and elusive as the wind as she swerved
hither and thither through the dusky glades, a light-
hearted but wary rider, not to be daunted by danger
or entrapped by the gentle deceits in which he was so
practised—the child of a king, a prize he had desired
first in wantonness, but now with a savage passion.
Perhaps he could win her with marriage. He had
sounded the envoys from Gwyneth; though they
demanded the girl back they did not say that Maelgun would not leave her in Caerleon as the wedded
wife of Conan. It would be the first step in a league
between Gwent and Gwyneth to master Cuneglas, the

king who lay between them full of envy and malice, eager now to summon Arthur to his aid, ready to let civil war blaze up in Britain if he could thereby strengthen his hold on the upper Severn. A simpler plan might be to defy Maelgun and come to terms with both Cuneglas and Vortipore. Then the three of them could fall on Maelgun behind his mountains. They could make an end of him or drive him overseas to Eiré; but simplest of all would be to send a hired assassin to strike down the Dragon of Gwyneth, and in that case what need for any bargain about Olwen? His mind fluttered swiftly from one piece of double dealing to another until he saw himself without a rival, overking of Britain. What was it but a game of chess in which he advanced first one piece and then another, taking here and sacrificing there? Meanwhile Olwen was only a pawn, the taking of which was little more than a gesture—a gesture of defiance, to be followed by a move in Powys and another in Dyfet. Why should he have scruples about a girl who had roamed over Britain in company with an outlaw, a girl who was utterly in his power? His brow darkened a little, He liked his dealings with women to be gilt with ease and laughter and mutual delight, and this approach to Olwen had a grimmer look, as when one sought to pick a flower that grew on some jut of crumbling limestone cliff above the Wye. . . . The trees thinned before them as they rode, and glades opened into slopes that were patched with springing corn, and beyond the clutching fingers of sombre forest rose the white, bastioned walls of Caer Gwent. Conan drew rein; he looked at Olwen and saw her eyes searching the hazy lowland that stretched to the right of the city, fringed far away by the broad glimmering wash of Severn. Beyond the water were dim flat-crested hills, and beyond those hills, he mused, were the marshy wastes of Ynys Gutrin, and beyond them the little round hill of Camelot, where Gwalchmei sat in the company of Arthur and Gereint. So a caged bird might look out between the bars towards distant woods where her mate sang in the branches of some round-topped oak. He bit his lips and wheeled his horse sharply.

"Let us ride back and rest the beasts awhile and find a forest spring to quench our thirst," he said. She did not answer, but turned obediently. The colour ebbed from her cheeks and her eyes were downcast, but she rode so close to him that their stirrups clicked together and their horses nuzzled at each other's mouths. Again the woods closed about them and almost at once they came to a little pool fringed with rushes and overhung by a dead tree with broken boughs. He dismounted and let his horse take a few mouthfuls of water, but Olwen sat languidly in the saddle, letting the reins slip through her fingers, overwhelmingly aware of the silence of the forest and of the quickening beats of her heart.

'If I had some magical power,' she thought, 'to make myself appear the woman I shall be fifty years hence, I could still his desire—I could be free from the torment he puts upon me and from the torment that begins to leap unbidden in my body, answering lust with lust. And yet when I am fifty years older shall I think it a dreadful thing that a king was fired by my beauty and forced me in Coit Gwent, among the enchanted oaks where Druids worked their spells? What can a woman do but yield, when she is beset as I am? Is it any shame to her, is her spirit sullied, any more than it is when she obeys nature's necessity? But do men understand that? Will Gwalchmei understand, when I tell him?' She sighed, thinking how little she minded if Gwalchmei found some girl to please him in Dyvnaint, so long as he came back to her in the end. And then she thought: 'If this happens to me men will avenge it, perhaps with murder or war; this little deed, done for a moment's pleasure, for pride of mastery, for wantonness, as a man will strike a beast because he has a stick in his hand—this will not wound my flesh, nor my spirit overmuch, yet it may cause all Britain to bleed.'

"Come Olwen," he said craftily, "you are not so light but that your horse is spent bearing you on his back. Hang your bridle over this branch as I do mine and let us sit awhile on this coverlet of primroses."

Again she obeyed him and left her horse tethered beside his. Without a word she threw herself down on dog mercury and pale primroses and the upthrust of bluebell leaves that stood out of the deep mould like little green swords. Her two hounds came from lapping the water and lay at her feet with quivering tongues. They did not even look up when Conan sank down beside her and laid a hand gently over her heart.

"Eager you are, Olwen," he said. "It is not fear that makes your heart leap under my hand, for no woman has so little fear in her heart as you have." She bit her teeth together and did not answer. His hands strayed farther and he watched her lips part, and her eyes close. 'How easy it was,' he thought, with a shade of irritation, even while his pulses quickened and his hands began to tremble. 'What a sameness there was in women, as there was in the taste of strong mead, though men did not cease to desire it on that account, . . .' She raised an arm slowly against his approach and something hard pressed against his lips. A gold ring slid down into view, and he twisted it about, reading the inscription. Now a brooding look came into his eyes—his mouth was a hard line. For a moment he no longer saw the fresh, quivering face pillowed in black plaits of hair and a scarlet kerchief, he saw this girl's father, a great bearded giant riding at the head of swaying masses of spearmen, a human torrent pouring through the mountain passes of Gwyneth. Dimly he heard words, Olwen's words, as he began to handle her roughly, impatiently, but they seemed to sound from great spaces beyond these woods of Gwent, from fire-lit halls where men sat gloomy-faced over their drink, while harps twanged in minor cadences, from the homesteads of Britain in ages to come: "There are three fatal loves in Britain; the love of Vortigern for Rowenna, the love of Medraut for Gwenhyvar, the love of Conan for the daughter of Maelgun."

"Thick clothes you have about you, Olwen," he said, setting his teeth. With a deep sigh she thrust herself up against him, wild-eyed and pale.

"Weak are my defences against such a man as you," she said in a low voice. "Let me be for a moment; go behind those great trees till I call; then you shall have your way."

Unwillingly he got to his feet.

"Have you learned to be so modest, Olwen, wandering in Reged's woods with a man such as Gwalchmei?" he said with a sneering smile.

"I am a King's daughter, and I have been taught what is seemly and what is not." She stared at him with smouldering eyes, and he went, round the pool and out of sight. She sat up quickly, she snatched her whip from the ground and sprang catlike towards the horses. In a moment she got their bridles free, vaulted upon her own beast and wheeled it round. She slipped Conan's bridle over her arm, she struck in her heels and rained blows on both creatures with her whip. Side by side they plunged off at a gallop. She heard a shout of rage behind her; a hunting spear whistled by, glancing against the stem of an oak. Ducking low under the branches she sank her face against the horse's mane and came with a thunder of hoofs into open glades. She heard a horn blown and saw some men running breast high through yellow-tipped gorse bushes. Now they were far behind, and the long low walls of Caer Gwent rose before her, cracked and ivy clad above greening willows. She swerved to the right and set the horses at a brook, gripping with all her strength, feeling a glow of exultation as mud and water splashed high about her and the wind caressed her hot cheeks. The hounds pranced joyously ahead; now they swept along a hard grassy road that dipped slowly to the wide silvery path of Severn. In a pool by the roadside was an old woman with bunched-up skirts, cutting reeds with a sickle. Olwen reined in the foam-spattered horses and slipped down from the saddle.

"Cut away these plaits of hair for me," she called imperiously.

The old woman came up on land, muttering through broken teeth. She shook her head sadly, but shore through the thick black plaits with her tool. Olwen pulled off her long skirted tunic and dropped it on the ground; she spread her shortened locks on the back of her neck and threw away the kerchief. Carelessly she tossed the bridle of Conan's horse to the old woman, remounted and whirled her whip in the air. Who would know her now from one of that band of haughty young men that had clattered through the gates of Caerleon? With the sun sinking behind her she rode on to a cluster of fishermen's huts by the waterside. Here coracles lay on the turf, nets hung up to dry, and gulls swooped and screamed over garbage. Shaggy-headed men clustered round, staring at the slim, angry-eyed youth and at the horse marked with slashes and dripping with sweat.

"I am a king's son; get me across the water," she said, keeping warily on the move and watching hands that hovered about knife hafts.

"We can put you across, Guletic, but you must leave your horse with us," said an old man in a soft, insinuating voice.

"You shall take me, my horse, and my hounds, on that barge," said Olwen, pointing with her whip to a broadnosed ferry boat aground in the mud. "If you fail me you will have cause to fear the sight of Arthur and his army when he comes from Dyvnaint. These huts will go up in fire and you will be thrown into the tide, bound hand and foot." The voices died down to a mumble; the crowd of men went slowly to the ferry and set about bringing it alongside a little quay. A young woman carried a bowl of milk to Olwen where she sat in the saddle, her eyes on the long straight road by which she had come. She drank, and ate some mouthfuls of cheese and oatcake. . . . Now there were figures on the road, horsemen riding fast. Calmly she rode on to the quay. She dismounted, stepped on to the barge and watched the fishermen hustle the horse after her; the hounds came to her side and licked her hands. Six men set to work with the oars and, now, churning the muddy water, they moved out from land. Soon there were shouts from the huts; riders cantered along the shore gesticulating, the rowers paused.

"Row!" said Olwen fiercely. "I shall not stint your reward when I am across Severn."

The boat gathered way again, fighting the incoming tide; the opposite shore mounted above the water, long shadows falling from trees and cabins that climbed on the green hills. Gwent drew away in a low blur of purple-crested woods and vague mountain shapes fading into the haze of sunset. They ran ashore and Olwen drew off the gold arm ring. She tossed it to the old man with the soft voice and the bushy, beetling brows.

"Gold!" he muttered, rubbing a grimy finger over the inscription. "Gold with some charm on it. The guletic is generous!"

Olwen climbed into the saddle and made the horse leap with her into the shallow water. She urged him up on land and looked over her shoulder. The boatmen were all clustered together in a knot, snatching and jostling; knives flashed, angry cries broke out like those of the gulls disputing over carrion; Maelgun's gift, she thought—it had brought her luck, but to these simple folk it would most likely bring hatred and murder. She called to the hounds, patted the tired horse, and rode away at a steady trot towards the darkening hills.

Next day she struck the road from Aquae Sulis and saw in the narrow vista of woods a host coming north, headed by a little band of horsemen about a standard. She drew in to the cover of the trees and watched. The standard swayed forward; a red image brushing the tender leafy tassels of birch—it was the Red Dragon of the Cymry, that she had last seen vanishing through the glades by Eamont, and below it rode a group of armoured men in gay cloaks and crested helmets. Olwen shook her reins and came towards them at a canter, the two hounds bounding before her and barking loudly. She saw grim, weather-beaten faces that lit up with a half contemptuous smile or remained impassive, brooding on things that had no place in these soft, steamy woods where folk rode unarmed, with shining eyes and splendid clothes. Arthur, Kai, Bedwyr, Mabon and Medraut—she looked round wildly as she urged her horse among them.

"What news, young man? Are you from Conan's house in Caerleon?" asked a gruff voice.

"News I have for all of you, but my best news is for Gwalchmei," she said breathlessly.

A warrior came knee to knee with her, staring fixedly in her face, and all at once she flung her arms round him.

"Olwen!" He pushed her back, caught her hair in his hand, slid his arm round her and felt the breasts under her tunic. She rose in her stirrups and kissed him on the mouth.

"Have you ridden all this way for love of me?" he said in a voice half tender, half exultant.

"For love of you and for fear of another; but now you have Olwen back as she left you." For a moment they clung to each other, and there was silence, and a light seemed to break on all the hard faces that looked on.

The trumpets blew; Arthur called a halt. Olwen and Gwalchmei sat their horses in a little space ringed on every side by crowding figures.

"The women that left the army in Reged are all living," she said in a loud voice. "Easy is the life in Caerleon for some, and perilous for others."

"Speak plainer. Are the Cymry welcome in Caerleon and is Conan making ready for war?" Arthur's voice sounded above a gathering murmur.

"There is one of the Cymry who will not be welcome, and that is Gwalchmei," she answered. "It may be that Conan gathers men to him, but most likely it is for war with my father Maelgun."

Arthur clenched his fist.

"It is a hard task to save those who have no will to be saved!" he burst out. "These princes of Britain are like butting rams who do not see the butcher standing over them with his knife."

"The wisest plan were for you to hold that knife, and let Cerdic be its sharp point," muttered Medraut in Arthur's ear.

Uncle and nephew stared at each other for a moment in silence. Arthur's brow darkened; he made no answer.

"I do but show you the way to power," said Medraut bitterly. "It may be better for Britain that you should have that power rather than another man."

"Vortigern used the Saxons against the Picts. Do you bid me use them against the Britons?" said Arthur in a low voice.

"You are a greater man than Vortigern, and desperate disease calls for desperate remedy. With Gereint and Cerdic in your hands like two keen daggers, you can destroy the kings beyond Severn and make a new Britain to your own design."

"Your counsel comes from hell!" muttered Arthur between his teeth. "Hear me, Cymry!" he said in a ringing voice. "To Caerleon shall we march and I shall not rest until Conan, Cuneglas, Maelgun, and Vortipore sit with me about one table. If God wills, I shall unite them so that they come into the field like a band of brothers; I shall make Cymry of all the Britons of the West!"

A long drawn out roar of voices answered him, spreading back from the foremost ranks of warriors to those far behind on that mighty highway, the road cutting across Britain, from Isca and Aquae Sulis over brown rolling hills and forests like seas of gloom to the walls of Lindum, rising like white cliffs out of a golden foam of gorse.

Broodingly Arthur turned to look on Olwen and Gwalchmei.

'These lovers,' he thought, 'these two, who warm our hearts, and delight our eyes, their joy may yet bring misery to thousands that have never heard their names. What is Olwen but our land of Britain in human form, lovely and beautiful, dear as life itself to those who cling to it and those who strive to win it for their own?'

"Turn back, Gwalchmei and Olwen," he said, smiling a little sadly, "adventure not with your happiness where we go to guest in cities by Usk and Severn. Safer will you be in the South by Coit Mawr, where none, perhaps, will grudge you joy. Then, if danger rolls in across the downs, you may fight, Gwalchmei, under Gereint's standard, and you can hide Olwen in the trackless combes of wild Dyvnaint."

Chapter XVII

Treachery in Caerleon

HAST NOT THOU, AURELIUS CONANUS, BY HATING, AS A DEAD-
LY SERPENT, THE PEACE OF THY COUNTRY, AND THIRSTING
UNJUSTLY AFTER CIVIL WARS AND FREQUENT SPOIL, SHUT THE
GATES OF HEAVENLY PEACE AND REPOSE AGAINST THINE OWN
SOUL?

—Gildas, *De Excidio Britanniae.*

Arthur sat with Gwenhyvar on a couch in the old house at Caerleon. Through a gaping window, that still had scraps of its glass lattice, could be seen the chase of April sunshine and shadow over waste ground with snags of ruin, fallen columns, yellow celandines blooming on limy mounds and pools of dark green nettles in every hollow. A little way off was the long ragged crest of the city wall over-topped by the ivied cylinder of the abandoned amphitheatre. The room itself had a tessellated floor mostly hidden by dirty rushes, the walls, stained with smoke and damp, still showed frescoes in red and black on a yellow ground—of hunters pursuing deer and boar, of legionaries mingling in battle with frantic barbarian figures that vainly hurled darts and stones. The ceiling was gone, replaced by rough joists and boards between which hung down wisps of blackened cobweb. The splendour of old days was faded, yet here was a living place that had not yet sunk to the level of the little beehive huts or the Saxon halls of upright logs and reed thatch.

Arthur's eyes glanced half unwillingly at the woman beside him—the glorious golden head of hair, the perfectly moulded profile, the petulant red mouth that drooped and then tightened suddenly when he laid a hand on her shoulder. 'This woman,' he thought, 'my woman, who carries my child, yet whose mind escapes me, like a fish gliding from clutching fingers into deep pools and dark shadows. It is enough for her that she has the child to brood on— no question does she ask me of what I have done since we parted in Reged, of risks taken, of wounds endured, of strange things seen in far parts of Britain. She does not speak of what lies before us, of the new war that may end wars and give our country peace—her mind glances away from me and from my tasks and follows a track of its own. It was different with Garwen'—a smile loomed on his grim features as he thought of Garwen ever ready to tend him, to talk, to hope with him, to be loved if the mood was on him. Then suddenly she spoke, in a level voice, without looking up, yet as though aware of his thought and of his smile.

"Where have you left the girl that you took out of London?"

He sighed and answered, "She is safe at Ynys Gutrin." He frowned and thought, 'Is this a thing that any can reproach me with, even Gwenhyvar, that I have given love to one British woman when I have striven to save thousands from rape and murder and slavery among the heathen?'

"There is no faithfulness left in Britain," she said in the same dull tone. "I know all there is to know of

how our rulers live. In the North, by the Clyde, there
is a fierceness in our folk that lends them the
strength of wild beasts, but here, among walled
towns and ploughed fields, there is ease and lust and
treachery—and we live in a nightmarish world that
dissolves in the coming of a new dawn."

"It is the dawn for which I work."

"Once I thought you more than man, a god
almost, with powers such as Christians claim for holy
men, but by your own deed you show yourself only
such as other men are."

"Sinful I am, yet God has favoured me many times
and may yet give me the victory I seek."

She shook her head. "To cast out the evil in this
land you must sin more deeply than other men or
else be without sin."

He turned away from her abruptly, seeming to
hear an echo of Medraut's words in Coit Mawr and on
the road from Aquae Sulis. Medraut and Gwenhyvar,
they two stood nearest to him and they both watched
him as folk watch a mighty tree when axes are laid to
its roots, knowing that all the strength and toughness
and the leafy crown shading the land, all will soon fall
with a crash. He rested his chin on his hands and
stared at the ground, aware of scraps of the mosaic
pattern showing under his feet and remembering how
he and Garwen had uncovered Hercules fighting the
Hydra that first night that they were together.

Gwenhyvar watched him for a moment. 'How this
man outshines all others!' she thought. 'And yet how
glad I should be if he were gone, and gladder still,
perhaps, if I heard that he had fallen like some great
hero in defence of his land. . . . The sameness of this
talk, how it wearies me! The dawn for Britain—it will
not come with a propping up of old ruins . . .' Absently her gaze wandered to the waste ground outside,
and slowly she gathered herself together, staring
fixedly at what she saw. A lean sow rooted among the

docks and nettles unconscious of the approach of two figures, a man and a boy. The man stood still, whistling a little air; the sunlight caught his profile and she knew it was Medraut.

'He does not come to see me,' she thought bitterly. 'My body does not tempt him now, or he is a man like other men, spellbound by the greatness of Arthur, unable to raise a hand against the Amherawdyr, now that this war moves towards a climax. But does that alter the longing that I have for him? Am I not as much his slave now as I was when he spoke to me in Bregion?'

The boy was busy picking up stones. Now he ran forward and began to pelt the sow. He threw with all his strength, and with a devilish glee. There were grunts and squeals as the bewildered creature rushed this way and that. Thump, thump, the missiles went home on its long, lean body. Now the boy was collecting more stones, gingerly picking some larger pieces out of a nettle bed; the man looked on impassively, but all of a sudden an old woman came on the scene brandishing a stout stick. A quavering voice mingled with the squealing of the sow and some very shrewd blows fell on the boy's backside. He fled and she pursued, stumbling heavy-footed among the heaps of wreckage. Now he was dodging behind a stump of ruin; he glared and spat, a knife flashed in his fist; all at once he darted out, thrust, and sprang back before the stick could reach him. The old woman turned and ran howling, clasping her belly, and the sow cantered away after her. The boy stood looking at the knife blade, he ran up to the man and showed it in triumph. The man stood with folded arms, as though preoccupied with the tune that he was now whistling in another key. Then he turned away and mounted a flight of steps to the top of the ramparts and went slowly out of sight. 'What is a sow and what is one old woman?' thought Gwenhyvar.

'And yet that was devil's work. A good woman should not look on it unmoved, but I am unmoved and so was Medraut. Alike we are in the face we turn on evil, and a sign it may be that we shall triumph by evil means when our chance comes. . . . All over Britain evil meets evil as steel meets steel, and if I betray Arthur with Medraut, has not he betrayed me with a wanton?' She glanced at the man who sat beside her and saw that he had fallen asleep with his head in his hands. And then she thought: 'How easily someone might slip in now and kill him where he sits—this man whose life weighs on mine like a great rock, crushing down the longing that I feel for Medraut, so that sometimes I could scream like a drowning man fighting for breath.' Again and again she sighed deeply while visions came to her of the deed that would set her free and again and again she blotted out these dreadful fantasies, thinking, 'Why should I be thrust down to hell, as the Christians believe, entrapped by a song that I have woven about myself? What I have woven I can break—if Medraut will help me to it—and what should help me more than to see him as I saw him just now? This is the madness of love, that everything, whether fair or hateful, seems to build a bridge for that achievement, that thing without which the flesh cannot rest, no matter how much the spirit may mock . . .' Her head turned sharply as she was aware of a figure in the courtyard, not a gaily-dressed figure with sunshiny eyes like Olwen's, but a figure in an old brown cloak with a broad-brimmed hat on its head; a man who stepped very quietly into the room and stood looking from her to Arthur and back again. She found it hard to recognise the shadowed face as that of Conan, King of Gwent.

Now her mind began to work feverishly, searching for clues which before had seemed dull, unimportant to her, like Arthur's plans for the Saxon war. What

plan had Conan in his mind when he came here gliding into the house like a dark shadow? What did
Arthur signify to him? Arthur, the friend of Gereint,
Arthur, bidden with the gift of a white mare to visit
Cuneglas at Lis Pengwern, Arthur, the cousin of
Gwalchmei. A league of princes against Gwent, a
league armed with the might of the Cymry, that was
what Conan had to fear, and from this, perhaps, he
hoped to free himself with a dagger stroke now and a
massacre to follow. Were not the Cymry spread out,
unsuspecting harm, some in Caerleon, some in Caer
Gwent, some back at Caer Gloui, guarding the Severn
bridge? The Saxons threatened in the east; but nearer at hand were the Cymry, ready, perhaps, to strike
in with Dyvnaint and Powys. What a prize was this
realm of Gwent, the last faded relic of Roman Britain,
left in the hands of a man who called himself Aurelius Conanus! She saw it all in a flash, and when
Conan took a step nearer she stood up and planted
herself between him and Arthur. As she did so the
light in the room dimmed and she saw that a crowd
of men leaned forward at the window opening, men
whose faces were dark against the blaze of April sunshine, whose hands were hidden in their cloaks.

Treachery, she thought; this was in the air at
Caerleon, it clung about the place, in the narrow passageways between high walls, in the waste spaces
with dark openings going down into broken vaults
and hypocausts, and now here it came, showing its
ugly face, the thing that she had played with in her
mind and which she had cast aside in horror as a
sleeper strives to wake from a ghastly dream. . . . And
then, all at once Conan drew back. Carelessly he
threw his cloak from him and showed himself in fine
clothes, blue linen embroidered with gold thread; he
sank back on a couch, stroking his chin, letting an
empty hand rest on his knee. The room was light
again; the row of heads had melted silently away, and

across the waste ground came champions of the Cymry—Medraut with Bedwyr, Kai, Mabon, the Gaelic warrior Coll, and Brude, the son of the Pictish King.

"The Cymry are awake even if Arthur sleeps," said Gwenhyvar, and as Conan smiled blandly she had a sudden intuition that he hated the sound of that word Cymry and all that it stood for.

"Who says that Arthur sleeps?" came a voice behind her, as the crumpled figure on the couch straightened itself out, the arms spread wide, the head sunken for a moment on one shoulder. A quiver of dread and distaste went through her—how like the figure of Arthur was to those Christian images of the Christ crucified—that symbol that filled her with horror rather than reverence, as being something which she could by no effort of the mind weave into her own way of living, or into that of those about her. But the vision faded abruptly as Arthur yawned and smiled, believing himself back in the timbered hall of Camelot, woken by Garwen for a day of hunting in Coit Mawr. He opened his eyes and saw Gwenhyvar and Conan, while from the window he heard Medraut's whistling—one of those sprightly sinister tunes from Eiré. The smile left his lips.

"I am come to take counsel with you, Amherawdyr," said Conan in a voice that was courteous yet carried a hint of menace.

"And I shall give you counsel, Conan, King of Gwent, to ride with me tomorrow for Lis Pengwern. There shall we all take counsel together, we men who have power in Britain, all except Gereint who awaits battle while we spend these precious days in talk."

"What security shall I have at Pengwern, in the hall of my enemy?" said Conan darkly.

"The same security that I shall have, and Maelgun, and Vortipore."

"Do you know that all these kings are raising armies?"

"It was I that urged them to make ready for war. My messengers went to them from Sarum, as they did to you also."

"And what if they make war on Gwent?"

"No party shall I be to any such war. I aim to make a league among the kings of Britain so that we may throw back the Saxon hordes."

"So men say. But in my lifetime I have suffered nothing from the Saxons. The men on the upper Thames have paid me taxes in corn and cattle, and if they have wrought harm to Gereint, that is not my affair."

"You have not seen what I have seen by London," said Arthur sombrely. "A nation moves against us, blindly, like a great wave rolling in from the sea. There is force in it to flood Britain to the farthest mountains of Gwyneth, and at its head is a man of our race who has the wit to ride this wave so that it bears him to power and us to ruin."

Conan shrugged his shoulders.

"Straightforward are your words, Arthur. You may know much of Picts and Saxons, but I doubt whether you know what I do of the British race, these hungry bands of spearmen that look down from their hills upon my plains of Gwent."

"Not all the Britons are as black-hearted and treacherous as you are, Conan!" burst out Gwenhyvar. "You think us simple folk, we who have come from the North, but we know better than most, perhaps, the weapons to which your hands are wedded."

"An unkind speech, lady, from one who has been a guest in my city, welcome though unbidden, these six months," said Conan with a twisted smile.

"A discourteous speech, maybe, yet it has some spice of truth," said Arthur gloomily.

Conan was silent; he thought to himself: 'The man is simple, but the woman not so simple. Does she draw her bow at a venture, or does she know what I had in mind for Arthur, does she know that I have sent a man to kill Gwalchmei, that I have offered the Saxons a passage into Dyfet and Powys, that I aim to destroy the Cymry and rule Britain side by side with Cerdic?'

Chapter XVIII

The Council at Lis Pengwern

IT HAS ALWAYS BEEN A CUSTOM WITH OUR NATION, AS IT IS AT
PRESENT, TO BE IMPOTENT IN REPELLING FOREIGN FOES, BUT
BOLD AND INVINCIBLE IN RAISING CIVIL WAR.
　　　　　　　　　—Gildas, *De Excidio Britanniae.*

The houses of Pengwern, pale with the pallor of new thatch and newly split oak timber, lay clustered on a ridge lapped by the Severn. Seen from the southern road that dipped from the uplands about Caer Caradoc, those homely buildings had a glamorous charm, almost a splendour, caught in a gleam of sunshine, amid an illimitable dusky sea— the forest plain that swept northward, a dim gulf of tree-tops, towards the sluggish waters of Dee, Mersey, and Ribble. Out of that plain, like some great cairn of forgotten significance, a waymark to wandering peoples in past ages, rose the dark whale-backed height of Vricon. Formerly it had presided over the Roman city of Vriconium, stormed and ruined in the Pictish wars and now abandoned to the evenly

flowing tide of trees. Owls and bats housed now in
the broken colonnades and cliff-like faces of wall dotted with black beam holes, ivy muffled the giant bulk
of baths and basilicas so that the old city was nothing more than a little hump of darkness in that great
realm of shadow, whereas the new town built by
Cuneglas rose bright and sparkling above red scarps
and tall stockades like a child's castle of shells and
pebbles on a weedy beach.

Conan's face was impassive as he watched Pengwern rise and sink and rise again out of that vast
landscape, but on Arthur's there was a reflection of
hope from that gallant show of man's handiwork in a
sombre world. Perhaps here was a sign of the New
Britain, the Britain of Celtic speech and fierce vitality
breaking away from the dingy foulness of Rome that
lingered within those monstrous walls of Caer Ceri,
Caer Gwent, and Caerleon.

Now the little company of mounted men rode
through great droves of sleepy-looking cattle where
the forest thinned to the reedy banks of Severn. They
ferried across, hailed by shouts of welcome from the
ramparts opposite, they rode up round the hill with
its bristling crests of thatch, in at a gateway, and up
a tortuous street with galleries and pent-houses and
colonnades of oak pillars, all new buildings grounded
in red mud and black layers of charcoal from a previ-
ous town burnt in the late civil war when Maelgun
had pursued his uncle into the land of Powys.

New as it was, the city stank with filth and slovenly ways of life, yet there was still a freshness about it;
a redeeming tang of wood smoke and of timber newly
split with wedges and shaped with adze.

Crowds thickened about the riders as they
splashed their way upwards to the highest point on
the ridge, where stood the sprawling buildings of a
palace—Lis Pengwern—and in an open space before
it they made out three woven standards floating

from tall poles—the Grey Hound of Cuneglas, the Black Dragon of Maelgun, and the White Falcon of Vortipore.

"We too shall plant our standards in this good company!" said Arthur gaily. A man made a hole in the soft ground with a javelin and Kai thrust in the pole of Arthur's Red Dragon. There was a cheer from hundreds of men gathered at the palace gates, fairer, wilder-looking folk than those of Gwent with their crisp curly hair black as pitch. Women and children pushed out from the low doorways, stared and pointed. "The Amherawdyr!" passed from mouth to mouth in a respectful muttering. And then Conan set up his banner of the Antlered Stag, and there was silence, followed by a sneering and spitting.

For three days the princes of Britain feasted in the hall of Cuneglas, they rode out hunting, they drank and whiled away time with women, and they took counsel with Arthur. They were all ready for war, yet doubtful whether it were worth while to muster so great an army to save Dyvnaint from the Saxons. Nor was Conan willing to give a passage through his country. The harvest had been bad on the lower Severn—he could not offer to feed thousands of warriors in addition to his own gathered at Caer Ceri. Let Vortipore take his warriors by sea and let the armies of Powys and Gwyneth march eastwards by the London road . . . Day by day the faces round the council table grew darker and more embittered.

There came a morning when they sat in a low-ceilinged room, dim with smoke, lounging on deer-skin rugs by a table marked with many circles from cups of mead. Conan had not come; it was rumoured that a messenger had reached him from the south, that he was busy with his men, that his horses were saddled as though for instant departure.

"If there were no Conan to bar the crossings of Wye and Severn, our business here might be soon finished," said Maelgun. He sat at the head of the table, an enormous figure, still youthful, but black-bearded, hatchet-faced, with cold blue eyes like some bird of prey.

Cuneglas struck his fist on the board; he leaned forward, a young man, splendidly handsome, tawny-haired, with the drooping moustache of the typical Celtic chieftain. "My plan," he said eagerly, "would be to pour through Gwent with fire and sword."

Vortipore regarded him sleepily from across the table and grunted. He reached out his hand for a cup and drank while his little dark eyes shifted to and fro from one face to another. He seemed a man cast in some uglier or more archaic mould than the kings of Gwyneth and Powys; his shoulders were like two great bastions flanking his thick short neck, his shaven cheeks looked as though they had been rubbed with soot, he had a huge fleshy nose and jet-black moustache continually twitched upwards to disclose long yellow teeth. His habits were beastly and no man there kept him close company, but his mind was subtle and seldom betrayed by his speech.

"Who shall rule in Gwent if not Conan?" he said, while his finger travelled among the pools of spilled mead tracing out plaits and spirals.

"Let Arthur have Gwent!" said Cuneglas. "As he is foremost among the warriors of Britain let him stand in the forefront to meet the Saxons, and I shall stand on his left hand and Gereint upon his right."

"It is no wish of mine to win land and power from you kings of Britain," said Arthur. He threw himself back and laid his hands on the table. "My task is to fight, to rid the land of its foes, not to sit at ease within the walls of Caerleon."

"Let us rid the land of Conan," urged Cuneglas. "He is the weak place, the patch of rotten wood in our shield covering the west from Dee to Sarum. Warnings I have that messengers go between him and

Cerdic, that out of hatred for us he will let the Saxons through."

"Nevertheless his forces are mustered on the Saxon march at Caer Ceri," said Arthur.

"All the better. Caerleon lies open to my host in Ercing," said Cuneglas with a chuckle.

"Nearer are mine by the banks of Taff," remarked Vortipore.

"Farther are mine in the Vale of Clwyd, yet a day's march will bring them in sight of Pengwern," said Maelgun, thrusting out his black beard.

"You princes!" Arthur sprang to his feet; his voice rose to a shout. He threw his red glazed drinking cup on the table so that fragments flew all over the room. "You sit here gambling for each other's goods while the house burns over your head—the fair house of Britain, the only shelter we Britons can find in a dark age lit by crackling fires of doom! Listen, you proud tyrants, reckoning up by how much you can strip each other of the good things that are left to us, I swore to my men, the Cymry, that I would sit with you round one board, that I would show you that there is at least one master of men in Britain who cares not who rules in Gwent or who in Gwyneth, who seeks no power for himself save the power to cast back the Saxons. Have you been east in the land, you, Maelgun? Have you seen the ruin there is there, the empty cities, the scattering of our people as slaves among the heathen, the land divided up among men who know not our speech, big men with blue eyes and flaxen hair . . . If you princes knew what they know in Dyvnaint, what I know, and the Cymry who stand by me in war, then you would pour out your strength to save our heritage, you, too, would join in that song that men sing from the Pictish march to the Narrow Sea—'Arthur our leader; Christ our King!' No longer would you be thinking how a Black Dragon might float over Pengwern or a White Falcon over

Caerleon; you would be taking an oath to plant the British standards afresh on the gates of London."

The three kings stared at him in silence, their arms folded on the table, their faces dark, withdrawn, unresponsive to his words save for a glint of malevolence. 'We understand each other,' they seemed to say, 'but we do not understand the language you talk. Who are you to threaten us? You a master of men! Cymry indeed! A few hundred warriors from the North . . .' Their gaze shifted furtively to each other, then away again, as though reviewing some ugly design not to be envisaged eye to eye. In the silence that followed the words of Arthur evil seemed to swell and flicker in the glances of those three men at the table, it whispered in the sharp intakes of breath, it was instinct in the clasping and unclasping hands. It was as though a light had been extinguished and vermin peered bright-eyed from their holes. Suddenly Arthur leaned forward and planted both fists on the table.

"I leave you!" he cried, and there was a reckless, fatalistic ring in his voice. He stared over the heads of the three kings as though at some vision that floated into the room through the close-set trunks of oak, a vision of magnificence and horror. "I shall go back to the South, where men love and trust me, Gereint's men from the combes and cliff castles of Kernou, where I was born. There it may be that the Cymry and I will fight our last battle . . . before the might of Britain lies in the hands of the Saxons." His voice died away; there was the sound of swift sharp footsteps, the rasp of a curtain drawn back, and Conan stood in the room. A stir went over the men clustered at the table, a flash, wary and menacing, like the quiver that passes through a skep of bees when a hand is laid on it. Conan in his fine Romanised dress, girt with a sword, the golden torque on his black curly hair; the steely, resolute figure of a man who had cast aside doubt, who was ready to look death in the face.

It was Maelgun who spoke first, in a gentle voice, with a smile that passed slowly into a grin of malice, while his huge form straightened up and loomed over the two other kings like some mountain crest emerging from mist above crouching hills.

"Late you come to the council board, Conan. Is it with pleasant women that you spend your time, or do you lay out gold on swift horses, on hawks or hounds here in Pengwern, or have you found better friends than us kings of the west and are now ready to ride and leave us?"

Conan's lips tightened. He reached out a hand and laid it on Arthur's shoulder.

"One man I see here whom I dare call a friend," he said sharply, "but well I know that you three kings would gladly flesh your teeth in the Stag of Gwent. So be it! To-day I stand ready to meet my doom; tomorrow it will be the turn of you, Cuneglas, and you, Vortipore. You, Maelgun, may last out a little longer behind your mountains, but in time men will see that the key to Britain lies not in Sarum or in Pengwern, but in the first bridge across Severn, at Caer Gloui on the road to Gwent."

Vortipore looked up from the smeared patterns of mead.

"Conan has news" he said. "Pale he is, as a boy at the first sight of blood."

"Tell us your news," said Arthur. "God grant that it puts an end to these plots of Briton against Briton. I can guess what you have to tell us."

"I too," said Vortipore, stroking his great fleshy nose, "for I had secret word this morning that the beacon fires are burning all along Dyvnaint. In full view they are from my shores of Morganuc."

"You knew that and said nothing!" Cuneglas flung at him, furious, yet daunted by the sight of the broad bestial face glooming across the table.

"Swords we have, plain to be seen, but daggers also that we keep hidden," said Maelgun with a dark smile.

"I have nothing left to hide," said Conan. "The war has begun. Cerdic has passed the Avon below Sarum. There has been such a slaughter as has never been seen since the fall of Anderida. Gereint's army is flying towards the west and the Saxons are burning their way through Durngueir. Bad news; but there is more that will prick your hides deeper, perhaps. A second Saxon army is on the move from the upper Thames; Sigbert's men out of London, and many thousands of fresh warriors newly come to Britain under a chief Erkenwine. With them are joined Engel from the east and Cissa's folk from the south—all save the Kentishmen are banded together against me, rolling like a flood past Caer Ceri and over the hills to the Vale of Severn."

"We must ride!" Arthur's voice broke the silence like a bell. "My horses are waiting. What men can do, that we shall attempt . . ."

Conan stared for a moment at the three kings, bitter hatred in his eyes, then he was gone and Arthur after him.

"He has failed with Cerdic," said Maelgun. "He has bought no safety for Gwent and now he will have to fight."

"We, too," said Cuneglas. "A storm is coming, such as the one that blew in the days of Vortigern."

"We shall have to save Conan." Vortipore got to his feet and reached for more mead. "I sent a messenger an hour ago bidding my men march into Gwent." The other two regarded him with respect and loathing. The Black Beast of Dyfet was swifter in action than in speech—a dangerous man, far more dangerous than his enemy, Conan. What luck if both of them perished in this new war! Then there would come a final trial of strength, to see whether Britain would be ruled from Pengwern or Deganwy . . .

"Now," continued Vortipore placidly, "I march to save, not to seize for myself. Can I trust you to do the same?"

"I am ready to swear that my weapons shall be turned against no British ruler till the Saxons are beaten," said Cuneglas. "Where are your men, Maelgun?"

"They will be here before to-night," said Maelgun. "Swift is the White Falcon, but the Black Dragon can match him."

"You aimed to burn Pengwern for the second time!" Cuneglas sprang up with a hand on his sword.

"Whatever I had in mind, whether against you or against Conan, I cast it from me. Side by side we must meet these Saxons."

"Side by side; yet one must be foremost," said Vortipore. "Beasts and birds may be all of one mind, but men must have a leader."

"Then Arthur shall be our leader!" said Cuneglas impulsively. "Arthur yr Amherawdyr, a man who fights for no private gain."

"We are well rid of the father—shall we raise up the son?" said Maelgun dubiously.

"If he rise too high, four kings should be able to pluck him down," said Vortipore, rolling his eyes so that the whites showed and thrusting up his brows in goblin-like merriment. "What is Arthur but a plough that we drive before us, cleaving the tough earth and burying the weeds that grow thick in Britain? And when the harvest is gathered in, the plough lies rusting in a corner of the field."

Chapter XIX

The Rising Flood

A VAGUE RUMOUR SUDDENLY AS IF ON WINGS REACHES THE
EARS OF ALL, THAT THEIR INVETERATE FOES WERE RAPIDLY
APPROACHING TO DESTROY THE WHOLE COUNTRY, AND TAKE
POSSESSION OF IT . . . FROM ONE END TO THE OTHER.
—Gildas, *De Excidio Britanniae.*

A warm, languorous breath of summer lay in the
Severn Valley and life streamed upwards from
the rich earth covering the face of the land with
a mist of tender greenery, with a white foam of fruit
and hawthorn blossom, with fiery plumes of gorse.
Bird song, the hum of bees, the heavy scents of flowery fields and of jungle sprouting from black slime
and iridescent pools—all this flood of vital forces
rolled over the plains like a sea imprisoned by a
phantom-like rim of blue hills. Birds and insects
busied themselves unperturbed in this fragrant
summer warmth, but mankind was aware of a vast
convulsion, a sudden turn of fortune's wheel that
dragged down their settled world in a blind onset of
chaos and terror. These people still lived a life that
was Roman in its essentials; they had not yet degenerated into the savage Celtic tribalism; they were

unconcerned about heathen Saxons living east of the hills. They had cattle, corn, fruit and honey; what matter that the big houses had been ruined in old wars? It was easy enough to build afresh in wood and the land was there, as bountiful as it had ever been. But it was hard for these people to realise that what they took as their right, the inheritance of their race from past centuries, land and goods to be enjoyed in security—all this was theirs only by virtue of the strong arm of Rome, moving fleets and armies to posts of danger, dotting the shores of Britain with fortresses and watch towers, enclosing her cities in mighty walls. Rome had struck and parried and struck again in their defence, and then, bewildered by the blows that rained upon her from every side, she had abandoned the unequal fight. "Defend your-selves," she had said, and immediately there appeared a band of upstarts: landowners, officials, retired soldiers, or men who remembered their descent from tribal chieftains. They seized power; they raised armies, it is true, but generally to war upon one another; they hired barbarians from oversea to fight the barbarians that were already in the land. As treacherous masters they found treacherous servants and they revealed the weakness of Britain to a race of men, brutish, ferocious, but faithful to their leaders, hardened by the rawness of life on the German plains—a people dimly aware that the good things of a well guarded world hung like ripe fruit on trees that any man might climb. The orchard was there; the gate was open, the guardians were gone . . .

It was not quite so easy a task as it had seemed at first. Enormous spoils had been taken, but now there were men rising up in Britain who fought desperate-ly, men with hatred in their eyes and their backs set against sea or mountains. A fresh effort had to be made to win what was left; a banding together of men who had won a foothold in Britain and men who came fresh from the sea, staring lustfully for the first time at British slave girls, crumbling the rich earth between their fingers, letting their rough guttural voices echo from great broken towers and in pillared halls. The armies feasted and drank, they boasted, shouted and sang, they shared out women for nights of lechery, they fouled the great buildings, the silent tokens of a power that had passed away. At last they set out, across heaths shimmering in the blaze of Spring sunshine, through woods misted with blue-bells and ringing with cuckoo calls—they set out to take the West.

* * *

There was a difference of opinion among the leaders. Cerdic wished to throw the whole army against the Britons of Dyvnaint, to harry them out of the forest combes and over the cliffs of Kernou. The Saxon chieftains were tempted by the wealth in the broad plain of Severn, cities to sack, the good land, women and cattle, the stores of well tempered weapons forged by smiths in the woods between Severn and Wye. Conan's country lay open to attack, and if the other kings emerged from their mountains one big battle might settle the fate of Britain. The army divided. Cerdic and his men swept Gereint from the Avon fords and poured through Durngueir; the other leaders went over Thames Head. Before them rose the grey walls of Caer Ceri lined with fugitives. Deep moats, stockaded ramparts, arrows whizzing from the parapets, shrill cries from women piling up stones and tiles to batter the assailants—the Saxons flowed round the place, consuming the countryside. They did not like the look of Caer Ceri. The stockades might be burnt with fire, but how were they to climb those walls or make an opening in them? There were men who remembered the taking of Anderida, when it had been worn down by famine. Caer Ceri was half-paralysed by terror, but still very full of life. Was the summer to be spent watching those walls and waiting for the folk inside to starve? Sulky and a little bewildered, the Saxons moved on over the forest hills and came down into the Vale of Severn. Their spirits rose at the sight of that glorious plain, surely the fairest in all Britain, rich in timber, rich in corn, full of flowery pastures and clustered dwellings, threaded by the shimmering links of a great river.

Eagerly the leaders scanned the long straight road ahead, expecting to see armies advancing to defend the land, but nowhere was there a sign of a human being, no smoke trailed upwards from the thatched houses, no cattle grazed in the fields. Food was not easy to come by. A growl of exasperation came from the tide of hungry warriors when they reached the river banks and saw vast droves of cattle, sheep, and swine across the water. A bridge was soon found, but it was covered by a walled city—Caer Gloui. Here was no horde of frightened countrymen and screaming women, but a dark silent mass of soldiery, shield to shield along the rampart walks, and over the south-eastern gate stood a Red Dragon standard, the like of one that Sigbert's men had seen before the walls of London. There was a brief and stormy council. Erkenwine resolved on trying to break in the gate with a battering ram. Piles of brushwood were pushed up to the stockaded outworks and set on fire, not without some loss, for a mangonel shot up from one of the flat-topped towers and pitched stones the size of sheep into the dense crowds of Saxons. A hundred men rushed forward over the glowing embers with a huge elm trunk poised like a lance against the wooden doors, but a sudden sleet of arrows struck the bearers, they stumbled, sagged and wavered; the tree came to ground a dozen yards short of the gate, crushing arms and limbs. Sigbert shook his head. The Welshmen might be smashed in the open, he said, but not behind walls and towers. It would be better to follow the river upstream and look for some other crossing place—eventually there would be fords, or a passage might be made on rafts. The swarming mass of Saxons streamed away to northward and from the walls of Caer Gloui rose a chant from a thousand voices, gloomy, menacing, and triumphant.

"It is Arthur we have against us," said Sigbert. "Were that man felled our task would be easy. It is he that holds the power of the Welshmen together like an iron hoop on a rotten cask."

For many a mile the Saxons followed the winding shores of Severn. There were no bridges, no fords. A raft was poled across, but scarcely had the crew set foot on the western bank before they were overwhelmed by a rush of Britons sallying from the thickets like infuriated bees from a hive. Now came the lesser stream of the Avon, edging the invaders away from the West. They climbed the great rounded bulk of Bredon and looked out over a vast forest. The good country had come to an end. Doubtless they could make a crossing somewhere and live by hunting in that dim unfriendly world of woodland, but were there women there, or weapons, or gold? Was there a chance of luring the Welshmen to battle, of striking a blow that would make the Saxon secure in these western valleys flanked by a surging mass of blue hills? These shaggy ranges were not like the smooth downs that made an easy path across Britain for wandering peoples; they had a grim, baffling aspect to men from the flat heaths of Saxony, ugly ramparts reared to shelter these fierce and cowardly folk who fought behind wood and water and stone walls and on cliff-like hillsides.

The host split and wandered this way and that in search of food. One party came on an old road, almost grown up, leading to a ford on the Avon and there, eating its way among the primeval oaks, was a settlement of Saxons, unmolested in the wilderness, men who had found their way in from the North Sea a couple of generations back. They had bred from British women and lost all touch with their kinsfolk in the East, a meagre, undernourished community, struggling with fevers and rheumatism, yet making some sort of living in the fringe of the great wood that they called Arden; one of those germs of a new people that was one day to make a mighty state in mid Britain.

Fresh life streamed into these small settlements as the Saxon host moved aimlessly along the upper waters of Avon, but the bulk of the host halted on a high hill encircled with old ramparts while the leaders took council again. They sat on the turf from which sprang cowslips and violets and bird's-eye trefoil; the air was sultry with the smell of hawthorn blossom, and a summery haze lay on immeasurable distances of gently rolling forest.

"We have turned our faces from the West," said Erkenwine. "In a while we shall strike the roads that lead back to London. We are strong enough to destroy any host that the kings of the Welsh can bring against us, and yet we are turned from our course by a river and a stone wall." He drew his sword and slice meditatively at the rising fronds of bracken, a young man, heavy-jowled, with a great mop of uncombed flaxen hair and the pale expressionless eyes of the seafarer.

It was Cissa, the South Saxon, who answered him, a burly figure still short of breath from climbing the hill, grey-bearded, with a bald dome-like head on which were several old scars crusted over with sweaty grime.

"The waves run up the beach and lap the cliffs," he said. "Little by little the land crumbles away. There are sandbanks now in the sea by Cymensora which folk tell me were once cattle pastures and fields of corn. So it goes with our conquest of Britain. A swift gain on level land and a slow one among the rising hills. Our strength still comes from the sea, and easier should I be in my mind if our eyes could reach from this hilltop to blue waters and ships under sail."

"Not so should I liken our enterprise to a high flood that runs far inland and is presently soaked up and dried away without trace save for heaps of wreckage," said Sigbert, methodically scratching out a tuft of cowslips with a spurred heel. "Rather are we the fire that sweeps the forest so that men may drive a plough between the stumps and turn up the good earth. Burning and hewing we shall waste away the life strength of the Welshmen so that they have no power to win back the land that we have trodden."

"The Welshmen keep beyond the reach of our swords," muttered Erkenwine, staring at the swathe of bracken he had cut down. "What can men do against those cursed stone walls?"

"Their walls and ramparted hills are the measure of their weakness," said Cissa. "They have no stomach to meet us hand to hand on open ground. Little by little we shall take their defences from them, even as we South Saxons have done, starving the cities and driving the country folk farther and farther into trackless woods."

"We did ill to part with Cerdic," said Erkenwine suddenly. "He should know, if anyone, how to break the fortresses. Let him show us the way into the place they call Caer Gloui and the river crossing is ours. Food we shall find in plenty on the farther side and there the Welshmen must fight or be destroyed."

Sigbert was not inclined to share power with Cerdic, a man of measureless ambition. He was better pleased to see the West Saxons swallowed up in the wilds of Dyvnaint, leaving him scope to master the rest of Britain. He knew that Cissa's strength was rooted on the shores by the Narrow Sea; that he thought only of plunder in the West. Erkenwine he saw as a dull-witted warrior, a hewer of wood for other men's needs, and it was he, Sigbert, who would take for his own what fell to the steel of this blindly flowing horde of seamen.

"I have a plan," he said; "let us go back swiftly to Caer Ceri and ring it in. It may be we shall have better luck there than at Caer Gloui. Arthur and Conan will come out to save the place and we shall crush them. What Welsh host can stand against ours?"

"In any case we turn our backs on these forests," said Cissa, his eyes glooming at the green sea of tree-tops, bounded now by little hills like islands of amethyst in the clearing air of sunset.

"Closer we shall be to Cerdic," said Erkenwine. "Breast to breast it goes in love-play, and in weapon-play hand is never far from head."

The three chieftains sat silent, looking out over the land of Britain with greedy, lustful eyes—this vast possession, theirs to take, share, and spoil, theirs to use for their delight and their necessity, a homeland for their children, a nursery for kings who would have power to shake the world. . . . The shadows lengthened from bush to brake, the air on that flower-spangled hill grew misty with the smoke of cooking fires. Axes crashed in the undergrowth, a brawling murmur came from thousands of human throats as from a den of wild beasts at feeding time, and here and there rose a wailing cry from some British girl run down in the woods and dragged up into the light of sunset to be a plaything for the conquerors of Britain.

Chapter XX

Badon Hill

THE SIEGE OF BADON HILL, WHERE TOOK PLACE THE LAST
ALMOST, THOUGH NOT THE LEAST SLAUGHTER OF OUR CRUEL
ENEMIES.

—Gildas, *De Excidio Britanniae.*

THE TWELFTH WAS A MOST SEVERE CONTEST, WHEN ARTHUR
PENETRATED TO THE HILL OF BADON.

—Nennius, *Historia Britonum.*

Events moved swiftly when the invading host returned to Caer Ceri. There was a fresh spirit about the place, for fighting men had poured into it. A roar of execration greeted the Saxons whenever they came near the walls; a desperate assault on a corner tower with scaling ladders was bloodily repulsed. But it was not the defiance of Caer Ceri that daunted the Saxon leaders, it was the difficulty of finding food in a countryside already scoured by both Britons and Saxons.

"Southward we must go," urged Cissa. "The Downs are full of sheep and cattle all the way to Sarum. When we have won a score of beasts for every man in our host, then we can talk about war.

If Arthur comes it is better that we fight him with full bellies."

The warriors tramped back over the woody flats of Thames Head, their eyes on the bare crests of Badon, a grey-green wall of turf, veined with trackways, rumpled here and there with mighty earthworks. Bleak and sinister those hills looked, thrusting out into the plains, a battleground and a graveyard of old civilisations, headland beyond headland, imprinted with the toil of forgotten races that had crowded upon them to escape from the dusky sea of swamp and forest.

As the Saxons drew nearer they could see that the highest hillside was blotched with dense masses of men and beasts. Right down to its foot were winding ramparts and stockades and on the crest, like some great citadel, a double ring of entrenchment, where even now work was going on in desperate haste with pick and spade and balks of oak.

"These folks have saved us the trouble of rounding up flocks and herds," said Sigbert exultantly. "Here is meat to feed us for many a week."

"There are men there that mean to fight," said Cissa. He sat on horseback, his feet trailing in the bleached moor grass, while he stared at the hill, shading his eyes from the sun. "Wiser it might be if we followed the road through the gap and took our toll of what lies beyond. There will be more cattle, easier come by, as we draw near to Sarum, and there we shall join hands with Cerdic."

"Hither it may well be that we shall draw Arthur from his post behind Severn. Let us fight and feast, and then make ready for a battle that will give us the West. Forward, men!" shouted Erkenwine, gathering up his reins. "Too long have we been tightening our belts on the roads of Britain! Shall we go by fasting and leave that pack of Welshmen drinking milk behind their palisades?"

"Kill! Kill! Hew the Welshmen!" sounded a growling roar of voices from the warriors behind. Thousands of spear heads swayed upwards, swords flashed out of scabbards and clanged on the high-bossed shields, a dull rustling of feet through long grass changed to a rumble on harder turf and strips of ploughland as the host took the slope like a wave glittering in sunshine.

"The place is one great fortress," muttered Cissa.

"It shall be ours by nightfall!" said Sigbert, setting his teeth and striking his horse hard with the spurs.

They were tough fighters behind the works on Badon Hill—black, curly-haired folk from the forests of Gwent, the old Silurian race that had followed Caradoc to war, and among them stood many a chieftain wearing the golden torque, reckless youths who had ridden out from the gates of Caerleon, flaunting green and scarlet cloaks around Conan's banner of the Antlered Stag. All that afternoon shout and counter-shout and the clang of weapons mingled with groans of the fallen, the dreary bellowing of cattle, and the bleating of ewes and lambs parted from each other in the turmoil. The Saxons swarmed about the ramparts on every side, they broke in, were thrust out, came on again, blinded with fury, unconscious of desperate wounds and spurting blood. Slowly the tide rolled higher and higher up the hill, and as the sun dipped to the dark banks of forest in the West, only the inmost ring of rampart was left in the hands of the Britons. There were enough of them left to line the whole circuit of the citadel. No matter where the Saxons flung themselves against it there was a dense mass of men brandishing blood-stained weapons, men without hope of life, maybe, but so inflamed with fury and despair that they stood firm like a living wall that could only be torn down stone by stone.

Dazed and spent, the half-starved heathen warriors recoiled at last, their swords drooped, the war cries died down, and all over that bare hill-top sounded only gasping breaths and a moaning of wounded men that rose and fell monotonously like the murmur of the sea, the eerie music of violent life waning and dissolving into oblivion.

"Let us leave them till tomorrow when they are parched with thirst, and their wounds are gone stiff. Life ebbs from a barked tree. To-morrow we shall finish in an hour what is beyond our strength to-night." So spoke Cissa, leaning against a broken palisade and running a finger over the dinted edge of his axe.

Erkenwine shook his head. "Fair weather at evening often turns to rain at sunrise," he said.

"Too many of our folk are dead," growled Sigbert, climbing out of a fosse half filled with the still-heaving bodies of fallen men. "A few more fights like this and our power is gone."

"Once in the bath one may as well wash oneself clean," said Erkenwine obstinately. "Better pleased should I be if our host overnighted within that rampart instead of lying spread out around it."

From the lower slopes came an agonised uproar from the cattle as men closed in upon them with axe and knife.

"We shall eat and drink, and some shall keep watch and some shall sleep," said Cissa. "A king I am by the Narrow Sea and my men shall do my will. Do you, Erkenwine, go on battering the Welshmen if it pleases you, but I have done with fighting for to-day." He strode away down the hill, blowing long blasts on a horn, and slowly the other two followed in his footsteps.

* * *

The Saxons had finished carousing in their scattered companies on the slopes of Badon and a greyness showed above the broad sweep of downs to eastward. The groaning of wounded men was fainter now, the petulant bleating of sheep had almost died away, and thousands of men lay silent on the dewy turf, both dead and living, beside the fires which had sunk into red heaps of embers. Dawn broke upon the bare heights, but night lingered on the plain muffled in dense mist, and suddenly out of the dusk to westward, where the Roman road struck through the hills to Cunetio, came loud shots, a confused murmur of voices, and the stumbling tramp of feet.

A man awakened Cissa where he lay with his head pillowed on a saddle. All round him in the chilly air he heard the words running through the camp like a ripple on a still pond: "Cerdic has come."

"The best news we have had for many a day!" said Cissa, getting stiffly to his feet. Everywhere folk were scrambling up and making way for a long, narrow column of men coming with a steady swinging step and the haughty bearing of warriors who had not yet met their match. Out from the ranks came a rider on a big bay stallion, cantering recklessly up the slope and waving a naked sword.

"Here am I, Cerdic!" he cried. "Follow me, Cissa, Sigbert and Erkenwine! Wake all of you and gather on the hills. Eastward we must go and choose a battle place, for the Welshmen are upon us. Wake, I say, and take your weapons! To-day shall decide the fate of Britain."

He rode on over the skyline, shearing away from the untaken fortress, his voice growing fainter amid the roar of voices and the clatter of arms that went surging after him.

On the slopes where Badon dipped eastward into thorny scrub Cerdic pulled in. A mass of men flowed after him like a torrent and among them came Cissa and Erkenwine, urging on their drowsy horses. Stirrup to stirrup they closed up beside Cerdic.

"What is there to fear?" they said in a breath. "We have lessened the Welsh to a handful. Let us turn now and make an end of them."

"It is not those men that I fear, Conan's champions licking their wounds on the top of Badon," answered Cerdic in a sombre voice. "It is what lies down there in the mist; the whole strength of the West marching from Caer Ceri. My spies have been among them already before they crossed the Severn; I know their plans and I have come like the wind leaving all I have won, leaving Gereint wriggling like a snake with a broken back among his shaggy hills."

"Conan's strength is broken too. A heavy blow we dealt him yesterday," said Erkenwine.

"He has more men than you have set eyes on, and with him come the hosts of Maelgun, Cuneglas, and Vortipore, and at the head of all is Arthur. A luckless day it was for us when the Bear of Britain slipped from our hands, west of London."

The sun threw a pale gleam over the jewelled turf and the snowy hawthorn brakes. Below them rolled the fog, tossing up wisps like swansdown in the morning breeze.

"Where lies Sigbert?" asked Cerdic suddenly.

"In the plain north of the hill," said Cissa. "He moves now. I hear his men driving the beasts together."

"He moves too late," said Cerdic. Out of a rumbling uproar down in the depths of the vaporous sea sounded the shrill notes of a trumpet. . . . Screaming cries, a thunderous yell, an answering shout of triumph from the fortress.

"Sigbert is being ground between two millstones. Shall we go to his aid?" said Erkenwine doubtfully.

"We shall fight, but not on ground of Arthur's choosing. Let us get away from this accursed hill," said Cerdic, grinding his teeth.

"Our plan was to draw Arthur across the Severn and then fall upon him," muttered Cissa.

"You have sown the wind and now you will reap the whirlwind." Cerdic gave a wild laugh. "Let us see

whether we can stand against it on that great hill circled with ramparts like a torque on a chieftain's head."

He pointed to a further stretch of down, grey-
green bosoms of turf shadowed in every fold and fading into dim featureless horizons. On the nearest
swell was the crater-like silhouette of an abandoned
fortress.

* * *

The mist had thinned away and battle was over on
the highest headland of Badon. Sigbert was dead and
the host he had brought from London had fallen
almost to a man. Eastward rolled the British army,
gay with standards and coloured cloaks, with bare
steel and helmeted heads flashing in the sunshine.
They moved on an old track between brakes of gorse
and forest copses, their eyes bent on a greyish
smudge eddying like a cloud shadowed on the next
curve of the downs.

Flushed with victory, the kings of Britain rode
beside Arthur on his white mare Lamrei. Perhaps
hatred of each other still lurked in their hearts, but
there were smiling faces and eyes that met with a
frank if grudging respect. For though Arthur had
planned the battle, the princes had no cause for
shame and none could say that the men of Gwyneth
had been braver than those of Gwent, or that Dyfet
hung back when Powys went forward. Nor had there
ever been a bigger slaughter of the Saxons with less
loss to the Britons, even in the Wars of Emrys, nor
had any British prince ridden at the head of such a
mighty host since the Roman legions had left the
land. All the same the murmur of exultant voices died
away as the next headland of Badon rose higher and
higher against the blue sky, spread with a carpet of
men lolling nonchalantly upon the turf as hunters lie,
unafraid of the beasts they mean to take and kill. It
was a sad-coloured multitude in rusty ring mail, in

leather jerkins, in dusty coats of wool or linen, but it had an air of insolent defiance, as though it had no call to stop chewing raw meat or slaking its thirst at the dew ponds when the Welsh standards had reached the foot of the hills.

The faces of the princes grew glum as they stared at those masses of men taking their ease on the skyline. Insensibly they closed up, drawn together for once by the kinship of blood and by a consciousness of dread and hatred at the sight of the spoilers of Britain.

"We have shorn them of some thousands," said Conan moodily, "but there are enough of them left to over-run the land from sea to sea."

"Cerdic has a good eye for a battle place. Shall we sweep round him to southward and take the gentle slope of the hill?" said Vortipore.

"He would charge us in flank and split us in two," said Arthur shortly.

"We men from the heights of Gwyneth are not daunted by such a hill as Badon," put in Maelgun.

"Nor are we of Powys daunted if Arthur tells us where to strike," said Cuneglas fiercely. "Set out our host, Amherawdyr! To-day we are all Cymry."

A growl of approval came from the warriors near-est and spread like the wind over the whole army, a great menacing roar of voices that woke a snarling echo from the Saxons on the hills.

"So be it," said Arthur. He rode out in front of the others and drew his long heavy sword. A hush fell on the thousands of sweating, rank-smelling men who had come to strike a blow for Britain; a sea of upturned faces watched the dark figure on the white horse raising aloft a sword that flashed in the sun. On the skyline the Saxons rippled forward into a dense dusky wall like an outcrop of rock on the smooth face of the downs.

"Gwyneth shall be our left wing and climb where the slope is steep," shouted Arthur. "Dyfet shall take the right where the slope is easier. Gwent shall be yet farther to the right and strike in where the slope is easiest of all. Powys shall be in the centre and climb that out-thrust ridge that leads like a ladder to where a standard waves on the ramparts of the fortress. That is the heart of the Saxon host, and against it shall I go with my Cymry as a spearhead before the ranks of Cuneglas. If God be willing we shall cleave our way across Badon till we come to a hollow stone by the roadside, and if I be alive I shall blow a bugle note from that stone that will be heard from one end of the battle to the other, proclaiming to friend and foe that victory is ours."

A band of men on half-foundered horses pushed their way through the eddying masses of Britons, they pressed up to Arthur, and the two foremost riders flung up their hands in the old Roman salute.

A look of joy came over Arthur's rugged features. "Welcome!" he cried. "Welcome to Badon, Gereint and Gwalchmei!"

"We have ridden hard in the track of Cerdic," said Gereint breathlessly. "Only a handful of men have I brought to the battle, but by the grace of God we are not too late. It shall not be said that Dyvnaint was absent when Arthur made an end of the invaders of Britain."

"Nor shall it be said that a kinsman of Arthur hid his head in the West when Mabon and Medraut stood by him on Badon." Gwalchmei's laughing face came nearer; he laid his hand lovingly on the shoulder of the hero, the man in the steel lorica, with the dragon-painted shield and the famous sword that had hewed the heathens in eleven great battles.

"How is it down in Dyvnaint?" asked Arthur, his eyes softening for a moment.

"It has gone ill with us, fighting from hill to hill and wood to wood—trails of blood and heaps of ashes as far as the headwaters of Axe and Tone, but Olwen and Garwen are safe among the meres at Ynys Gutrin," answered Gwalchmei.

The British army flowed out into four masses at the foot of the slope; the standards and the champions of the Cymry urged their horses up to the group beside Arthur.

"Forward, forward!" shouted Mabon. "Gwyneth breasts the hill and the sun is past noon."

"Cuneglas presses behind us; Conan is already out of sight in the combe to westward."

"The Saxon horns are blowing for battle."

A clamour of voices broke out, harsh and fiery; the ranks of the legionaries thrust their way out of the heavy fragrance of the gorse on to springy turf, the green flowery quilt of the downs that for untold centuries had given life to mankind and had been a deathbed for contending peoples. Medraut sat silent in the saddle, his drawn sword resting on his horse's mane.

'This is the trial of strength,' he thought, 'between the old Britain and the new. My arm strives for what is passing, but my mind works for what is to come, not through Cerdic, but through me. Cerdic is one Briton leading on the blind forces of destruction; if he triumphs our race will perish; but if he falls it will one day be my turn to wield the strength of both Briton and Saxon, to be the Amherawdyr both of kings in the west and kings in the east.'

The trumpets spoke shrilly and haughtily above the hum of voices and the hoarse droning notes of the Saxon horns, the Cymry moved upwards on to an out-thrust spur of Badon, the mounted men slipped from their saddles and clustered on foot round Kai with the Red Dragon. Again the trumpets sounded and the legionaries swept on, a dark silent column,

shield to shield, followed by the shouting ranks of
Powys. Steadily they climbed the great swell of the
down till with a sudden crash they struck the dense
mass of Cissa's South Saxons swaying to meet
them—grimy warriors with matted hair falling over
their shoulders, a glint of madness in their blue eyes,
and a stink about them hateful to British nostrils,
kinsman fighting beside kinsman, bellowing uncom-
prehended words like a monotonous incantation.
Slowly and rhythmically, like a man rolling a stone up
a hill, the Cymry gained ground, the lines of helmeted heads rising in a wave as they strode over the fall-
en; short stabbing strokes answered to the wild slash
of Saxon axe and sword. The Red Dragon dipped into
the great fosse of the fortress and rose again on the
ramparts, drawing nearer and nearer to Cissa's standard rocking on the windy heights like some pennoned
mast on a ship beating out a storm at sea. . . .

Meanwhile Maelgun and Erkenwine were in desperate conflict on the ridge to eastward. Three times
the spears of Gwyneth thrust the horde of seamen
back from the steep brim of the down, and three
times they went staggering down the slope again. On
the right Vortipore advanced under cover of an arrow
blast that pinned shields to the bodies of those that
held them and transfixed arms and thighs as though
they had been cheese. The men of Dyfet drew the
strongest bows in Britain, but their aim grew wild
and they sagged backwards as the West Saxons drove
down on them with whirling steel. "Kill! Kill!" burst
out a roar of guttural voices; like a great wedge
Cerdic's men clove the mass of Britons about the
White Falcon, hewing at the pale desperate faces,
coming on with wild leaps over the swathes of dead
and the wounded rolling on the turf grappling for
each other's throats. On and on they went until their
weapons crashed among the snowy boughs of
hawthorn that swallowed Vortipore's host at the foot

of the hill. And then a horn blew afresh, they turned their heads and saw another wave of men sweeping behind them along the skyline, the host of Gwent headed by the Antlered Stag and the splendid figure of Conan galloping on horseback.

Too late the West Saxons regained their post on the brow of the hill. Conan's warriors had slipped past them and charged into the turmoil where Arthur stood like a rock among beating waves on the ramparted crest of the down. To the left he heard the exultant yells of Erkenwine's men, to the right a fresh roar of gasping shouts as Cerdic clashed with the rearmost ranks of Gwent, but before him the surging mass of Saxons began to reel backwards. It was as though a door against which he threw his weight had suddenly been unbarred.

"Forward!" he shouted, striding out of the ranks and swinging his great sword aloft. Hundreds of voices answered him with the chanted words:

> "Arthur our leader;
> Christ our King!"

Faster and faster the battle rolled away from the great blood-soaked earthwork over the level sward of the downs. A blind panic was seizing the South Saxons, struck in flank by the charge of Gwent. They had had their fill of the hard hand play, they began to run, thinking of their homes above the shingly beaches of the Narrow Sea. Erkenwine's men were caught by the rush and swung round; they stared about them, looking for fresh assailants, but could see only a Red Dragon standard swaying far off above a surf of helmeted heads and rising and falling weapons. Cissa's banner was gone and Cerdic's was out of sight behind the fortress, though the notes of his horn still sounded on the wind freshening from the west. Bewildered, the sea folk broke backwards from the crest of the hill; a mass of them streamed away with the South

Saxons, but more gathered about Erkenwine in a dense ring, still confident of victory. Arthur, Gereint, and Cuneglas were pressing on side by side into the heart of the host that dissolved over the southern face of the downs. Before them lay combes dipping towards vast sweeps of woodland, bare hilltops pale in the sunshine, and blue distances verging on the sea. There was shelter in that low country, dark with the tangled crowns of oak, deep in ling, interwoven with briar and bramble; but meanwhile men who had no more heart for fight jostled and stumbled against men who still strove to make head against the champions of Britain. The fallen lay so thick that the green turf was hidden under tumbled bodies, cast-away shields, and pools of blood. Out of this undergrowth of dead and dying rose a stubborn knot of men like weather-beaten trees in a heathy brake, and thence came hard strokes and there were grim, brutish faces with clenched teeth and gleaming eyes, rugged fighters resolved not to give back another foot before the Welshmen. Arthur marked that cluster of warriors growing in the drift of battle like bees beginning to swarm on a bush; he dashed upon it with a shout. Before him sprang Gwgawn of the Ruddy Sword. Up went the axes, swords whirled and bit, Gwgawn fell cloven through the face, but Arthur burst in. Covered by two shield bearers was an old man whose helmet had been knocked off; his bald sweaty head shone in the sun, his eyes under bushy brows looked like wolf holes in a crag, he gripped an axe with both hands and hewed rhythmically to right and left. A stroke took Arthur on the helmet and brought him down on one knee, but Medraut lunged in with his sword through the matted beard. The goblin-like figure of Cissa went backwards like a falling tree; the group of Saxons reeled and vanished under the rush of the Cymry. Here and there a head showed up like a rock among breakers—steel flashed and blood spurted—and then there was nothing before the uplifted weapons but the smooth down dotted with running men.

"Victory!" shouted Arthur, wiping the blood from his eyes. Almost at his feet lay a block of sandstone bedded in the turf. He stooped and put his mouth to a hole. In a moment a deep note boomed across the down; it was as though the discordant shouts, the rattle of weapons, the twanging of bowstrings and the thud of blows were harmonised for a moment into a horrid yell coming from the earth itself, a shuddering outcry of triumph and anguish from the tormented land of Britain, like the voice of a woman at the climax of her travail.

At once an answering roar swelled up to east and west. Maelgun charged again into Erkenwine's ring of seamen, Conan turned with redoubled fury upon Cerdic. Vortipore's archers swarmed up the hill a second time, Cuneglas swung to the right and crashed into the West Saxons as they tried to regain the shelter of the great earthwork. Above the guttural rumble of Teutonic voices sounded louder and louder the British shouts, echoing Arthur's cry of victory. The battle of Badon Hill drew to its end as the sun dipped like a blood-red ball into purple haze; the downs glowed, then faded into ashen tints, a leaden greyness sank upon vast and desolate horizons. The Cymry leaped upon their horses and galloped with Arthur on his white mare Lamrei, trampling down a terror-stricken remnant of the great host that had sailed up the Thames with Erkenwine, but Cerdic and his men burst southwards into the woods, ever melting in the blast of steel that followed, them, yet shaking off pursuit by many a desperate stand in darkening glades.

Chapter XXI

The White Horse

THE BOLDNESS OF THE ENEMY WAS FOR A WHILE CHECKED,
BUT NOT THE WICKEDNESS OF OUR COUNTRYMEN.
THOU CHARIOTEER OF THE BEAR . . . CUNEGLAS.
                              —Gildas, *De Excidio Britanniae.*

That night the victors camped on the place of battle. When morning came they dispersed over the down, taking all that was worth having from dead and dying—weapons, clothes, mail, arm rings, jewelled belts and scabbards. With bandaged wounds and haggard faces Conan, Maelgun, and Vortipore came to meet Arthur and what was left of his champions, a little group standing silent about the Red Dragon. Moodily the kings drew together and looked from afar at the man who had delivered Britain; with a stab of fear they saw that Gereint and Cuneglas were already by his side. They flashed glances at Medraut who stood alone on the ramparts, his hands thrust in his belt, his eyes lifted from the wreckage of war to the cloudless vault of the sky and a lark singing overhead.

"Are we three of one mind?" said Conan in a low voice. "Are we agreed that as Arthur has lessened the

Saxon power so we shall strive to lessen his power over us?"

"Dangerous is the man who unites Dyvnaint and Powys; dangerous most of all to you, Conan," said Maelgun, biting his lips. "Honour we must do him, but let it be empty honour."

"Shall we hail him as Pendragon of Britain, as his father was?"

"The folk will follow Arthur as they never followed Uther," put in Vortipore. "Amherawdyr they call him, and if he goes farther in this war and drives the Saxons into the sea, all Britain will lie in the hollow of one hand, as it did in the hand of Maxen Guletic. It may be that he will gain power such as the Amherawdyr of Rome had in olden days and there will be no more kings in Gwent or Gwyneth. The tallest heads in Britain will fall at his bidding and the people will see us kings for what we are, wolves that take their toll of flocks and herds in every valley of the West. A new Britain he will make, guarded by the might of Cymry from the Forth to the Narrow Sea, but it will be a Britain that knows us not." Vortipore smiled and spat; he jerked his thumb towards Medraut. "There," he said, "is the man who can eat out the greatness of Arthur like a worm in the core of an apple. Let us push him on by secret means. Power he has in his tongue and in his harp, but the people have no love for him. If we set him up we can bring him down again and all will be as it was. Children we have, we three, and they shall follow in our footsteps, they shall have our heritage, maybe a greater heritage . . ." he pursed his lips and nodded in the direction of Cuneglas and Gereint. "No servants shall they be to a son of Arthur and Gwenhyvar." Slowly the three kings sauntered up to the group below the Red Dragon.

For an hour Arthur reasoned with these men, the masters of Britain, who had come together in dread of the Saxons, but who now breathed freely again. He told them that this was their chance to free the land, to win back all that had been lost in a hundred years of war. Let the army march on London, hold the passages of the Thames, and then work through southern Britain, destroying the Jutes and the Saxons. After that they could turn north and clear the east coast right up to Berneich.

"Who is to rule these new realms that we shall conquer?" asked Maelgun in a tone of subtle mockery. "Who is to people them if we slaughter the Saxons?"

"Great champions you have under your standard," said Vortipore smoothly, "but less is your host by many a warrior lying on Badon. Have you strength to take the East in your own hands, Arthur? For we cannot hold it with the folk that dwell behind Severn and Coit Mawr."

"I would gladly stretch the British power to the end of the Narrow Sea," said Gereint, "but it is useless for me to try alone. We have shaken the South Saxons and killed their king, but not a man have we mown down of the Jutes on Ynys Gweith or the Jutes in Kent, and for all that we know, Cerdic and Erkenwine are still alive."

"I see no reason to help Gereint to greater power," remarked Conan. "An evil neighbour he has been to me for many a year."

"Were I to set out eastward from Pengwern," said Cuneglas, "in a hundred miles of heath and forest I should find nothing worth taking."

"Did I not tell you, Arthur, that there is no Britain left?" said Medraut, breaking an uneasy silence. "There is only Gwyneth, Dyfet, Gwent and Powys, and there is Dyvnaint, and there is Reged, Elmet, and Strathclyde. True it is that a man may yet ride on British ground from Alcluyd to Caer Isc, but from each knot of cloudy hills hatred streams out on the wind, and Briton points his weapon at

Briton, disputing his share of the western wilderness and forgetting that the land out eastward is filling up with new people. And from those plains in the east, the good ploughing land and the sheep walks of the bare hills, was Britain ruled in the past and so she will be again."

The kings scowled and turned their backs. They walked away in a group from which the voice of Cuneglas sounded loudest and angriest. Arthur and Medraut stood alone under the Red Dragon; they looked at each other doubtfully, their eyes wandered away to the corpses lying grey and stiff on the green turf, to distant horizons harsh and sharp like sword edges under rain clouds drifting from the sea.

"It could be done," said Arthur at last, "but I am not the man to do it. I cannot make them trust me, these tyrants; their hearts are heavy with hatred and guile. Each thinks only of how this victory will profit him, not of what it may do for the British race."

"You have given them peace for many a long year; that will be the fruit of Badon Hill: but how will they use it?" said Medraut, smiling.

"They will use it in war against each other." Arthur stood with downcast eyes, his hands resting on his sheathed sword.

"And you will stand by and watch ruin swallow the West as it has already swallowed the East?"

"What strength have I to do otherwise?" said Arthur, staring at the shrunken companies of the Cymry sitting listlessly on the ramparts.

"The people are for you if the kings are not. Even among them you have friends. Gereint and Cuneglas would come to your side. Your name is famous in Pictland and Eiré. You have power if you care to use it, power to raise armies, power to be the master of both Briton and Saxon."

"As Satan tempted Christ on the top of a high hill, so you tempt me, Medraut. Shall I save our people by

stirring up a war ten-fold greater than the one that
has fretted the marches of Powys and Gwent these
many years; a war that might make me guletic over
valleys full of graves from Reged to Kernou?"

"I shall say no more than this, Arthur. Since we
raised the Red Dragon on Moel Fre I have stood by
you in battle and in council. It may be I saved your
life yesterday when Cissa's axe rose and fell like a
smith's hammer on the heads of the Cymry. I have
been content to see your fame grow till you have
become the foremost man in this land, a man whose
name will be on our people's lips while the British
race endures, but I have a foreboding that your star
has reached its zenith. The Arthur of the twelve battles has finished his course. Men will say of him that
he turned back the tide of ruin flowing from the East
for a few years, perhaps for a generation. He did
more than any Briton has done before or since. But
that is little beside what he might do if he had the
will, the hard heart and the daring spirit. A fresh
course you must set yourself, Arthur. There must be
one Amherawdyr who stands alone, high above the
heads of all other men as this Red Dragon stands
high above the hosts on Badon. King you shall use
to beat down king, and the Saxons you shall make
your servants, not the servants of men like Cerdic.
You shall send priests among the heathen, not warriors with spear and torch, you shall blend East
with West and build a new Britain, a Britain at
peace from sea to sea, strong in her own might, like
some island crag unshaken by the waves that have
swept the old world of Rome. Begin to-day! Sound
your trumpets and speak to the army from these
ramparts; tell our people as much as it is good for
them to know, and thousands will come to your
side. As for those that stand against you, Maelgun's
men, or Vortipore's, we shall hew them down on top
of the slaughtered Saxons."

"And what if I stand aside and keep my hands from the shedding of British blood? What then, Medraut?" Arthur looked fixedly at his nephew—the man with sombre eyes in a face of girlish beauty.

"Then others will make the attempt. Perhaps Cerdic, perhaps Maelgun . . . but to none will the task be easier than it is to you on Badon Hill."

"To-day comes the parting of our ways," said Arthur. His face had the set, stubborn look that it wore when he stood before the people on Moel Fre. "A man may take it upon him to do as you counsel me to do and good may come of it; but for good or ill I am not that man."

'The hero,' said Medraut to himself, 'the man of principle, the man who is too proud or too dull-witted to use the weapons dear to the Briton, lies and treachery—the saint, perhaps, most certainly the fool . . .'

Back came the kings with smiling faces. Vortipore spoke first:

"Though we are against you, Arthur, in your plan to lead our armies eastward, we all say with one accord that yours is the glory for the battles on Badon. Your work it is that our realms are safe and our foemen fled."

"A gift I offer you," said Gereint. "My palace of Camelot and land around it to support the men of your army in days of peace."

"And I bid you to Pengwern. A guest you shall be in my halls as long as it pleases you," said Cuneglas.

"And the gates of Caerleon are open to you," said Conan.

"Let us set a mark on Badon that shall be seen in ages to come," said Maelgun. "With our axes let us pare away the turf down there on the steepest slope, where Arthur led the attack. We shall cut into the chalk and make the white figure of a galloping horse with the head turned to the east—Arthur's mare, Lamrei."

"My task it shall be to lay out the figure," said Cuneglas gaily, "for I have here a model from ancient times . . ." He drew off a gold chain from about his neck and showed a coin on it—a gold coin of Cunobelin, on which was embossed a galloping horse copied perhaps from some design minted in far-away Macedonia.

Arthur looked gloomily from one face to another—fear or malice veiled by jovial adulation. Behind the princes in their soiled finery moved a column of shaven monks chanting dolefully in Latin. The melody faded away on the wide spaces of sunlit down as they dispersed to succour the wounded and comfort the dying. Women followed them with a miserable clamour, searchers for missing husbands, sons, brothers, or lovers. Overhead circled black birds: there was a cawing of crows, the occasional hoarse croak of a raven.

Badon Hill was a battlefield like other battlefields, he thought, only a greater slaughter, a greater victory, but to what purpose? It might have been the turning point in Britain's story, the beginning of a new age; but these men whom he had brought together for a day, these Celtic chieftains, the tyrants of the West, they had lost the splendid vision of Britannia—the peaceful land of Roman days, armed against barbarous invaders, secure in the strength of fleets and fortresses, full of industrious folk: cultivators, merchants, and craftsmen. What were they but men greedy for power, reckless squanderers of the nation's strength in raid and rapine, in bickerings among those blue hills that still daunted the sluggish Saxons? What he had done on Badon had saved these men from destruction; they thanked him by cutting an image on the down, and then all would be as it was . . .

* * *

The British army had turned its backs on Badon. Above the smooth skyline drifted a cloud of birds, and a sweetish stench of unburied bodies tainted the warm breeze that spread abroad the heady summery smell of hawthorn and gorse, Farther and farther the masses of tribal soldiery rolled away through the cool woods, turning their heads to look back from each rise at the pale line of downs sinking towards the horizon, a grey wave with a gleam of foam, the grotesque figure of the White Horse—a bleak enigmatic imprint from the death struggle of a nation.

The gates of Caer Ceri were thrown wide; an exultant roar of voices came from the walls—voices of old men, women and children. From the archway emerged a ramshackle chariot drawn by two dispirited horses, covered with sores and with ribs standing out like scythe marks on a meadow. Arthur got down from Lamrei and mounted the chariot, Cuneglas took the reins, and they drove into the old city, the huge figure of Kai marching ahead with the Red Dragon, Maelgun, Conan, Vortipore, and Gereint following behind on horseback, and behind them standards and slanting spears and shaggy heads and grim faces as far as the eye could reach. Trumpets blared out and horns boomed in the tunnel-like entry through the walls, a crude and childish echo of Imperial Rome, the dying notes of Mediterranean culture in the darkening world of the West.

The column swayed from side to side of the broad street, avoiding masses of ruin that had collapsed forward into the roadway. Half-starved cattle chewing at docks and nettles scuffled out of the track, a flock of geese hissed and cackled beside the chariot wheels, savage and brutish faces looked out from smoke-blackened doorways like vermin lurking in their burrows. Here and there above the wilderness of sagging roofs rose precariously some carved façade, garlanded with fern and corded with ivy. The Forum was nothing but a vast rubbish heap surrounded by cliff-like fragments of great buildings. Pigeons nested in the rows of beam holes, and goats climbed over the screes of fallen stone stripping leaves and bark from innumerable ash saplings. The chariot halted, and Arthur stared about him over the heads of the army crowding into the open space like sheep blindly flowing into a fold.

"This place has been one of the brightest jewels in Britain," he said, half to himself. "What is it now but stones and filth?"

Cuneglas looked at him as though uncomprehending. It was of no interest to him what Caer Ceri had been once, any more than it was to the pigeons and goats that housed in its desolation.

"Here we have food and drink, women, and roofs to sleep under," he said in a tone of ferocious gaiety. He dropped the reins on the backs of the horses, stretched himself and yawned. "Our work is done. We shall feast here and then it will be every man to his home."

Chapter XXII

The Shadow of Sin

Hints from the *Vitae* of Saint Cadoc and Saint Carannog, and from the *Red Book of Hergest.*

It was an autumn morning with gleams of sunshine and ragged clouds trailing from the tops of Cantuck and Exmoor across the channel. The tide was running out; a northerly wind whirled the sand on the beaches of Morganuc and flecked the dark sea with little crests of foam. From the salt-bitten copses along the shore came an old man, bare-headed and bare-legged, with a patched cloak girt about him by a belt of raw cowhide. Slowly and laboriously he rolled a round table towards the sea, oak boards pegged to heavy battens, that taxed his strength to the utmost as it plunged into heaps of seaweed and sank deeply in the sloppy sand. He paused to take breath and his eye fell upon another man coming along the desolate beach from the east, a man in the rough dress of a shepherd or woodcutter; there was, however, a defiant flash in his dark blue eyes and he carried a naked sword in his hand.

"Is there room for two on your raft?" said the newcomer, his handsome face breaking into a smile.

"This is no raft, but an altar to set before God," muttered the old man in answer, as he wrenched the table forward over crackling shells into the shallow, swirling water. "I shall set it afloat and if God wills I shall see it drift away on the sea."

The younger man put his shoulder to the table and forced it on through the breaking waves. He let it fall sideways and float. With boyish zeal he thrust it into deeper water and watched it beginning to drive out on the tide.

"Gulls and shags are the only priests that will serve at that altar," he said with a tolerant laugh, coming up dripping on to the sands.

"You are no peasant," said the old man, regarding him gloomily. "You have the look of some guletic living in strife and sin, but you have done me a service and I thank you."

"The service was small, yet I will ask for one in return. Are there fishermen on these shores, men who have a boat that would carry me over the sea?" He jerked a thumb towards the blue, clouded hills that rose dimly above tossing waves and gusts of spray.

"There is a boat in the next river mouth," said the old man, pointing westward. "I have begged the men that own it to take me across the water, but they fear the wind and they fear the folk that dwell on the other side. My purpose is to go ashore in Dyvnaint and seek until I find my altar cast up by the waves. There I shall build a church and preach to the people, who I hear are little better than heathen."

"I shall persuade those fishermen to take us, either with gold or with this sword! You are right, a guletic I am reckoned, cousin to Arthur, Gwalchmei by name, and Conan's men would take my life if they had the chance. If we get safely across I will help you to find the altar, and I will speak for you with Cadwy, Gereint's son, who rules among those hills. True it is that we in Dyvnaint have little cause to welcome folk from Gwent or Morganuc, but you are doubtless a holy man, who can work wonders by the grace of God. Different you look from the haughty monks in Bangor ys Coit who seek favours from Maelgun with great gifts of corn and cattle."

"The humblest of God's servants am I, Carannog. From Dyfet I come, driven forth by Vortipore because I reproved him for his evil life."

"I would reprove him, not with words, but with sharp steel! An enemy he has been to Arthur these twelve years since the fight on Badon Hill."

"Vain and foolish are the tyrants of Britain, battling together like blackcock in some forest glade; but worse it is when those with power are enemies of God as well as of man."

"You are old, Carannog," said Gwalchmei, as they walked westward along the edge of the wet sand, "your strength is nearly gone, you are not moved by the red lips and shining eyes of women; the smooth flank of a girl does not tempt your hand any more than the shining bark of a birch tree. Your eyes are not turned outward to the splendours and perils of the world, but inward to the spirit contending with the will of God as an unruly horse struggles against its master. Vain and foolish we seem to you, we men who have fought the Saxons and who now have our fill of all the good things that are left in the land of Britain, the glitter of gold, swift horses, hounds and falcons, fine clothes and keen weapons, the joy of music and storytelling and witty talk, the glory of famous deeds, and the love of fair women. Shall we leave all this and spend our days in fasting and our nights in prayer, we men whose blood runs so hotly that we do not feel the pricking of sin?"

He turned his gleaming eyes on the old man and laughed, throwing up the sword and catching it by the hilt. Something there was in him of the brightness of the sun, the violence of the wind, and the harshness of breaking waves—the man of his time, clutching with greedy fingers at the good things of life in a darkening world.

"It is easy for me to read your mind and the minds of men like you," said Carannog quietly. "I am the son of a guletic who wore the golden torque; I have felt all that you feel, pride, lust, and hatred, but now it has been revealed to me that all this is no more than a fire crackling in dry twigs—in a moment it is gone and nothing remains but sparks and ashes whirled away by the winds of God."

* * *

Arthur and his champions, Bedwyr and Kai, rode along the shore towards the hills of Cantuch, escorted from the palace of Dindraithov by Cadwy and a couple of armed men. Deerhounds and boarhounds padded beside them over the shingle, but the party were not out to hunt in the swampy forest that rolled away inland, a sea of russet-coloured oak and full green alder; they were in quest of an outlaw who had his lair in some combe among those high wild hills. He was a Saxon, Worm by name, left behind when Cerdic raided Dyvnaint, and for twelve years he had maintained himself in Cantuch as a hunter and plunderer, ravishing girls in the forest cots and killing not a few of the men who came in search of him.

It was a lowering autumn day with squalls whipping the spray from the breakers that fell with a sullen crash on the beach. The horsemen pulled their flapping cloaks round their knees and bent their heads to the wind, pushing on in silence with set, indifferent faces. It was little pleasure to Arthur to ride with five men hunting one Saxon; he still hoped to lead armies against the invaders of Britain who sat firm if inactive in the East. There had been peace in the land since Badon Hill, but now there were rumours of a stir among the heathen. Every year saw fresh shiploads of men, women and children putting in at the river mouths on the North Sea. Erkenwine had been hailed as king over all the land between the ruined cities of London and Camalodunum. There the East Saxons, as they were called, were building up a state that bid fair to rival the older and more prosperous settlements of the Jutes in Kent. The West Saxons had been driven from the upper Thames, but Cerdic had saved a remnant of his people by retiring to the sea, fusing them with the Wightwaras on Ynys Gweith and the Meonwaras on the mainland, Jutish settlers who had won a foothold there in the days of Emrys. The land he held was too small for the host that dwelt in it, and as more and more men flocked to him from abroad the war bands came plundering up to the gates of Sarum and lapped once more about the downs where the grass grew green over the graves of Badon. It was time to strike again at these folk who did not know when they were beaten, but the eyes of the Britons were turned in another direction—they watched anxiously the growing power of Maelgun and, forgetting the Saxons, they nerved themselves for a fresh trial of strength between Gwent and Dyvnaint.

A changed man was the Arthur who rode the old war horse Lamrei along the featureless shores of Carrun. Some splendour had gone from him, the exaltation of a mighty enterprise that had shone in his face, kindling the people as by a supernatural force and bending the princes against their own will. Now he was the battered warrior brooding on the failure of his hopes, plunged alternately in gloom or in ferocious gaiety, squandering in trivial adventure the energy that might have ruled Britain.

A bank of rougher shingle made the riders turn towards the sea. The horses splashed through pools left by the ebbing tide and threaded their way among heaps of weed and driftwood.

Suddenly Arthur drew rein. He pointed to a great disc stranded between green-scummed rocks—thick boards of oak wrought together and trimmed by skilful carpentry. Kai dismounted and wrenched the woodwork out of the sand; he stood it up on edge and said laughingly:

"A table, Arthur! The sea has cast up a table for you to sit at and feed your champions!"

"A table it shall be such as we made for ourselves on the turf by Eamont Water," said Arthur. "I will have it sent to Camelot; a worthy board it is for my men to sit by—the men who delivered Britain." His voice dropped to a sullen note.

"Let us eat here," said Bedwyr. "It is a hungry air that blows across the water from the land of Vortipore."

Cadwy's servants propped the table on the low rocks; from their packs they took out chased silver cups and cakes of oatmeal and set them round the board, but a sudden spray-laden blast whirled everything off on to the sands. In a moment the table was bare again.

"The thing is bewitched!" exclaimed Cadwy. "Let us leave it where we found it."

"To Camelot it shall go!" said Arthur, striking the board with his fist. "If I am stinted by the rulers of Britain I shall at least take what the sea casts at my feet. A sign it may be that our fellowship shall endure and yet prove fruitful, that Britain shall some day have need of the champions that live in ease on the round hill under Coit Mawr."

Kai and Bedwyr took the disc of oak between them and carried it up the beach above high-water mark. The others broke the food with their hands and ate in the blustering wind; they clashed the silver cups together and drank the sharp-tasting mead poured from a leather bottle. The pair of warriors came back and pointed along the beach to a solitary horseman coming at a fast trot from the direction of Dindraithov, a dusky hump with smoke trails rising against the tumbled heights of Exmoor.

"Here comes Gwalchmei!" said Arthur, his face lighting up with a flash of gladness. "Seldom he comes without news to stir our blood in these days of idleness. Welcome, cousin! On what perilous quest have you been, faring away from wife and child and our company at Camelot?"

"From Gwent I come," said Gwalchmei gaily. "Perilous indeed was my mission in Conan's land; my life hung by a hair, yet I have had my fill of feasting and love, and I bring back to Olwen the gold she lost when Conan snatched at her beauty, years ago before we rode to Badon." He pulled up his sleeve to show a golden arm ring with the lettering MAGLOCUNI DONUM.

"A treasure indeed, with some strong spell graven upon it, doubtless," said Cadwy, looking enviously at the gold.

"With this Olwen paid for a passage over Severn, when Conan's huntsmen chased her to the shore. Now that time hangs heavy on our hands and the battle trumpets are silent on the Saxon march I resolved to go adventuring and win it back. Disguised I rode through Gwent, west from Caer Gloui, till I found the fishermen who had taken Olwen on their boat. The gold was theirs no longer; it had been the death of several men and Conan had robbed them of it, giving it to a girl of his choice at Caerleon. A guest I was for weeks in Conan's halls; the women liked me, for I have a ready tongue and no grey hairs on my head as Conan has. They laugh at the long faces of the monks, those girls in Caerleon, for lust is their delight as it is mine, and what can a guletic do in days of peace save make love where it is welcome? A free gift I had of the gold and more besides, all that a girl can give to the man that takes her fancy, but we were spied upon, and swift and secret are the servants that do Conan's bidding. I got a good horse from Conan's stable and rode him till he dropped, and then on the shore of Morganuc I found a holy man seeking a passage to Dyvnaint. I helped him to launch a wooden altar in the sea and we followed after in a fisherman's boat. On these beaches of Carrun we parted, he to look for his altar and I to find Olwen at Camelot. I gave her the gold, but she gave it back to me, saying it was the gift of her father Maelgun Gwyneth, and that it might some day help me to make my peace with him."

"Did she like your way of winning it?" said Bedwyr with a smile.

Gwalchmei shrugged his shoulders. "What am I but as other men? Is there faithfulness in Britain today save the faithfulness of us warriors to our Amherawdyr, Arthur? From Camelot I rode to find him at Dindraithov, and now I will follow him again wherever he goes, to war as I hope, for Gwent is like an angry hive of bees and it will not be long before Conan's standard is seen in these sleepy combes of Dyvnaint."

"Gereint's bow shall bring down the Antlered Stag!" said Cadwy fiercely. "Let Gwent beware; we are strong enough to take everything from them this side of Severn."

"This Conan is the bane of Britain," muttered Kai. "Uther would have taken him from his days long ere this."

"It was the charge of Gwent that turned the tide on Badon," said Arthur. "The tide will come again, and from what I see the men that have to battle with it will be few and weary, looking over their shoulders lest comrades stab them in the back. These people of

Britain, how can they be saved? They are a flock of sheep whose shepherds are no better than wolves."

"Break the princes and rule yourself," said Kai bluntly. "The folk will follow Arthur today as they followed him when we raised the Red Dragon on Moel Fre."

"The folk love you, but they hate one another; envy and hatred burn like a fever in the blood of the Britons from Penwith to Strathclyde. Kinsman stands by kinsman and blow will answer blow . . ." said Cadwy, thrusting his spear viciously into the sand.

"It could be done," muttered Bedwyr, "and there are men that have a mind to do it."

"Our race grows to a mighty power in Armorica," said Gwalchmei. "Go there, Arthur, and raise an army that may win back what we have lost to the Saxons. At its head you can overawe the kings so that they walk beside you like hounds on leash beside the huntsmen."

"We bow to Arthur in Dyvnaint, but we bow to no host that he may bring from overseas," said Cadwy, staring challengingly at Gwalchmei.

"Once more I will try what may be done by words of warning—at Lis Pengwern and at Deganwy," said Arthur gloomily.

"It needs a wolf to reason with wolves," said Kai.

"Or a serpent, such as Medraut, he who sits with Conan, biding his time at Caerleon," put in Bedwyr.

"Too subtle is the mind of Medraut, too rash is yours, Gwalchmei. With Kai and Bedwyr shall I go, men honoured for glorious deeds, ill-wished by none in Britain; but first shall we seek this evildoer in Cantuch." He pointed to the dark hills blurred by mist and spray blowing from the sea.

"Two folk I see coming westwards along the beach," said Cadwy. "It may be that they can give us news."

The group turned to the horses and leaned upon the saddle, ready to mount, and as they did so a gleam of sun broke out through the racing clouds and fell on the newcomers, a frail-looking, grey-bearded man who held in his hand a slip of willow plaited round the neck of his companion.

"A strange huntsman walks here with a stranger hound on leash," said Cadwy. "What make you of that yellow-haired monster walking tamely with empty hands?"

"He is none other than Worm the Outlaw," said one of the servants. "I should know him again after exchanging blows with him on a forest path by Longborth."

"And I know the old man," said Gwalchmei. "He is Carannog, the hermit with whom I sailed from Abertaff. Welcome, holy man! A worker in magic you must be that you can lead the Yellow Beast of Cantuch on a band of willow!"

"What power I have is of God's giving," answered Carannog. "It avails more than heathen magic or the might of swords in the hands of warriors. I have spoken with this man Worm and he has given himself into my hands to make his peace with those he has wronged. For years he has lived in blindness and sin, but now, by the grace of God, his eyes are opened."

"He sees well enough that his time is up, now that Arthur has come from Camelot to make an end of him," said Cadwy scornfully, stepping forward with levelled spear. "We shall fix his head on the highest rooftree in Dindraithov."

The great brawny figure of the Saxon stood impassive, but his dull blue eyes wandered anxiously from the armed men to the hermit.

"You shall do him no harm," said Carannog in a stern voice. "Where God has been merciful, shall man be less so? A curse I lay on him, whether prince or peasant, who strikes at this man now that he has put aside his garment of sin, confiding himself to the humblest of God's servants."

"A Saxon!" said Arthur, lowering his bushy brows. "Too many marks I have on my body from Saxon swords and axes; too many heaps of British bones there are under brake and briar!"

A sudden growl came from the knot of Cymry; their teeth showed in their beards, their eyes gleamed wolfishly as hatred clouded their minds like the fume of strong drink, hatred for this race of blond, slow-witted men whose heavy hands had battered down the old Brittannia. Carannog took a swift step forward; his eyes flashed too, reflecting a fierceness of spirit that matched itself against the warriors' blind lust for killing.

"They are one flock, those who put faith in Christ! It is not for you to shed the blood of men that bow to the living God!" he cried. "You princes that boast of slaughters you have made in years gone by, what have you achieved? You are as men threshing the seas with flails. The sea of heathendom flows deep over Britain and will flow yet further; it is not to be turned back by the blowing of Arthur's trumpets nor by swords wielded in sinful hands. I say to you that Britain shall not be delivered till men of our faith go out among the heathen and spread the word of our God upon the waters. Let this be a sign to you, that I, a feeble old man, have taken captive this outlaw who has defied you men of the sword for twelve years; I have cast out the devil that made him no better than a savage beast of the forest, I have broken his proud spirit, not with sharp-edged steel but with gentle words, promising him God's mercy and the fellowship of Christian men."

Arthur stared grimly at the impassioned face of the hermit and at the heavy-featured Saxon, comprehending nothing except that his enemies were baulked in their desire to take his life. He stood there inert and incurious, scratching after lice in his beard, as a horse stands flicking its tail at flies when freed of its rider's weight, the nagging bit and the sudden thrust of spurred heels. Could a nation of men such as these be turned from their deadly work by the preaching of a few monks? Yet perhaps it was equally impossible that they should be subdued with the sword by a people that sucked up sin and treachery with their mother's milk. He gave a bitter laugh and vaulted into the saddle.

"Come, Bedwyr and Kai!" he shouted. "Our business is not to reason with holy men, but to gather the Britons to war. God's favour we must seek, not by ringing bells and mumbling prayers in the wilderness, but by daring deeds that shall prove us worthy to keep our heritage and hand it on to our children, begotten in sin, maybe, but blood of our blood, and not the brood of these wild beasts from overseas. Farewell, Cadwy and Gwalchmei! You shall hear of us soon in the North, guesting at Pengwern and Deganwy."

The three riders went off at a gallop and were soon lost to view among the fringes of wind-tortured scrub that crept down to long banks of seawrack and driftwood.

"Your altar is here, Carannog," said Cadwy, a shade of mockery in his voice. "Arthur found it. He would have had it taken to Camelot, a board for champions to feast at; but here it lies. Build a church on Carrun's shore if you will, and pray for us sinners in Dindraithov."

"That I shall do with this man's help," said Carannog, lifting the willow band from the Saxon's neck. The outlaw seemed to breathe more freely now that the grim-looking warriors were out of sight; he stood looking from face to face truculently, his hands thrust in his belt, but as Carannog turned away he turned also and walked behind like a well-trained hound.

* * *

At sunset Arthur and his men rode out of the woods on to a little green hill: the last boss of the uplands declining to the great tidal swamps that lay in sheets of leaden water and yellow reeds, dotted with scrubby islets—a domain of birds and fish as far as the faint blue rampart of Coit Mawr. At the foot of the hill was a grove of gnarled fruit trees and in it a farmery from the old Roman days, where broken walls still supported roofs of thatch and firelight shone out from gaping doorways.

"The house of Indec, the harlot," said Bedwyr, with a laugh. "No bad place for overnighting, as many travellers have found."

"I have not set eyes on her," said Arthur, pulling in his tired horse and staring absently at the plain out of which rose with vague and occult significance the solitary tor of Ynys Gutrin.

"A lovely woman, still young, but childless. Her husband fell in the war with Cerdic twelve years ago. They say she cares little for the pleasure of lying in bed with strange men, but longs for children. . . ." The words came to Arthur on the breath of sour marshland air, dreamy and melancholy, stirring in his mind old visions of tenderness and delight that had faded in bitter years of war. Children—what children had he to be inspired by their father's powers, carried forward to fame in the radiance of what was fast becoming a glorious legend among all the Celtic peoples of the West? He remembered his carefree youth in Kernou, passing swiftly from place to place in hunting or in war, how women had given him love—a black-haired girl going barefoot on green pathways in the gorse brakes of Trevalga. . . . They had met often and clung together, tormented by a passion that seemed unappeasable in that drowsy warmth of springtime, breathing in the fierce scent of gorse and hearing the gentle murmur of a glittering sea. Gwyll her name was, and for a year or two when he thought of her soot-black head of hair resting on his arm and her body fretting impatiently against his, there came to him afresh the smell of gorse and of sun-dried seaweed. Perhaps she had borne him a child—he had hardly thought of it till now. There had been other women whose names he had forgotten, and there, across the marsh was Gwenhyvar, sitting gloomy-eyed and childless in the hall at Camelot; Gwenhyvar whose beauty was sung by all the bards of Britain, the woman who was his, but who brought him no joy now that power had slipped from his grasp. It was as though her proud spirit would not let her rear a child for the man who had been great enough to save Britain, but too simple-minded to make himself master of what he had saved. . . . She had lost his child. And so there was only Lacheu, Garwen's son, a boy brought up in Gereint's household at Sarum, slim and lovely as a young tree in spring, delighting in music and horses and skill with the bow, a little flickering torch kindled in the windy dusk of Britain, and how easily blown out in the first gust of war!

The glow in the west faded, withered leaves rustled sadly in the skirts of the forest, earth, water and sky began to fuse into greyness under the full moon. The horses shivered and tugged at their bits, turning their heads with pricked ears towards the lights in the harlot's house; and Arthur felt an oppression of dark ironic powers brooding on man's futility, powers that looked with the same indifference on the saint praying by his altar and on the warrior pitting himself against hopeless odds. 'The trees shed their leaves and green again in the spring,' he thought, 'but what man creates is all torn down in a little while, his purposes are blotted out as footsteps on a beach vanish under the flowing waves.'

"Weary men are we, Amherawdyr," said Kai. "Let us go down and take our ease in yonder firelight."

"Where shall we go to escape our fate?" muttered Arthur.

"There is a saying among the heathen that a doomed man's death is everywhere," laughed Bedwyr, "but we three have luck with us and have proved it in many a desperate hazard. Come, which of us shall sleep with the woman to-night?"

"Let it rest on a throw of the dice you carry with you," said Kai.

Bedwyr took out dice from his pouch. In turn they shook them in hollowed hands and stared at the result on outspread palms in the pale moonshine. It was Arthur that got the highest throw.

He laughed indifferently and gave Lamrei her head.

As they rode down the hill he said to himself: 'If I fail now to knit the kings together and a new war comes of Briton against Briton, I will follow Gwalch-mei's counsel and strive to build up a fresh power in Armorica. I will take Lacheu with me and keep him safe awhile across the sea.'

Chapter XXIII

Anir

An interpretation from the *Mirabilia* of Nennius.

A young man rode up to the outer gateway in the stockades of Camelot. His face was handsome and crafty, with the furtive look of some savage animal in unaccustomed surroundings, his hair had that glossy blackness most often seen in the far west, his clothes were coarse and dirty like a peasant's, and he rode a pony so small that his feet all but touched the slough of mud and filth that lay in the sunken entry to the fortress. For arms he had a heavy-shafted spear and a naked knife stuck in his belt. Glewlwyd, a grey-haired warrior from Reged, scarred with wounds taken at Badon and the Broch of Guinion, stood in the path of the rider like some battered tower.

"What is your business in Camelot, young man?" he said in a tone half-mocking, half-surly.

"I seek Arthur," said the other, with a flash of defiance in his dark beady eyes.

"What is your name?"

"It is Anir men call me."

"And what have such as you to say to Arthur yr Amherawdyr?"

"That is for Arthur's ears and not for yours."

The old legionary grinned and laid a hand on the pony's bridle as a blow of the heel urged it into the gateway. He looked hard in the face of the young man and his jeering smile faded.

"By your voice you are from Kernou," he said questioningly.

"From Kernou I come, and I must see Arthur!" The soft voice rose in sudden passion.

"Then turn back, for Arthur is not in Camelot."

The youth sat motionless in the saddle; then suddenly he said: "I will see Gwenhyvar."

Slowly and doubtfully the watchman stood aside and let the rider go past, pressing his beast impatiently up the curving road under the inner rampart. Other men came stooping out of a beehive hut and stared likewise.

"A stranger from Kernou," muttered the northern warrior, "riding like a peasant, but haughty as some guletic famous in war. His face made me think of Arthur as I saw him first, under the standard on Moel Fre."

Anir drew rein on top of the hill; he got off the pony and let it wander away among the huts and rubbish heaps. With his head in the air he strode among snarling dogs and through groups of children pelting each other with filth, kicking bladders about, shooting blunt arrows at cattle that grazed hungrily on the short turf. From a taller building of wattle and daub came the sound of a harp and of men's and women's voices rising and falling in some dreary chant about Maxen Guletic. Rhythmically came a few words in unison, sometimes in a murmur of despair, like some magical incantation of dubious meaning, hypnotic in its effect as the fruitless pulse of breakers on immutable sands. The young man stepped through the open doorway into smoky gloom. He saw couches of fern spread with deerskins, dusky figures lolling against the walls with a glow of firelight upon their faces, hands that held drinking horns, hands that flitted monotonously about distaffs. The smouldering oak logs burst into tongues of flame at the thrust of a spear shaft, and Anir found himself standing before a woman whose hands lay in her lap, toying with two great plaits of golden hair, a woman lovely, calm, and disdainful, whose upturned face had the freshness of apple blossom, whose dark eyes regarded him steadily, with a brooding stare as though he had been of no more account than some dog that had strayed in from the courtyard.

The voices died away, the harper played a few full chords and there was silence in the great hall of Camelot. Awkwardly Anir went down on one knee.

"I seek Arthur," he said. His voice was loud, but trembled a little. He had not thought that there were women like this, as different from the lively, easygoing women of Kernou, as a stately beech tree is different from pliant birches swaying in the wind.

"You must seek for Arthur elsewhere than in Camelot," the woman answered after a long pause.

"Do I speak with Gwenhyvar?"

"I am she."

"Lies cannot fall from your lips, though I would not take the word of the man at the gate. . . . Tell me, lady, where I may find Arthur."

"He is far away, maybe in Caer Isc or Dindraithov. Speak out; what message do you bring us? Is it war with Gwent?" she said with sudden impatience.

"The land is quiet where I come from, far west in Kernou; there is no talk of war. I bring no news, but I ask a favour that none but Arthur can grant."

"Few ask favours of Arthur in these days and few he has to grant. Go rather to Conan or to Maelgun

if you would serve a master of armies," she said
bitterly.

"Arthur is the Amherawdyr of Britain and I am his
son Anir, born within the walls of Dinmelioc in Kernou,"
he said in a ringing voice. There was dead silence, then
a muttering of voices all round the hall.

"If what you say be true, then some women, it
seems, are luckier than I, Arthur's wife sitting alone
in Camelot."

The face of Gwenhyvar flushed darkly; she raised
her hand as though to thrust the young man away
from her.

"The son of Arthur and of Gwyll I am, and I can
prove it by this ring on my finger, that Arthur gave my
mother when he lay with her by Trebarwith Strand!"

"A ring proves little, but your face proves much,"
said Gwenhyvar venomously. "What is the favour you
will ask of the man who spends his days drinking
with Cadwy and his nights in the arms of dirty harlots?" A murmur sounded along the lines of forward-
craning heads, and all of a sudden the harp rang out
to Medraut's melody on Moel Fre. "Cymry in victory;
Cymry in woe."

"I shall ask of him the golden torque of a guletic," said Anir firmly. "A good horse, a sword that
will cleave the shields of the Saxons. It is I that
shall lead the Cymry to war when the arm of Arthur
grows weary."

Gwenhyvar laughed scornfully. "You strut well
like a young gamecock! Perhaps you will ask Arthur
to find you a wife, some girl with king's blood in her
who is not too nice to teach a peasant woman's son
the arts of love," she said, wrinkling her nose.

"I have chosen already the woman who shall be
my wife and she is the match of any in this hall save
you, lady."

"What is her name, then?"

"Indec is her name; broad lands she has and many servants by the mere-side beyond Longborth," he said with boyish insolence.

There was a titter, a mumble of angry voices that Gwenhyvar silenced with a gesture of her hand.

"You have chosen well, Anir!" she said coldly. "Let base blood mate with filth; and now begone from Camelot."

* * *

Late that night Anir, riding the trackway that pointed towards Dindraithov, turned in among the scraggy apple trees about Indec's farm. He knew the place well for he had spent ten days there on his way up from Kernou. Indec had been his from the first night, and the simple promptings of lust had grown swiftly in his untutored mind to a violent passion. A beautiful woman, practised in all the arts of beguiling inexperienced manhood, elusive, yielding, gay, melancholy, lively in wit, dainty in her habits: every aspect of her was strange and exciting to a boy brought up among half-savage villagers between the great moors and the Atlantic cliffs. He longed to prove his worth before Indec, that he was not only Arthur's son, but one who could pit himself against champions, endure pain and deal out mighty blows. The only chance he had got was when an ugly old man rode up to the door and called out words that made Indec turn crimson with shame and anger. Anir understood little of his meaning, but he struck the old man with his fist, knocked him off his horse into a midden and trampled him down till he was nearly suffocated. And when the old man was gone in a cloud of stink, Indec had taken him indoors and washed him from head to foot in hot water, a thing that had never been done to him in his life before. With tenderness, with subtleties she had begun to turn him from a brutal and ignorant peasant into a man in whom she could take pleasure, for Indec, for good or ill, had cherished a few sparks of the old Roman culture lingering in obscure corners of Britain long after its self-consuming fires had been trodden underfoot by Scot, Pict, and Saxon. She had made her mark upon Anir; he was enchanted and bewildered, and he hurried back to her like a moth to the candle flame after his glimpse of jeering savagery at Camelot. Gwenhyvar's taunting words had glanced off from his simple mind leaving only an angry inflammation of the senses, a furious resolve to go his own way and climb to power. Arthur's son—was he to be mocked about his choice of a woman? He would gather folk about him; there was magic in his blood to stir the British race, the magic that had raised his father to a pinnacle of glory. Armies would bow before him in some long hall on a ramparted hill, with harpers to strike up at his bidding and Indec beside him in the high seat. . . .

Anir got off his pony and knocked with his spear shaft on a door behind which was red fire-glow. He heard voices within, Indec's servants, no doubt, who slept in the outer room. The door was lifted away and he saw the stooping figures of two men, great dark silhouettes against the light.

"A messenger," said one.

"With bad news, likely enough," said the other.

The warmth of the room flooded out into the windy night, but a chill fell on Anir. These were not men who worked for Indec, shepherds or fishermen who lay with their girls round the fire when she slept in the inner room; their voices had the sharp surly tone of warriors such as he had seen at the gates of Camelot.

"What is your business here?" he said furiously, clenching his fists and stepping swiftly over the threshold.

"Not so fast, stranger! What is your business? Give us your news," they said warningly.

"News? I am master here! I come to see Indec."

There was a chuckling laugh.

"Turn back, young man," said the nearer figure good humouredly. "The harlot's bed is full for tonight."

A red mist floated before Anir's eyes; he bared his teeth like a vicious horse and snatched the knife from his belt. Before he could do more he got a blow in the face that tumbled him backwards. His head struck a stone quern lying on the floor and he lay still.

"Quick you are with your fists, Bedwyr," said Kai admiringly. He glanced at the fallen figure and stirred it with his foot. "A boy with some spirit in him, but the night wind will cool his hot blood." So saying he gathered Anir in his arms, threw him out into the mud and darkness, and made fast the door again.

It was a long while before Anir came to his senses. He sat up slowly and felt his head; he got to his feet and found his mouth full of blood and several teeth missing. For a while he stood trying to think what had happened to him, then he took a step towards the door, but had to grope forward and support himself against the house wall. His hand fell on something soft and shaggy—the pony standing there patiently with its tail to the wind. Smothering a groan, he got on its back and rode away at random through the dyked fields and along the edge of the marsh. He could not go back to Indec in this state, but when he had got shelter and food somewhere . . . then surely he would find means to kill that man who was with her now. Fury blazed up in him like a fire in dry wood suddenly fanned by the breeze, his senses reeled again and he fell from the saddle just as the pony stopped by a beehive hut on the verge of reedy water that glinted frostily under the moon.

* * *

Arthur and his friends sat at breakfast over freshly caught fish, oatcake and ale. The happenings of the night had passed from their minds; they hardly noticed Indec setting food before them and filling their cups, the beautiful complaisant woman with smiling lips and sombre eyes. They talked eagerly of the way they should ride, round the marshes to the Roman road, of what passage they should seek through Conan's country, avoiding Caer Ceri, where folk would know them . . . Suddenly a frown settled on Indec's face; she leaned across the table and said to Arthur: "Will you not tell me your name? It is easy to see now that you are a man known to many, though a stranger to me."

Arthur looked at her with a steady, not unkindly gaze, much as a man may lay his hand in friendly fashion upon horse or dog while his thoughts are elsewhere. He did not answer; but Bedwyr said roughly: "It is not for you to ask who we are. To you all men are alike in the dark and it is best that you forget their faces when daylight comes."

"It matters to me more than you think," she said, flushing hotly and turning away lest they should see that her eyes were brimming with tears.

"There is danger everywhere beyond Aquae Sulis, perhaps even here," said Kai. "The youth who drew his knife on us last night, he might well have been set a task by Conan."

"Did someone come to the door in the night?" Indec's voice broke in. "I saw blood on the ground. . . ." Her face turned ghastly, a cup slipped from her fingers and broke on the floor, but no one heeded her.

"Folk will hardly recognise us if we are clean shaven," said Bedwyr. "The woman shall take off our beards and lend us peasant cloaks. You," he nodded to Kai, "are bald enough about the head to pass as a monk; a black cloak and a few words of Latin are what you need."

"There are too many scars on my face to suit a monk," said Kai, with a laugh.

"We can rub some dirt on them. You," he looked at Arthur, "must leave the white mare behind and ride a beast from Indec's stable. There is a little gelding that might carry your weight."

"Swift is Lamrei, even in her old age, and unless we travel fast I fear we shall come too late to Lis Peng-wern," said Arthur moodily.

"Mare and rider are too famous in Gwent. Too many men there are now that wish you ill in the vales of Severn and Wye," said Bedwyr, getting up from table.

"Lamrei," muttered Indec. Had she not heard the name before on the lips of guests? A sickly dread weighed upon her heart; her well-tended body was inured to sinful usage, but now for the first time she felt a horror for what had happened to it.

"Get busy, woman, and rid us of these beards!" Bedwyr stared suddenly and thrust at her with his foot. He took a handful of little silver coins from a pouch and said: "We shall pay you well for what you have done for us, first in darkness and then in daylight. . . ."

She went out quickly, hating to hear the plain ugly words that followed, words that called up dark smiles from Bedwyr and Kai, but left Arthur unmoved.

'There was a time,' he thought, 'when I rode at the head of the Cymry and withstood all sin that I might find favour with God. Favour I had, but I slipped into the easy-going ways of the flesh and my task remained unfinished. Shall I succeed better now, when sin is become of no more account to me than dirt on my shoes?'

* * *

The three travellers avoided the best-known track from Caer Gloui into the land of Powys and swung west through lonely forests—so likely it seemed to them that Conan's spies would discover their plan and that an effort would be made to take Arthur in some ambush. For Arthur and his legionaries, friendly to Gereint and Cuneglas, were reckoned as by necessity the enemies of Conan. All went well; there came a day when they rode unscathed into the low country of Ercing with its vast oak trees and deep red mud and saw far behind them the blue waves of hill that marked the frontier of Gwent. All was well, indeed, except that their pace grew slower and slower, for the little gelding taken from Indeg was failing under Arthur's weight.

They rested the beasts by a spring where a stream oozed out in a glade thickly strewn with glossy acorns. In all directions the grey, lichened trunks closed up in dim barriers under a motionless canopy of brown leaves. There was a silence in these woods, infinitely oppressive to the mind; for the trees were masters of the land and turned a gloomy indifferent face to man's desires. Here and there in the course of thousands of years some spasm of human life force had made axes ring cheerfully upon the stubborn old trees and had sent spirals of wood smoke floating over the forest tops, but again and again nature's rhythm had healed these puny scars and with the wilderness there flowed back the breath of an ancient world in which neither beast nor man had left a mark.

Arthur, Kai and Bedwyr sat in the faded bracken watching their horses drink and begin to pull eagerly at the tufts of deer grass. Now that they had nothing to fear from any folk that might meet them (for this was reckoned the land of Cuneglas), their spirits grew sensitive to the gloom of the forest under leaden skies, and the silence seemed to them a foretaste of that greater silence of death and decay towards which was set the course of every man, no matter how strong in body and nimble in wit. For a long time they sat without speaking, and then Kai and Bedwyr got up and went to catch the horses. Arthur lay back with his head on the ground and almost at once he heard the faint thud of hoofs coming from the south. A single rider, pushing along fast, he thought—danger perhaps, but for once his mind was unresponsive, busied with a vision of futility. What could he do for this land of ruined cities and empty woods, this people that were resolved to turn arms upon each other? What did anything matter any more? For suddenly the truth came upon him like a rumble of thunder from dark clouds; he would come to his end without achieving the task he had set himself. He had not been great enough to bind the kings together or to break them, not great enough to renounce the stupid lusts of the men he strove to lead, not great enough to win the love of the most beautiful woman in Britain. . . .

There was a shout from his companions where they stood on the far side of the little stream. He turned his head and saw a rider on a white horse coming towards him at a gallop, a spear poised for throwing. Arthur sprang up. There was no time to reach for the shield he had laid down in the bracken, but he drew his sword. As he did so the spear flew through the air. It seemed as though it would pass over his head, but it swept down in a curving flight and glanced from his thigh, leaving a great gash spurting with blood. Almost in the same instant the horse was upon him, swerving against the will of the rider, and went by in a flash, but not before Arthur had lunged out with his sword. He turned and saw the rider slip from the saddle and fall in a heap by the spring. The horse went on with flying stirrups, circling round the other beasts with a loud whinny of recognition. There was no mistaking the big white mare—she was Lamrei, but who was the man that had fallen from her back? Hardly conscious of his wound, Arthur gazed at a boyish figure lying face downward, with a trickle of blood soaking into the green-scummed mire about the spring. Already Kai and Bedwyr were turning him over and pointing their naked weapons at his throat. The youth opened his eyes; speechless, but with a glint of hatred, he stared up into Arthur's face.

"This is no stranger!" exclaimed Bedwyr. "This is the fellow who burst in on us when we sat that night in the harlot's house. See, his face still has the bruise from the blow I gave him!"

"Why did you try to take my life, young man?" said Arthur heavily.

"Are you he who lay with Indec?" came a gasping answer.

"I am; and who are you?"

The lips moved, but no sound came from them. Arthur took water in his cupped hands and let it stream into the sagging mouth. The fallen boy raised himself suddenly on one arm.

"I am Anir, son of Arthur and Gwyll. . . . Had I lived I would have been king . . . of all Britain. . . ." The dark curly head fell backwards, the features sharpened as the contours of a hill spring out in the light of sunset.

"My son!" said Arthur. He gave a groan and sank to his knees. Suddenly he pressed his lips on those of the dead.

"Black he is where you are golden, but he may well be your child, Arthur; your face is mirrored in his," said Bedwyr. "Brow, nose, mouth and chin are fashioned alike. Aye, if he had lived. . . ."

Kai said nothing. He was busy tightening a halter round Arthur's leg to stop the bleeding. Presently they buried Anir under a mount of sods torn from the banks of the stream; then Kai and Bedwyr lifted Arthur on to Lamrei.

"A heavy load of grief and sin you have to carry now," said Arthur, laying his hand on the mare's neck.

"Kindly you are with women and with beasts," said Bedwyr, "but deadly is your sword to your kinsfolk. First Modron and now Anir."

"Heavy is God's hand against us," said Arthur. He rode forward, but again and again he looked back at the heap of red earth. That night they reached a cluster of peasant huts by a ford over the Wye. They ate and drank and lay down to sleep, but next morning Arthur's wound was swollen up and he was in high fever. For ten days they stayed there and when at last they pushed on to meet Cuneglas in the loop of Severn the news overtook them that Conan and his army had broken into Dyvnaint.

Chapter XXIV

The Decline
of the West

SAW I OF ARTHUR'S
BRAVE MEN HEWING WITH STEEL,
MEN OF THE AMHERAWDYR, DIRECTOR OF TOIL.
AT LONGBORTH THERE FELL OF GEREINT'S
BRAVE MEN FROM THE BORDERS OF DYVNAINT,
AND ERE THEY WERE SLAIN, THEY SLEW.
    *   *   *   *
I WAS THERE WHEN LACHEU FELL,
ARTHUR'S SON, WELL SKILLED IN SONG.
             —*Black Book of Caermarthen.*

It was early morning; Gwenhyvar sat on the ramparts of Camelot looking out over the swampy levels to low hills in the west where plumes of dun-coloured smoke spurted up in the soft, bluish haze. The legionaries were all gone to fight for Gereint, joining in with a horde of warriors hastily summoned from the Saxon march. Only women, children, and old men were left in the fortress; they had armed themselves as best they could, but now their courage had ebbed away. A

rumour spread that battle had been given somewhere behind those western hills and that it had gone
ill for Dyvnaint. What other meaning was there in
that smoke from burning houses that sprang up
nearer and nearer to Camelot? If it had been Conan
alone coming by the road from Caer Ceri, things might
have gone differently, but another host had landed on
the shore at Carrun, scattering the levies raised by
Cadwy and Cystennin, Gereint's sons at Dindraithov.
It was Vortipore, who had struck in suddenly, resolved
to share the plunder with the men of Gwent.

A trickle of fugitives had begun to leave Camelot
for the fastnesses of Coit Mawr, but Gwenhyvar sat
unmoved, watching and waiting, borne up by the
intuition that out of the ruin of the West she would be
able to take what she desired from life. The old order
might be ready to fall and bury those that sheltered
within its tottering towers—the Celtic kingdoms
undermined by the flow of Saxons from the east like
some desolate cattle on the seashore—Arthur's work
might be in vain—but a new order would rise in its
place, a new order in which she might again be the
foremost woman in Britain instead of a neglected wife
sitting in Camelot. . . . The bent figure of an old man
came along the rampart, gazing at her mistrustfully
under puckered brows.

"What is it?" she said impatiently.

"A warrior has ridden up to the gate. He asks for
you. Shall we let him pass?"

"What manner of a man?"

"A dark man on a dark horse covered with foam.
He has a hat pulled down over his eyes. I doubt he is
the bearer of bad news."

"Bring him to me." She glanced at her dress of
blue silk, the finest she had; she felt for the golden
chain about her neck and rubbed the dull and grimy
jewelled rings on her fingers till they shone. Then she
spread her cloak on a heap of sling stones and sat

down, watching Medraut coming towards her through a crowd of muttering women. She said to herself: 'He has the same stealthy tread, the same elfish beauty as when I first saw him, yet he is different; there is a light of triumph on his face that I have never seen before.'

He dropped on one knee before her and raised her silken dress to his lips in a gesture of homage; reverent yet ironical, his face looked up at hers, and he said:

"First on the ramparts below Alcluyd, then at Bregion, and now at last at Camelot, fate draws our lives together, Gwenhyvar."

"For thirteen years you have not come to me. Why do you come now?" she answered distantly, but on an overmastering impulse she put her hand in his. He stood up, a dark figure with dark, burning eyes, and pointed to the west.

"The first blow has been struck, the blood has begun to flow, blood on which my ship will sail into its harbour."

"The battle has been fought . . . was Arthur there?" she said. Her lips parted, the colour left her face, her whole body grew tense with awakening joy and horror.

Medraut shook his head. "Arthur is gone, no man knows whither, but Gereint has fallen, fighting at Longborth, and with him the old warriors that followed Arthur from Abergleinwy to Badon Hill. Back to back they stood, hewing with steel, too proud to fly. The sharp sword of the Cymry is broken at last, the sword that I forged on Moel Fre, and Arthur is stripped of his power."

"Did you help in the work? You were with Conan, were you not?"

"My mind is a deadlier weapon than any I might have used in that clash of steel. It was my counsel that launched Conan and Vortipore upon this conquest of Dyvnaint that will leave Arthur like a rootless tree."

"Is it to win me that you seek to bring him down, or to win power over all Britain?" she asked, as she had asked years ago when she sat by his side looking across the sea to shadowed mountains on Mull.

"I cannot have the one without the other. The time is near when folk shall see us for what we are, one man and one woman exalted above prince and peasant, Briton and Saxon, grasping at power to shake the world from the Pictish hills to the gates of Rome."

"Others have grasped at that power and failed, as the old songs tell us of Maxen and Cystennin," she said doubtfully.

"Never before in Britain has there been a pair the like of us, more splendid in beauty, more daring in spirit, more stained in sin. Listen, Gwenhyvar; it was Arthur that strove to save Britain sinlessly. He is my kinsman, he was my friend, my good companion, and I beat down my lust for you and my hopes for power. I gave him all the help that a man may give another, in war and in counsel; I urged him hard to do what I had a mind to do myself, and he achieved what no man of our race has achieved before, for never was there such a victory in Britain as the one we gained on Badon. The time came when he could advance further only by guile, by ruthlessness to Britons such as he had already dealt out to Pict and Saxon. He stood aside and would not use the power that lay in his hand, but the power was there to hinder me from stepping in where he had failed. The Britons do not love me as they love Arthur; the old warriors from the North were like a sheathed weapon, his to draw and strike with if he chose; Gereint was his friend, a master of mighty hosts. Now all is changed; the evil-minded men have triumphed, Conan and Vortipore, but I in turn shall triumph over them, for the strength of my sin is greater than theirs. By unnatural means I came to life and by unnatural deeds I shall gain my desire, for wherever we look in this land, in east or in west, the weapons of hell outmatch those of heaven." He stared at her and suddenly laid a hand on her head. "Do you stand by me or do you stand by Arthur?" he said in a voice, gentle as the light caress of his fingers on the golden hair.

"By you, for you are the only man who can bring love into my life—it matters not to me whether you be cruel or treacherous or steeped in deadly sin—you are Medraut, the man I have worn in my heart ever since we were together in Bregion." Her eyes dropped and the words seemed to come from some realm of her consciousness that had never found outlet in long years of indifference to the life that went by her. 'All is changing,' she thought, 'soon this place will be burnt and lie desolate; folk will look at this round hill and say: there lived Arthur among his champions, and there was feasting and song and lovemaking in the days when Britain drew breath again after long wars, and there, in the pride of her beauty, her jewels and silken clothes, sat Gwenhyvar, the woman that betrayed Arthur and went out from the cheerful firelight of Camelot like a werewolf into the darkness where she belonged. . . .' A sudden murmur aroused her, a wailing cry from a crowd gathered on the highest point of the hill. Flames were going up from an old house buried in apple orchards at the far end of Camlann. It was Olwen who came with a hard, resolute face to speak with Medraut and Gwenhyvar. She was in man's clothing with a spear in her hand and spur on heel.

"You stand here with folded arms watching ruin come to Arthur's Hall," she said fiercely, "you, Medraut, who come from Caerleon like a black bird of evil omen. Is it in your power to turn back the men who make towards us with lust and murder in their hearts?"

"It is not," he said. "Too much has Gwent to avenge, for the Cymry died hard at the waterside by Longborth."

"What of Gwalchmei?"

"Dead, like many another champion of Arthur."

"How came he to die? He had always luck with him."

"It was gold that undid him. He lay there wounded and offered a man a gold arm-ring to hide him away. The man would have done it, but Conan came by and recognised the ring. With his own sword he struck off Gwalchmei's head." Medraut stared at her curiously, but Olwen only gave him a look of hate.

"This is your work!" she said, then she turned to the women who thronged after her and cried: "Save yourselves, all you of Camelot! Our men have died in battle, but let us see that their children live to avenge them." She ran to the stables and a moment later she was riding out at the gateway with a curly-headed boy in front of her on the saddlebow.

"Her elder children are safe in Kernou," said Gwenhyvar, watching Olwen with cold, envious eyes. "Where is the woman here who has not given suck except only Arthur's wife?"

"Take comfort, then, that Garwen's son lies dead at Longborth, Lacheu, the idol of the Cymry, who would not be parted from them when they went into battle," said Medraut with a devilish smile.

"Lacheu!" A qualm went through Gwenhyvar, a sudden ache from breast to throat. "I did not guess that you were so hard-hearted as to wish him dead, that lovely boy who has done no harm save to goad me with the thought that I am childless."

"Hard-hearted we must be or we shall not endure what lies ahead. Think no more of Arthur shorn of all he holds dear, but mount your horse and ride with me, Gwenhyvar. Is it your wish to see Camelot afire and let yourself be passed from man to man in Conan's camp?"

Chapter XXV

The Villa

THE ENEMY LEFT OUR PEOPLE, BUT THE PEOPLE DID NOT LEAVE
THEIR SINS.

—Gildas, *De Excidio Britanniae.*

It was nearly noon when Medraut and Gwenhyvar rode at a gallop along the copsewood paths far to the south of Camelot. A thick fog had rolled up from the great marshes and hung heavily on the hills; the tunnel-like passages through over-arching hazel were unfathomable to the eye and the taller tree-tops were lost in a grey void. The clamour of panic-stricken people had faded away behind them and the only sounds breaking the dreary stillness of the forest were the gasping breaths of the horses and the thud of hoofs in the sodden carpet of fallen leaves. Higher and higher they climbed through seas of yellow bracken, treading down the withered foxglove spires and the stout rods of mullein, ducking their heads under low sweeping boughs, till all signs of a track were lost, and at last they came to a standstill among ever-thickening underwood twined with honeysuckle and briar on a hill mounting steeply as a house roof. Gwenhyvar sat passive in the saddle with no thought for the beast under her, head drooping to the ground and flanks streaming with sweat, or for the fog and forest that narrowed her vision to a little patch of ground with Medraut standing up in his stirrups, turning his head this way and that for a hint of wind or sun. Her mind was filled with the one idea that she was free, free to have what she wanted from life as she had never been before. For the best part of her youth her will had been bent like a sapling caught in a snowdrift, but now a hand had released it. . . . Suddenly she laughed and let the whip fall on her horse, urging him up alongside Medraut.

"We are lost, it seems," she said gaily, "but does it matter? We are together, you and I, with none to hinder us, far beyond human ken in this forest, secret as a locked bower in the dead of night."

Medraut looked at her, his perplexity broken by a gleam of amusement. Women only saw one thing at a time, he thought, whereas to him every instinctive action was something to be weighed over and considered with artistic detachment. Perhaps he had been more tempted by Gwenhyvar long ago, when she, the young bride of Arthur, had asked him to adventure with her, sailing out from Bregion into unknown seas; nevertheless all these years he had told himself that he would take her when he had the power, and now the power was his. Abruptly he swept the thought from his mind. Other matters had to be attended to first.

"If you are content here, I am not," he said, watching her flush at the coldness of his tone. What ardour the woman had to think of love in such a place as this! "Here we sit on tired horses, with nothing to eat but a few frosted blackberries, perhaps, and with every chance of wandering out of these woods into some village full of Conan's men. My plan was to take you into Durngueir, south of the hills, where war may never reach us, but now who can tell which way it lies?"

"Let us get to the top here; the mist may be thinner on the high ground," she said sullenly, and began to ply her horse with the sharp prick spurs, driving him upwards into the stony thickets.

"It will take a stout horse and rider to make that passage; let us look for some better place," he said, but in a moment she was out of sight high above him and he had to follow as best he could.

'Savage she is when her will is crossed,' he said to himself. 'Arthur has been too gentle with her to break her spirit, but she may have to humble herself before me.' He went up slowly, getting down from the saddle to ease his horse and going before it with the bridle over his arm. Gwenhyvar, for all her spirit, was a poor companion on an enterprise of this kind, as much out of place riding in the wilderness as she had been in the ranks of the Cymry when Bregion was stormed. What did women know of weather or woodcraft or what a horse could endure without being foundered? Women in these days of turmoil began to think themselves the comrades of men instead of servants and playthings . . . He came out on the top of the hill; the mist was still thick, but the trees were gone. His horse was up to its belly in deep heather, and instead of the dusk of the woods there was a drift of white vapour through which the sun showed as a little silvery disc. There, straight ahead, must be the South, though a moment ago he could have sworn that it lay over his right shoulder. After all, Gwenhyvar had given good counsel, but where was she? He rode on and the mist dimmed as though he were coming up against high forest or a hillside, and then it brightened again and there was nothing, only the rusty heath rising in billows against dark islands of bramble and furze. His horse stumbled over an old dyke buried in undergrowth, and he thought: 'Here have been plough lands that have gone back to waste. Perhaps we are not far from some living place.' "Gwenhyvar!" he shouted again and again, but there was no answer. He pulled in irresolutely, spitting out curses. What blind folly of the woman not to wait for him! Perhaps in her bad temper she had gone on at a gallop and the horse had fallen under her. She might be lying stunned somewhere in this endless tangle, as hard to find as a jewel dropped in a hayfield . . .

A ring of men leaped up around him; out of the thickets rose long spears levelled at horse and rider like the spokes of a wheel. Brushing through the dew-laden gossamer of the gorse bushes came the stooping figures, closer and closer, with a growling shout. At once his sword was out of its scabbard; he gathered up the reins and turned his horse, looking for a place to break through. In a moment he saw that it was hopeless to make a fight—whatever he did, some of those spears would be through him before he could move a yard. He sheathed the sword again and sat still. Hairy arms locked round his waist and pulled him from the saddle, grim faces were all about him, jabbering in some unfamiliar dialect; he saw knives raised threateningly, but he said with cold indifference: "Do me no harm, men! I am a guletic, a kinsman of Arthur."

"Let him be," said a tall sinewy fellow with a horn slung from the shoulder. He looked keenly at Medraut and said: "We do not harm such as you, but you must go with us to our lord at Castel ys Coit, now that you have come so far. Few come our way and those that do fare either as guests to the house, or as slaves to the village, or they leave their bones on these hills that hide us from folk without."

"Trusty watchmen you seem to be," said Medraut approvingly. "Tell me, have you taken a woman here on the heath, a woman with golden hair, riding a black horse?"

"We have her safe," said the head man with a grin. "As for women, we do with them as we please."

Medraut smiled slowly, but his eyes had a glint of devilish passion.

"The woman is in my charge," he said. "If any mischief is done to her there will soon be an army coming to avenge it."

"Armies have come and gone without finding Castel ys Coit," said the headman. He laid his hand familiarly on Medraut's arm and drew him away through the bushes. Soon they came to an open space ringed with blank fog. The grey film of moisture on the grass was broken by many footsteps; a dark object loomed up—it was the body of Gwenhyvar's horse, dead, with blood oozing slowly from spear thrusts in breast and flank.

"She rode through us when we first came on her, but the beast was too blown to carry her far," remarked the peasant. A few steps further another ugly sight emerged from the fog: three men crouched round the motionless form of a woman. Her skirt and shift had been pulled up over her head and tied with a cord so that she was helpless to resist anything that might be done to her.

"So we deal with women that show fight—we break them in quickly enough at Castel ys Coit."

Outwardly unmoved, Medraut listened and looked. The scene was familiar enough to him during years of war and stirred his senses pleasantly because of the cruelty in his nature, but never before had this happened to a woman who was more to him than a means for the quenching of lust. A new emotion struggled in him, something that for years he had not felt for woman, child, or beast, or any living thing save Arthur—and that was pity. 'Tender I was once,' he thought, 'gentle with girls, forbearing some-

times when it would have profited me more to be
harsh, but what I was when I rode with Arthur into
Reged has faded away since the desire came to me for
power. I walk alone and all the pleasures of common
men have lost their savour; what delight have I any
longer in heady drink, in talk and song, in a galloping horse, in the scented air of spring, or in kindling
a woman to love? All grows dim to me except this
vision of power, but now all at once it is as if there
was a rift in the fog through which I go and a glimpse
comes to my eyes of sunlight falling on pleasant
places far away. . . . Pity,' he thought, 'why should I
pity one who is but as other women?' He bit his lips,
staring at the uncovered limbs and breasts that quivered under the cold caress of mist-laden air. 'Why
does it make my heart ache to see her proud spirit
crushed by violence, the treasure of her body laid out
under the eyes of brutish men? Power I have over her,
but I did not guess that she had power over me, that
she could break through the steel with which I guard
my spirit and play upon my heart like sad music or
sunset colours above blue hills.'

"Set her free!" he said hoarsely; his face went pale
and his teeth chattered together. The peasant nodded
with a glooming smile; he cut the cord, raised up the
woman and pulled back her dress. Without more ado
he swung her up on to the back of Medraut's horse
led by one of his men.

"She shall ride and you shall walk," he said craftily. "Together we shall go in a body down to Castel ys
Coit. One or other of you might break away from us
on the forest paths, but hardly the two of you together. Safest, though, it will be to take that bright sword
from you, guletic, and those bloodstained spurs from
the woman's heels, for I see that you are folk of a high
spirit and reckless as some wild beast taken in a trap.
You need not fear; hospitable is my master to such as
you. Hungry you are now, but good food awaits you

at Castel ys Coit, aye, and a soft bed to sleep on," he added with a leer.

It was evening, after hours of travel along tortuous pathways in primeval woods, when the little band came down into a valley with stubble fields and green pastures. The mist was gone when they reached the southward-flowing streams, and a blaze of golden sunshine swept over the forest tops, throwing long shadows from a cluster of low buildings with tiled roofs and walls covered with yellow stucco. Blue smoke eddied upwards in the still air against a grove of mighty elms and sycamores, beehives stood in a long row facing south, stacks of hay and corn rose beside a barn whence came the dull thud of flails. Further away were the conical roofs of a village, peeping up above sheep folds and cattle pens; a chanting of women's voices at the milking, a grunting of swine, a cheerful barking of dogs racing to meet the new-comers—a sleepy air of peace and comfort lay like an unruffled pool in depths of enchanted gloom.

"The old Britain," said Medraut, looking up at Gwenhyvar riding beside him. "I had heard that one could still get a glimpse of it here in Durngueir."

She did not answer. Folktales painted pictures of the life in old times and as a girl she had thought vaguely that when wars were ended she would spend her days in such a place as this, not in a cluster of thatched hovels like worm-eaten mushrooms on the turf, ringed round by the mountainous ramparts of Camelot. Like a bad dream the past faded from her mind: the stink of low smoky rooms always crowded with the unfriendly faces of warriors sitting glum over their mead; Arthur coming and going amid a clatter of hoofs and a roar of voices, a smile on his harsh face for the men that loved him, but with fewer and fewer words for her as the years went by; war again, and all the wretched scenes that had darkened her girlhood in Strathclyde; distracted women battling their way through fortress gates, the shrill clamour of children, cattle struggling along under a rain of blows; then the sudden realisation that she was free; galloping joyously beside Medraut, a gust of anger, shock-headed men springing up in the mist, and terror such as she had never endured before—thrown on the ground half naked, a knife point touching her skin here and there and pressing harder and harder till the pain and the dread of more pain plunged her mind in darkness and made her body a squirming, sweating, uncontrollable mass of flesh like that of a tormented beast . . .

She got down from the horse and gazed at the buildings whose yellow walls seemed to radiate a friendly warmth; they stood there assured, dignified, well tended, and she thought: 'Fate has brought me out into sunshine at last from a life of darkness and horror,' and then a qualm came over her as she looked at Medraut and a voice seemed to say within her: 'Nothing is so pleasant as sin; but the greater the pleasure the greater the price that must be paid for it in the end.'

A flight of worn stone steps led to a terrace in front of the house door and there stood a man in a white toga scattering corn to pheasants that came stalking towards him from the cover of bushes clipped into the form of walls and bastions. He raised his arm courteously in the old Roman salute as Medraut and Gwenhyvar mounted the steps, he first and she following. The peasants stood below, leaning on their spears, a little sinister group in a setting that mirrored only peace and security.

"Are we guests or prisoner here?" said Medraut, looking hard at the man among the pheasants as though to find some hint in the master of what had been plain enough in the servants.

"That may depend upon who you are."

Medraut nodded, saying to himself: 'Things here are not what they seem.' "I am Medraut, the nephew of Arthur," he said aloud.

"Your name is well known indeed," said the other. "I am Caius Aurelius Milo and this is Castel ys Coit, though once it had a better name." The man in the white toga tossed out the last of the corn to the confiding birds; he cast only a fleeting glance at Gwenhyvar, but looked long and measuringly at Medraut. "You have fled from the fighting north of the hills?" he said in a grave but not unfriendly voice.

"I thought that we should be among friends here, for you are Gereint's men, are you not?"

Milo smiled and shrugged his shoulders. His eyes had a steel flash that Medraut liked very little. This quiet clean-shaven man who had more the look of a monk than a chieftain and who called himself by a Latin name in keeping with his house, his costume, his air of cultured indolence, he was perhaps as dangerous a man to guest with as any of the princes in Britain . . .

"Come within," he said. "You will be glad to bathe and change your clothes before you sup. Afterwards we shall talk."

"We shall," said Medraut significantly. "They are heavy-handed fellows, those men of yours that came on us when we rode into the hills."

"Rough men are needed to guard such a place as this," said Milo unconcernedly. They passed through an archway into a paved courtyard with colonnades thickly draped in autumnal vine foliage. In the centre played a fountain from a little group of statuary. The figures of three boys were the work of a skilful artist, lively and graceful, but contrived with a startling disregard for decency. Medraut looked at them with an inscrutable face; Gwenhyvar laughed aloud. Her half-barbarous spirit responded naïvely to this shamelessness, the ingenious presentation of a spectacle that mankind does not obtrude upon public gaze; but to the keen-witted Medraut it was clear that they had left Christian Britain behind on the other side of the woods and had strayed into the mockery and cynicism of the old pagan world.

"The shadow of Rome still lingers on Castel ys Coit," he said with a subtle smile.

"Say rather the sunshine," said Milo, watching the pair with a slight nod of comprehension.

They entered the dusk of the colonnade and pleasant-faced young women led Gwenhyvar away to the bathrooms. She accepted the unaccustomed ministrations, bewildered but happy, hardly conscious of the meaning glances exchanged by these silent and gentle-handed girls, so different from the lively, chattering, and slovenly women of Caerleon and Camelot. Presently she was on a couch with food and wine set before her: a lamp burned on the table and through an open doorway she heard quiet footfalls on the paved court and the monotonous plash of the fountain. No fire was visible, but the floor was warm to the touch; a drowsiness came over her as she drank eagerly the unfamiliar Gallic wine, and she felt that here at last was the materialisation of those daydreams conjured up years ago at Alcluyd, visions of luxurious ease that might await the bride of Arthur. . . .

Not far away Medraut lay in the triclinium looking across a lamp-lit table at Milo pouring red wine from a leather bottle into glass beakers. Washed and changed, satisfied by a meal of excellent venison, he lay propped up on one elbow, all his faculties intensely alert now that they were alone in the dim room with smooth, frescoed walls and heavily curtained doorways.

"If all Britain could have the peace that you preserve in this little valley . . ." he said tentatively.

"What hinders it?" Milo passed him the wine.

"The Saxons, surely. Have they not reached you here?"

"A little band got into the lower valley when Cerdic crossed the Avon. We took some of them alive and crucified them by the sea shore. The Saxons would not trouble Britain if Briton could agree with Briton. It was not the sword of the Saxon that made the slaughter yesterday at Longborth."

"News comes swiftly to you here!" said Medraut.

"There are many men that watch for me."

"A powerful chieftain you seem to be, but I have not heard your name before now."

"The land is mine from the hills to the sea, but few strangers have found their way to this house. On every side lies Coit Mawr; what paths there are we guard day and night, and so it has been for a hundred years. Neither Scot nor Saxon has set foot in this courtyard, nor have the tax-gatherers of Gereint. My men are trusty, for I can give them abundance of milk, meat and corn, and they know that they would not fare so well under any other master."

"And you are content to be master of this one valley like a man on a little isle in a great waste of sea?"

Milo looked at him steadily; he drank out his cup and set it down.

"I have what few Britons possess today—a house such as this, land that yields more than it did a hundred years ago, folk that love me. I have ships in the river mouth that barter goods for me in Gaul and bring me iron from mines that I own in the forest west of Glevum. I have books, music, horses and hounds. Why should I wish for more? . . .

"It is three hundred years since an ancestor of mine bought this land when he retired from a military post in North Britain. He built this house in place of an agent's cottage overlooking the village, he cleared some forest and bred a new kind of sheep on the hills. In time his family acquired great wealth; they became mine-owners in different parts of Britain, working lead ore in the Brigantian valleys—a road was made across the mountains and a fortress garrisoned to keep order—they bought estates much larger than this in Cantium and east of London. Now all is lost except this place where they first took root, and some mines worked for me in Gwent; but I am richer for having learned men in my household, and in the village are skilful smiths, men who understand corn and men who understand cattle, potters, ploughmen, tanners and carpenters, all gathered from the ruin that has fallen on land and cities farther east. I say, I am content with what I have."

"The gods have been generous to you, for I take it you are no Christian?"

"I trouble about no gods, and what has faith in Christ done for Britain? I pay reverence only to my ancestors whose masks hang in this house."

"And are you blessed with a wife who values all this as you do?"

"I am bound to no wife, but women are here in plenty and I have a score of sons. Each I have trained in some duty that will be of advantage to all; one has charge of cattle and one of sheep, one of the ships and one of the folk when they are armed for war, and the eldest shall be master of all when I am gone."

"Brother is often jealous of brother," remarked Medraut.

"All my children are trained to be comrades."

"It was Arthur's plan to make all the princes of Britain into a band of brothers."

"Make him the true Emperor of Britain and it could be done. The people love him; let them come to him both from the North and from the South; let him put himself at the head of an army, as great as that he led to Badon Hill, and those that stand against him must either bend or break."

"So I have advised him more than once; but he has no heart for such a task. Is there any other man who could do it, think you?"

"While Arthur lives, there is no other man that the Britons will hail as Emperor," said Milo slowly. He leaned forward, his chin on his hand, staring fixedly at Medraut.

"You are for Arthur, then, and against the princes?" said Medraut, yawning sleepily.

"*Quidquid delirant reges plectuntur Achivi*," said Milo with an ironical smile.

"I know only a few words of Latin learnt from monks."

"Those are older and wiser words than any they gabble in monasteries."

There was a long silence. Suddenly Milo's voice broke in on the gathering murmur of a great wind in the trees:

"The woman you have brought with you—is she your wife or mistress for whom you seek a refuge in this time of troubles?" he said.

"She is my mistress," said Medraut readily. "With no shame I say it, she is my woman."

"And so you would sleep with her to-night?"

For a moment Medraut hesitated. Was not all this what he had planned—his whole purpose in taking Gwenhyvar out of Camelot and hiding her for a while so that they could have their pleasure together? And yet he might have done the same thing in loyalty to Arthur, putting his wife in some safe place such as this where her honour might be preserved. He could have done this even against her own will, turning a blank face to her offer of love, as he had done that day in the deep forest. He could still do it . . . and for that matter he could go back to Arthur a guiltless man; he could say: 'Gwenhyvar is unharmed; come, let us ride together through the kingdom of Britain and speak to the people, let us gather men from

Powys, from Gwyneth, Reged and Strathclyde, let us put down the tyrants and make you Emperor. What you cannot accomplish alone we shall attempt together, as we did under the standard on Moel Fre.' *It could be done* . . . Deliberately he let another vision form in his mind and there came to him, as a slave comes at his master's call, that strange ecstasy of pity and desire born of an ugly deed done on the misty hills.

"Surely I shall sleep with her," he said, and for an instant the glass cup quivered in his hand.

"Lies flow easily from your tongue," said Milo calmly. "You asked whether you were here as a guest or as a prisoner, and now I tell you that you shall be a prisoner."

"What have I done to harm you? I thought you were my friend, Milo. You who have fathered so many bastards, do you take it amiss that I have my woman?" Medraut's voice was gentle, almost pleading, but his eyes glanced at the curtained door, at a window high in the wall.

"Do you think that I have had no spies in Camelot? This is not your woman—she has never slept in your arms, for she is Gwenhyvar, the wife of Arthur."

"Even so; it is by her choice that she comes to me."

"And it is your choice that you betray Arthur, not only with his wife, but by raising war against him and against those that are his friends."

"Arthur!" Medraut's mind began to turn and twist like a coursed hare. "Are you, too, under the spell of this man? Do you see him as the one saviour of our country? I tell you he is no more than a simple-minded soldier with a strong right arm, stumbling helplessly through this darkest age of Britain, a blood-stained figure whirling a sword blindly for a cause that has perished. He has no vision beyond the battlefield, he can build nothing, preserve nothing, for our heritage is become a quicksand sinking under the Saxon sea, and in it our leaders tread each other down to death."

"The quicksand is the lust for power and the lust for women, and in it you are stuck fast, Medraut; but not so Arthur, for he is the one man in Britain who seeks nothing for himself." Milo leaned forward, his hand on a little bell that stood on the table.

"Power I have," answered Medraut in sudden desperation. "And you, who have great possessions, should think twice before you challenge my power, Milo. Those ruffians that guard your march, can they withstand an army? Thick is Coit Mawr, yet men can cross it when they know the way."

Milo smiled, but in the light of the little lamp his face seemed harsh and terrible, etched in black shadows.

"Why should I fear you?" he said slowly. "Can a dead man guide armies through Coit Mawr? Gereint may find avengers, but not Medraut. Does any man love you, for all your gift of words and your skill with the harp?"

Medraut stared down into his empty cup. He found nothing to say. 'Death,' he thought, 'how swiftly I have rushed to meet it, caught by the lure of a woman! I have matched myself against Arthur and it is he that strikes me down through the hand of this Milo. Dangerous it is to threaten men who have much to lose, and powerful, indeed, is he who is loved by his fellows. I have the love only of one woman; she it was who urged me on the path I have taken, sitting beside me on Bregion's walls and gazing out on mountains rising from the sea. Without her I might have turned back—even in this last hour it was not too late—but I betrayed myself, I fell into the trap set for me. What is it worth, this delight in possessing one woman above all others, this drunkenness of the spirit and this brief pang of the flesh that is love—this madness that over-rides all other lust?' He set his teeth and glanced round the room again. 'I could put out the lamp, I could make a struggle, but the gates are closed and guarded; what could I do weaponless in the house of Milo?' Suddenly he laughed bitterly.

"Wiser are you," he said, "you who mate without passion and who breed sons as you breed sheep and cattle to serve your ends. Slave girls are alike to you and none will grudge you their possession. No woman will tempt you to set at stake your life and your good fame among men."

"The eyes of Britain are upon you, Medraut; rumours spread that you will follow in Cerdic's foot-steps—that you will swim in the Saxon sea rather than sink with your countrymen and that you work for the downfall of Arthur. I heard these tales; I doubted their truth till it was plain that you would betray your uncle with his wife. The death of Gereint, the slaughter of the champions, the rape of Gwenhy-var, the sending of Brude to Pictland and of your kinsman Brawdbach among the West Saxons; it all fits into one design like the coloured stones of a paved floor, now that you have revealed the woman in its centre. I know now what others only guess at—that you are the deadly enemy of the West. To raise your-self to power, to gain possession of one worthless woman, you would bring the barbarians over us, undoing Arthur's work, blotting out all that the British race builds afresh and all that men such as I have saved from Rome."

"Do what you will, the storm will come, and it will be worse for Britain if I am not there to temper it."

Milo shrugged his shoulders. "You will not leave this place alive to work our destruction. Sleep well to-night, Medraut. To-morrow you shall die."

"How shall I die?" Medraut licked his lips; he reached out his hand and took a harp from the wall.

"I will send you a cup of poison or a sword—whichever you prefer," said Milo indifferently.

Medraut tuned the harp without replying. He played the sprightly fatal-sounding air which he had played that evening years ago in Din Uther. The hard beating of his heart died down, his eyes glittered, reckless and undismayed, his brain was full of whirling visions, of scenes in which death had been near him in the past: Eadwald swinging his axe at Afon Coch, a Pictish warrior poising a great stone on the ramparts of Bregion, clanging blows as Cissa laid about him on Badon Hill. Slowly on the dusky frescoed wall he saw the paleness of water, a hill against the sky with a few stunted thorns. 'The race of Uther shall perish,' he said to himself, 'but not here, not yet.'

"Deft fingers, but barbarous music," muttered Milo. He lifted the bell and rang it.

CHAPTER XXVI

March, the
Son of Milo

THE SIN OF LUST, WHICH IS FOULER THAN ANY OTHER.
                              —Gildas, *De Excidio Britanniae.*

A thick-set, heavy-browed young man entered the room at once and bowed before Milo. He stood with folded arms, eyes bent on the floor, gloomily subservient.

"Take this man to a bedroom, lock him in and set a guard at the door," said Milo shortly. "The courtyard is watched, the gates are closed, there are no windows in the outer walls," he said, staring at Medraut without either pity or vindictiveness.

Medraut laid down the harp on the table; he got up and went out of the yellow lamplight into the cool darkness of the colonnade. The young man walked beside him, a drawn sword in his hand. They had turned the first angle of the courtyard before Medraut spoke, slowing his steps and laying a hand on the arm of his escort.

"Are you a son of Milo?" he said.

"I am," said the young man warily.

"Are you his eldest son?"

"There is another a few days older than I am."

"So one day he will be your master and you his servant?"

"So it seems."

"What is your task at Castel ys Coit?"

"I have charge of the swine that feed in our oak-woods," said the young man unwillingly. He moved on, but Medraut sensed in him an eagerness to talk.

"What is your name?" he said gently, again reaching out with his hand.

"Marcus is my name, but the village folk call me March. You must be some famous harper," he said impulsively. "I have heard much music in this house, but never playing such as yours."

"I am more than a harper; I am Medraut, nephew of Arthur the Warrior. Listen, March, your father says that I shall not go out of this house alive, but will you take a price to set me free?"

"We sons of Milo are not to be bought with bribes; together we stand to defend what is ours." March threw off Medraut's hand, he stepped back, but stood there motionless in the darkness. A cold, clammy air blew through the covered walk and withered vine leaves stirred with a faint scratching along the pavement.

'No moon and a mist hanging on the hills,' thought Medraut. 'All is in my favour if I could win over this boy.'

"Hear me, March," he said in a whisper. "In a little time—if I live—I shall be the master of all Britain. I shall have the power to break the kings one after another as Conan has now broken Gereint. Nimble are my fingers on the harp, but still more nimble are my wits in carrying forward a great design, in shaping a new Britain. Think, I will take an oath to make you ruler of all Dyvnaint; would not that be more to your fancy than herding swine in Coit Mawr?"

March was slow to answer. Medraut whispered again: "Men will build you a palace in Sarum, another in Isca, another maybe in Aquae Sulis; you will ride at the head of armies, you will pick and choose among the loveliest women of the West. Have you a girl here in this household? Do you know the delights of love?"

"Girls we brothers have that our father chooses for us, but mine brings me no delight," muttered March. "Come!" he said in a rougher tone, "you must go in at this door."

"Do you not trust me?"

"Who would trust in promises from a man who battles for his own life?" said March shrewdly.

A sudden rage boiled up in Medraut. For a moment he nerved himself to throw himself upon his companion, wrench away the sword and die fighting the guards at the gate, the men he could see across the courtyard, grouped in a doorway with lamp-light behind them. Then the thought: 'The night is still mine.'

"Take me to the room where my woman lies," he said. "Her door you may bar and guard as easily as any other. Can it profit you to keep us apart for these last few hours?"

"I doubt Milo did not mean that you should be together," said March uncertainly.

"Surely one favour you will grant me, friend, as man to man?" Medraut's hand rested on the young man's shoulder.

There was something hypnotic in the touch of those fingers that would soon be stiff and cold. "As you will," said March in a dull voice. He led the way a few yards farther and opened a door noiselessly. Light streamed out into the velvety darkness; Medraut set one foot in the room and looked. There lay Gwenhyvar asleep, pillowed in her golden hair, with one bare arm trailing downwards to the tessellated floor. A little oil lamp burned on a table beside her. 'This is the woman who has brought me to my end,' he thought—'what is a woman's beauty set against life—forty years of life, maybe, forty springs and forty summers, pleasure and power . . .' His desire drooped like a flower in a frosty wind, the breath of the grave that would soon open and take him in its cold embrace, but his mind grappled with a last desperate enterprise. He beckoned to March.

"Look," he said in a whisper, "here is the most beautiful woman in all Britain. Think how it would be to lie in her arms instead of in the arms of some slave girl with foul breath and sweaty limbs. Set us free, March, after you have lain with her in my place; go with us, and I swear to make you a king."

For a long time March stood silent in the flickering lamplight, his eyes seemed to become glazed, his mouth sagged and dribbled. Then he stepped back into the colonnade.

"Does she please you? Is she more than a match for the women your brothers have to sleep with them?" came Medraut's voice, cold and lascivious.

"She would resist me—scream—folk would come to us—my father would have me flogged if I, the least favoured of his sons, were to snatch at such a woman as that," whispered March hoarsely.

"How can she tell you from me in the darkness? I shall put out the lamp and wake her with my voice and you shall take your pleasure on her. No one will know. . . ."

"Yes . . . that way . . ."

"How will you get us out of Castel ys Coit?"

March thought for a minute. He said haltingly: "At the end of the walk there is a staircase leading to a loft where we store wool. You shall both go up there. A little door opens to the outside of the house. A man stands below on guard, but I shall go out at the gate and take his place. When I am ready I will give a hoot like an owl. Then throw down fleeces of wool and jump on top of them. A hundred yards over a field and we shall be on a forest path."

"Come," said Medraut. On tiptoe he entered the room and blew out the light. March closed the door and locked it with a key from his girdle.

"Wake, Gwenhyvar!" said Medraut. He drew the rug that covered the sleeping woman. "A little time we have for love and then we shall go out into the night. A dangerous lodging it is for me in Castel ys Coit."

The warm body stirred under his touch; a voice said, heavy with sleep: "You come late, Medraut. . . . Twelve years we have waited, and now . . . I am afraid—I have had fearful dreams. It seemed to me the door opened and something ugly stole in upon me . . . I think this is an evil place—can we not go now?"

"Soon, soon," he said, "but first what must be must . . ." He felt March thrusting past him and he stepped back soundlessly and leaned against the wall. He set his teeth and tried to silence his deep breathing; he tried to hear nothing, to think of nothing but the lifting shadow of death.

At last he was aware that March was beside him again, groping for his unbuckled sword on the floor, turning the key in the lock.

"You must not leave me! How shall I find you? Are the gates opened?" called Gwenhyvar. Her voice sounded frantic, bewildered, hardly human.

"I look only to see if folk are about in the courtyard," muttered Medraut. The door opened and March slipped out. It shut again. "Put on your clothes quickly. We shall go now," he said in a fierce tone.

"Help me then—this darkness . . . if only the lamp had not gone out . . ." she said petulantly, half sobbing now.

After a little while they stole out into the colonnade. Medraut felt his way to the corner, he found the opening where a stair went up. With one hand stretched before him and one clasped in Gwenhyvar's, he climbed till he stood on a floor and breathed in the heavy smell of sheep's wool. He felt on among the soft fleeces, greasy to the touch or harsh and dry where caked with dung; a gust of cold air blew in his face and he found himself at a little door, half open to the outer darkness. Voices sounded below, March speaking haltingly to another man. He felt for Gwenhyvar crouched down by his side; in a mingling of rage and exultation he caught her to him, smothering her face with kisses, the face that was still clammy from the touch of other lips. She lay back sighing, shielding herself a little against his violence; slowly her arms began to tighten instinctively about him. An owl hooted and he pulled himself free, snatching at the rolled-up fleeces and throwing them out at the open door. They fell soundlessly. Presently the owl hooted again.

"Jump!" he whispered savagely.

She hung back, clutching at the wall, protesting, beginning to sob again.

"Be quiet!" he spat out. "Do you want us to get our throats cut?" With a sudden push he tumbled her out into the chilly darkness full of a fine drizzle of rain. A moment later he jumped himself and landed up to his thighs in wool.

"Which way do you want to go?" March's sullen voice sounded beside him.

"Eastward," said Medraut.

Huddling close together the three of them set off across prickly stubble towards a deeper darkness. They climbed a stake fence and began to twist this way and that among enormous tree trunks. The forest fringe was open, cleared of brushwood and hard grazed by animals. Soon they were out of it, turning

left-handed and scrambling over dykes and through
a shallow stream. A dog barked nearby and there was
a fragrance of wood smoke in the air. March led the
way faster. Dripping twigs brushed their faces; they
plunged upwards into copse, seeming to battle with
an untrodden jungle, though March said that they
were on a path. All night they stumbled forward in
his tracks, up hill and down, always touching bark
or sodden foliage as they thrust out their hands
into blackness.

Sometimes they squatted down to rest for a few
minutes, silent, listening intently; there was nothing
but the low moan of wind in the forest and the inter-
mittent thudding of heavy drops on fallen leaves.
Gradually they were conscious of a greyness about
them, of branch patterns above their heads, and a
faint twittering of birds. It was dawn and the rain had
stopped. The woods thinned to a scattering of old
trees in a rusty sea of bracken; they stepped out on a
long glade of green turf, rising and falling, straight as
an arrow and ending at last in a waste of rush tufts
and black ooze.

There above lush grass and faded ragwort rose the
stuccoed walls of a villa—the image it seemed of Castel ys Coit, so that for a moment Medraut stared at it
suspiciously, thinking that March had led them in a
circle. Then he saw that the long, low roofs were
almost gone, reduced to a crazy skeleton of beams
and rotted rafters. They went in over the fallen stone
of a portico into a courtyard full of rubble heaps and
glistening dock-leaves. Monstrous nettle beds mounted against the broken walls of buildings where cattle
looked out through ragged openings, and in one corner smoke billowed up from a newly kindled fire.
There were people here, savage-looking peasants
crowding out with their dogs from dark rooms with
middens banked up under the windows. March knew
them. He asked for food, for the loan of a pony to

carry Gwenhyvar. For some time he argued amid a babel of gruff voices, barking dogs and bellowing beasts, while Medraut and Gwenhyvar stood apart from the rest, aware now of cold, sodden clothes and a leaden fatigue in their limbs.

"Some day Castel ys Coit will be like this," said Medraut.

"I was happy when I first saw it, but I was glad to go," said Gwenhyvar artlessly. "They were evil folk there, I think."

"No," said Medraut, "they were wiser than most of us Britons, acting according to reason, unmoved by the passions that make us prey to our enemies." She did not understand him and lapsed into dispirited silence.

Grudgingly the peasants gave what March demanded. He came up to Medraut.

"Which way?" he said in an undertone.

"Sarum."

March went back to the peasants and began asking the best way to Durnovaria and the sea to the south.

"Shall we not eat and sleep?" said Gwenhyvar, turning up a haggard face from where she sat on a stone slab by a filthy pool, that had once been the ornamental pond.

"We shall be followed," said March to Medraut. "My life is at stake as well as yours. I am for pushing on and resting in some solitary place with thick cover."

Gwenhyvar scrambled wearily on to a shaggy pony, then splashed through the swamp to southward and followed the green track pointing towards the sea. After a while they broke away eastwards again over chalky uplands patched everywhere with gorse brakes and thorny thickets. Avoiding flocks of sheep where there might be shepherds watching, they hid themselves in a grove of yew trees. After some of the food had been shared out they stretched themselves on the hard, dry ground. Gwenhyvar slept, Medraut tried to keep awake. He dozed from time to time; once he sat up with a start and saw March crawling towards Gwenhyvar, his heavy face alight with a lustful curiosity.

"I have kindled a fire in this young man that will not easily be put out," he said to himself, clenching his teeth and feeling instinctively for his sword. He remembered he was weaponless and looked thoughtfully at the short, heavy sword dangling from March's belt. For the first time he began to consider seriously how he should deal with the man whom he had sworn to make king of Dyvnaint.

'There is mettle in him,' he thought, 'a son of Milo is someone to be reckoned with—a good comrade he might be to me in the war that is to come, but he is like a dog with a bone; once he has set his teeth in it he will not let it go. Yes, my friend, those few minutes with Gwenhyvar will bring you death, and the sooner I can contrive it the better.'

Gwenhyvar woke shivering and sick. Stiffly she threw a leg over the pony and got on its bony back. She had no saddle and twice she would have fallen off from sheer weariness if March had not supported her. For a while she hardly noticed his hand steadying her over rough ground, clasping her waist, straying over her body in tentative caresses.

'Love,' she thought bitterly, 'love for Medraut has given me little joy since we set out from Camelot. What do I mean to him? No more, perhaps, than a hundred other women, except my being Arthur's wife, that famous jewel of Britain, that he lusts to have in his possession like some swift horse or well-strung harp. Here he trails me through the wilderness with never a word now that he has done to me what he wanted; a thief dreading only that what he has stolen be taken from him . . . and yet, were he walking beside me now instead of this ugly youth, his touch would soothe away all the fever from my body and the misery from my mind; I could be gay as a bird singing in spring.'

They came into a valley and saw above them bared out in the chalk on a smooth down the huge figure of a naked man with a club in his hand.

"Do you wish for children?" said March, staring hard at Gwenhyvar and walking close so that her knee brushed against him.

"What is that to you?" she said so sharply that his eyes dropped at first crestfallen and then took on a strange glitter.

"Lay yourself to sleep up there between the giant's thighs if you would bring forth," he said with a gloating laugh.

Gwenhyvar turned away from him with a qualm of fear and disgust. She remembered hearing this figure spoken of among the folk at Camelot, but no one had dared to hint about it to her, the childless wife of Arthur, no one had laid a hand on her and looked her in the eyes as this man was doing. . . . There was Medraut walking behind, seeming to notice nothing, his gaze on the ground. Then she remembered that March knew the way through these desolate places and Medraut did not, that he had a sword at his belt and Medraut was weaponless. Her cheeks flushed and tears came to her eyes as she stared hopelessly at the long rolling hills and the colourless sky, the hateful figure of the giant that seemed suddenly to symbolise man in all his arrogance, brutishness and stupid complacency. It enraged her to think that her life was grey and dreary as that sky unless Medraut came like the sun to kindle it with warmth and passion. . . . Abruptly she kicked the pony into a trot and went jogging painfully ahead towards forest horizons dissolving in a fresh haze of rain.

Towards noon they were on the flanks of higher hills, making quicker progress on short turf, but finding it hard to keep out of sight of human beings. Unmistakably they were drawing towards the great open downs dotted thickly with old villages, and still stocked with a vast wealth of sheep and cattle in spite of Saxon raiding. Suddenly March rushed to Gwenhyvar's bridle and wrenched the pony round. In frantic haste he led it into a winding alley among red-leaved brambles.

"Pursuit?" said Medraut, looking back at a long slope dotted with juniper bushes.

"I saw a man on a white horse ride out of that wood—Milo, for certain. I saw spears moving in the brake lower down; I never thought he would pick up our track so quickly. . . ." March stared from Medraut to Gwenhyvar, fingering his chin, his jaunty manner overcast with a rising despair.

"They head us off from the eastward-going tracks," said Medraut thoughtfully. "We must make North. I remember seeing a strong fortress at the gorge of Stour; most likely there will be folk in it now and there we could seek shelter."

"They will be Gereint's folk; no shelter will they be for me against my father. We should be safer with Conan."

"Maybe; but his forces are on the far side of Coit Mawr and heading towards Isca."

"What plan have you in your head?" said March, beginning to scowl and clench his fists. "I have no mind to be taken back to Castel ys Coit and crucified there. You swore to make me King of Dyvnaint; where is your power?"

"My power has other roots besides those in Gwent and Dyfet; but my first concern is not with you but with Gwenhyvar. She will be safe wherever Gereint's men can hold out."

"A woman is safe anywhere—it is the man who pays with his life!"

The blood rushed to Medraut's head; he foamed at the mouth and stooped as though ready to spring.

"You will put yourself before my woman, will you?" he snarled.

"Ready enough were you to put your life before her honour," said March grimly. He unsheathed his sword. "I am master here—I have a weapon and I know the way; she is as much my woman as yours. . . ."

"You, a swineherd, laying claim to Arthur's wife!" They eyed each other in blazing hate and contempt. Gwenhyvar watched them curiously; again a qualm went through her at the sight of March, coarse-featured like a peasant, strong as a bull, vicious as a young stallion. Medraut might have power in the palaces of kings, but March had power here on the hills of Durngueir, until he was pulled down by the hounds that came after him from Castel ys Coit. He would take her if he had the chance—the thought had been goading her ever since they passed below the giant cut in the chalk, and now the nagging soreness had become a hot pleasure. Here, surely, was a weapon she could use against the chilly subtlety of Medraut—the man who had never laid his hands on her since they left Camelot save for a few moments in Milo's house, among the bales of wool. 'How little I am to him!' she thought, 'and yet I shall never have peace while he is alive. Better perhaps for me if March kills him here and takes me with him, wandering from forest to forest as Gwalchmei took Olwen out of Deganwy. . . . Here stands a young man, fiery with lust, pitted against an elder man practised in guile, and they strive for me, forgetting that death follows fast in their footsteps!' Sitting on horseback she could see over the top of the brake how a company of riders spread out fanwise over the down.

"They come!" she said with a laugh.

Instinctively both March and Medraut turned their heads; they pulled aside the brambles and peered out at the open country. Without more ado Medraut struck the pony with his open hand and March pricked it with the sword. With lowered heads they ran along the narrowing glades keeping the beast to a canter. Breathlessly they came up on a brow where a great barrow stood out dimly in driving mist. On a lower spur of the hill was a fortress, pockmarked with old camp fires but now desolate. On they struggled through gorse and ling, hurrying back into scrub at the sight of men ploughing a terrace on the face of the down. High woods closed round them again; they slowed to a walk, continually looking over their shoulders. The hills dipped more and more steeply; they abandoned the pony and burst their way downwards into a level sea of undergrowth. March hewed some sort of passage with his sword.

"There should be a trackway here, but I have missed it," he said, dashing the sweat from his eyebrows.

He fought the tangle with maniacal fury, gaining a few more steps, and then they saw a greyness of water ahead through the interlocked branches. Now they were among willows and alders, already sinking knee-deep in the mud where flags stood up like green sword blades. March clambered out on a fallen tree. Here was the Stour eddying swiftly in the trough of the hills and across it was a huge dim slope carved at the top into banks and ditches. Faintly he saw people standing in clusters like little black stakes against the sky.

'Now we are at the crisis,' he thought. 'How shall I save myself and tear this woman out of Medraut's hands?' Once they had baffled the pursuers from

Castel ys Coit a mad desire leaped up in him again, the fire that had been smouldering all these long hours while he went beside Gwenhyvar, watching her lovely sullen face taking colour in the dawn, her slim body stretched out under the yew trees, the disdainful gleam in her eyes as she surveyed the obscene figure of the giant. Gradually he had lost interest in the vague hope of power held out by Medraut; his mind was set upon bending this woman to his will again, upon making her body welcome his in knowledge as it had done in ignorance. What was possession of land and warriors beside the possession of golden-headed Gwenhyvar!

He looked broodingly at the water flowing past; his eyes followed it, that silent glassy stream dimpled with little eddies, frothing here and there in a chain of bubbles that sailed away and vanished like dream pictures chasing each other on stealthy currents of thought. . . . All at once his gaze fell upon a little creek where a boat was moored to an overhanging branch, a boat with oars sticking out over the stern. In a flash a plan shot into his brain. He would get on board the boat with the other two, he would kill Medraut with the sword and row away with Gwenhyvar. Downstream they would go and into Avonmouth. There were sea-going fishermen there, so he had heard, much harried by Jutish raiders from Ynys Gweith. It might be easy to persuade some of them to make the passage to Armorica. . . .

He turned back along the tree trunk and found himself alone. He called, but the only answer was a rustling and snapping in the undergrowth further along the bank. They were hurrying away from him and towards the boat; perhaps they had already seen it—

March dashed after them. Here were their footprints filling up with water, a scrap of Gwenhyvar's cloak hung on a broken branch. . . . The shore curved in under the out-thrust trees; he saw a great log lying across an oozy place—he ran along it, but it crumbled into tinder under his weight; he slipped into the mud, sank deeper and deeper, threw himself on his face and wriggled frantically, dragging himself forward by clutching at reeds and rushes. It seemed as though he would never get to the rising ground, but at last he did, covered with black slime from head to foot and carrying the sword between his teeth. The boat was just beyond that thicket of bulrushes—he stumbled dizzily down to the water's edge and saw it was gone. There it was, however, far downstream, and drawing steadily nearer to the opposite shore. Medraut was rowing; Gwenhyvar sat in the stern looking back over her shoulder. They both saw him, but they made no sign. A moment later they were in under the bank, they sprang out and let the boat swing off and drift away. March stood motionless.

If he could have swum he would have followed them, but there had been no chance of learning to swim, herding swine in Coit Mawr. Slowly his eyes wandered away from the man and woman mounting the slopes towards the fortress; he saw a firm grassy track winding through the woods from which they had come, a track which began at the place where the boat had been moored. He remembered now that he had come here years ago with his father and Lucius, his elder brother. A boat had been here and they had got into it to cross the Stour. He had been made to row and Lucius had jeered at him for his lack of skill. . . .

A rider on a white horse came thundering down the path at a reckless gallop; behind him were more horsemen with lowered spears and heads ducking under the canopy of branches. He saw again the coldly staring eyes of his father, Lucius with fiery cheeks and lips drawn back in a malevolent grin, and many other faces that he had known ever since he could remember anything at Castel ys Coit. For a moment he raised the sword thinking: 'No son of Milo has my strength, none is a match for me in sword play; let the servant show that he is a better man than his master,' then he threw the weapon on the ground and folded his arms.

Far upon the hillside Medraut and Gwenhyvar paused to look back.

"Milo has come, but there is no boat for him," said Medraut. "We are beyond his reach."

"What are they doing there, all in a knot by the waterside?" said Gwenhyvar with a slight shudder.

"They are digging a grave for March," he said, beginning to whistle softly.

"He might have been a famous man if he had lived."

"If he had won the love of Gwenhyvar he would have been more famous than the March who died in battle west of London—Cunomor, the slayer of Drystan—a grave there is for March, a grave for Gwythyr, a grave for Gwgawn of the ruddy sword . . ." he said musingly.

"A grave for Gwythyr, my father!" she said, turning pale.

"He fell at the gate of Alcluyd when the Picts began war again a little while ago. Friendless you are now in Britain save for me, Gwenhyvar, yet you will be safe enough in yonder fortress."

"And you?" she stared at him, fascinated, yet with horror dawning in her eyes.

"My course lies in the track of Brawdbach among the Saxons and of Brude among the Picts. Farewell for a little while, Gwenhyvar." He turned abruptly and went in long swinging strides across the face of the down eastwards into the gloom of coming night.

CHAPTER XXVII

Maelgun Gwyneth

O THOU DRAGON OF THE ISLAND . . . THE FIRST IN MISCHIEF,
EXCEEDING MANY IN POWER AND ALSO IN MALICE, MORE LIB-
ERAL THAN OTHERS IN GIVING, MORE LICENTIOUS IN SINNING,
STRONG IN ARMS, BUT STRONGER IN WORKING THINE OWN
SOUL'S DESTRUCTION, MAGLOCUNE!
                                —Gildas, *De Excidio Britanniae.*

Arthur, Kai and Bedwyr had fared well in their
mission to Cuneglas. The King of Powys had
entertained them with splendid hospitality; a
beacon had been lit on Vricon to call the tribesmen to
arms, a messenger had gone on a swift horse to seek
out Conan and bid him turn back from the harrying
of Dyvnaint on pain of war. Now they were on their
way across Mon to confer with Maelgun in the palace
of Din Ligwy.

The riders drew rein on a heath and looked back
at the stormy sunset, at the great mountain mass of
Arvon, blue shadowed, its peaks grey with new-fallen
snow, its western faces flooded with red light, a realm
of desolate splendour brooding over the low country
chequered with little fields and stunted copses, misted with smoke trails in the windy dusk.

"Here," said Bedwyr, "beats the heart of the British race, cheery with milk and mead, locked in by mighty ribs of mountains; a good land thick with folk, Mon mam Cymru."[1]

"Strongest in arms but blackest in heart of all the princes is Maelgun Gwyneth." said Kai gloomily.

"The glory of our race fades like yonder sunset; but it may well be that here in Gwyneth we shall out-live the fury of our enemies, a brood of folk nesting like eagles among the mountain crags, savage of heart and sudden in warlike deeds." Arthur turned his horse and they rode over the crest towards thatched roofs and firelight and a gathering hum of voices. "It is from Caer Ebrauc and London that Britain will be ruled in years to come, as it was in the old days of Rome, from the rich lands in the East, not from places such as this, a warren of little huts, nor from the tumbled stone walls of Deganwy," he said with a sigh, stroking the stubbly beard on his chin, and looking sombrely at the swarm of people rushing to meet him, men, women and children swept by hys-terical ardour, with glassy eyes and gaping mouths, like a pack of hounds acclaiming a master:

"Hail, Arthur yr Amherawdyr! Welcome to Mon!"

The riders threaded their way through the squalid confusion of a camping place, they went by a grave mound broken open by treasure seekers, a ragged hump of trampled turf out of which emerged a vast table-like stone set over a black cavity, they swung themselves from their saddles by a pair of tall lime-stone pillars in a wall made up of undressed blocks of stone as children might build in miniature with peb-bles on a beach. Arthur stepped into a narrow alley packed with shouting people; a tall conical roof loomed up wreathed in smoke, with gusts of sparks

[1] Mona, mother of the Cymry, so called because of its fertility.

flying in the wind, and beyond it the clamour of voices and the confusion of man's handiwork ended suddenly on a cliff edge. Like a pale, frosty plain the sea stretched away silvery-grey into a fume of mist and sullen cloud-masses heavy with rain.

The round hall of Maelgun held a huddled circle of guests—dark-browed men and laughing women, and the king's hand rested amorously on the waist of a girl with flushed cheeks, full red lips and eyes black as sloes, eyes that had the veiled unspeculative look of animal contentment. Lazily her fingers twisted the dirty locks of a sheepskin rug and a naked foot rubbed its instep persistently on the king's shoe. On the other side of Maelgun sat Arthur, erect and grim, his weatherbeaten face expressionless, unchanging, as from a hundred throats came a chanted chorus: "Glory to the Dragon of Mon! Glory to the Eagle of Arvon! Long life and victory to Maelgun Gwyneth!" All round the hall hands shot out clutching mead horns; the liquor splashed over the grimy fingers and fell sizzling on hot ash and glowing embers; the folk drank, every face turned towards the huge figure of Maelgun leaning back with a brooding smile.

Suddenly there was a commotion in the doorway. A young monk thrust his way on to the floor and stood by the fire raising a clenched, trembling fist—a lanky, youthful figure, hollow-cheeked, with straight beetling brows, a straight, sharp nose, and a mouth that was a hard straight line. His whole bearing had the tenseness of a wild beast confronted with its enemies; his eyes burned with passionate hatred, and the company gazed at him spell-bound, hypnotised by a spirit that flamed out so fiercely in such a frail body.

"Woe to you, Maelgun Gwyneth!" he shouted. "Woe to you, mightier than other kings in stature and in arms, and mightiest of all in sin! Do you remember that God's eye is upon you, where you sit exalted

above your company of bloody-minded men? Have
you no ears for the words of the prophet: 'Woe be to
thee who spoilest! Shalt not thou thyself be spoiled?'
What has your life been from boyhood up but a horrid trail of lusts, treacheries, and abominable murders, and why are you today still foolishly rolling in
that black pool of your offences? In warlike fury you
have oppressed your fellow Christians, even your
kinsfolk, grasping for power and pleasure; strong
with the weapons of hell, you have triumphed over
those that wore the armour of light: the just and the
innocent. By whose hand has your wedded wife come
to her end? Aye, you tyrant, you may smile in your
might, knowing that none in our nation dare take
vengeance upon you, but none the less know that
God's vengeance is certain; for has he not said
through the mouth of his prophet: 'The bloodthirsty
and deceitful men shall not live out half their days?'
Why do you heap fresh sins upon your kingly shoulders so that you are bent down from low to lower,
from bad to worse, letting your lust consume that
woman who is your nephew's wife, dragging her
down with you into the foul pits of hell? I say to
you, Maelgun, that not only you and your partner
in guilt shall bear God's punishment; our whole
nation shall reap what you have sown: misery and
desolation! The flames of war and the stinking
abomination of pestilence shall lay waste this lovely land of Britain, the fields of the valley and the
strong places on the hills. On just and unjust, on
the humble peasant and on the proud master of
warriors shall God's displeasure break like a thun-
derstorm on a smiling cornfield, not once, but
again and again in centuries to come. Woe to
Britain! Woe, I say, for the crimes of Maelgun
Gwyneth!" He passed a hand over his eyes, tottered,
and sank down in a heap by the fire.

A low murmur went round the hall, a murmur of anger tinged with dread, but Maelgun's voice broke out, undismayed, filled only with a kindly contempt.

"It is the young monk, Gildas," he said. "I know his face from the days when I dwelt among the brethren at Bangor ys Coit; a dreaming mind is his in a sickly body. Do him no harm; doubtless he has walked here fasting day after day over moor and mountain. Such men have visions and they babble folly; their words are meaningless as cloud shapes in the wind. Who has not seen monstrous beasts and toppling towers in the sky, and mountains that are stained with blood or that glow like iron in a furnace? Yet we whose feet are planted in the earth, we who live in health and strength, with food in our bellies and hot blood in our veins, we know that these spectacles are no concern of ours, portending at most a fine day or a shower of rain. So it is with the ravings and vapourings of those that lead unnatural lives, at war with their own bodies. Do not raise your hands against him, I say! Give him food; for hospitality he shall have who comes to me in Din Ligwy, be he a crazy monk or the Amherawdyr of Britain."

A woman got up and scraped out a stew of meat from a cooking pot into a chipped red bowl embossed with naked figures from the days of the Empire. She put it in the youth's lap and laid a hand pityingly on his shaven forehead. The savoury steam rose to his nostrils; slowly he lifted his head and began to eat with his fingers, at first mechanically, then with a shame-faced ravenousness.

Maelgun turned to Arthur. "The monks give us ugly words till we stop their mouths with meat," he said. "It is the same from the bishops downwards, and yet how do they live at all except by the strength of men such as us, who go through life taking the women we desire and clearing enemies from our paths as a woodcutter lays low the thick trees? For we are the men, Arthur, that broke the might of the Saxons on Badon Hill, we are the deliverers of Britain."

The mead horns rose afresh amid a shout:

"We drink to Maelgun Gwyneth and Arthur yr Amherawdyr!"

"God bore with our sins and gave us victory over the heathen," said Arthur slowly. "Yet how do we use the peace that we have won?" His eyes wandered round the circle of fire-lit faces and rested on that of the woman leaning drowsily against the king's shoulder. 'This is the wife of Maelgun's nephew,' he thought. 'This is mortal sin, so says the Church. Are the priests right, that our race is poisoned by lust, and that a natural vice, being indulged, sprouts quickly into uglier growths: unnatural vice, murder, and war? Evil comes boldly into the light of day when a nation is shaken to its foundations, as nettles smother the wreck of a fallen building. . . .' Suddenly he laid his hand on Maelgun's arm. "Put forth your strength, King!" he said. "Deliver Britain afresh from the war that rages where no heathen have yet set foot! Use your might to make peace in Dyvnaint; let us bind our wounds and forgive the men that dealt them. Let us turn our faces once more to the East and fight a new battle of Badon."

Maelgun shook his head. "Your mind dwells ever on the Saxons," he said with a laugh. "They will always be with us, do what we will, like flies coming after meat, like the lice in our houses, and the wolves in our woods; we need not live in fear of them. More deadly to us in Gwyneth are the weapons wielded in British hands. It is not sorrow to me that the cats of Gwent and Dyfet have set their claws in the old rat of Dyvnaint, and that the dog of Powys shall worry the cats; for then men will see that I am the master of the dog, and mine will be the power over prince and peasant, from the cliffs of Penwith to the sands of Dee.

Hear me, men! The day comes when Maelgun Gwyneth shall be overlord of Britain!" A roar of voices answered him: a savage exultant yell, an echo of the hatred of Celt for Celt from far-off days when the chieftains stood back and allowed Caradoc to struggle single-handed against the might of Rome; a portent for the murder of Urien at Dinguardi, for the dreadful strife of Briton against Briton on the field of Arderydd in days to come . . . .

Naked steel flashed aloft in the firelight, the woman thrust herself into the king's embrace, only Gildas, sitting over his bowl of meat, muttered the words: "The wages of sin are death."

In a low voice Kai said to Arthur: "Dangerous it is for the Amherawdyr of Britain to sit in the house of Maelgun, as it was for Uther in the hall under Moel Fre." In silence the three men stood up, Arthur, Kai, and Bedwyr; they crossed the floor and went out into the night, wrapping their cloaks round them against the driving rain.

"There is no help to be got here," said Bedwyr. "Shall we take ship for Eire or ride to our friends in Reged?"

"We shall go to Cuneglas and urge him to bring this war to an end." Arthur stood with his face upturned to the overcast sky, while Kai led out the horses.

"What then?" said Bedwyr.

"My only hope is to gather folk in Armorica, to use their strength against the Saxons and save our nation even against its own will."

"The sooner we are out of Mon the better; a king is jealous of the man who stirs the hearts of the people," grunted Kai.

It was noon next day when they came to the shores of Conwy and waited in a group of fishermen for boats to ferry them across. A cluster of small craft made towards them, the rowers pulling hard against the incoming tide. A young man in a steel helmet stood in the prow of the leading boat, angry-eyed, twirling a javelin impatiently. Even before the keel grounded he sprang out and waded ashore ahead of his men.

"Here comes Meredith, Maelgun's brother's son, with folk from the east," said one fisherman to another, "back from some warlike errand on the Saxon march."

"A dangerous guest he will be at Din Ligwy."

"Too long has he been away from Bronwen's bed."

"A wife is soon consoled in the house of Maelgun Gwyneth!"

The young man went by with hardly a glance at the bare-footed fishermen and the three gloomy-faced warriors sitting their horses under the dripping trees. In a moment a crouching figure darted out at him, something gleamed in a knotted fist, and Meredith stumbled forward with a knife planted in his back.

When his men raised him up he was dead: unsheathing their weapons, they looked round for his murderer, but the man was gone in a flash behind the fishermen's huts. Like a darting bird he vanished among glittering hollies and shining rods of hazel.

"A sturdy young man brought down by a foul blow," said Bedwyr grimly.

"Deadly is the ill-will of Maelgun Gwyneth!" said Kai.

Arthur said nothing. As he rode to the water's edge the word SIN rang in his ears with each clash of Lamrei's shoes on the shingle.

CHAPTER XXVIII

The Dyke

THE MAGNANIMOUS ARTHUR.

—Nennius, *Historia Britonum.*

The war which had flamed up in Dyvnaint came suddenly to an end. Conan and Vortipore had met with a tough resistance when they pursued Cadwy into the West; a raid on Sarum had been beaten off, the threat of invasion from Powys determined them to make peace. For a week the kings camped in the overgrown buildings of Aquae Sulis where tall columns rose above the green-scummed pools of the great baths, once the fashionable pleasure resort of Roman Britain, now a haunt of pike and moorfowl. By hard bargaining with Cadwy, by the gift of a lovely girl who tempted the ungovernable passion of Cuneglas, Conan was able to push his frontier southward. Vortipore, deserted by his ally, got nothing and went back to Dyfet meditating on a fresh bond with Maelgun.

It was a hard task to make a limit to Conan's claims on the vast grazing grounds north of Sarum. In the end it was Cuneglas who said: "There is but one man in Britain who will decide this business without favour either to Conan or to Cadwy, and that is Arthur. Let us abide by his decision."

So, Arthur, who stood aloof from the threats and intrigues of the treaty makers, rode out with the kings from Aquae Sulis by the Roman highway that pointed towards London. From hill to hill they rode over the bare downs, into deep woods, and out again to a beaconstead where the land reached its highest point between the Thames and the Narrow Sea. Men followed, planting stakes or marking the old mile-stones and forest trees. A line was drawn from Avon mouth along the hills to Aquae Sulis and thence east-wards for near on forty miles, and men were set to labour at a great dyke with its fosse to the north, the new frontier of Dyvnaint for all time to come, so the kings swore before a priest, and Arthur sat there on Lamrei thinking: 'This is the best I can do; I have taken no vengeance for the killing of the men who loved me best: Gereint and Gwalchmei and the son Garwen bore to me, the son who might have been a greater man than his father. I have shorn land from my kinsfolk and given it to a man whose greed and wickedness have made him hated far and wide, but I have bought peace between Gwent and Dyvnaint that will endure, maybe, so long as this dyke shows above the ground.' He left the company of the three kings in a downland village, sitting at ale round a parchment shakily inscribed in Latin by a priest. They could not read what was written there: the forgiveness of injuries, the vow of peace, the way-marks of the new frontier— but they set their seals below the lettering: CVNE-GLASSVS, CATHOVIVS, AVRELIVS CONANVS.

Southward Arthur rode with Kai and Bedwyr in the pale winter sunshine, over the gently rolling hills and up to the beetling stockades of Sarum, that mighty bulwark of British power on the Saxon march. It was fourteen years since he had ridden in at Sarum

Gate with Garwen at his side, with a host of men chanting the grim Song of the Cymry. Then his mind had been clouded with anxiety, thinking of the tide of destruction flowing from the East, yet he had been light of heart, for about him he felt the trust of men with whom he had shared deadly peril, and the love of a girl that seemed like bird-song in sunlit woods, a breath of sweet contentment, of hope, and ecstasy. Now he could tell himself that his labour had not been in vain for Britain, but his heart was heavy for all that he had lost in these few weeks since he had thrown dice on the hill above Indec's house.

"We three are all that are left from the fellowship that came on a winter's day to Sarum, that made the passage of Coit Mawr, and housed for the first time at Camelot," he said sadly, as the horses scrambled up the steep chalky track to the city. Kai nodded, but Bedwyr said with a wan gaiety: "Mabon lives in Reged; and not all the men of the legion fell at Long-borth; some had gone into Kernou before the battle and some are here in Sarum—aye, and Garwen is still a beautiful woman, unwedded at Ynys Gutrin. A bright face you wore, Arthur, when she rode her pony among the champions."

Arthur was silent. The old horse Lamrei slowed to a walk. She had carried him to Badon Hill and on many a wild ride through Dyvnaint, sallying out at daybreak through the elder copses that grew on the slopes of Camelot, but now her strength had ebbed away. She would carry him to the sea when he took ship for Armorica and there he would have to part from her. . . . A great weariness came over his own spirit. Young though he was in years and strong in body, he felt no zest for the tasks that lay ahead of him. His ambition had been to build a new Britain founded on valour and comradeship, and now he saw that it was beyond his power. The kings had been too strong for him, they had struck the weapon from his hand; Medraut had gone beside him like a dark shadow, prophesying failure, working secretly for a plan of his own. Slowly that plan was emerging like some mountain peak from clinging mist. . . . He remembered now that it was Medraut who had thrust Garwen into his arms, Medraut who had shown him to Gwenhyvar as a man like other men . . . "Arthur our leader, Christ our King"—those words had a gleam of splendour when the Cymry listened to them on Moel Fre, but now he saw that Medraut had sung even then in a spirit of irony. Who was Arthur, the man who had given himself carelessly to lust, the blood-stained warrior, butcher of his own brother and of his own son, who was he to have his name coupled with the Saviour of Mankind? Armorica—that was his last hope, the faint chance that he might find a new weapon in the folk who had fled from their homeland; and meanwhile Medraut had loosed the bond of blood—he was gone to arm himself with the might of Britain's enemies.

That evening Arthur sat in the old frescoed building that had once been a Christian church, in the very room where he had once lain with Garwen, but which was now the lodging of Gwenhyvar. They sat facing each other, yet avoiding each other's eyes, each with a vision that they had no mind to reveal in words.

"For many months you have not shown yourself to me," said Gwenhyvar listlessly. "Where have you been while war swept across Dyvnaint, your men fell by the sword, and your house went up in flames?"

"I have been at Lis Pengwern, in Mon, and at Aquae Sulis. I have made peace—I have healed the wound which for years has drained life-blood from the West."

"You come here a homeless man with two companions. Where is your power? What profit have you for victory in the North and victory in the South save the figure of a horse on Badon Hill and an empty title—Amherawdyr of Britain?"

"Profit to me there is none," he said with a shrug of the shoulders. "I can reckon only the loss of friends and kinsmen; yet I have given the nation a breathing space."

"Power you had once, but it was little gain to me. Little more than a roof over my head you gave me in Camelot while you rode abroad in wanton adventure. The wife of the Amherawdyr did not fare as well as a mistress of Conan or Cuneglas. Now even Camelot is gone and I live on the charity of Cadwy."

"A new hall shall be built at Camelot. . . ." he said, but his thoughts were elsewhere. 'Would Garwen have spoken thus to me if I came to her a lonely man, fallen from power?'

"Much thought you give to the welfare of our nation, but did you think of my welfare when you rode away to the North and left me to shift for myself amid the clash of armies?"

"It was the chance of war—the Cymry fought and fell, and Camelot fell with them," he said mechanically, while a new thought grew in his mind. 'She, too, is glad to see my glory dimmed, my friends shorn away. Her mind follows in the track of those that hate me. Bitter is the heart of the childless wife and easily given into another's keeping.'

"Long ago, at Alcluyd maybe, I told you that I would not live content, housed in a hut on some ramparted hill, as women and cattle are housed while enemies are in the land. Our wars ceased, but did I have what was due to the foremost woman in Britain—a life of ease, servants to wait on me, warm rooms where no soot lies on the walls and no rain drips through the roof, baths and flowers and a fountain playing in the court?" she said dreamily, twisting a ring upon her finger.

"Who can give you such things in Britain today?" said Arthur, gazing at her broodingly, his chin on his hand.

"I know well that you cannot, even if you had the will," she said in an angry voice, while suddenly the colour rushed to her cheeks. He found his heart beginning to beat heavily. 'How beautiful she is,' he thought, 'and yet she brings me neither comfort nor desire, for though we sit together in this little room I am sundered from her by the sinful vision of a better woman and she from me by some discontent, some secret and deadly thing that has fretted her spirit from the first days of our wedded life.'

"Is that all that you wish for, Gwenhyvar?" he said with the flicker of a smile. "I might well give it you across the sea in Armorica. There is a land without strife, they say, and folk live as they did in Roman days . . . Or was it the husband, rather than the home, that weighed upon your heart all those years at Camelot?" he said gently, yet with a spice of grimness.

She did not answer; suddenly wary, she thought: 'What would he do to me if he knew? My secret is in Olwen's keeping—she hates me, but she is not here.'

"Silence may give as good an answer as the spoken word," he said, and thought: 'Why should I torment her with my presence here—a woman who is hungry for love, but not for my love? There is a change in her since we were together in Camelot, the gloom in her eyes has surely changed to fear and hate.'

"Unfaithful you have been to me, not once, but many times. Did not a son of yours fall among the Cymry at Longborth?" she said in a toneless voice, thinking: 'Here is my keenest weapon against Arthur, this horrible bear, this iron hammer. Such is my defence for what I did in Milo's house, and yet it is a defence that puts me to shame. Only a woman could

taunt a man with the death of his son—a son such as
Lacheu. Hard are men in their dealings with us, but
we women are crueller and more pitiless when we
strike back.'

"Weak we are, all of us, Gwenhyvar; our whole
nation sinks under its load of sin and God gives it the
wages of sin. In my pride years ago I thought that I
was chosen to show our people the path to power. I
thought that I should knit the nation together in a
bond of blood and make it strong through sacrifice,
deserving of justice at man's hands and favour from
God. I thought little, maybe, of sin; I loved the people
and the land that was theirs, as a man may love a
woman more and not less because her soul and body
are blemished. I even thought that the sin in us
would add fierceness to our strokes against the enemies of Britain. It may be so, yet the weapons we use
turn in our hands and bring us to destruction. I have
gone my way; men reckon that I have achieved much,
but you reckon it at little. You are right; my hopes are
blasted, even as they deserve to be in the eye of God.
But beware, Gwenhyvar, lest your desires be guided
by powers of darkness! There are mighty men in the
land climbing to greater and greater power, men who
exult openly in lust and treachery; splendid figures
they may seem to you beside the man here whose
course is downward, yet beware of casting in your lot
with men such as Conan, Maelgun, and Medraut."

He rose to his feet, stared at her for a moment as
though he would have said more, then passing a
hand over his brow he went out of the little room,
leaving her alone with the figures on the frescoed
walls: men with mournful eyes and haloes round
their heads.

A sudden terror came over Gwenhyvar. She knew
now that Arthur made her ashamed of the evil in her
nature, while Medraut drew it out caressingly, and
made it a thing of delight. The haunting beauty of his

face, the swiftness of his mind, the soft tones of his voice, the music that sprang from his harp, gentle as the first rhythms in love play, or leaping to the clash of galloping hoofs on some ocean beach, a vision of sea and storm and desolate earth—all this drowned her senses like the heady perfume of meadowsweet in marshy woods. She knew that the sweetness that flooded into her was not of love; it was of lust, cruelty, and vicious imaginings—a radiance from the fires of hell.

'If Arthur loved me,' she thought, 'he could break this enchantment in which I am caught fast, but his love faded away when he found Garwen and will never green again for me—and I have no will to blot out those visions which began on the walls of Bregion and brought me at last to Milo's house, and will lead farther yet to joy, horror, and death. . . .'

* * *

There came a morning soft with a foretaste of spring when larks winged their way upwards against the blue vault of the sky above the broad grey downs. In a long line of stooping figures, men hacked and shovelled to make a dyke, mounting steadily towards the green beaconstead, the symbol of peace in the West. Up the slopes from dim scrub and fire-blackened gorse came two riders on white horses, a man and a boy. They drew rein by the stake that marked the dyke's end and looked at the line of white earthwork stretching west as far as the eye could reach.

"A mighty task, Father! What is the meaning in it?" said the boy in the guttural tongue of the Saxons. Letting the reins slip through his fingers as his horse lowered its head to crop the sweet downland turf, he sat at ease in the saddle, watching the swing of mattocks and basket-loads of chalk being carried up the rampart.

"There is no meaning in it, Cynric, for us West Saxons," answered Cerdic. His lean, hatchet face was now sunk in to the bone by wasting illness following on a wound got in the retreat from Badon Hill, but his eyes still had their hawk-like brightness and in his mind was still the vision of power glimpsed as he stood alone on the Broch of Guinion. "Those folk labouring there are like ants toiling blindly in the path of a marching army that will trample them underfoot," he said with a swift gesture of contempt. "I shall not see the day, but it will come in your time or in the time of your children, when all that we look on here will be Saxon earth, far away to the Severn Sea and the western mountains. For our race it is that shall break the power of the British princes and undo the work of Arthur."[1]

---

[1] It was Cynric who stormed Sarum in 552; his sons
Ceawlin and Cutha broke through to the Severn in 577,
destroyed Lis Pengwern, and carried their arms into the plains
of Dee.

Chapter XXIX

Sunshine on Aleth

A HINT FROM THE *Geste des Bretons.*

For seven years Arthur stayed in Armorica, the guest of Hoel the Great, his mother's kinsman. With Kai and Bedwyr he had gone from one end of the land to the other. He knew the settlers of the north, dark sullen folk whose gloom seemed partly the aftermath of their flight from Britain and partly a resonance from the primeval oak forest that overshadowed their new homes; he knew also the gayer, more barbarous tribes of the Atlantic seaboard, where faith in the druids lingered on among the great stone monuments of an earlier race. But wherever he went he found the same disunion, the same regional feuds that were the bane of Britain, and on the eastern frontier was the menace of Frankish conquest. The Franks, indeed, were now Christians and had evolved far beyond the ferocious invaders of Britain; for the moment their energy was being absorbed by a rapid expansion over Central and Southern Gaul, but the time was coming when they must surely attempt to dominate Celtic Armorica. Hoel's mastery of the land was too uncertain for him to unite all the princes against Childebert, the Frank, and though he bore Arthur nothing but good will, he could hold out no hope of sending armies across the Narrow Sea. As viewed from Armorica, Britain was clearly a ship drifting rudderless in a gathering storm; the crew were deserting her, even Arthur, the hero of the twelve battles . . .

It was a summer's day in Aleth, an old city planted on a hill where the sandy bays of Rance opened out into a sea studded with gorse-covered islands and eerie humps of rock. Within a circle of Roman walls and towers clustered slate-roofed houses of dark stone or peeling stucco, and paved streets radiated out in orderly fashion from a forum or struggled up towards the citadel in a labyrinth of narrow lanes among creeper-covered walls and hanging gardens. A few ships were moored at the quays, fishermen's boats sped over the land-locked waters, and on a bleak ridge across the harbour was the tiny dome of a hermit's cell. A holy man was newly come there from Dyvnaint and his preaching had diverted the rough country folk from druidic rites on an island in the open sea.

Arthur leaned over the parapet of the citadel looking northward to the white-flecked distances of the Narrow Sea. Up here a fresh breeze blew, driving little sand storms along the deserted footwalks of the fortress; down below there was a stifling air in the city streets and the slate roofs quivered in the blazing sunshine. Somewhere down there in that warren of old houses never yet sacked by an invader were Kai and Bedwyr, whiling away the day with dice and women and the harsh-tasting wine of Armorica, but Arthur stood alone, his eyes following the slow approach of a beaked galley rowing in against the wind, a ship possibly from Britain, though few vessels nowadays risked an encounter with Saxons pirate craft nosing along the coasts of Dyvnaint. It was the extreme danger of a voyage across the Narrow Sea that made it necessary to leave Gwenhyvar behind in Cadwy's charge. The ships in Aleth's harbour seldom left the sight of Armorican cliffs when they put to sea. Most often they went up the winding reaches of Rance, under the rolling heights, billowy with oak woods, to Dinan, where Hoel had lately been carrying on an ineffective struggle with Comorre, a protégé of Childebert.

Arthur lost interest in the galley, which to his mind had too much of the old Roman pattern about her to have come from British harbours—he looked idly at the glittering water, the rusty grey sands where children ran to and fro, the quiet town sweltering in the heat, the hovels creeping out beyond the gates towards green cornfields and ripening hay at the forest edge. War eddied fitfully through the land not very far away, perhaps, yet here was peace; Armorica had a fast-rooted people that would weather the storms of tribal hatreds and Frankish ambitions. Britain might be doomed—despite Badon Hill, despite the seed that he had sown in creating the Cymry—but in Armorica something might be saved. He had come here planning to lead the British race back to Britain, but was he not fighting against a racial impulse as a keeper of bees might strive vainly to prevent a swarm from leaving a hive and seeking fresh quarters?

'Perhaps my work lies here,' he said to himself. 'From Gaul our races came in past ages, so men say, and to Gaul it is returning, now that its power has gone down in sin.' Pictures streamed through his mind of the land which the Briton had enjoyed for a while and which was now slipping from his grasp—the great plains in the east streaked with grass-grown roads and studded with burnt-out towns, the valleys of the West with their clustered huts taking the place of crumbling cities, herds of cattle wading in green seas of bracken where once had been cornfields, blue hills rising wave beyond wave under sunset skies . . . a lovely land, but fertile in tyrants, choked with foolish pride, with lust and savagery as by a monstrous growth of thistles.

'I will have some good ships manned with warriors; they shall sail to Dyvnaint and bring Gwenhyvar to me here in Aleth,' he thought. 'Here we shall begin life afresh, a happier life, maybe, than that we led together in Britain.'

He leaned back against the wall in a patch of shade thrown by an ivied turret. The heavy scent of gorse came up to him from sunbaked slopes and a gentle murmur from the sea. He fell asleep and dreamed that he was lying beside Gwyll on the cliffs by Trevalga. Slowly she turned her face towards him and he saw that it was Garwen in the little vaulted room at Sarum. The gloomy-eyes saints stood behind her raising warning fingers, and he thought: 'This girl is my heart's desire, but she tempts me to sin, she robs me of God's grace. Either I may have Garwen and be as other men, or I may thrust her from me and become one of that band of saints. To those that tread down the lusts of the flesh is given power to work miracles in this world, and everlasting glory in the world to come,' And then comfort flowed into him as a voice seemed to say: 'There is no sin between you and Garwen, for your wife is gone; she is yours no longer,' and then a chill fell upon him, for he seemed to hear the mocking laughter of Medraut and a wailing cry that rose from end to end of Britain . . .

He awoke with a start and sprang up, for a growing murmur of voices was in the air. Along the rampart walk came three men—Kai and Bedwyr and a stranger, a man with dark-piercing eyes and coal-black hair, wearing a seaman's tunic. Behind them at a distance came a throng of townsmen, anxious-faced, making a threatening clamour to which the stranger paid not the least heed.

"A man has come from Britain to speak with you, Arthur," said Kai, and even his impassive face showed signs of excitement. "Lucius, son of Milo, is his name and he has sailed hither with a cargo of goods from Durngueir. He brings news and a summons to you from Cadwy, and not only from Cadwy but from Cuneglas and from Maelgun Gwyneth."

Lucius raised his arm in the old Roman salute; he looked keenly at Arthur, a long, measuring stare that betrayed nothing of his mind. There was a silence on those dusty, sunlit ramparts, but an uneasy murmur still sounded from the town below.

"Speak, you bird of ill omen!" said Arthur gruffly. Between blue sky and glittering sea he had striven to forget that cloud-swept land of Britain, but Britain would not forget him. . . .

"Your work is perishing, Arthur," said Lucius in a calm, business-like tone, an echo from past ages when the fortunes of Britain were not swayed by the windy eloquence of the Celt. "The Picts and Saxons are united against us in the West. They have taken hostages from Maelgun and they have harried in Powys; Conan is their friend, and now their main force is encamped on Cadwy's border. The kings offer to submit in the hope of saving something from the wreck, but the common people call for Arthur."

"Who is the man who has raised this power?" said Arthur in a dull voice. At once they all spoke:

"Need you ask? Have you been blind all these years?"

"There is only one man who could have done it."

"Your kinsman, Medraut."

"We have held off Saxons and Picts before this. Has the spirit of our rulers sunk so low that they cannot strike now as they did at Badon Hill? Why must they yield to Medraut when they did not yield to Cerdic?"

"Medraut has split the nation by his league with Gwent," said Lucius. "He has Britons as well as Barbarians under his standard—men from the midland forests and the fens, and men whose blood is blended with the Saxon. No king is resolute to challenge him, for no king dare trust his neighbours. Vortipore will not move because Medraut swears to him in peace; nothing pleased Maelgun more than to see Cuneglas overthrown."

"If the kings will not defend the nation, what can I do? I who have no more than two men to stand at my side, Bedwyr and Kai."

"You are the one man who can turn the tide. If you set up your Red Dragon in Britain men will flock to it. Rather than be ruled by Medraut and his pagan hosts they will leave the kings and follow you. As things go worse for us, so the seed you planted grows to a mighty tree."

"The Cymry are not dead!" Bedwyr struck the parapet with his fist. "The next generation of Britons shall be Cymry from the rock of Alcluyd to the cliffs of Kernou."

"To my mind," said Kai sharply, "Arthur has as much call to stand by his kinsman Hoel, adding strength and glory to Armorica. Twelve great battles he won for Britain and what thanks did he get? A white horse and a wooden hall on the hill of Camelot. Not so easily will you take him back with you, Lucius, for the people of Aleth will sink your ship rather than see Arthur depart in it."

"In all those battles Medraut stood by my side. Little heart have I to turn my sword against him and save kings from their own folly," said Arthur, looking dreamily at the ivory-bosomed thunder clouds mounting the sky to northward.

"Cadwy and Mabon are your kinsmen as well as Hoel," said Bedwyr.

"Think not of the kings but the nation," said Lucius urgently. "Something has been saved here across the sea, but in a little while all will be trodden out in Britain."

"You work for your own ends, Lucius," said Kai bitterly. "We know of you here in Aleth better than we did in Camelot—you and your father and your band of brothers that keep to the Roman ways and have possessions hidden in Coit Mawr that might be envied by any king in Britain. You have good cause to dread the coming of Pict and Saxon, for yours is a frail tree like a pine that snaps before the blast, while we men of the beehive huts and ramparted hills, we are like stubborn willows that rise again when the storm is gone and shoot up swiftly after the axe has laid us low."

"If Arthur will not come for love of the people, let him come for vengeance on the man who has carried away his wife," flung back Lucius. "All Britain knows that Gwenhyvar is the prize that brings Arthur's nephew questing to Dyvnaint."

"Has Cadwy yielded her up?" Arthur's voice rose to a shout, but in his heart a small voice seemed to say: 'Is it a greater matter to you, the fate of a woman who loves you not, than the fate of a people who call on you in their agony?'

"She is part of the price that Cadwy must give if he will have peace. The Saxons shall have what they will between Exe and Tamar and Medraut shall have Gwenhyvar to keep him company at Camelot," replied Lucius in a hard voice.

Kai and Bedwyr looked away, thinking dubiously of what path led through these mazes of guile, dishonour, and sin. Arthur said: "Have you a message for me from Gwenhyvar?"

"I have," said Lucius, after a moment's pause.

"Why did you not give it first?"

"In Coit Mawr we do not lay much weight on women's words." Lucius folded his arms with a show of indifference; his mind was busy behind his unfaltering gaze. 'This is the bait that will lure Arthur to Britain, that will bring war, and maybe victory for the West. On this woman hangs the fate of Milo and his sons and the sons that follow them in Castel ys Coit, this woman, who betrayed Arthur already when she had the chance after Longborth; but he does not know of it any more than he knows that she is now with Medraut in his camp by Aquae Sulis.'

"The message from Gwenhyvar to Arthur is that if he value the wife he has left these seven years let him come and deliver her before it is too late."

"Let not your mind be bent by a woman, even by golden-headed Gwenhyvar," said Kai bluntly. "What luck has come your way from the daughter of Gwythyr? What proof have you that Lucius speaks the truth?"

"Glory fades for the man who lifts no hand to shield his woman from rape and incest," muttered Bedwyr.

"The truth is hidden," said Arthur slowly, "but each of us sees a vision of that which he most desires and strives towards it. For my part it is as though God has sent me a sign, setting me one more task that may redeem my wasted years of sin and failure. We shall sail to Britain, Kai and Bedwyr. No army will go with us from Armorica; the most we can do is to set up the Red Dragon, call on the Cymry, and let our fate rest in God's hands."

Chapter XXX

Camlann

GUEITH CAMLANN IN QUA ARTHUR ET MEDRAUT CORRUERUNT.
—*Annales Cambriae.*

"HAVE YOU COME TO TAKE AWAY THE KING?" Somersetshire
rustic to party of archaeologists at Cadbury Castle.

Gwenhyvar sat alone in a great hut of woven
branches roofed with bundles of reeds. All
round in the deep valley, in the glades where
short bracken and yellow ragwort were trampled
down by thousands of men and beasts, lay the camp
of Medraut's army that for the moment dominated
Britain from sea to sea.

There was a surly hum of insects in the moist,
windless air and a deeper rumble of voices rising and
falling like the sea. Pillars of blue smoke swayed up
out of clefts in the forest canopy, that rolled over the
hillsides like a vast green avalanche, glistening after
a night of gentle rain. Through the door of the hut
Gwenhyvar looked out on shaggy droves of ill-used
horses, listless save for their switching tails, on cattle
standing knee deep in river pools, and on Saxons
clustered together like swarms of vermin on the

fouled ground. There they lay, big silent men, gorged
with meat, torpid after a drinking bout that had last-
ed all night round spluttering fires, while the vaulted
spaces of the woods rang to a brawling uproar of voices, the instinctive, monotonous repetition of a few
alliterative phrases, a protective incantation against
the ill-will of land spirits among these glooming hills.
Haunted ground it seemed to the simple-minded folk
swept together from the moors of Deivr and the flat
shores of eastward-flowing rivers, for there, in the
bend of the valley, rose immense walls of squared
stone, splitting and tottering in the clasp of ivy, porticos smothered in tufts of fern, and pediments on
which could be made out sculptured figures of an
aloof and arrogant dignity. To the barbarians these
carvings were almost as incomprehensible as the fos-
sils that showed in cliffs and quarry faces, yet dimly
they saw them as the symbol of a great power over-
turned by invaders in past ages, a power that might
still lurk vengefully about these scenes of shattered
splendour. In the eyes of Gwenhyvar the wreck of the
old city had another significance; it stood for the irre-
trievable collapse of that world that lingered at Castel
ys Coit, the world that found its last prop in the stern
figure of Arthur and the ranks of men in helmet and
lorica, the legionaries hewn down at last in the fratri-
cidal strife of Briton against Briton. Now her life was
joined with that of the man who was resolved to make
an end of every link with Rome, of the Christian faith,
of the haughty guletics who reckoned their descent
from great officials and landowners, citizens of an
empire that reached from the Persian plains to the
Atlantic. 'I have the man I love,' she said to herself,
'Maybe I shall give him a child. His power mounts
over Britain by the might of men that come from the
sunrise, and Arthur's has faded away like a sunset in
the west. The Bear of Britain has gone down before
the Serpent, fallen he is like those great columns

lying under sedge and slime, never again to be reared up by the hand of man. . . .'

The doorway went dark as Medraut stooped and came in. He stood by the dying embers of the fire, a splendid figure in a blue embroidered cloak and saffron-coloured breeches, his well-combed hair falling in ringlets below a horned helmet, his long fingers thrust into a belt with a buckle of gold. Suddenly Gwenhyvar went down on her knees before him, her hands touched his timidly, her face was turned up to his as though imploring a caress. Medraut raised her up gently as was his way with women, but there was no smile on his face, no tenderness in his eyes; rather they had the steely, glittering reflection of horrid spectacles in his climb to power—multitudes of brutish faces turned towards him, kindling at his words to raging blood-lust, the gloating look of men stooping to rape or torture, frantic faces amongst the smoke of burning huts.

"Do you remember how I clasped you when you stood over me in Bregion, after your dagger had pricked me in the breast?" she said, trying desperately to rouse his passion. "It came to me then in a flash that my spirit thirsted for you, that my body was all afire to have you, that no man could give me pleasure but you."

Side by side they sat on a log of wood covered with sheep skins and Medraut said: "Was it pleasure for you, when the time came in that little dark room under Milo's roof?"

A sudden qualm went through her, a feeling of horrid defilement that had hung about her in nightmarish fashion all the way through the wilderness, past the figure of the giant to the passage of Stour. She stared at him without speaking, aware of the undercurrent of evil in the man's nature, but no longer exulting in it. Instead of a stealthy delight, it now filled her with a foreboding of doom, with a sickening terror akin to what had come to her in Milo's house.

"Is it pleasure for you to have me now?" he muttered, pressing her hand mechanically.

"Yes, yes!" she whispered. "Are you content with Gwenhyvar? Is it a joy to you that you have cast down the work of Arthur and taken his wife?"

It was his turn to be silent. The woman wearied him, now that he had achieved his purpose with her and set her up beside him, a token of his triumph in the eyes of all Britain. His mind turned away impatiently from those stirrings of pity and love that had first come to him on the hills above Castel ys Coit. So far every plan had run through to success; he had cowed Gwyneth, crushed Powys, held Dyfet at bay, made an ally of Gwent, and dictated terms to Dyvnaint. But now a little cloud had appeared on the horizon of an empty sky. Word had reached him that Arthur had come ashore in Durngueir. Woman-like she divined some preoccupation in him that made her caresses untimely.

"Is your seat firm, Medraut, ruling this rough host as a man masters a vicious horse? Will you ride yet further in among your enemies?" she said gently.

"There is no need to ride far beyond Camelot. From that round hill I shall rule the West, secure in the friendship both of Conan and Cynric, with a great host of Saxons planted beyond Exe and another of Engel on the wasted lands where I have broken the power of Cuneglas."

"What of Brude and his Picts?"

"A dangerous beast I have under me in that body of savages. Yet they have served me well, striking terror into all that they come against, and I may yet give them work that will tame their spirit, even as a rider sets a fiery horse at steep hills that will break his heart."

"So many enemies you have, Medraut, do you dread none of them? Will you sit at peace while the kings live, while Arthur forges a new weapon in Armorica?"

He laughed and said indifferently: "One nest of enemies I will root out and that is Milo and his brood of sons on the other side of Coit Mawr."

"Let us take that house and live there instead of on the dreary top of Camelot! Let us save for our-selves the servants and the soft couches, the fountain and the tame birds—let us have joy there that will wipe away the remembrance of seven years ago!"

"A strange fancy you have, Gwenhyvar!" he said, his mind busy with other thoughts.

"What should content you more than to live as a Roman in a land sunk down into savagery? Are you not perverse in all your pleasures, liking to see grief rather than joy, to fit lovely music to dreadful deeds, to bring down your kinsfolk, to mingle cruelty with love. . . ." Her voice dropped from a note of playful taunting to a breathless whisper as she stared at the set face under the horned helmet and felt again a wild longing blended with terror.

He got suddenly to his feet. His eyes were on her now, coldly appraising, he lifted a lock of the golden hair in his hand and let it fall again.

'Love,' he thought, 'can love grow in my heart while I do the things I have to do? Can a flower blos-som on sands swept by the salty waves?'

"Your face is grim, Medraut; your mind is trou-bled. Take your harp and play, and you may find ease."

"I have laid aside my harp now that I am master of Britain. Dangerous are the spells cast by music— when I gave myself up to it I saw many a vision that I took to be of things to come; but now that I have closed my heart to music my mind is clear and calm, and I laugh at what were childish fancies."

"It was the man with the harp that won me from Arthur," she said, half to herself, but Medraut did not heed her any longer. He went hastily to the door of the hut where Brawdbach was just getting down from a horse covered with foam and sweat. He took the youth by the shoulders, drew him away, and looked him in the eyes.

"Is the Bear moving?" he said in a low voice.

Brawdbach nodded. "Towards Camelot," he said.

"Do folk gather fast to him?"

"As hounds to a master; but as yet he has only hundreds where you have thousands. I have other news, not good."

"Ah." Medraut's hand tightened on his half-brother's shoulder.

"Cadwy has ambushed the Saxons who were to take the land from Exe to Tamar. They are all dead."

"He breaks his word—he plucks up courage now that the Bear is in Britain again," said Medraut, clenching his teeth. "Well, we can loose the Picts upon him." An answering gleam lit up the swarthy face of Brawdbach.

"We shall see women with their guts ripped out on the grass and children tossed from spear to spear," he said with a dreadful chuckle.

* * *

The Red Dragon came out on to the pastures at the foot of Camelot, and following it came a swarm of men with matted hair and faces shining in the rain, upturned to the grey sky, after the long march under the dripping boughs of Coit Mawr. In the midst of them rode Arthur on a big black horse from Milo's stables and elbowing their way close beside him was a little knot of legionaries chanting the old song "Cymry in victory, Cymry in woe," men who remembered the march to Abergleinwy and the Round Table by Eamont Water. Among the elder copses on

Camlann stood another cluster of folk, peasants and fishermen from the mere sides with a show of spears and round shields, monks from Ynys Gutrin raising their hands in prayer, a woman on a pony. They set up a wavering shout of welcome as Kai planted the standard in the deep, black earth; the woman rode forward, dismounted and went on her knees beside Arthur. She kissed his foot as it rested in the stirrup; her great dark eyes gazed up at him in wistful adoration. A murmur went round: "It is Garwen, the mother of Lacheu."

Arthur bent down and laid his hand on her head, on the thick brown hair that his waking eyes had seen on the pillow beside him many a morning in the West Country, years ago when kinsmen and champions greeted him with cheery faces and Britain nerved herself for deliverance at Badon—the happiest days, maybe, in his life of toil and bloodshed.

'Is it sin,' he thought, 'when a man and a woman love each other as we do? Perhaps it is but a step from this sweetness and tenderness to the dark passion between Medraut and Gwenhyvar, and to the vile lust between Vortipore and his wife's sister, the foulness between Maelgun and his nephew's wife, and my own unwitting crime with Indec. A man who loads himself with such a task as I do must be hard against his enemies, but harder still against himself.' He rode to the standard and gripped the ash shaft that carried the Red Dragon. All around him now the people went on their knees; there was a long drawn out cry: "Save us, Amherawdyr! Save us from the Pict and the Saxon!"

"A thin host we have here," said Kai gloomily.

"It will grow fast. Men say that Cadwy hastens to us from the west," said Bedwyr.

"Medraut is at Aquae Sulis. Too near have we come to one that knows the art of war," put in Lucius, sitting impassively on a restive stallion.

"Hear me, men of Dyvnaint!" shouted Arthur, rising in his stirrups. "You folk born and bred between the White Downs and the breakers on Penwith, who know me as I know you! I have given you victory and I have given you peace, but the powers of evil are mighty in the land and they cast down my work. Once more I shall stand forward as a shield for the British race, and while I live I will hold that shield over your heads. Few we are and our enemies are many. For our sins it may be that God will let them devour us, but let us pray for a miracle, that worthless as we are, our little strength may prevail against theirs that is armed with the might of devils."

He lifted off his helmet and bent his head. A sobbing murmur came from the kneeling people on every side of the little group of horsemen, and then a fierce cry from the monks of Ynys Gutrin, raising their arms towards the lowering clouds:

"Domine, miserere nobis! Christe, miserere nobis! Miserere Britanniae!"

Next morning a man came riding hard through the warm summery showers, across the flat country and up the hill into Camelot. He brushed his way through the crowds about the gateway, sprang off his jaded horse and went into the new hall where Arthur sat with Kai, Bedwyr, Lucius, and a few other men of mark. They sat over meat and ale, with thoughtful faces, for though they had news of the massacre of the Saxons in the west, there was news, too, that Medraut was on the march southward from Aquae Sulis.

"Here come I, Brawdbach, with a message for Arthur," said the newcomer boldly.

They all turned to stare at the bushy-browed young man with the long, dangling arms, who came striding through the hall, splashed with mud and dripping with rain.

"Let him not go forth alive!" exclaimed Kai, reaching for his sword, but Arthur waved him back.

"What words have you for the Cymry, Brawdbach?" he said. "You who went everywhere with us from Caer Ebrauc to Badon."

"I bring words of peace from my brother Medraut."

"On what terms?" said Arthur grimly.

"He will send Gwenhyvar into your camp if you will quit Britain again for Armorica."

There was a silence; then Kai muttered: "There is a path that way to an honourable peace."

"Not unless he send away the Picts and the Saxons!" burst out Lucius.

"It is a good offer," said Brawdbach with an ugly smile. "Many men we can put against one of yours, yet Medraut has no wish to raise his sword against Arthur."

"'Why, then, did he lay hands on Gwenhyvar?" said Bedwyr.

"She came to Medraut of her own free will."

"A lie!" said Lucius hotly.

"It is truth as you know better than most men, and it is not the first time."

"If that be true, why do we fight for a woman who is worthless as dirt?" said Kai.

"What woman can resist the enchantment of Medraut?" said Bedwyr. "The evil is in him, not in her; and no peace can we make with him, the man that boasts he will rule Britain by the swords of its deadliest enemies."

"It is to Arthur that I speak," said Brawdbach, shrugging his shoulders.

"Is there love between them?" said Arthur, breaking another tense silence.

"Is blood to flow because a woman burns to lie with one man rather than another?" said Brawdbach contemptuously. "If you value her, Medraut will give her back. But you, Arthur, shall leave Britain to

Medraut, to shape after his own fancy, as a potter takes clay in his hands and prints his will upon it. Once the power was yours; you had your way with Britain and did as you thought best—now it is the turn of another man."

"You shall have your answer," said Arthur in a loud voice. "I shall make no bargain with Medraut over a woman's body; the sin is done and cannot be undone. I would have hindered it, but I will not avenge it. Another task rests upon me: I have laboured at it in twelve great battles, I have laid it down in despair, but the people call me afresh and God has sent me a sign—even a lying message from you, Lucius, that brought me here, too late to save Gwenhyvar from deadly sin, but not too late to beat down the deadly purpose of Medraut, and beat it down I will while I can strike a blow with this right arm; for Medraut will give our men to the sword and our land and women to the Saxon, building a new Britain indeed, of which he may be master as Satan is master of the devils in hell."

"I had hoped to hear Arthur speak more like a soldier than like a priest," said Brawdbach jeeringly. "There is no fear of sin or devils among the Saxons; we measure a man by his weapon play, his wit, and what he dares to do. Both Saxon and British blood I have and I know that what is Saxon in me makes me the overman of you folk who dread the shadow of a cross, following your lusts in terror as a dog steals its master's meat with its tail between its legs. The day will come when you will be thrust out to live like goats on the mountain crags and we men of mixed blood shall have the good land of Britain!" He turned to go, but Kai leaped after him with a drawn sword.

"We shall have one devil the less to fight when the Red Dragon goes forward!" he shouted. The blade whistled in the air, but quick as lightning Brawdbach snatched a board from the trestles and raised it above his head. The sword bit and stood fast; with a jerk he wrenched it out of Kai's hand and flung both board and weapon across the hall. He stood there poised warily on his toes, his hands resting on his hips, his teeth bared in a grin of hate and contempt.

"So we deal with the strokes of the Cymry!"

With a wolfish glare of rage the others sprang to their feet, but Arthur shouted: "Let him be! We shall not soil our hands with treachery, even against the sons of Modron."

Brawdbach turned without a word, he walked out of the hall, vaulted on his horse and drove his heels into it with brutal violence. The thud of flying hoofs died away across the hard turf of Camelot, and Kai said gloomily: "I doubt that man will do us much mischief in tomorrow's battle."

* * *

In the early morning Arthur's army moved out from Camelot across the gently rolling country to the ford of the Brue, where the Roman road came straight as an arrow from Aquae Sulis pointing towards Ischalis and Isca, the great highway through Dyvnaint. The rain had stopped, but mist was in the air and the steep hills scattered about the marshland were banks of bluish gloom. Some miles to northward Medraut's host was known to be encamped on the ridge of Pen Ard, but fog lay low in that direction and all was silent and dim, with no more sign of life than an occasional flight of moorfowl above the alder copses. The Cymry looked over their shoulders again and again in the hope of seeing Cadwy's standard coming to meet them from the south-west, but there, too, were only empty plains of bog and brushwood stretching mile on mile toward the heights of Durngueir. There was little evidence that Celtic Britain was aware of the struggle impending that day, save for the arrival overnight of five hundred bowmen from Dyfet—proof

that Vortipore was inclined to throw his weight
against the new tyrant.

A faint radiance of sunshine came through the
slowly drifting clouds and Arthur, taking a last long
look at the Isca road, had the trumpets blow challengingly in the direction of Pen Ard. At once he
moved two thirds of his army on to the low woody
slopes that flanked the marshes of Brue, there to lie
hidden until a fresh trumpet blast should give the
signal for attack. With a little band of the most
trusty men he had, he stood his ground on the slope
to the ford, Kai foremost of all with the Red Dragon.
He had not long to wait. A low murmur sounded to
northward and suddenly the scrub across the river
was alive with lurching figures, wild frowsy-headed
men splashing and squelching in the oozy ground,
grinning over their little round shields, swaying forward under a waving forest of spears. They were
Picts, the advance guard send on by Medraut to
draw the first blood.

Every bowman under the Red Dragon began to
shoot steadily into the dusky mass of warriors that
halted irresolutely on the edge of the black water. On
they came at last with a horrid yell, churning the
river into foam, but the ford was deep and many lost
their footing and were trampled down or stuck helplessly in the reedy mud. When some hundreds were
across the Cymry charged and drove them back into
the water and so it went on time after time till the
bank was covered thick with dead and dying and the
river became a sludge of corpses. Now, however, the
Picts came on mingled with more resolute fighters,
Britons from the midland forests, and men of Gwent
carrying Conan's banner of the Antlered Stag. Slowly
the Red Dragon moved backwards on to higher
ground; it left the Roman road and turned into the
thickets, following the marsh along the riverside.
Continually the rearmost ranks turned about and

showed a bold front to the men that streamed after them through hazel tunnels and on winding cattle trods knee-deep in bracken. Medraut and Brawdbach rode ahead to where Brude still led the advance.

"Arthur withdraws himself towards Ynys Gutrin," said Medraut, watching the Red Dragon moving further and further from one tuft of trees to another down the shores of the Brue. His strength is small, yet he may well make a stand on the bridge, waiting for Cadwy to come to his aid. Ride to the Saxons, Brawdbach, and lead them round by the western end of Pen Ard and so to the Tor of Ynys Gutrin. Then we shall have him in a trap."

"Arthur has more men than those clustered about the standard, so I judge by what I saw yesterday in Camelot," muttered Brawdbach.

"Once Arthur is fallen, Britain drops into our hands like an over-ripe apple; it matters nothing about other men that contend with us here or elsewhere. Ride, Brawdbach, and you Brude, press on hard to the bridge; the Bear is in the toils."

"Heavy was the stroke of the Bear's paw at the ford of Brue," said the Pict, rubbing the sweat from his brows with a hairy wrist.

"The man is mortal; one thrust over the top of his lorica and the day is ours."

"I doubt it," said Brude. "To my mind he casts a spell upon our people and his blows have the strength of magic." He plucked a spray of rowan and wove it into a green wreath about his helmet, then with a shout he rushed on with the remainder of the Pictish host. The copses gave place to pastures yellow with buttercups, then came tussocks and a spongy earth full of white cotton grass and red sundew. A trestle bridge mounted out of the marsh, and crossed the sluggish water to the rising ground of Ynys Gutrin.

Arthur's standard halted and there stood champions with laughing faces mowing away with mighty
strokes at the trickle of foemen pouring on to the
bridge. A rumble of voices swelled up above the crash
of blows and the splash of bodies falling in the water;
thicker and thicker grew the crowd of men trying to
force a passage. Now Brude was on the bridge swinging an axe, and there sprang to meet him Coll, the
Isleman, a champion who had got away with the Red
Dragon from the field of Longborth and had been hidden in Indec's house while his wounds healed. The
hosts paused and stood to breathe while the two old
comrades exchanged blows, a friendly light in their
eyes and grunting approval of each other's toughness
in this match with death. A glancing slash shore
away the rowan from Brude's helmet, he slipped on
the bridge planks, now slimy with blood, and fell
headlong into the Brue with Coll's dagger sticking in
his throat. There was a yell of triumph from the
Cymry and suddenly Arthur's trumpets pealed out, a
long strident blast echoing from the dim hills and the
dark walls of foliage across the marsh. Now came
arrows whistling upon Medraut's host from the bows
of Dyfet, a rush of fresh warriors from the woods in
their rear, and in a moment the battle became a massacre. The dense crowd of Picts and the men with the
Antlered Stag of Gwent rolled helplessly this way and
that, plunging ever deeper into moss and reeds and
bubbling pools, and the Cymry closed in on them
treading down the corpses into the mud, driving the
panic-stricken remnants of the army into open
water. The drowning dragged down those who could
swim and behind came hard-driven arrows and
flashing steel. . . .

"Longborth is avenged!" shouted the champions
on the bridge as the ranks of Gwent, stuck fast on the
treacherous banks of Brue, went down like meadow
grass before the scythe.

"This is the worst sight I have seen—Briton slaughtering Briton," said Arthur gloomily. He stood on the bridge watching the outcome of his plan of battle—a victory for which he had hardly dared to hope—but his lips quivered and tears came to his eyes as he turned his gaze from the unavailing struggle of Conan's warriors. There were faces among them that he remembered well from that day when the united forces of the West went up against the roaring crowds of Saxons on Badon.

"It is an evil work to which I have set my hand," he muttered. "Never again shall this sword be wielded against the bond of blood!" He swung up Caledvulch and hurled the great weapon into the Brue.

"Too soon, too soon you part from Caledvulch, the bringer of victory!" said Kai. "See, Medraut swims his horse to the other side. We have not done with him yet; two javelins he has thrown at us—the Picts and the men of Gwent, but he still holds the best one in his hands—the Saxons."

"Let us get away from this dreadful place!" shouted Arthur suddenly. "We shall march back to Camelot and eat and drink. There we can stand at bay on those great ramparts if Medraut comes to challenge us again."

"I wish Cadwy's host were in sight," said Bedwyr. "Few we seem here, a little band of weary and bleeding men, lost in this wide marshland. A better shelter we might find on Ynys Gutrin."

"The monks have fled to the west; there is nothing there for us but an empty church and empty huts," said Arthur.

"Too late it is to hold Ynys Gutrin!" Kai pointed to a dark mass of men coming towards them through apple orchards below the great cone of the Tor, cloud-shadowed above the low country gleaming in watery sunshine.

"Hew down the bridge and let us march!" ordered Arthur.

In a little while the army was reunited and moved away on the southern side of the Brue, turning their backs on the scene of carnage and the oncoming Saxons baffled for the moment by the broken bridge. The spirits of the men, inflamed by victory, drooped again as they left behind them scores of comrades helpless on the ground, too hard wounded to follow the march to Camelot, with nothing to expect but death at the hands of the Saxons. Already Medraut could be seen dispersing his folk along the shores of Ynys Gutrin in search of boats, of material for mending of the bridge. There seemed to be an immense number of them, all fresh men and undaunted by the disaster which had overtaken the rest of their army. Pursuit was certain, and Camelot looked very far away in the summer haze, a little green hill against the dark wall of Coit Mawr.

There was still no sign of Cadwy when, late in the afternoon, they reached the Isca road, but now there were enemies in front of them as well as behind, men who had come down on the ford of Brue after the battle had rolled away to westward. There were woodlanders from the Midlands, relics of the Pictish host, flaxen-haired bands of Engel from Deivr, and among them moved the sinister figure of Brawdbach. The men of Dyfet began to shoot again, the opposing ranks recoiled, and the Cymry burst through. Now they were swallowed up in a trackless waste of scrub and reeds; they struggled on desperately aware of horns blowing behind them, of shout and countershout as here and there a knot of weary men faced round to fight. Louder and louder grew the uproar of guttural voices, the thundering yells of "Kill! Kill! Hew the Welshmen!" The archers had shot away all their arrows; now they hung their shields on their back and ran; a panic spread among the men who battled

their way head down through the thorn brake, tangled with heavy-scented honeysuckle, who dragged
their feet out of black slime and stumbled on through
myriads of wiry bracken stalks. Clegs and midges
hovered in clouds above the creamy foam of meadowsweet; monstrous banks of briar and bramble
withstood the flowing tide of humanity like rocks
splitting the course of a river. The Cymry trickled
away by a hundred different channels through that
fragrant, inhospitable wilderness, and when the
ground rose at last into high forest the half of
Arthur's host was gone beyond recall, struck to earth
by the Saxons or scattered far away, running for life
aimlessly in untrodden glades. Only the stoutest-
hearted still thronged about the Red Dragon and
Arthur on the black horse as they came out on to the
bare crest above Camlann and saw the Saxons mass-
ing already in the green valley in front of Camelot.
The sun was going down among ragged cloud shapes
that shredded away in wisps of gold; long shadows
fell across the plain and the stockades of Camelot
were like walls of rosy amber crowning an enchanted
hill. Arthur had the trumpets blown—one more defiant blast at the day's end while death reached
towards him in the cool shadows of evening. Far to
the west sounded faintly an answering horn.

"Cadwy comes!" shouted Bedwyr.

Kai pointed to the long crest of the hill now
swarming with Saxons.

"We shall all be dead men before Cadwy's host
sets foot on Camlann," he said, leaning his weight
wearily on the standard. Lucius stood beside him,
biting his lips and staring moodily at the far-flung sea
of forest behind which lay Castel ys Coit.

"A man on a good horse would still have time to
ride southwards and save his life," he muttered.

"What is one life out of all that is left of the
Cymry?" said Kai.

"On Arthur's life hangs the fate of Britain." Lucius' gloomy eyes turned towards the mighty figure that sat motionless in the saddle looking out over his men, who had thrown themselves down on the turf, gazing apathetically at the Saxons closing in on hill and plain. "If we die now it will not be in vain," said Arthur. "A man's death should be worthy of his life; so shall his story become deathless among his countrymen and his fame leap up like a bright beacon when darkness lies over the land. The strength of our nation is in the heights—in the green hills of Britain. Let us go forward now with a good courage, and strive towards the hill of Camelot that blazes in the sunset as though lit by the eye of God."

He rode down the slope, through a scattering of old stunted thorns, towards the valley floor where the Saxon ranks stood in a great dusky arc amid a yellow sheen of buttercups. Mechanically the army rose and poured after him with set, haggard faces; Kai lifted the standard so that the sun still shone on the Red Dragon while the men plunged down into shadow. Bedwyr swung up a dinted sword and gave a shout: "Arthur our Leader; Christ our King!"

Medraut and Brawdbach stood behind the Saxon line on the far side of a little brook. They watched the shrunken band of Cymry struggling towards them encompassed on every side by a sea of Saxons. Nearer it came, but more and more slowly amid a louder and louder roar of voices and a furious clashing of weapons.

"Their strength is spent, they are wasting away like a lump of wax in the fire. Their feet will never tread the hill of Camelot," said Brawdbach exultantly.

"So perishes the Glory of the West." Medraut let his sword point sink to earth; he stared fixedly at the low hill with the weatherbeaten thorns standing out against the sky that now glowed like a great furnace.

'This is the vision,' he thought, 'the vision that came before my eyes years ago when I played on the harp and gave rein to my lust for Gwenhyvar; the vision that has left me since I rose to power, yet here it comes again in the hour that Arthur draws to his end.'

"The Red Dragon is down at last!" Brawdbach's face lit up with a devilish radiance; his thin lips rolled back from the clenched teeth. "Britain is ours!" His voice rang out like the croaking of a bird of prey.

The rising and falling weapons clustered about a vortex in the heaving waves of men and then out of it came two figures reeling forward and stumbling through the brook. Nearer and nearer they drew, as great boulders rolled from some mountainside come scarred and battered to rest in soft ground. Bedwyr fell crumpled up in a bush of loosestrife by the water's edge, but Arthur still came on, gasping for breath, streaming with blood from head to foot but still gripping the sword which had been Kai's.

Brawdbach leaped at the dreadful figure; his sword went through the broken armour with a deadly stroke, but at the same moment Arthur's weapon whirled and bit on that scowling face, cleaving through teeth and skull to the brain. Slowly he wrenched the blade free and stepped over the frantically writhing corpse, coming upon Medraut like a toppling tower. Once more the sword swung up. . . .

Medraut gazed into those eyes that regarded him with a glassy stare, unspeculative and uncomprehending, the eyes of a man whose spirit has fled while his body still obeys an impulse of will, like a horse bearing on a dead rider. Images rushed through Medraut's mind—he saw that grim face alight with joy at Afon Coch, drunken with triumph above the ship's prow at Dinguardi, the face of the man whom he had loved, hated, and resolved to destroy, the saviour of Britain, the husband of Gwenhyvar. His hand gripped the hilt of his sword, but as in a dream he could summon no power to avert the stroke of doom that came like a bat's flight against the evening sky.

* * *

It was growing dusk when Bedwyr slowly raised his head and looked dazedly about him. His wounds chanced to be of little account; he had fallen insensible from utter exhaustion rather than from loss of blood. He rolled over, plunged his face in the brook and drank. For a while he stared unseeingly into the muddy water, then he heaved himself up on one arm and turned his face towards the pale yellow sky in the west. Far off at the foot of the hill he saw hurrying masses of men; spears and standards sweeping forward. There was a distant shouting and a braying of horns. Cadwy had come at last, and away to the north were scattered companies of Saxons, a confused leaderless rabble, uncertain whether to fight or fly.

Bedwyr got to his feet and gazed long at the bodies of Brawdbach, Arthur and Medraut. He knelt by Arthur and lifted the cold right hand.

"A deadly hand has this been for the enemies of Britain, and a fatal hand for the house of Uther," he said to himself. "What man was like this in his love for the British race? Heavy were his blows in defence of our land, but heaviest of all they fell on his own kith and kin, the men who sought most eagerly to bring him down."

A figure on horseback came slowly across the plain, from the direction of Camelot, a cloaked figure moving like an uneasy spectre in the rising mist. It was Garwen who drew rein beside him.

"Here was the fight," she said. "Are all fallen except you, Bedwyr?"

"I am the last of the champions left alive," he said.

"What of Arthur?"

"Here he lies; but in his fall he has crushed the life out of the two serpents that were the bane of Britain: Brawdbach and Medraut."

She dismounted hastily, got water in her cupped hands and washed the blood from Arthur's face where it lay upturned to the greening vault of the sky. She bent and kissed him on the lips; she laid her hand on the curly auburn hair and said:

"Of all the heroes that have come up out of the race of Britons, this man sought least for himself and was most basely betrayed. Who is left to carry on his work? What is left for us to live for, we who loved him?"

"Life is empty for us," said Bedwyr, "we who know that the sun that warmed us has gone down for ever, but Britain does not know what we know—let Britain live in hope that Arthur will come again when she is in desperate need. We shall leave the bodies of Medraut and Brawdbach here for all men to see, but we shall hide the body of Arthur."

Together they lifted the corpse on to Garwen's pony and made their way to the elder copses at the foot of Camelot. Here were shepherds' huts whence the folk had fled at the coming of armies. They tethered the animal, went inside and ate and drank in silence. Bedwyr found a mattock and they went out into the moonlight. Walking among the bushes with their great drifts of bitter-smelling blossom, they came to a place where the hill rose suddenly in a dusky wall.

"A tale I heard from an old man years ago that the hill is hollow," said Bedwyr. "He stood by me here when I was a boy, with a bow in my hand, watching for hares on just such a moonlit night as this, and he said that here had been a door, and that he had seen the men of Eiré break in and bring out gold and silver buried with some guletic of Roman times . . ." He struck with his tool, tearing away the turf and laying

bare a mass of fallen stone. A strong earthy smell
streamed out into the still air and the blows of the
mattock set up a dull boom. Presently they could
pass their hands into a cavity, and lifting away the
rubble laced with elder roots they felt a low, round-
arched opening. For a while they sat on either side of
it, resting, then Garwen crawled in on her hands and
knees. A paved passage soon led to a wide space
where she could stand upright. Her hands touched
the clammy overhanging walls and snapped off sta-
lactites that sprouted from the mortar joints. She felt
on the floor, but there was nothing there except bits
of broken pot, from urns, no doubt, that had held the
ashes of some line of land-owners living in the fertile
country between the meres and Coit Mawr. She came
back, with deep sighs and thinking dreamily, 'Here,
far overhead, Arthur lay in my arms, sleeping
through spring nights in the hall of Camelot, and now
in this black silent place I shall take his body in my
arms for the last time. Here he will sleep at peace
while in the world outside life springs and fades and
springs again, and joy and sorrow pass like sun and
shadow over the green land of Britain. . . .'

Together they carried the corpse into the vault
and laid it there with the bloodstained sword beside
it. Then they put back the stones, spread turf on top
and trod it smooth again.

Afterword

Arthur and his companions have been the subject of literary enterprises for at least eleven hundred years, so it might perhaps appear superfluous for one more writer to retell a story which has already produced something of a best seller in the early twelfth century, a magnificent fantasy in the fifteenth, and some of the most famous English poetry of the Victorian age. When Geoffrey of Monmouth constructed his tale of early Britain to divert his Norman patrons in the reign of Henry I, he set the fashion for portraying a chivalric Arthur, which has persisted to the present day. Professedly a serious history, his book is a mass of ingenious anachronisms and absurdities, but its merit as drama has crystallised a conception of Arthur which can have only a very faint relevance to the dim sixth-century hero.

Ever since I was a child of ten, imbued with a fanatical devotion to all losing causes, it has been an obsession with me to reconstruct the historic as opposed to the romanticised Arthur. I must confess that, whereas there are voluminous materials for the latter figure, the real man continually eludes the student. His very existence has been doubted; the silence of the earliest writers, both British and Saxon, is in strange contrast to the torrent of mendacious information offered us when the Arthurian legend took its place in the annals of chivalry. Nevertheless there is a small residuum in the work of the British monk, Nennius, which may well fit into the meagre historical framework linking Roman Britain to the England of the Heptarchy. Further, one need not be so sceptical as to disregard all hints from Welsh poems and folk-tales, and from the lives of certain obscure saints. The poems, notably those in the Black Book of Caermarthen, do almost certainly preserve fragments composed by bards, the Cynfeirdd, or 'old singers' of the sixth century. Even Geoffrey's monstrous accretions to the Arthurian legend may contain a few independent grains of genuine history.

It is from these early materials that I have produced a picture of sixth-century Britain in which are set, harmoniously, I hope, the figures of its defenders and assailants—not the colourful medieval tapestry of Malory nor the gentlemanly Victorian décor of Tennyson, but a grim and bloodstained pageant of the darkest age in our island's history.

For the general picture we have substantial materials in the contemporary treatise of the British monk Gildas, *De Excidio Britanniae.* Unfortunately he concerned himself mainly with the cowardice of his countrymen and the wickedness of their rulers, and from this it may be understandable that he makes no reference to Arthur, or perhaps only faint allusion, for when Arthur first appears in the *Historia Britonum* of Nennius, nearly three hundred years later, he is already the progenitor of the familiar 'blameless king.' This is not the place to discuss the sources from which Nennius drew his record of Arthur's victories over the spoilers of Britain—suffice it to say that he may have had a written record from the first half of the seventh century, and that he drew, no doubt, on oral traditions. Nor do I propose to say much about the location of the twelve battles. For many reasons it seems to me difficult to dissociate the earlier ones from Northern Britain. There is a remarkable concentration of Arthurian legends and place names in Cumbria and Southern Scotland, and, as a personal name, Arthur appears most often in Scotland and Ireland during the centuries immediately following on the hero's lifetime. Badon, however, the last and greatest victory, mentioned already by Gildas and enlarged on by later writers, obviously lies in the South. I follow the Arthurian scholar, Mr. E. K. Chambers, in placing it on the Downs near the border of Wiltshire and Berkshire. There may be some significance in the close juxtaposition of Baydon, Badbury, and Beedon. Possibly the name Badon was once applied to the whole range of hills later known as Aescesdun or Ashdown. We may compare Brendon, the hill name in Somerset.

In the middle of the tenth century come the brief and fragmentary *Annales Cambriae,* providing us with dates on an uncertain reckoning and with the first mention of Arthur and Medraut perishing in the battle of Camlann. This again is developed in later Welsh literature and forms the climax in the courtly medieval drama of Arthur and Guinevere. Camlann has usually been placed in Cornwall, but it is hardly probable that the Arthurian legend sprang originally from that remote and barbarous corner of Britain. More likely it receded thither as Celtic dominion shrank under the Saxon attack and was ultimately driven across the Tamar. There are many clues that point to Somerset as a centre for Arthur's activities, especially the Glastonbury legend and folk-lore associating Camelot with Cadbury Castle. Here we have Queen (or East) Camel, West Camel, and the little river Cam. The earliest recorded form of Camel is Cantmael, evidently a Welsh name, Cant Moel, meaning 'the

---

[1] For this interpretation I am indebted to Professor A. Mawer.

round bare hill,' which would appear to refer to Cadbury Castle nearby. Cant Moel may well be the root of 'Camelot,' 'Camalat,' and 'Camalack,' first mentioned by Chrétien de Troyes and other French metrical romancers in the latter part of the twelfth century as the residence of Arthur. So also Camlann may be a contraction of 'Cant Moel Lan,' the field or enclosure by the round hill, or merely the field by the Cam, though that river name is possibly a backformation from Camel. The lives of St. Cadoc and St. Carannog, sixth-century saints recorded in the late eleventh century, also associate Arthur with Somerset.

As to the Wansdyke in Somerset and Wiltshire representing the frontier between the British kings of Gwent and Dyvnaint during the Arthurian period, I have the authority of Sir Charles Oman.

The outline of my story has been designed from any scraps of material which seem to be of historical value. Here and there, like Geoffrey, I have had recourse to pure, but I think not unreasonable, invention. I have preserved the central romance of Arthur, Medraut, and Guinevere (more correctly Gwenhwyvar), not only on account of its tragic splendour, but because intuitively one feels that it springs from a germ of truth rather than fiction.

Finally I should like to express my gratitude to Miss Harriet Middleton for assistance in constructing the episode at 'Guinion,' to the Rev. T. Wilson for his book on *The Stow of Wedale,* and to the Rev. H. Poole for much inspiring discussion of Arthurian problems and for the loan of maps and literature.

—E.F.
Ravenstonedale, 1940.

About the Author

Edward Percy Frankland was born in London in 1884. After completing his Ph.D., he lectured in chemistry at the University of Birmington until he resigned because of ill health. He started writing fiction in 1922, making frequent use of the Cumbrian setting where he made his home, and continued to publish until his death in 1958.

About the Series Editor

Born in 1941, Raymond H. Thompson lived in many different parts of the world before emigrating to Canada, where he is now professor of English at Acadia University in Wolfville, Nova Scotia. His fascination with Arthurian legend dates from student days. He has written *The Return from Avalon: A Study of the Arthurian Legend in Modern Fiction,* and he is an associate editor of *The Arthurian Encyclopedia* and the *New Arthurian Encyclopedia.*

Pendragon™ Fiction

The Arthurian Companion

by Phyllis Ann Karr

Written in a warm and entertaining style, *The Arthurian Companion* contains over one thousand entries, cross-referenced and annotated. It is an alphabetical guide to the "who's who" of Arthurian legend, a "what's what" of famous Arthurian weapons and artifacts, and a "where's where" of geographical locations appearing in Arthurian literature. The many appendices include a chronology of Arthur's reign.

5 3/8" x 8 3/8", 576 pages, stock #6200, ISBN 1-56882-096-8; available from bookstores and game stores, or by mail from Chaosium Inc., 950-A 56th Street, Oakland CA 94608.

Percival and the Presence of God

by Jim Hunter

From the traditional tale of Sir Percival, one first told by Chrétien de Troyes in twelfth-century France, Jim Hunter crafts a novel of dual quests for Arthur and for the Holy Grail. The completion of Percival's quest becomes the story of a young man striving to understand himself and the world around him, told vividly by an author at the height of his powers. First paperback edition.

5 3/8" x 8 3/8", 192 pages, stock #6201, ISBN 1-56882-097-6; available from bookstores and game stores, or by mail from Chaosium Inc., 950-A 56th Street, Oakland CA 94608.

To the Chapel Perilous

by Naomi Mitchison

This novel relates a new version of the story of King Arthur, the Knights of the Round Table, and the quest for the Holy Grail, as seen through the wide and wondering eyes of a pair of reporters working for the *Camelot Chronicle* and the *Northern Pict*. More than just a lively story, it concerns the twisting of historical truth in the interests of various powerful groups. First paperback edition.

5 3/8" x 8 3/8", approx. 224 pages, stock #6203, ISBN 1-56882-120-4; available in 1999 from bookstores and game stores, or by mail from Chaosium Inc., 950-A 56th Street, Oakland CA 94608.